Too Long T

Too Long To Die

Pat Jackson

Too Long To Die

ISBN-13: 978-1502386762
ISBN-10: 1502386763
Too Long To Die
Text copyright © 2014 Pat Jackson All Rights Reserved
No part of this book may be reproduced, copied or transmitted in any form without the written consent of the author.

Too Long To Die

To my great friend, Rhonda Fraser Brown,
without whose constant support and encouragement
this book would never have been completed.

Too Long To Die

Too Long To Die

Chapter One

Leaning into the wind, the solitary man hugged the wolf skin tunic to his body, more through fear than cold. He peered over the wide expanse of rocks and sand which led down to the distant, blue Salt Water, where powerful gusts were whipping the waves into a frenzy. Wind like this, he knew, should be accompanied by dark skies and the promise of torrential rain blowing in over the water, but today was different. A cloudless, azure sky, with no hint of menace, capped the scenery and the rays of a bright sun glinted off the peaks of icebergs visible on the horizon when the waves abated. The only sound was that of the wind and the response of the land and water below. The clamour of the great white birds that usually circled overhead was absent. The startlingly blue sky was devoid of life and yet not empty.

He fought the urge to look skyward but his eyes kept returning to the unnatural sight. The back of his neck prickled and he tried to control the tremors that coursed through his body. Above him, beside the glowing sun, shone the silver ball of the moon, a perfect circle, which even he knew had no right to be there. His knowledge of the workings of nature was limited; full teachings were kept amongst the Enlightened Ones, but one fact that every child learnt was that Sun and Moon should never be seen together. If these opposing forces were meeting, it foretold no good for the creatures that inhabited the land below. It was a fearful omen. The tribe would be in turmoil.

'Lonell!'

The man took a deep breath and looked back towards the cliffs as he heard his name, distorted by the wind. His eyes searched the rocky outcrops, struggling to find the source of the call until he saw Valon's arm waving urgently. He sighed and signalled back, aware that he must return to the cave and face the fear of the tribe.

He started to walk but one foot slipped on a loose stone and the wind blasted sand into his eyes, as if to remind the man of its power. The thong that tied the deer skin footwear around his leg had torn through the fixing holes.

'Sacred Stones!' he cursed and retied the thong lower down the ankle, hoping it would stay in place until he reached the cave.

Valon was running towards him. Lonell frowned. Either the situation must be worse than expected or Valon needed to tell him something away from the eyes and ears of others. Lonell reluctantly picked up his pace. They met and Valon half raised one arm, his open palm facing the other man, in the casual gesture of friendship, used only between members of the same tribe. In his left hand he carried a short spear. Like Lonell, he bore the two dark, wavy scars over his left eyebrow which showed he belonged to the Pescovari tribe.

'Lonell, everyone is looking for you,' said Valon, breathing deeply. 'The Guardians blew the Summoning Horns and everyone came in except you. They sent me out and I've been searching everywhere. I saw you from the top of the cliff.'

Lonell saw fear in his friend's blue eyes and the tightness of his light skin over a clenched jaw. Valon nervously pushed his blond hair away from his face.

'Why did you come down to the Sands? You're not even carrying a weapon.'

Lonell looked down at his hands, horrified at the potentially fatal oversight.

'My mind was on something else.' Lonell hesitated. 'I woke early this morning, before Sun Wake. I could feel something was wrong.'

The dark head turned back towards the crashing water and Valon only caught some of his friend's mumbled words:

'... come here to think ... needed ... alone.'

Valon glanced up at the sky and quickly looked down again, superstitiously touching the centre of his brow.

'You were right. I've never seen anything like that.' He shivered. 'But you know it's too dangerous to come out without your spear.'

There was a short silence before he remembered why he was there.

'We must return or they'll send out a Guardian. Then we'll be punished.'

He took a few steps but Lonell did not follow. He was still staring out, over the crashing waves of the Salt Water, his dark, inset eyes focussed on something only he could see.

'No, Dreamer. Now is not the time,' Valon shouted. 'We must return.'

His friend's voice brought him back to reality, snatched out of his thoughts by the urgency of Valon's cry.

They started to climb the steep path that led up from the beach to the High Pasture, Valon striding ahead, his blond hair whipping round his head. Lonell stared at the figure ahead and wondered briefly why his own dark hair and olive skin gave him a lower tribal status than his friend. He pushed the thought out of his mind - there were more serious worries that needed his attention.

Valon came to a sudden stop. He turned and stared down at Lonell.

'There's more you must know. None of the Enlightened Ones has left the cave this morning except Tordano, and he wouldn't tell us about the others.'

Lonell looked at him, shocked.

'What? They didn't attend the ceremony?'

Valon shook his head in misery.

'We must hurry,' urged Lonell, his concern deepening. He could think of no other occasion when the Enlightened Ones had not performed the Sun Wake ceremony. Although tribal members were not permitted to take part, they were woken each day by the procession that passed the entrance to their cave, so Lonell was certain that he would remember.

They clambered to the top of the cliff and ran over the flat ground of the High Pasture, their eyes straining for any unexpected movement, always aware that danger could be nearby, but no predators stalked in the tall grasses on this day. Plants and flowers of every hue created a vivid carpet of colour in the warm summers, which attracted a multitude of small animals, birds and insects. This was a natural garden which provided many of the plants used for food and healing remedies. Although Lonell knew little of their medicinal properties, he was aware of their importance to the tribe's survival. Few trees survived on this beautiful but exposed plateau but those that did were doubled over, shaped by the wind that so often blew in off the Salt Water, howling and battering the land. Today was no exception and the two men fought to keep upright as they were blown along in the direction of the cave.

The friends reached the path that descended to their home and Lonell's eyes scanned the unusual formation of the deep mountainside crevice where the two caves faced each other. The only approach was a natural ledge, cut into the rock face. The ledge was wide but dangerous: two people could walk side by side but, if anyone did fall over the edge, there would be no return from the long drop down to the rocky base of the cliffs below. Lonell and Valon walked close to the rock face, a habit deeply ingrained in each tribal member.

Beside the dark opening in the rock that formed the entrance to the tribal cave, stood a man. Lonell and Valon stopped at the sight of the tall, unmoving figure of Tordano, one of the Guardians. He wore bleached white skins but it was his physical appearance that set him apart from the others. Out of his pale, almost translucent face, framed by snowy white hair, stared colourless eyes which were the marks of an Enlightened One. Even though the Guardians held the lowest rank of the spiritual leaders and were not, themselves, beloved of the Gods, they still bore an air of mystery and authority. Tordano turned his head, eyes expressionless, and motioned the two men to enter.

Lonell and Valon moved rapidly into the cave where they found the tribe sitting in terrified silence, all eyes fixed on the entrance to the White Cave, the home of the Enlightened Ones. Lonell remembered when the High Priestess, Saretta, had given the order for the entrance to the tribal cave to be left open, but the appropriately named White Cave retained the gleaming, bleached skins that hung over its entrance. It added to the mystique of the Enlightened Ones and also provided them with warmth and comfort in the cold months which was denied the tribal cave. This command had sparked the first, almost subconscious, feelings of concern within the tribe but Lonell, alone, had recognised it instantly as an unwelcome change in the relationship between the two groups which comprised the Pescovari. His thoughts were interrupted by an angry voice.

'Where have you been, Lonell?' asked Kadell, the Leader. He rose swiftly from his stone seat and crossed the cave to face them, running a nervous hand through the light ginger hair of his beard. Despite his short stature, the Leader possessed a natural air of command but now his usually calm disposition was shaken by anger and fear.

'Why do you always go out by yourself, Dreamer? You were needed here.'

Lonell was surprised at the accusing tone Kadell used when addressing him as 'Dreamer'. Long past were the days when he had frightened people by drifting into his trance-like state of deep thought. Only when the others had finally realised his ideas could be useful and that his particular intelligence was helpful to others had he been affectionately given the tribal name 'Dreamer'.

'Why did you need me? There was nothing for me to do here,' retorted Lonell.

'I don't know,' admitted Kadell, shaking his head, 'but it does seem that you're able to help sometimes. The way you see things - it's different. I don't understand why …,' he said. Then, remembering his position as Leader, he added in a commanding voice, 'We should all be together when there is danger.'

'Is there danger?' asked Valon.

Kadell shrugged, his anger passed.

'We don't know,' he admitted. 'Even Tordano refuses to tell us what is happening.' He hesitated for a moment. 'I'm not certain that he knows, but something is wrong,' he whispered.

Kadell glanced at Tordano who, unnoticed, had moved and was now standing just inside the cave. The Guardian was still staring at the opposite cave, the light striking his stark, white tunic.

'In the sky, the Sun and Moon are talking,' announced Lonell.

There was an intake of breath as every member of the cave touched their brows to ward off evil. Some of the women seated around Kadella, the Leader's sister, began to sob, upsetting the children. Keeping her voice controlled, she spoke to them and pulled a wailing child onto her lap, soothing her fears. She looked over their heads and saw Lonell watching her. He felt a deep admiration for her, understanding the fear that she was hiding from those around her.

'This is an ill omen but we must not panic - in time I'm sure we will be told,' said Lonell, glancing at Tordano.

He saw the Guardian watching him from the corner of his eye and the tribesman wished he felt as calm as he sounded. He moved towards the pale figure. Tordano was the only one he would have dared approach - no other Guardian would have deigned to talk to a lowly member of the tribe unless to give an order. However, it was known that Tordano was more friendly - there was even some suspicion that he would have been happier in the tribe but, as soon as he was born, his fate had been sealed. He had the clear white skin and colourless eyes of an Enlightened One and, at his birth, his mother began to mourn the fact that he would be removed from her keeping after five winters.

Lonell stood beside the Guardian.

'Something serious must be happening,' he said, his voice hushed.

Tordano nodded without turning his head.

'Are you able to say what it might be?' Lonell worded his question carefully and hoped he had not spoken too boldly.

'No. In truth, I am unaware of the full facts. I am here only to ensure that the whole tribe is gathered.'

Lonell's attention was snatched away when, suddenly, the coverings of White Cave were pulled aside violently to reveal Saretta, the High Priestess. Her once tall, elegant body was now slightly stooped but still she made an imposing figure. She had long, white hair which framed a face that showed signs of strength rather than beauty, now more than usual. Her ankle length robe, made from the softest goat hide, was covered entirely in white seashells which glinted in the sunlight and, over her shoulders, she wore a white, winter fox cape. Surrounded by the three Attendant Priestesses and two Guardians, at the woman's side stood an enormous wolf, its white fur raised along the ridge of its back, and yellow eyes which stared intently at the crowd across the other side of the crevice. However, no one looked at the animal; all eyes stared at the High Priestess who wore a headdress of pure white feathers. None of the tribe had ever seen the Kalia Headdress - named after the first Priestess to create it. All knew that it was only worn at times of tragedy and stories were told of it but most had doubted the very existence of such a headdress.

However, Saretta was wearing it and the look of fury in her eyes dispelled any hope that the crisis might have passed.

She flung her arms open.

'My children, a disaster has struck us,' she cried. 'Our beloved Narthan has vanished and only this was left.'

Saretta sobbed loudly and dramatically as she held aloft a broken shell necklace which all recognised as belonging to the missing Guardian.

'Some evil has befallen him,' she pointed into the sky. 'Even our Gods are disturbed - they search for an answer. And we must search also.'

She stopped, head tilted, as though listening. No movement, the tribe held its breath.

Her head spun back and serpentine eyes pierced the distance across the abyss.

'All men, led by the Guardians, will go out to find Narthan - alive, if the Gods are kind.'

Lonell wondered why the women were not also expected to go out.

'The Gods have spoken to me,' Saretta screamed, as if reading his mind. 'Only the men must search. Go, go now, I command!'

The wolf, startled by the rage in her voice, showed its teeth and a rumbling growl came from deep in its throat. Saretta's head twisted round to look at the oldest Attendant who took a step forward and put her hand on the animal's neck - there was instant silence.

No one considered disobeying the order but it occurred to Lonell that, had the missing person been anyone but Narthan, there would have been a greater enthusiasm and feet would have moved faster to the task. If he were never found, there would be few who would regret his disappearance.

'Come, Valon,' he said. 'Let us go.'

Too Long To Die

His eye was caught by a tall, young man who was sitting at the hearth, waiting. His closely cropped head and two livid scars above his eyebrow revealed that he had recently become a man and Lonell could sense his eagerness, his hope that someone would remember he was no longer a child and invite him into their group.

'Sim, will you come with us?' he asked. 'You have now completed the Rite of Shadows so you no longer have to stay with the children.'

Sim nodded gratefully at the older man, clearly pleased that he had just passed the terrifying and physically demanding series of trials that was the path from childhood to manhood. He jumped eagerly to his feet.

'Wait!' commanded Sarril, the senior Guardian, his voice deep and guttural, different from the more gentle lilting voices of most of the Pescovari. 'Lonell, Valon and Sim will search around Mountain Water. Valt, you will accompany them.' He spoke quietly to the other Guardian before moving off to organise the other groups.

Valon looked at Lonell with a raised eyebrow.

'They have no trust in you, do they? They think you'll wander off by yourself!'

Lonell considered Valt the most remote of the Enlightened Ones and it was generally thought that he had never actually had an unnecessary conversation with any member of the tribe; he kept his contact with them to a minimum. Valt was the smallest man in the tribe and his delicate features reminded Lonell of a woman – even his facial hair was thinner than most.

Lonell watched him move towards them and noticed that the Guardian seemed even more uncomfortable than usual; his normal expression of discontent had been replaced by something else but Lonell was unable to work out whether it was anger or fear. The dark man frowned; he disliked the confusion. He could usually read what others were thinking by their movement or expression, but not now.

He looked at the Guardian and noticed, in addition to his facial expression, a stiffness in Valt's gait. His body showed more tension than even the unsettling loss of a brother Guardian should cause.

A question instantly rose to Lonell's mind but he tried to ignore it. If it had been Tordano with them he might have asked but he had no intention of questioning Valt. However, the Guardian's manner did nothing to settle Lonell's uneasiness which he could not shake off.

'Before you leave, Lonell, Saretta will speak with you. She is waiting.' Valt's high-pitched voice was heard by everyone and the cave came to a stand-still.

Lonell felt a thumping in his chest. His eyes moved to the other side of the crevice where the High Priestess stood, staring at him. He swallowed and made his way towards the entrance.

'Mother, she never talks to any of us. Why does she want to see Lonell?' A child's clear voice rang out in the silence.

His legs shook as he followed the ledge round to the White Cave, keeping his eyes to the ground. A tightness in his chest constricted his breathing and he was aware of small stones crunching loudly beneath his feet.

'Lonell.' The name, almost whispered, brought him to a halt. 'Why did you not return to the cave when the Summoning Horns were blown?'

'I did not hear them,' he replied, his voice hoarse. 'I was on the Sands.'

He slowly raised his eyes to the white face of the High Priestess. The anger appeared to have lessened but the smile on her lips contradicted the slit, pale eyes which stared at him, unmoving. His eyes dropped to the ground once more and he heard her intake of breath. He waited, expecting a tirade, screamed threats to eject him from the tribe, but nothing happened. Silence. He looked up again. A tremor ran over the woman's face, her head twitched to the side.

Lonell took a step backwards and one foot slipped, knocking pebbles off the ledge which clattered down to the rocks far below. He threw himself towards the rock face and felt a bead of sweat run down the side of his face. Looking back at the High Priestess he saw that she had been joined by Lexana, the senior Attendant Priestess. There was no wolf with her now, only Saretta, still unmoving, the pale eyes staring out of a frozen face.

'Go now!' ordered Lexana, quietly. 'Don't wait!' Her arm waved him urgently away.

Lonell ran, not stopping until he reached the tribal cave. Valon was waiting for him and caught his friend's arm when he ran in.

'What happened, Lonell? What did she say?'

'Nothing,' he answered. 'Look.'

He pointed a shaking finger at the ledge opposite where Lexana was holding a wooden cup to Saretta's lips. Then she shook her, calling her name until the High Priestess took a deep breath, smiled vaguely and allowed herself to be guided back inside the White Cave.

'I was waiting for punishment but she didn't say anything,' continued Lonell. 'She smiled but she had a look on her face ... Do you remember the day we saw the snake with the rabbit?'

'Yes. The rabbit froze with fear - it couldn't move. The snake killed it. Why?'

'Out there,' Lonell stared across the crevice, 'I think I was the rabbit.'

The two friends joined Sim and Valt and the four figures crossed the High Pasture. The wind suddenly died, bringing a complete silence except for the insects which began to rise, taking flight as the men's footsteps disturbed the grasses. They walked quickly, each of them looking around for any tell-tale signs that Narthan might have passed that way or for anything that seemed out of place – not an easy task after the wind had swept through the area bringing its inevitable chaos.

'Here,' shouted Valon, known for his skill at tracking. 'More than one person passed this way recently. See, the grasses have been trodden down.'

They started to run until they reached the path that led down the hillside. Picking their way carefully, even though they saw it frequently, it was hard not to stare at the sight of the crystalline water gushing from the side of the mountain and pouring into an exquisite, deep blue lake at the bottom. The lush vegetation spoke of the warmth of the summer they were enjoying and the bright colours of the many species of flowers that thrived at this time of year usually caused people to stop and admire, but the men had other things on their minds.

'I think they went in that direction,' said Valon, pointing to the right. 'We should follow the path back to the lake.'

'No.' Valt spoke his first word since they had started out and the high-pitched roughness of his voice caused Lonell to look at him sharply.

'Valon, you will come with me along the hillside and approach the lake from the far side,' signalling the opposite direction. 'Lonell, you and Sim take this path. Lonell, you must lead and watch out for Sim.'

As Lonell nodded, he could see the fury on Valon's face, quickly hidden as the Guardian turned in his direction and gestured him to move on. His unease deepening by the moment, he led Sim down to the flat meadowland that bordered the lake, where they stood side by side looking at the scene before them. The beauty of their surroundings brought out Sim's youthful exuberance, making him temporarily forget the gravity of their task and, first ensuring that Valt had completely disappeared from view, he cried:

'I'll race you to the lake, Dreamer!'

'No,' replied Lonell, too late, for Sim was already well ahead.

He sighed and began to run after him, smiling, despite himself. Suddenly he felt his footwear come loose. With the traumatic events back at the cave, he had forgotten to replace the broken one and the makeshift ties had fallen off. He stooped to retie them and stood up to see Sim laughing and waving at him from the lake side. He signalled for the young man to wait but Sim had turned and was peering at something that Lonell was unable to see.

Sim's frozen stance suggested fear and the older man covered the distance between them rapidly. Lonell followed the direction of the young man's eyes and saw the foliage of a tall shrub whose large palmate leaves measured the length of a man's stride. He moved towards it and squatted down, pushing the branches apart with an outstretched hand. From underneath one of the leaves protruded an arm, white and unmoving. When Lonell touched the ice cold flesh, all hope of finding life disappeared.

Too Long To Die

Chapter Two

'Quickly,' Lonell said to Sim, who stood immobile in his terror, 'Help me pull him out.'

The two men touched their brows before dragging the corpse into the clearing beside the lake. Lonell saw the boy's shaking hands and pale face. He wondered what he could do to keep the boy active - he would be no use to anyone if he lost control.

Looking around, he took in the surroundings, the waist-high grasses of the meadowland bounded on all sides by rock walls, accessed only by steep, pebble-strewn paths at various points.

'Sim, go, find the others and bring them here,' he said, trying to keep his voice calm.

He spoke, pointing to the other side of the green swathe and Sim looked at him gratefully before speeding away.

Lonell knew time was limited so, quickly, he took the opportunity to inspect Narthan's body, incongruously wrapped in an old, dark, wolf skin cloak. If anything, the face was whiter than in life and the stiffness of the body reminded Lonell of animals he had seen in the depths of winter, caught unaware, frozen to death in the snow.

'The weather's too warm,' he thought, 'and although the skin is cold and rigid, it's not the same, it's not solid. Why is that? When I return to the cave I'll ask Endorina. A Healer might know.'

Lonell remembered the times he had seen human death - something not easily forgotten. When members of the tribe returned to the earth, the Enlightened Ones always dealt with the bodies rapidly, removing them for disposal. He had always been thankful they did but, as a result, he had never before had the opportunity to study a corpse. Now he took a detailed look at the one in front of him. The back of the skull had been caved in by a powerful blow and, where the fur wrap had fallen away when they moved him, he studied carefully the bruising around the neck and shoulders, deep purple marks showing clearly on the white skin. The hands and arms bore no visible injuries, except for some slight blistering on the finger tips. He peered closely at the face. A bitter odour emanated from the swollen mouth and he tried to prise the jaws open to look inside but the clenched teeth would not part.

Lonell rearranged the cloak and returned to the place they had found Narthan's body, under the leaves. He looked around thoughtfully, taking in the details of the ground where the corpse had lain and the area nearby. His brow furrowed as he tried to understand the events that had taken place. He knew he was missing something but his brain could not recognise it.

Hearing the sound of running feet, he quickly emerged from the undergrowth and joined Valon and Sim. Valt said nothing, he asked no questions, but took up his position over the body in the traditional mourning stance of the Enlightened Ones, imploring hands held upwards towards the sky. The Guardian threw back his head, gave a great cry of grief and then brought his gaze down to bear upon the other three members of the group who stood with their heads lowered in respectful silence. From the distance, the chattering shrieks of cave hyenas cut through the stillness.

Lonell looked up suddenly. The hairs on his arms stood on end; Valt was staring at him with what could only be described as a look of triumph on his face.

'The three of you will carry Narthan back. Treat him with the respect that is due to an Enlightened One. I shall go on ahead to give the tragic news so they can prepare to receive him,' said Valt, his insincerity clearly audible.

Lonell watched the effeminate Guardian walk away, his mind filled with unanswered questions. Then he shrugged and bent down to tidy the body, beckoning Valon to assist him. There was little they could do but the cloak was pulled tight and kept in place by the skin belt that he had been wearing around his white tunic.

'I can't touch him,' said Sim, as they prepared to hoist him onto their shoulders. 'When he was living he always scared me and maybe I should not say so, but I often wished that he would ... leave the tribe; but such a death is ... unnatural. It's not right...' His stumbling voice trailed off into silence.

Lonell noticed that Valon was carefully observing the young man beside him as though aware for the first time of his tender years. He had drifted away into his thoughts when Valon reached out a comforting hand and placed it on Sim's shoulder.

'Don't worry. Lonell and I can carry him. We'll need someone to guide us up the steep paths. You'll be honoured when we return to the cave - it was you who found Narthan. I wonder what reward you'll get. What do you think, Lonell?'

He grinned at the young man. When there was no reply from Lonell, they looked round.

'He's thinking again. Look at him, staring at nothing. He hasn't heard anything I said,' laughed Valon. 'But I know he'll agree,' and, raising his voice, he insisted, 'Come on, Dreamer!'

Lonell started, his eyes focusing once more on his surroundings and he looked down at the corpse.

'They'll wonder why we're not coming,' continued Valon. 'I'll take the head, you hold the feet.'

They hoisted it onto their shoulders and, although a heavy burden and its bulk obscured their vision, it was strangely easy to carry the rigid body. Even so, the climb up the slope to the High Pasture proved difficult despite Sim's efforts to guide their footsteps over the loose and uneven pebbles. Half way up, Lonell lost his footing and tumbled off the path, slipping away down the hillside, almost taking the corpse and the others with him. As he slid by, Sim managed to catch hold of the back of Lonell's tunic, preventing them from ending up, once again, on the meadowland at the bottom of the slope.

'Sacred Stones!' cursed Lonell, as he heard his wolf skin tunic rip in Sim's grasp and felt his elbow graze against a boulder. He struggled to his feet, still clinging desperately to the corpse. Back on the path he turned his head to look at Sim out of the corner of his eye. He was about to thank him when the young man stuttered, 'I'm sorry, Lonell. Your tunic - I tore it. I'll replace it when I next go hunting.'

Lonell smiled to himself. His instinct had been correct - this young man had a good spirit and he would grow to be a valuable member of their tribe.

'You saved us, Sim. You have no need to be sorry. We'll hunt together for a new skin.'

Although he could not see his face, Lonell was certain that the young man would be pleased, having momentarily forgotten his fear of the terrible burden they carried.

Lonell carefully tried to balance the body. He winced at the pain in his elbow, and grimaced at the thought of the walk back to their cave. However, crossing the High Pasture proved a simpler task than expected. The wind no longer obstructed their movement and it was an efficient but respectful group that approached the tribe, all gathered, waiting for them. Despite his bowed head, Lonell was watching and took in the reaction of the two distinct groups. Huddled together, the tribe stood in their dark wolf or deer skins, children pulled close to their mothers, their fear tangible. In contrast, the whiteness of the Enlightened Ones, dressed in their gleaming tunics and skins, seemed to cast an aura around their group. They stood apart, to one side of the tribe, each distanced from the next, as if in their own private space, not wanting any personal contact. The High Priestess stood in front, motionless, waiting.

The bearers approached and every man, woman and child superstitiously touched their brows to ward off evil. No one liked to be in the presence of death and Lonell knew that each person there was relieved that they had not been given the task of carrying the body. Like all members of the tribe, Lonell was only too aware of the dangers which surrounded them and everyone knew that life was often short, but death was a mystery few desired to understand. The presence of a lifeless corpse reminded them of their own mortality - Lonell could see the fear etched onto every face - and their unease was magnified because, for the first time in living memory, they were dealing with an unexplained death.

However, Lonell's eyes were drawn to the Attendants. Instead of the expected grief that should have shown on their faces, he could only see signs of fear. He studied each of them in turn.

Lexana was the oldest, a few winters older than Saretta. Everyone had hoped and expected her to succeed the last High Priestess as she cared deeply about the tribe and was well loved. Her face, once pretty and smiling, was now deeply lined, as though grief had been permanently etched into her skin. Nowadays she rarely left the White Cave except to attend official duties. The tribe missed her and longed for the time when the Enlightened Ones had guided the tribe with love and kindness, and punishment was only doled out in the most extreme of cases. Lexana kept the wolf beside her which also seemed uneasy as though, thought Lonell, he could pick up on the sense of agitation which surrounded them all. Tied around the neck of the animal was a cord which Lexana held tightly to keep it under control. She muttered, stroking its head with a shaking hand, but her eyes did not stray from the High Priestess.

Beside Lexana stood Talia, a tall, thin young woman. Of all of them she appeared the most unnatural, giving the impression that she might blow away if the wind blew too hard. No one knew where she came from; the pale child had staggered into the cave one evening, unable to speak and starving, and had instantly been adopted by the White Cave due to her colouring. She had never gained the use of her voice and this, together with her constantly faraway expression, made people avoid her whenever they could. As she stood there on the hilltop, she appeared more haunted than usual.

Finally, there was Minaya, a young girl who had been initiated only two summers before – until then she had served her time as an Attendant Priestess in Training. When Minaya was taken away to the White Cave after her fifth winter, her mother fell ill and eventually succumbed; it was generally believed that she had grieved to death. As a small child, Minaya's beauty and gentleness charmed everyone, even Lonell, who did not encourage contact with children. However, once taken away from her mother, although still beautiful, her radiance had dulled and whenever he saw her, Lonell was aware of a deep sadness that hung over her. Despite that, on this day he was shocked at the change; the skin was drawn tight over her hollow cheeks and dark rings circled her eyes. She shuffled her feet and frowned at the horizon with wide eyes as she chewed her bottom lip and wrung her shaking hands.

'There's no doubt, they're as frightened as the tribe,' thought Lonell.

The High Priestess stepped forward, no sign of her recent affliction. She still wore the white headdress, its white feathers fluttering in the wind. She paused dramatically.

'Place Narthan on the ground and step away,' she ordered.

The bearers obeyed and backed away, relieved to have completed their task and happy to return to the relative security of the tribe.

'Narthan has returned to the earth. The Gods have taken him,' announced the High Priestess. She walked slowly around the body, starting at his head and when she had completed a circle she turned around and repeated her actions in the opposite direction, muttering an incantation.

'He brings no evil spirits with him. You may now approach,' she declared to the Enlightened Ones. They ringed the body and, as if one, threw their arms in the air and cried their grief to the sky. At the same time, the wolf threw back his head and howled, startling the already frightened observers. The mourning came to an end and the tribe started returning to their cave. A shout from the High Priestess brought them to a standstill.

'Wait. There is more to be said. You,' she pointed at Lonell, 'found where Narthan was lying. The reward for that is ...'

Her dramatic pause allowed Sim enough time to shout out. At the same moment she shrieked the word 'Death', his words of 'No, I found him!' were heard by everyone.

If the tribe had been quiet before, they were now completely silent, not a breath to be heard. The stillness was finally shattered by the cries of a small child. Then shouts of 'No!' 'Death?' and 'Why?' erupted from the tribe and the High Priestess turned to Valt.

'But you informed me that it was him!' she shouted.

Valt looked at Lonell with terrified eyes.

'It is not true!' he yelled. 'You were with the body - you found it! I saw you!'

Valon stepped forward.

'It was Sim who found the body. He was pleased to have served and we thought he would be rewarded. This isn't right ... I don't understand...'

'You would say anything to help your friend,' sneered Valt.

Too Long To Die

'I did. I arrived at the lake first and saw the body before Lonell - he was far behind me...' Sim's brave words, the shaking voice, brought silence once again and everyone turned and stared at his terrified face.

Lonell turned to the High Priestess, anger overcoming the usual nervousness that he felt before her.

'Valon is correct - this is ... wrong. Why does the man who found the body deserve death? We thought he would be honoured.'

'Are you questioning me, Lonell? How dare you!' she shrieked, causing the wolf behind her to growl menacingly.

She closed her eyes dramatically and faced the tribe.

'I shall tell you all why Sim must face death. It was obvious to me that some evil had befallen Narthan and only one person would know where to find him. It was for this reason that we sent you all out, knowing that the man who killed him would reveal himself, and he has done so. That boy took the life of Narthan, our well-loved Guardian.'

She pointed a long, white finger at Sim who was cowering on the ground, shaking his head and sobbing.

'No, no, it wasn't me, I did nothing, I swear!'

'When the moon has twice shrunk and returned to full circle,' the High Priestess continued, ignoring him, 'this boy will be sacrificed to the Gods. We shall offer Them his blood at the Darkening ceremony when the Gods decide what hardships we must suffer through the cold times. Perhaps in this way we shall appease Them for the dreadful crime that has been committed against Narthan and They will take pity on us.'

She paused, her face devoid of any of the pity she expected from the Gods.

'Sarril, Valt, escort the sacrifice to the Pit and take the wolf. The rest of you, return to your hearths. No one is to leave the area for the remainder of this day.'

Too Long To Die

'Oh, please, no. There must be some mistake. My boy would not ...,' begged Sim's mother, launching herself at the feet of the High Priestess. Saretta looked down with glassy, merciless eyes and, kicking the weeping woman away, looked furiously at the tribe.

'All of you, to the cave now!'

For a moment, nobody moved, as though an unseen force held them back. Then slowly they began to shuffle away. Ancient Pel, the longest living member of the tribe, helped Sim's mother to her feet and guided her away. Lonell, one of the last to file down the narrow path, looked back to where the High Priestess, her three Attendants and Tordano were circling the body on the ground. To his left he could see a shattered Sim being led to the Pit by the two other Guardians. Valt was holding the wolf by the cord, trying to control it, but the animal seemed relieved to be away from the noise of the people and, wanting to run, was pulling away and shaking its shaggy head. At one point Valt almost fell and, despite his anger and confusion, Lonell smiled grimly at the struggle – perhaps the wolf would punish the feminine man who, Lonell realised, had been part of a plot to trap him.

The strange group took the easiest but longest route to the Pit, over the High Pasture to the end where a short path led down to the tiny opening in the rock face which stood far above the caves in which they lived. Another, but far more dangerous route, took the ledge between the two caves to the furthest point, followed by an arduous climb up on a narrow, rocky path. The Guardians had chosen the former.

He thought of the Pit itself - aptly named, it was a tiny cave, that sloped downwards away from the opening. It was just long enough for a person to lie out at an angle but not quite high enough for man of average height to stand up fully. The opening was sealed by a gate, made from a framework of wood and cords from the creeping plant that grew down the cliff side, which created a near impregnable barrier. A person incarcerated there was allowed no fire; the only items permitted were the clothes the captive was wearing, one skin cloak and the soil bowl which had to be emptied each morning by the man or woman who brought the day's food. In this case, it would be Sim's mother who would have to perform all the duties associated with looking after her son, although there would be little she could do to make the days more tolerable for him for she would always be accompanied by a Guardian during her visits. No one else would be permitted to speak with him. Sim would be uncomfortable and lonely while he waited for death; his only companion would be the fierce, white wolf tied to the gate.

From his own experience, Lonell knew how dreadful that cramped, tiny space could be and that was before the wolf had come to live with the Enlightened Ones. He had spent five days in there when he had not obeyed Narthan quickly enough and he had been sent there to 'think on his disobedience and improve his character'. In truth, the only change that this containment had brought about was that, instead of disliking the Guardian, after five days he hated him to a point where he had hoped that one day he would get his revenge. He slowly realised it was a childish emotion and, as time passed, his hatred mellowed to a dull loathing but one thing was certain, he thought, the tribe would be much happier without him.

Lonell wondered if anyone in the tribe had hated Narthan as much or more than he, enough to take his life, and he was suddenly overcome with a certainty that he had to find out the truth. It was the only way that Sim would live but Lonell was filled with dread. He doubted his ability to accomplish the task but he knew that, without him, the young man would surely be sacrificed to the Gods.

Chapter Three

When Lonell entered the cave, Valon was standing slumped against the wall, beside the wide entrance. Sounds of distress filled the air but Lonell headed straight to the back, without speaking. On his right he passed the High Hearth, located nearest to the entrance, and the two smaller hearths. As the days became colder the High Hearth would be moved further back into the cave, away from the open entrance, and the other smaller hearths would be moved to allow for the change, but now it benefited from some natural light which reached into the front of the cave. To his left was the storage area where communal implements where kept, and the working area where skins were hanging on stretching frames and half-made wooden utensils lay, waiting to be finished.

Lonell saw none of it. He walked straight past, his eyes fixed ahead as he made his way through the cave. He retrieved his bed skins and threw himself down, dragging his hands through his dark, curly hair. He sat numbly, back against the cold cave wall and looked around, his eyes settling on Valon, aware of his grief. His friend's blond hair was tied back with a narrow, rabbit skin thong and his face, usually so quick to smile, was distraught.

Most people were sitting around the High Hearth in groups, trying to console each other but there were no words that could remove the pain they all felt. The hearth was large enough to accommodate the whole tribe as they sat on the surrounding stone seats. Ancient Pel held the sobbing figure of Verina, Sim's mother, in his wrinkled, skinny arms. Despite being the longest lived person in the tribe, which granted him the title 'Ancient', he was remarkably strong and able. Lonell saw his gentleness and fervently hoped that he would survive many more winters before passing the title on to Endorina, their Healer. Kadell, the Leader, was talking to his sister, their heads close together and then they separated, moving from person to person, trying to calm and support.

Lonell remained by himself in his preferred position at the rear of the cave. He did not mind the lack of any natural light; it was the perfect observation point from which he could watch the activity and people in the cave without getting involved. Others knew he liked the spot and usually left it free for him although he had no claim to it as they could all sit or sleep anywhere they wanted. Sometimes people even forgot that he was there which was useful when he needed to think or had no desire to interact with others.

Lonell watched the reactions of the members of the tribe. Some sat silently, wrapped in grief, and others talked in hushed voices, sadness and confusion equally evident.

'Poor Verina.'

'Sim would never have done anything like that.'

'I don't believe it.'

'It must have been an Outlander.'

Lonell listened to the snatches of conversation, thinking that no one else had realised the truth, that Saretta had planned for him to be held responsible, not Sim. That had certainly been a mistake. 'Why?' he asked himself. 'What have I done to deserve the blame?'

Lonell tried to work it out. He had always been aware that he was different. He could form unexpected solutions to problems and understood things that others were unable to grasp. He was also one of the few men who liked his own company, perhaps because of his very difference. However, Lonell recognized this and took a fully active part in the life of the tribe, contributing all he could but, whereas others *belonged*, there was always a part of him that felt somewhat isolated, an observer rather than an integral member of the group. He sometimes wondered why Valon put up with him but, he had to admit, he was glad he did. Valon was one of the few men whose company Lonell actually encouraged. Was his individuality the reason he had been selected by Saretta, he wondered?

After a while, with Kadell's encouragement, the overwrought tribe started to go about its routine duties. Fires were lit and food prepared and cooked, but Lonell was oblivious to the activity. He stared at the storage area. Something was different. The wooden shelf on which the dried foods, nuts and fruits were kept was built up off the ground on stone walls, in an attempt to keep small rodents away, while the communal plates, spoons and baskets were stored underneath. He watched as a hazelnut rolled to the edge of the shelf and dropped to the floor. It was at an angle, no longer a flat surface.

He pushed himself up from his bed skins and strode towards the shelf, unaware that everyone was watching him. He squatted down beside the structure and when he stood up, Kadell and Valon were beside him, enquiring expressions on their faces.

'The shelf's not safe. One of the supporting walls has collapsed.' Lonell shrugged his shoulders and walked slowly back to his bed skins, where he sank deep into thought. He did not even see the men fixing the damage and, later, when Valon went to tell him that Kadell wanted to talk with him, there was no reaction, no indication that he had heard. Valon returned to the Leader.

'He's thinking. We should wait until he comes back to us. Leader, did you think there was something unusual about what happened? I mean, when we brought back the body?' Valon was unsure how to word his suspicions.

Kadell frowned and cleared his throat.

'It did seem to me that Saretta thought it would be Lonell who found the body. She was ...,' - he searched for the correct word - 'disappointed that he didn't. If Sim had not been so eager, it would be Lonell in the Pit waiting to be sacrificed.'

'That's what I thought,' agreed Valon. 'Why?'

'I wish I knew. As it is, I think Lonell's in great danger. I only hope he knows something that we don't.'

Valon stared at his friend through the glimmering light of the hearth fires and fish oil lamps that were now illuminating the cave. It still amazed him how his friend sank so deeply into his own thoughts that he knew nothing of his surroundings, especially at a time when everyone else was so full of grief that it was hard to think of anything. Valon selected a wooden plate from under the newly repaired shelf and took it to the High Hearth where food was being served. He filled it with a selection of meats and took it back to Lonell, placing it on the floor in front of him. There was no sign of recognition. Later Valon removed the untouched food and left him, knowing that he could do no more but hoping, like Kadell, that the Dreamer would come up with the impossible - a solution to their problems.

Lonell remained in his trance until late into the night. He ate nothing and, long after everyone else had finally gone to sleep, he wrapped himself in his skins and slept fitfully for a short time, waking to darkness. He waited for a while, until the very first vestiges of light began to show at the cave entrance, timing his actions carefully. Then he got up quietly and went to the storage area, where he found a small rabbit skin bag which he filled with a selection of berries, pine nuts and hazelnuts. He also took another larger skin bag with him. Tying the food bag to his belt, he slung the larger one over his shoulder and left the cave, making no sound. Along the ledge he went into the cave that served as the weapons store. He picked out his own bundle of weapons, known to him instantly, even in the near darkness by the shape and feel of the dyed piece of skin that wrapped them. He quietly removed a spear and put the rest back. As always, he carried a flint knife in his belt and a small bag tied round his waist.

Lonell heard rustling in the grasses as he ran but recognised the sounds of rabbits that infested the plateau. There was nothing to fear, at least, not from these animals. He retraced his route of the day before and quickly found himself beside the lake, close to where the body had been found. Aware that he had little time, he began to search the area. He did not know what he was looking for but he felt sure that something must be there that would give him an insight into how Narthan had been killed.

Suddenly, through the dim light of the early morning, his eyes spotted a stone, larger than the others around it. Lonell picked it up, turning it over. On the rough underside he saw the outline of darkened blood. He weighed the stone in his hand and realised that, although not overly heavy, it was large enough to have inflicted serious damage if used in anger. He was certain he had found the weapon that had cracked Narthan's skull and wondered why he had failed to see it the day before. He knew something was evading him and his brain struggled to find the missing details.

He knelt down, dug into the bag that he always wore tied round his waist and took out his hangbone. He unravelled the cord, made from very fine, treated and greased goat's intestine and allowed the piece of bone attached to it to hang free underneath. He held the cord delicately with his arm out in front of him. Despite Saretta's ban on the use of these objects - she had declared them instruments of the Gods and claimed they were dangerous for those lacking spiritual instruction - the hangbone was a tool Lonell often used in decision making. When the bone moved from side to side the answer to his question was positive, backwards and forwards negative. He found the accuracy of the answers hard to ignore. However, in the search for Narthan's killer, Lonell's questions were getting no clear answers. Lonell quickly wrapped the cord round the bone and tucked it back into his bag.

He looked round him once more, relieved he had not been seen, and realised that there was nothing more to find in this place. Whatever was missing, it was not there. He dug a hole under a tree, laid grasses and leaves in the bottom, placed the stone inside and covered it up with more vegetation before smoothing soil over the top. He did not know whether the stone would be necessary in the future but he understood the need to keep it, in case it might become important. He sprinkled a few more leaves and twigs around to disguise the moved soil and then washed his hands in the lake.

The cool water was too tempting. He stripped off his clothes and plunged into the blue water, gasping as the cold took his breath away. He dived under and felt the cleansing water run through his hair, wishing that he had some of the small mauve flowers to clean his hair and skin but he knew there was no time for that. He made one quick circuit of the lake, his easy swimming stroke sending small ripples across the surface and then, feeling refreshed and invigorated, he rapidly pulled on his leggings and tunic over his wet body.

When Lonell straightened up, he saw the tall, pale figure of Tordano walking rapidly towards his position. He felt a thumping in his chest and picked up his spear and waited, his body taut with tension, only relaxing when he saw Guardian give the open handed greeting, which he returned, still holding the spear firmly in his other hand.

He realised he had been holding his breath.

'I saw you leave the cave.' Tordano spoke quietly. 'I could not follow immediately – I had tasks to do – but I desired to talk to you.'

Lonell had to strain to hear what the Guardian was saying.

Too Long To Die

'I came to swim....' His words were silenced by Tordano, putting one hand up quickly and the other over his own mouth, to signify that Lonell should not speak.

'You are in danger,' continued Tordano, almost in a whisper. 'I am certain that you are trying to discover what happened to Narthan. You must not. You must stop looking and accept it as it is, for your own sake and for others.'

'But Sim did not kill him,' Lonell whispered back in response. 'I cannot leave him to be sacrificed when we all know he did nothing.'

'If you continue, you will take his place. That was what they wan...' He stopped mid-word, as if realising that he had said too much.

'Why, Guardian? Why do they want me to go to the Gods?'

'I have said too much already,' said Tordano, backing off. 'I have warned you. The rest of the Enlightened Ones will be here soon for the ceremony. You must leave now and it must not be known that we have met or my life, too, will be worth nothing.'

Lonell moved quickly, leaving the blue Mountain Water behind, and, when he was certain that he was out of view, he sat down on a grassy bank and opened the bag of nuts and berries. He ate and stared into the sky as if searching for inspiration, scratching his short beard and trying to make sense of Tordano's words. However, all he could understand was that the Enlightened Ones did not want the truth to be uncovered and that, somehow, they considered him a threat. He felt the early morning sun on his back and turning round, he lifted his face to its warming rays, feeling comforted by the power directed towards him. If he had been able to, he would have offered a prayer to the sun; it would have been a plea to help him unravel the mystery, thereby saving a desperately frightened, young man. He would also have prayed for a return to the peaceful, contented times he had heard about from the older members of the tribe. However, only the Enlightened Ones were allowed to address the Gods but, he hoped, maybe they would understand his silent thoughts.

He opened the large bag of fresh water he had filled with the clear liquid that flowed from the mountainside and took a deep drink. Lined with the stomach of a wild horse, the bag was waterproof and, if asked, Lonell would be able to say that he had come to the lake to collect some water for the cave. It was a task that all tribal members had to carry out constantly and it would be impossible to say that he had gone to Mountain Water for no reason. He also intended to catch something for breakfast on his way back and he would then declare that this had been his primary reason for going out.

Indeed, he arrived back at the cave, having replaced his spear, clutching two plump, skinned rabbits and the almost full water skin which he handed over to the pleasantly surprised women who were starting to prepare breakfast. Lonell headed to his place at the back of the cave and took out the rabbit skins which he started to scrape down; they would be very useful as footwear linings when the weather turned cold. Usually, tasks like this were enjoyable because they gave him time to think whilst doing something useful, but this time the thought of the rabbit caused Lonell to admit that he was now ravenous for he had not eaten since the same time the day before.

'You went out early.' Valon's voice made him start. 'I was beginning to worry about you.'

Lonell turned and looked at the man in front of him for a few seconds before making up his mind.

'You must no longer talk to me. It will put you in danger; you must pay me no attention.'

'I thought you might say that. I saw the way Saretta looked at you and, although I can't understand things like you, it's obvious that she wants you to ... return to the earth. Most of us realise that they wanted you to find the body and take the blame. That's the very reason you need someone to look out for you.'

Valon's face had taken on a familiar, stubborn look and it was clear that Lonell would be wasting his breath trying to talk him out of it.

'And,' continued Valon, 'it is possible that I might be useful at times for you to share your brilliant ideas with!'

'I doubt it,' laughed Lonell, his eyes shining with gratitude, as he grabbed his friend's arm. His face became serious again.

'If it weren't for Sim, I would leave and try to find another tribe that would take me in - perhaps the Fillari - but I can't leave him now. So I'll be glad to have your companionship through this, my friend, but you must be careful and keep a watch out the whole time for .... anything! Truthfully, I don't know what they might do.'

As he uttered this last sentence, his eyes flickered over to the covered entrance of the opposite cave. There were no signs of activity but it was unnerving how the Enlightened Ones always seemed to know what was going on, even when they were not around.

'Come, let's eat some food,' said Valon. 'Then we can go hunting. I want to get away from the cave where we can talk without fear of being overheard. I also need to practice my tracking skills on animals rather than humans.'

'That is true,' replied Lonell loudly, in case anyone was interested enough to repeat their words to a Guardian. 'I need some new skins; I have torn my tunic.'

He put his hand behind his back and touched the flap of wolf skin that had been hanging down since Sim had stopped him from falling further down the slope. Suddenly he was filled with an intense sadness.

'Do you think you'll be able to find me a wolf or bear?' he asked, trying to keep his voice steady. 'You are supposed to be the Tracker of the Pescovari – you must prove it!'

'Yes, and I've heard that Davoril is going to challenge me for the title soon so I do need to practice.'

Lonell remembered how proud Valon had been when he had earned that title. Some names like his 'Dreamer' came about just because it highlighted a characteristic, but others like 'Tracker' had to be earned and retained.

Davoril heard the comment as he sat at the High Hearth. He pushed his blond hair back from his forehead and stood up, towering over those standing nearby.

'Actually, Tendo and I wondered if you and Lonell would like to compete against us at fish catching,' he said to Valon. 'We could make it a new title. I'm tired of just being Runner. It's too easy with these long legs.'

Davoril laughed loudly and then, remembering it was the wrong time for frivolity, he blushed.

'Perhaps, when all this is over,' he said solemnly, but his words had already started others to think about Challenges and a hum of conversation broke out around the cave.

Lonell nodded at Davoril approvingly as he headed towards the food. Passing those seated, he heard them talking about a range of Challenges from bear hunting to spear making. He wondered how long it would be before any of them might be taken up but it was irrelevant; although the sadness remained in the cave, the terrible weight of despair had been temporarily lifted.

Lonell and Valon helped themselves to a filling breakfast of goat stew, prepared with wild onions and carrots, and rabbit cooked on the spit, all accompanied by Lonell's favourite, flat bread made from ground acorns. Not only did he enjoy it, he appreciated it because of the hard work that it took to prepare the bread. Lonell always volunteered for the expedition to harvest the acorns in the forests that lined the lower slopes of the mountains. Then came the shelling and endless leeching to make them edible but, now, Lonell was only thinking about the delicious taste as he took a huge bite of the bread.

Having eaten, the two friends were about to leave when their path was crossed by a small, dark woman, her shoulders hunched as if in pain.

'You!' cried Verina, Sim's mother. She stared in hatred at Lonell. 'It should be you in there. You killed him. Sim didn't do it. My boy will not survive this and it's your fault!'

Quickly surrounded by three other women, Verina was led away sobbing, but Lonell saw that one of them, Mila, turned and stared at him with what he read as uncertainty.

Valon grabbed Lonell's arm and dragged him from the cave. They went to the weapon store and silently selected their spears. Lonell also took a net and they both picked long flint knives which they tucked into their belts.

Lonell did not look at Valon.

'If Verina keeps saying things like that,' he said, 'it won't take long until the whole tribe believes I killed Narthan. Even Mila has doubts. I could see it in her eyes and she knows me as well as anyone here.'

'No,' replied Valon. 'No one will think like that; certainly not Mila. We all know she likes you. Her face turns red when she looks at you, and I know that you two spend some very active nights together!'

He nudged Lonell and winked, trying to lighten the mood.

'Come, Lonell. Let's get away from here. I can feel a cave bear calling me!'

Lonell felt Valon pushing him forward as they ran up the sloping path and, at the top, he almost crashed into Tordano.

'Where are you going?' the Guardian questioned them.

'Hunting.'

The Guardian's right eyebrow arched, doubt on his face.

'I want some new skins. My tunic was torn as we carried Narthan back,' explained Lonell, watching for any reaction to his words, 'and the cave needs fresh food, so we're going hunting.'

He searched the man's pale eyes for some sign of a bond between them but there was none, no recognition of the fact that shortly before he had taken a grave risk to warn the tribesman. Tordano's face appeared emotionless.

'Very well, but listen out for the Summoning Horn – Saretta may want everyone to return, at any time,' he said.

The two men nodded and turned away from the Guardian, eager to escape. Lonell had taken two paces when he heard a quiet voice behind him say:

'Sarril and Valt are also out hunting. They have their bows with them.'

Chapter Four

'We must change our plan.' Lonell turned to his friend. 'In the cave we said we intended to hunt for wolves or bears, so they'll expect us to go towards the high mountains inland. I think we should take the path towards Sun Sleep instead.'

He pointed to the west.

'We could hunt mountain goats instead, or we may still have luck and find a wolf. I think it might be safer.'

'We didn't bring the right weapons for hunting goats but we do have the nets. Yes, we could do that. But they may still be watching us to see where we go.'

Valon looked around him and Lonell could see that his friend was nervous.

'Come on,' he urged. 'I know a way – follow me.'

At a run, Lonell led Valon over the High Pasture towards the inland mountains which rose majestically behind the dark forests, stretching skyward, their ragged tips disappearing into misty clouds. The men dropped down into a gully close to the tree line where they were out of sight from prying eyes. Then they headed in the direction they wanted to go. The trail was tortuous; they were not following an established path so their footing was uncertain, and their flint knives had to cut the way past shrubs and bushes, which caught at them with their long thorns, scratching arms and legs and tearing at their garments.

The sun was high by the time Valon and Lonell joined up with the well-used track and followed it to the lower slopes of the hills that stretched down to the Salt Water. Small white clouds were scudding across the blue sky, casting shadows that touched the land briefly and then disappeared. Up above them on the rocky hillside they spotted what they were looking for – a small herd of shaggy goats, unaware of any danger, was grazing peacefully on the tufts of hardy grasses that grew out of the inhospitable ground.

The two men studied the situation carefully and made their plans, drawing lines on the ground to point out potential positions. There was no need to talk. They hunted together so often that each knew what the other would do and, if there were a need to communicate from a distance, it would be done with a sign language that every hunter understood.

They started to climb quietly and slowly, placing their leather-bound feet with care so that no small stones rolled down the hill, alerting the animals to their presence. They kept the wind in their faces so their scent did not carry to their prey, for goats were naturally wary of humans and able to move extremely fast and with an agility the men did not possess which made hunting them a skilful task.

After a long climb, Lonell selected the position that he had shown Valon, where he thought the goats would run once they had been startled. He stopped to unravel the net and noticed with annoyance that it had not been mended properly on its last outing – he would bring that to the attention of the Leader. Everyone was responsible for replacing communal implements of any sort in a perfect condition, ready for the next person, and failure to do so showed a lack of respect and consideration for their fellow members of the tribe.

He spread the net out on the ground to look at it carefully. It was a large triangle made of the same cord as the bindings on the Pit gate. Lonell, like all members of the tribe, had spent many hours harvesting the creeping plant that grew in great abundance down the cliff sides throughout the vicinity of the caves in which they lived, for it was used in many ways, but its primary purpose was as rope and cord. As long as it was picked before it became woody, the stems were pliant, extremely strong and grew to a great length. In addition the tendrils could be used as small ties and delicate bindings. Known simply as the Cord Plant, one of the tasks the tribe had to perform before the long winter set in was to harvest as much of the plant as possible, without depleting it completely, so that it would grow again the following year.

Lonell noticed that some of the net's strands were wearing and one was broken. It had been quickly tied with grasses, obviously whilst hunting, but not repaired before being replaced in the store. He sighed – it would have to do. He checked the stones; at each point of the triangle was a stone tied into a small grass basket and attached to the net. The lead stone was larger than the other two and the hunters had developed a method of throwing the net neatly over an animal, the stones aiding its flight and also bringing it down quickly in the correct place. It required years of practice to perfect the skill, as Lonell knew well, for, although he was not one of the acclaimed hunters in the tribe, he was extremely adept with a net. It was a useful weapon in a hunt for most species of animals, for they could be brought down and then killed neatly with a knife in the neck which preserved the whole skin – there were no great holes in it where it had been struck with a spear. Of course, there were times when there was no choice; when the hunt became too dangerous or they wanted to take more than one animal, then spears or bows had to be used.

Whilst he prepared the nets, Lonell remained aware of the progress of Valon, who carefully continued further up the hill, stealthily avoiding the goats, until he found himself above them. Suddenly, Lonell felt his neck prickle and he turned to look over his shoulder. He thought he saw a flash of white but then, nothing.

Too Long To Die

There was no sound, no movement, but Lonell knew they were not alone. They were hunting the goats but someone was hunting them.

Lonell looked up the hill and saw Valon in position. He rapidly gave the signal and saw his friend move down towards the animals until they caught his scent on the air. Valon flapped his arms and the ensuing panic drove them downwards, for there was no escape further up, and they turned back towards where Lonell was waiting. He launched the net into the air, bringing it down on top of a large buck with impressive horns. The unfortunate beast lost its footing and tumbled over, its struggles only serving to tangle it further in the cords. Lonell was on it quickly and almost immediately the beast lay motionless, a single knife cut to the throat. As Lonell looked up, he saw a spear launched by Valon who was running headlong down the hillside after the animals. The flint spearhead sliced into the side of another buck, younger than his but still a good size. Valon, breathing hard, finished it off with his knife, before removing the spear carefully.

Once blood had stopped pumping out of the goats, the two men pulled the carcasses together.

'I give thanks to you for your sacrifice, that we may eat. I honour your life and I honour your death,' Lonell addressed the lifeless animals.

The men smiled at each other. For a few moments the activity had taken their thoughts away from their problems, the exercise had refreshed their bodies and their minds, but reality instantly came flooding back.

'These are large animals and we only have one net. It'll be hard to carry them back if we have to go the same way we came,' said Valon.

Lonell looked around and noticed an outcrop that jutted out of the hillside nearby which would afford them protection from anyone following them.

'I agree,' said Lonell, suddenly realising that the hollow feeling in his stomach was a mixture of hunger and fear. 'I think we should prepare our catch and eat before we start back, but not here.'

He pointed to the outcrop. They carried the carcasses into the safety of the shelter and, while Valon started to skin the goats expertly using his long knife, Lonell collected wood and dry grasses to start a fire, glancing around constantly. At one point, he was sure he heard a twig crack in the nearby undergrowth but he could see nothing. He tried to stop his hand from shaking as he took a little of the goat's fine hair and placed it in a circle of the grasses. Then he opened the small, waterproof bag which he always carried on his belt, and took out a cylindrical piece of grey stone and a smaller piece of flint. The nodule had a groove cut down the side and Lonell struck the flint against it, scraping down the groove which resulted in a tiny piece of the stone breaking away and igniting. He sent the spark onto the hair and grass kindling and leant down to blow on it. He smiled as the flame grew and, before he replaced the stone into the bag, Lonell uttered the words, 'My thanks to you.' The Marcasite nodules, when broken open, revealed a pattern which the Pescovari tribe considered proof that the stones had been given to man by the Sun God – its rays emanating from a central point within the stone. This, together with the fire it provided, left them in no doubt and, consequently, they were named Sun Stones.

As the Sun Stones could not be found near their cave, the tribe regularly sent traders south to exchange salt, shells which were highly desirable for decoration, skins and a variety of other goods for these plain, grey nodules, which made them valuable possessions to be treasured. Every person owned at least one Sun Stone and most had a second in reserve, for they were fragile and easily rendered unusable if not looked after correctly. Together with a person's weapons, these stones were vital for survival and thanks were always given when they were used, for fear that the Sun God might take away His gift if the people showed themselves to be ungrateful.

Lonell built up the fire and constructed a small framework. Strips of goat's flesh were hung over the flames, the smell of cooking meat making the two hungry men salivate as they sat waiting to eat. They stared out over the rocky terrain in front of them and the great expanse of the Salt Water beyond.

'I hate bows,' said Lonell suddenly, breaking the silence.

Valon looked round, one eyebrow raised questioningly.

'Well, you could be shot without ever knowing where it came from.'

'I know,' replied Valon. 'That's why it's so good. Think of how much easier it is to hunt since Delina made those first bows. If only we were all allowed to use them ... ' He shook his head with annoyance.

'I wonder what Ancient Brano would have thought if he could see what his mistake has turned into.'

Despite his worries, Lonell had to smile when he thought of how the bow had come about. It had been the great event of the summer before which started when Ancient Brano, now returned to the earth, wanted to make himself a shade under which he could sit to work on some nets. He tied a cord to the top of a sapling and pulled it down, attaching it around the middle of another shrub. Then he pulled the cord back again and tied it to the base of the sapling. Balancing a long stick from the shrub through to a branch of the small tree, he draped the cords over it which were needed for the net; Ancient Brano's eyes were no longer sharp but, with the cords hanging within reach, there was no need to search around for them. As he turned to sit down, he missed his footing and stumbled into the shrub, breaking the cord and sending the stick gliding through the air, albeit not very far.

All this might easily have passed without comment - just an

embarrassingly clumsy mistake by the old man that no one would have mentioned, but the projectile landed beside a young woman just missing her. Delina turned in anger, thinking that someone had thrown it, but seeing Ancient Brano struggling in the bushes, she smothered her laughter and went to help him. Afterwards she thought about his muddled explanation and an idea came to her. Her love of hunting was well known and she often commented on how much more effective and less dangerous it would be if they could bring down an animal from greater distances. This might just be the answer.

Over the next few days people wondered where she was disappearing to by herself, because she refused to tell anyone. Just as the Leader was beginning to seriously worry about her, Delina arrived back at the cave with a crude but workable bow. She had cut a long piece of pine – it had taken her time to find the right wood that could bend enough – and then tied a thin length of cord, making notches on both end to hold the cord. She had her bow; now she had to look for a stick that would travel when fired. She found the answer at Mountain Water, where the tall reeds grew high and straight. She cut one down, flattened an end and sharpened the other to a point, thereby creating the first arrow. The weapon was basic but everyone could see its potential. When Delina told the tribe the whole story, their laughter turned to great admiration; even Lonell was impressed by her determination and initiative.

Since then, the weapon had been refined and it had become a fearsome weapon – so much so that Saretta declared that only the Leader, the Enlightened Ones and Delina, known thereafter as Bow Maker, were allowed to use them. It was Lonell who had suggested that a small piece of sharp flint could be introduced to the end of the arrow which would allow it to cut through flesh more efficiently. When Delina discovered the method of gluing the tip with a thick mixture made from goats' hooves and then binding the end with cord until just the sharpened blade stuck out from the end, it became a truly deadly weapon.

Unfortunately, Ancient Brano did not live long enough to see the bow perfected - he returned to the earth, passing on his title to Pel - but his last days were filled with the development of the new weapon and he sat grinning toothlessly as everyone laughed about his unusual method of invention. He would forever be remembered as the inventor of the bow and arrow, and Delina, as the weapon's developer.

Although he could see the advantages of such a weapon, at this moment Lonell wished that Ancient Brano had stayed in the cave to make his nets. He knew that someone could be aiming an arrow at him right now and he would not even know it. He tried to concentrate on other things, but the feeling that he was being watched would not leave him.

The clouds had thickened, becoming more menacing, as they raced over the waves below.

'Do you know why they want you to return to the earth?'

Valon did not look at his friend as he bluntly asked the question that had been on his mind since the moment they had brought Narthan's body back.

'I've been asking myself the same question. I don't know anything that I've done so I can only think they must be worried that I'll discover who did kill Narthan. Tordano found me this morning and warned me not to try to find out,' added Lonell.

'Did he? It is true that if anyone can find out the truth it's you, but there's something I don't understand - surely the Enlightened Ones must want to know the truth of what happened to their Guardian. And what they've done to Sim ... none of it makes sense!' Valon's confusion was clearly written on his face as he looked at Lonell, hoping he would have some form of an answer.

'Sim is only in the Pit because he said he found Narthan. They thought I found the body; they didn't expect Sim to come forward and, when that happened and everyone heard Saretta shout 'Death', she couldn't change what she'd already said. She was forced to follow it through even though her trap had caught the wrong person.' Lonell spoke quietly and deliberately, voicing his own thoughts rather than giving an answer to the question.

'Do you think she deliberately set a trap to catch you?' asked Valon, aware that Lonell was, as he called it, 'talking his thoughts'.

There was a silence and Valon had to repeat his question before Lonell looked at him.

'Yes, I do,' he replied. 'I can't think of another explanation. But I agree with you - the real question is, why don't they want to find out what really happened to Narthan?'

While he waited for the meat to cook, he peered into the distance where he thought he saw a shadow move and heard stones rolling over the hard ground, but the bright sun shone into his eyes. When it was ready, a distracted Lonell took some of the food on a stick from Valon who then helped himself. They sat in silence, chewing the succulent goat meat and thinking.

'We must make our way back to the cave soon,' said Lonell, jumping to his feet. 'The less time we spend out here, the safer I'll feel! Are you aware that we've been followed ever since we left?'

'Who is it?' asked Valon, his voice rising in concern. He looked round, quickly searching the hillside with frightened eyes. 'I don't see anyone.'

Lonell stamped out the fire.

'No, but they are there,' he said. 'I've heard them and seen someone moving on the hillside but I couldn't see who it was. We must go now.'

Valon did not need the instruction repeated. Lonell almost laughed at the sight of his friend as he rushed to wrap the carcasses inside the skins and put them all in the net. Valon's hands became caught up in the cords in his haste and he cursed as he tried to shake himself free. Lonell came to his aid and, placing an assuring hand on his Valon's shoulder, he calmly disentangled his struggling friend. The blond man gritted his teeth and, pulling his hand free, straightened up. Embarrassed, he picked up the load, showing a strength that seemed out of proportion to his build.

'I'll carry this; you take the spears. We can change over later. Which direction shall we take? Back the way we came?' Valon's voice betrayed his emotions and he cleared his throat, staring into the distance.

Lonell turned his head and looked back up the track. A frown furrowing his brow, his eyes scanned the surrounding scenery but he could see nothing. Suddenly he stepped to one side and felt a sharp pain in his right upper arm. An arrow passed by and struck the ground, skidding to a halt, just in front of him. Its darkened tip was stained with Lonell's blood. Instantly he stooped and picked it up.

'Quick! This way!' he shouted, and the two men hurtled down the hillside, skidding on the slippery stones, in the direction of the Salt Water.

Too Long To Die

Chapter Five

Lonell and Valon ran to the edge where wind and rain had eroded the hillside away over the ages, creating a sheer cliff. With no second thought they jumped, landing on the sand below. Lonell rolled and got to his feet quickly, relieved that he had broken no bones from the long fall, but he could see that Valon, with the weight of the two carcasses on his back, had been severely winded and was lying, gasping for air. Lonell dragged the burden off his friend and hefted it onto his shoulder.

'You should have thrown them down first. Are you injured?' he asked.

Valon shook his head, unable to speak, and Lonell pulled him to his feet with his one free arm.

'Come. I know where we can hide. We must get to shelter. I don't know if they're still hunting us.'

Lonell thought quickly. Should they walk through the Salt Water where they would leave no tracks but be exposed to further attacks or keep hidden close by the cliffs which offered some protection? He chose the latter.

'We'll be safer this way,' he said, 'but keep your feet on stones where you can so we don't leave a trail.'

He could hear Valon gasping for breath as he led the way along the beach until, after what seemed an age to both men, they came across a vast boulder that had broken off and fallen from the cliff above.

'In here,' said Lonell.

Too Long To Die

He pushed past the large rock, dragging the carcasses behind. There, hidden from view, was a cave. It was only small, accessed by squeezing through a narrow gap but in the gloom there were signs that it had been used recently. A hearth still had the remnants of a fire in it and there was a bundle of kindling lying beside it. On a ledge at the side was a wolf skin which belonged to Lonell and some deer bone platters.

'I didn't know this was here,' said Valon, looking around. 'You've used it before.' It was a statement, not a question.

'I come here many times,' admitted Lonell, 'when I need to escape from the noise; I need to be alone sometimes. I found it when I was a boy.'

'You keep things here,' stated Valon, still breathing deeply.

'Yes. Things I don't want anyone to know about. Recently I've brought more down here.'

'What sort of things? Why?' asked Valon, looking around him curiously, and Lonell realised that his friend, so open and trusting, would not consider hiding anything from the tribe.

Lonell stared at the man in front of him for a moment, as if weighing him up. He went to a niche in the cave wall and pulled out some more skins which he spread on the ledge.

'Come, sit. It's time I told you something I've never shared with anyone before.'

They settled down on the skins, hardened through lack of use.

'It's not easy to tell,' said Lonell, after a short hesitation. 'You'll understand why when you hear what I'm going to say. But, before I go on, you must swear on your Sacred Stones that you will never repeat what I tell you to another person. Do you swear?'

His clenched jaw relaxed slightly when Valon stood up, put his right fist to his brow and declared formally:

'I swear on the Sacred Stones of my kin that I shall never repeat to another person what you are about to tell me.'

He sat down again and stared at Lonell, waiting expectantly.

Lonell took a deep breath.

'I first knew when I could count four winters although I had no understanding of it but, after seven winters had passed, I had no doubt that I was different. It wasn't happening to other children.' He lapsed into silence, wondering whether to tell the entire truth, including the find he had made as a child.

'Tell me, my friend. What was happening to you?' urged Valon, interrupting his thoughts.

Lonell looked hard at his friend, deep lines furrowing his brow.

'There are times when I hear someone talking to me but it's in here.' He tapped his head.

Valon frowned and opened his mouth to ask but Lonell shook his head and held his hand in front of his mouth to silence him.

'There's no voice,' he continued, 'no sound that others can hear. I feel as though someone is looking after me – someone I can't see. They ... send me warnings and sometimes tell me what I should do.'

He could read doubt on Valon's face.

'This is difficult. I've never put it into words before - it's hard to explain.'

He thought for a moment.

'Do you remember the time I almost ran off the cliff when we were hunting in the mountains? The reason I stopped was that I was told to – quite clearly a voice in my head told me to stop, so I did. And sometimes I just get a feeling. It tells me when people are sick, when they need help.'

He grinned sheepishly.

'I call it my 'helper', he added.

'Well, it didn't tell you someone was going to shoot an arrow at you,' argued Valon.

'Not exactly,' replied Lonell, 'but it did tell me to move to the side. If I hadn't, I think I would have returned to the earth now.'

He knew that Valon had seen his strange movement and had no doubt wondered what he was doing, but it had been forgotten as they ran. Valon was now looking at him in concern. Lonell was sure that he was fighting the urge to touch his forehead for protection.

'Look, I know it's difficult to believe. If someone told me they heard voices, I would think they were head-sick.'

The gloom in the cave seemed to thicken as the two men sat without speaking.

'Can't you ask this voice to tell you who killed Narthan?' Valon asked suddenly.

Lonell smiled grimly and shook his head.

'It doesn't work like that. I have tried to ask questions but I get no reply. I just have to wait for messages and it doesn't tell me everything that's going to happen. I don't know how it works. I don't understand it anymore than you.'

He shook his head again and suddenly knew, without doubt, that now was not the time to reveal his discovery to his friend. The warning in his head was almost a shout: *He is not yet ready.*

Lonell was surprised how important it was to him that Valon believe his words. He just wanted the man beside him to accept it, not to question too much.

'Well, it does explain some of the things you've done,' said Valon, 'It doesn't make any sense to me but, if you don't understand it either, I won't even try.'

He laughed and put his hand on his friend's shoulder but stopped when he saw the tension still lining Lonell's face.

'Is there more?' he asked.

'I want you to think about something.' Lonell hesitated. 'When Saretta became High Priestess, everyone hoped it would be Lexana, so why was Saretta chosen? No one wanted her.'

'Because she talks with the Gods, she hears Their words.' Valon blanched, his hand flew to his mouth.

'And she has become evil and head-sick. You see why you mustn't tell anyone,' insisted Lonell, urgently. 'Everyone would say I was head-sick. They think I'm strange enough without hearing this.'

'Is it the Gods? Do They talk to you?'

'I don't know. I don't think so. It can't be.' Lonell's tortured voice filled the cave. 'But you mustn't say a word to anyone.'

'No one will hear of this from me. I have sworn,' Valon reassured his friend.

The silence that descended once more, tense and suffocating, was finally broken by Valon.

'You are a good man, Lonell. If the Gods are talking to you I know you will use it to help others, not like Saretta. It is not the same,' he said determinedly.

Lonell's rough hand surreptitiously wiped a tear away before Valon could see it. He cleared his throat, glad of the gloom of the cave.

'And no one else knows about this cave, so don't mention it either. The reason I come here and keep some things in the cave is that ... I've been told to.'

Lonell pointed at his head again.

'I don't know why yet, but I have the feeling it will be needed soon. I'm sure I was led to this cave for a reason and I think we'll soon be shown why.'

Lonell leant back against the cold, damp wall of the cave and watched Valon, relieved that, finally, someone else knew his secret but also fearful that it might be too much for his friend. He watched Valon stand for a moment before kneeling to light a fire in the cold hearth and knew he was trying to process what he had just been told. The kindling was damp and the sparks from the Sun Stone were instantly extinguished as they landed and Valon soon gave up. He stretched and tried to look around him.

Lonell was aware that Valon desperately wanted to see what he was keeping there but with no fire, only a little light came into the cave. Lonell stood, took down a fish oil lamp from a high ledge, and lit it, using more of the goat wool as kindling. As he turned to put it back up Valon reached out and took the lamp from him, shining it on his arm.

'Your blood is running,' he said, 'and the arm is very red. Did you know the arrow hit you?'

'I forgot about it when we started to run. It only just caught me and there's little pain. When we leave here I'll wash it in Salt Water.'

'Good idea,' agreed Valon. 'How long do you think we should stay here?'

Lonell thought carefully. There were two times each day when everyone knew exactly where the Enlightened Ones would be. At Sun Wake, as the day started, and Sun Sleep, when darkness fell, the ceremony was held in the meadow at Mountain Water. As a boy, he once had crept out to see what they did and the sight of the pale figures in the waning light, chanting unintelligible words, had seemed so unnatural that he had broken out into a cold sweat of fear. Suddenly the High Priestess had stopped and looked up in his direction and he had run shakily back to the cave, not waiting to learn what happened and the vision had haunted him for many days afterwards. She had not said anything about it and he never did find out if she had really seen him but the memory had stayed with him since that day.

'We can go back safely when the Enlightened Ones are at the Sun Sleep ceremony, so we must wait until the light begins to move away. It will not be long.'

'So, are you sure it's one of them trying to kill you?' Valon's voice began to crack slightly, revealing the fear which was growing inside him. 'Why?'

'Sure no, but I think it must be. Valt guided me towards the body and expected me to find it, so that I would be held for the killing. And we know from Tordano that Sarril and Valt are out hunting with bows and it was an arrow that hit me. There are few who can use the bow and I can't imagine that any member of the tribe would want me dead.'

Lonell stopped. He realised that when he said 'the tribe' he did not include the Enlightened Ones, even though they were Pescovari - they had become so entirely alienated from those he saw as his people. He shook his head to clear the thoughts.

'But, when I think about it,' he went on, 'they might do - almost everyone's afraid that I'll find out the truth in case the killer is someone they're close to.'

'Only two people in the tribe know how to use a bow and neither Kadell nor Delina have any reason to harm you,' insisted Valon.

'Are you certain of that?' asked Lonell, who had gone to the rear of the cave and came out holding a bow in his hand.

'I can use it quite well now.'

Valon gasped in horror.

'But if they catch you ... Why did you do it?'

'Why? Because everyone should be allowed to,' Lonell replied angrily. 'This can save lives when we're out hunting. We should be told to learn how to use it, not stopped. The Enlightened Ones use them on hunts because it keeps them safe but we don't matter. I don't like being told I can't do something which might save my life.'

He sat down heavily, turning the bow over in his hand.

'But that's not why I'm telling you. Think about it, if I'm learning to use this, others may be doing the same.'

Valon thought for a moment.

'That may be true,' he said, 'but I can't believe anyone in the tribe wants you ... gone, surely.'

'Someone does. I'm a threat to the killer. It could be anybody, except you. I don't think you'd be able to shoot at me when you're with me!' Lonell laughed, and Valon visibly relaxed for a moment at the sound.

'No,' continued Lonell, looking upwards. 'I have to go back to the beginning and forget for the moment about who's trying to kill me. I need to work out who would want to kill Narthan. If I can answer that, the rest will become clear, ... I hope.'

'It could be anyone,' said Valon, running a hand through his blond hair. 'Nobody liked him - in fact, many people loathed him for some wrong he had done to them.'

Lonell nodded and thought about the utter lack of mourning in the cave. Not one person had shown any form of grief for the dead man.

'Normally, when even the most difficult person returns to the earth, someone grieves for them.' He voiced his thoughts out loud.

'Do you remember, you once said you hoped his life would come to a bad end?' asked Valon.

'I did, and I meant it then, but it was a long time ago – I was only a boy. I never trusted him after that though. No, it wasn't me,' he smiled. 'But, you're correct, it could be anyone.'

Lonell's forehead settled into frown lines once again.

'Flamina – she became head-sick when Marita returned from her Journey to Womanhood. If Kadell and his sister had not held her back, I think she would have gone over to the other cave and killed Narthan then. She might have been planning how to get her revenge all this time,' offered Valon, as a first consideration.

Lonell said nothing as he considered the possibility. He had been a young boy when Saretta became High Priestess and moved herself and the other Enlightened Ones out of the tribal cave and into their own White Cave. At the same time she created new laws and customs which had to be followed without question. The Journey to Womanhood was one such innovation - Saretta announced that every girl who had experienced her first blood loss must undergo 'education' which would develop her and turn her into a perfectly trained woman.

No man of the tribe was allowed to touch the learner, as she was called, during this time. Lonell had watched as the women of the cave instructed a series of young girls in the finer arts of cooking, making clothes, preparing skins, cleaning and collecting food and herbs. The learner also had to help to look after another woman's baby and be taught about the basic forms of ailments and how to cure them. The first time a baby was not available, Lonell had laughed to himself as he watched the actions being played out using a bundle of old skins with explanations from the women. He thought much of it ridiculous and unnecessary because children, as they grew in the cave, were exposed in a general sense to most of this information. However, all the women had to take part in the teaching and it lasted for three of the moon's cycles. At the end, the learner had to pass an extensive test, conducted by the Enlightened Ones, in front of the whole tribe and each time, Lonell felt a great sympathy for the shaking young girl.

The first time he watched, he was surprised that, when he thought it was over, the terrified girl was led away to the White Cave and he asked Endorina, who was sitting at his side, what was happening. She explained to him, trying to hide her anger, that the learner was taken to the White Cave for another three moon cycles where one of the Guardians became her 'Guide' and, in this phase of the education, she was taught how to please a man. What she had not added to the young Lonell, but he knew now, was that this was the most frightening part for the learner because she was then completely at the mercy of her Guide - he could do with her as he wished. Usually the girls were treated kindly as long as they behaved, but Lonell was now thinking about a Journey where the learner had been cruelly abused. It left a lasting impression on him, as it had on everyone.

He remembered Flamina's immense pride when Marita announced that it was her time but he knew she was nervous, as all mothers were. No one doubted that this fun-loving, intelligent girl would pass every part of the ordeal and emerge a successful and extremely desirable, young woman. Lonell, like many a tribesman, looked forward to spending some time with the latest adult member of the Pescovari.

Not long after Marita was led away by Narthan the tribe began to hear the screams and cries coming from the opposite cave. They heard them for many nights and sometimes during the days. The tribe tried to keep Flamina busy to distract her but it was an impossible task and the chilling sounds went on day after day. Then the silence fell and no one knew if this was better or worse.

When Marita finally returned to the tribe, gone was the beautiful, smiling child. In her place came a thin, terrified girl who looked out at the world through haunted eyes. From that day she had not spoken a word and if a man went anywhere near her she cringed and clutched at her mother who was always by her side. She never left the cave unless forced, took no part in activities and spent her time staring inwardly to a place of unimaginable horror. Lonell felt his nails digging into the palms of his hands as he relived the anger and helplessness they had all felt.

'You're right,' said Lonell, his voice echoed in the cave, making Valon jump as he wondered for a moment what he was right about.

'Neither Flamina nor Marita will be sorry at his death. We don't know whether Marita is able to plan anything but, if she can, she certainly has more reason to want revenge than most.'

'Everyone hated him for what he did to her. If that's the reason for his death, it could be anyone. Even Saretta knew that Narthan had gone too far. I think that's why he hasn't been selected as a Guide since, but then, he's not been punished for what he did either. Maybe she thought he'd disgraced the Guardians ...?' Valon let the question hang in the air.

Lonell thought it unlikely but it could not be completely discounted.

'The problem is the time that's passed since it happened. Surely the killer would have acted sooner, or did they wait so that no one would suspect them?'

'If Narthan always behaved in that way with women, maybe he hurt someone else who never told anyone. Anyway, why does it have to be a Guardian who guides the girls to womanhood? They never used to have to go through such an ordeal.'

Lonell could hear the fury in his friend's voice and his hope of finding the killer sank; if Valon and he both felt such hatred for Narthan, then so would everyone else.

Suddenly he remembered a thought that had come to him when Jadilla, another young woman of the tribe, had started carrying a baby shortly after she returned from her Journey. When Jadana was born with white skin and pale eyes his suspicion seemed to be confirmed but until now he had not mentioned it to anyone else. He found the whole idea repulsive and was sure that others would have the same reaction.

'I have wondered if Saretta hopes these girls will become mothers shortly after their stay in the White Cave and that the babies might have pale skins,' Lonell slowly put his thoughts into words.

Silence filled the cave and Lonell could see Valon trying to grasp the full meaning of the words.

'What do you mean?'

'Think about it. The only pale babies born have been to women after they return from their Journey - Jadana, Tordano and we know Delina's baby would have been pale if it had lived.'

'Do you think that being in the White Cave makes a difference? Is that why she makes them take the Journey? No! Even Saretta! She wouldn't ... ' Lonell could hear the disgust in his friend's voice.

'I think she would,' insisted Lonell. 'Jadana will be taken into the White Cave after the next winter.'

'If what you're saying is right, why don't all the women have pale babies when they come back?'

'I don't know,' admitted Lonell, frustrated. 'All I'm saying is that the babies born much later are never pale, so there must be ... a link.'

'Saretta must be doing something to them while they're over there, trying to create more Enlightened Ones. She's using our women and they're not even given a choice. Sacred Stones, until now I've never understood why they had to be treated like that.'

Valon's face was a mixture of astonishment and horror but Lonell began to realise that he seemed to be looking at his friend through a fog.

'Oh yes, there's something else I forgot to tell you,' he heard Valon say, as though from a distance.

'Not now,' mumbled Lonell, in a low voice. 'Tell me later.'

His legs were beginning to shake and he could hear a thumping noise from his chest. He put a hand to his forehead and felt the cold, damp skin.

Hiding his concern, he stood up and went to the entrance of the hidden cave. He could feel a difference in the air; night was coming on. Even during a glorious summer the nights brought a distinct drop in temperature which drove people back into their caves.

Lonell's mind was whirling in a mist filled with large animals covered in thick, waterproof fur and spear-wielding men fighting them for their skins. Why had the Gods not gifted man a luxurious fur covering? It would have made life so much easier.

He shook his head, trying to clear his mind.

'Come,' he said to Valon. 'The light is beginning to move away. We should be safe to go back.'

The two men moved down to the water's edge where Lonell cleaned off his wound. He cursed quietly as the salt made the long cut on his arm sting viciously, but he knew it was the best way to clean it and the pain cleared his head for a while. They walked along the sand, constantly glancing around them and up at the overlooking cliff edge and, as they did so, the beach became wider and more rocky. The grey clouds being blown across the darkening sky were silhouetted by a deep orange glow and the light was starting to fade.

They made their way to the place where Lonell had been when Valon had come searching for him only the day before. How much longer it seemed; so much had happened in that short space of time. With each step, Lonell was feeling worse; his chest was tight, making breathing uncomfortable and his cold, clammy skin was sweating. He pulled himself up the steep path to the High Pasture but it was becoming difficult to walk, his feet weighing heavy and his sight blurring. He pushed himself as far as he could. He was not sure at what point he dropped the spears and arrow but, half way across the High Pasture, Lonell collapsed, hitting the ground hard. Through the fog and maelstrom of enormous beasts and frail humans, he heard Valon shouting his name.

'Lonell, come on! Stand up! We must return to the cave. You need help!'

He was being shaken and tried to move but he had no control over his body. He felt himself being picked up. He tried to speak, to say he could walk by himself, that he did not need help, but no sound came out of his mouth. He saw, through the grey mist, the ground racing past as he was carried at a run, over Valon's shoulder. He felt them scrambling down the path to the cave, sliding, almost falling, one shoulder scraping against the rock wall.

They rushed into the cave and the last thing Lonell saw was the fear and shock on the faces of his fellow tribesmen and women when they noticed his inert body slumped over Valon's shoulder. He heard a wail go up from the women which echoed round the cave but he had disappeared into the foggy depths of numbed sleep before the men, who were hastening towards them, managed to relieve Valon of his burden.

'Help! Healer, please help us!' shouted Valon over the noise, to an older woman who emerged from the back of the cave, limping towards them. His voice shook with anguish:

'I think he's returning to the earth!'

Too Long To Die

Chapter Six

'Take him over there,' she said, her voice raised to penetrate the noise echoing around the cave. She pointed to where Lonell usually slept.

'Tell me. What happened?'

Someone - Valon could not remember who it was afterwards - rolled out Lonell's bed skins and he was placed gently onto them.

'He was hit ... shot by an arrow,' Valon spluttered, his eyes dark with concern. 'It didn't seem bad at first but then he just fell down and couldn't move.'

Even as he spoke, the Healer was examining the wound. She looked up at him, concern etched into her lined face.

'This sickness comes from more than this small wound.' She shook her head, smelt the wound, and muttered, 'Salt Water and ... Death Juice. They have used Death Juice on the arrow.'

'Death Juice?' repeated Valon, his voice cracking. 'What's that?'

He stood up, running his hand through his blond hair as he always did when worried.

'The liquid from many plants can return us to the earth. The arrow must have been covered in one of these juices,' the Healer explained as she continued to examine the sick man.

Kadell, who had been watching silently from the middle hearth, desperate to be close but not wanting to intrude, strode towards them when he heard this.

'Can you heal him, Endorina?' he asked, struggling to appear calm in front of his tribe.

'I need to know which plant was used but I can't tell because of the Salt Water. I can give him something but it may not help if it's the wrong plant.'

She looked around in desperation.

'We should get Lexana - she will know more.'

'Wait,' interrupted Valon. 'Lonell was carrying the arrow with the spears. He dropped them all. If I can find them ...'

He looked around as though searching for help and his eyes landed on two men, one tall and slim with brown hair, the other short, stocky and immensely strong.

'Davoril, Tendo,' he called. 'Will you come with me?'

They needed no second invitation. While Valon explained what they were looking for, Tendo scratched his large nose in thought, his dark eyes on the ground, and Davoril moved from foot to foot, itching to be on his way.

Someone lit burning torches and handed them to the men. The three left the cave at a run. The light from the flames flickered on the ground as they sped over the High Pasture and they almost stumbled over a large bundle. Much to Valon's amazement, it was the forgotten carcasses which were untouched. The thought that they might have been guarded by Lonell's 'helper' flickered into his mind, but Valon told himself not to be ridiculous. A little further on, the wavering light picked up the shape of the spears lying on the ground and, holding the torch high, Valon searched the area until he found the arrow which he picked up carefully, now aware of the danger that it presented.

When they arrived back at the cave, Valon headed straight towards Endorina and handed over the offending arrow, while Davoril and Tendo took the meat and skins away. He saw them hand the pelts to Kadella who started rolling them carefully to await his attention when he had the time. Vellisco, the cook, took possession of the goats and, before he turned back to Lonell, he saw the carcasses being divided and many people stepping forward to help. Food and skins were a valuable commodity, as were other parts such as the hooves, horns, intestines and bladders. Nothing would be wasted and the work would give people something to do to keep their minds off the man who was lying close to death.

Endorina peered at the arrow, brought it up to her nose and sniffed deeply. Then she nodded.

'From the colour of the arrow and the smell I think it's the juice of the Hanging Flower that's been used – the one that grows on the tall plant with the long, white flowers that close up at night. If it's eaten it can be very dangerous - you're unlikely to live if you eat some of that.'

She stopped and stared hard at Lonell, lying motionless beside her.

'He's lucky the arrow did not stay in his body,' she continued, 'and that it struck him far from his centre. He will have a struggle this night. If he lives until Sun Wake he may survive but it will be a long night.'

She was talking quietly, more to herself than the others, as though reminding herself of the facts. She looked into a skin bag that she kept by her side and rummaged through it.

'I'll give him a drink of this Sweating Root which should help clear out the Death Juice that's inside him.'

She held up a long, dried rhizome, deftly cut some thin slices and walked over to the fire where a bowl, made from a bear skull, was lying beside the flames.

'When you went out I started to heat some water,' she said as she poured some into a horn cup and added the root slices.

'What is that?' asked Valon, doubts niggling at the back of his mind.

'It's the root of a small plant with pink flowers. It doesn't grow around the cave. If you break the plant itself, it leaks white, sticky liquid – you have to be careful. I have to walk far to find it, but it's very useful for many sicknesses. It can be dangerous if it is not used properly but, don't worry, I know what he needs.'

She put one hand on Valon's arm and her wise eyes looked reassuringly into his. He nodded, feeling a lump in his throat, and turned his head away.

'While that's getting ready, I'll treat the wound with Cleansing Flowers,' she held up some small mauve flowers, each with five petals, which Valon recognised instantly. They grew in abundance in the area including the High Pasture and the meadowland beside Mountain Water. Valon was amazed to see them being used in healing for they were the same flowers that everyone used for washing. He knew that other tribes they met did not wash as frequently as the Pescovari, who considered it an important part of their culture. He had always assumed it was because they had so many of these flowers nearby that turned the water into a soft, soapy liquid when they rubbed the petals. Like most of the tribe, Valon hated it when they were not allowed to wash in the days before a tribal hunt, when the scent of the flowers could alert the prey to their presence. He had never thought to wonder if the plant could have another use.

Seeing the surprise on the faces watching her, Endorina smiled.

'Yes,' she said. 'They are the same ones we use for washing our bodies, but they work very well on cuts and injuries like this. Luckily I still have some.'

Valon looked at her questioningly.

'The High Priestess has told Endorina that she cannot heal us,' explained Kadell, 'that she can no longer be called 'Healer' and they took all her healing plants. They tried to take the bear bowl, too, but she hid it.'

'Well, not quite all my plants,' said Endorina, as she busied herself over the wound, her face hidden in shadow.

Too Long To Die

'All my life I have dedicated myself to finding plants to cure or help sickness. Then, two moons ago, Saretta came to me with no warning, saying I could no longer treat people – that anyone who needed healing plants or potions must go to the White Cave and ask Narthan for them. I know over there they have more knowledge but I look after you all ...'

She stopped suddenly and caught her breath, trying to control her emotions.

'Now I do what little I can at the back of the cave here so Saretta won't find out what I'm doing.'

Valon could hear the bitterness in her voice and knew she was harbouring a fury and sadness inside her. Just for a moment, he wondered what she would be capable of doing.

It was only then that the full gravity of the situation hit him. Endorina was willing to call Lexana, one of the Enlightened Ones, and, in doing so, she risked Saretta's discovery that she was still healing and the inevitable consequences. Valon's stomach went cold as he realised that, despite Endorina's encouraging words, his friend was dangerously sick.

Endorina held Lonell's head and helped him drink the draught she had prepared. She stood up and turned to the others.

'I have done all I can for the moment but I must speak to Lexana,' she said quietly.

'I'll go and ask her to come over,' offered Kadella, glad to be of some use. She too was aware of the gesture that Endorina was making.

Valon watched as she left the cave and made her way around the ledge. She slapped her hand against the white hide that covered the entrance and he breathed a sigh of relief when Talia responded, not one of the Guardians. He could see Kadella explaining the situation and the tall, silent girl disappeared, only to return almost immediately with Lexana, bearing a large skin bag.

Kadella led the way back and when Lexana, the sad-faced, kindly Attendant walked in, the tribe came to a standstill. Watched by everyone, she approached Kadell and asked permission to enter the cave, bringing smiles to their faces. It had been a long time since any Enlightened One had shown any respect and the tribe took her to their hearts once again. The older members of the tribe were reminded of the days before Saretta had split the Pescovari people, bringing fear and mistrust of the Enlightened Ones.

Valon sat beside his unconscious friend while Lexana talked to Endorina, their brows furrowed. He could see the Healer explaining what she had done and the relief when Lexana nodded in agreement. He moved aside to let her examine the sick man and she shook her head in disgust when shown the arrow. He suddenly became aware that the cave had fallen silent, each person's eyes on the Attendant, waiting to hear what she had to say.

'Endorina has done everything possible for Lonell,' she announced, her voice loud in the heavy silence. 'Now we must wait to see if he survives the night.'

By the morning Lonell's arm had swollen into a hard mass of burning heat and the sick man's initial silence gave way to an internal battle for life where he groaned and sweated in his bed skins, tossing from side to side.

'We must cut out the Death Juice or he will die,' declared Lexana after examining it and Valon saw Endorina pale at the thought.

'Have you cut into someone before?' she asked the Enlightened One and when Lexana shook her head, Valon felt a knot of fear in his stomach for his friend. He jumped when Lexana called his name.

'Valon, can you find us the sharpest flint in the cave, please.'

He jumped to his feet and went to find Pallo, the cave's flint knapper, to ask him for his finest blade. He returned with a slither of stone, so sharp that Valon carried it back with great care, marvelling that such blades could be found within lumps of stone.

Lexana nodded appreciatively as he handed it over and he backed away to observe from a distance. The Assistant Priestess looked upwards and called on the Gods to help save the sick man and then looked hard at Endorina, kneeling on the other side of the body, who nodded back.

'We need people to hold him down,' requested Lexana of the silent men and women, watching. Valon and Tendo were the first to step forward and while Valon held his friend's shoulders firmly, Tendo took up position at his feet. Endorina held down the arm on her side and Lexana put her knee firmly on Lonell's free hand.

Lexana's hand was slightly shaking as she held the blade to Lonell's skin. It did not surprise Valon - he had never heard of a healer cutting into a person's skin. Cures were only put on the outside or drunk, in his experience. She hesitated and then withdrew the knife.

'We must move him into the light. It's too dark here.'

They laid him down gently in the cave entrance and, once more, Lexana bent over the swollen arm. Valon heard her deep breath as she pushed the blade into the red, hard skin, close to the wound. As she cut, blood began to seep, followed by an ooze of thick yellow pus which covered Lexana's hand.

'Hold him still!' she shouted as the sick man began to thrash around. He was instantly pushed down and she continued to cut, one tiny movement at a time.

With the pus released, Lexana stopped slicing and washed the wound out with clear water. She peered down at her work and Valon saw her frown. She took the knife and inserted it once more and, using one finger and the blade pulled out a thin sliver of wood. She cleaned the wound thoroughly and covered it with large green leaves, tying them round the arm with soft pieces of hide. Then she sat back on her heels and let out a long breath. Her face was shiny with perspiration.

Valon, like everyone else, was looking at her in admiration but it was Endorina who had the courage to ask:

'Will he now live?'

'Only the Gods know the answer to that question. It is in Their hands. I can do no more.'

Valon and Mila stayed beside Lonell through the nights. During the day, the women of the cave took turns in sitting beside him, doing what they could to make him comfortable and Valon was pleased when Verina, Sim's mother, appeared to regret her words to him and offered to help in any way she could. As he drifted off to sleep after his night's vigil, Valon realised how much he loved his tribe, their willingness to help another member and their natural kindness, even in difficult times.

On the third night a scream jarred everyone awake. Mila leant over Lonell, shaking him.

'He has returned to the earth,' she wailed. 'Look, he's not moving!' She fell against Valon, sobbing.

Endorina rushed over to Lonell and put her hand on his chest; a hum of mourning began to fill the cave.

'Quiet!' she shouted. The hum stopped instantly. Valon watched as she put her ear to his chest and saw her relief when she heard a low but steady beat which she knew was the sign of life. She put the back of her hand in front of his mouth and felt the gentle tickle of shallow breath against her skin. Smiling, she stood up and addressed the tribe.

'Lonell still has life. I think he is winning his battle with the Death Juice which has been long and hard. He is now sleeping deeply and must become strong again. It's not yet over but now I feel ... I hope he will live.'

A relieved murmur went round the cave and everyone settled down again. Valon still held Mila, now crying in happiness rather than grief.

'You get some sleep now,' he said to her. 'I'll watch for the rest of the night.'

Lexana spent most of her time in the tribal cave, leaving only for ceremonies and late at night. Valon started wondering whether she really preferred to be with them. She made no reference to the ban on Endorina's healing and the two women worked together in harmony for the good of the sick man. They talked incessantly about plants and cures, sharing new ideas, learning from each other.

Valon's thoughts were finally confirmed while he sat resting, his eyes closed. He was tired. The emotion and hours of watching over his friend had taken their toll. The women's voices droned on nearby but, through his drowsiness, he heard Lexana say, 'I wish I could come over here more often. I had forgotten how good it is to be surrounded by ... other people. I'm sorry that Lonell was injured but I have enjoyed these past days.'

Valon's eyes opened in surprise and he thought he saw tears well up in Lexana's eyes as she turned back swiftly to check on the sick man.

A shout of laughter from the High Hearth drew his attention. Davoril and Tendo were there. At gatherings they could always be relied on to start off the games and tell hilarious stories, most of which bore little or no resemblance to the truth, but no one worried about that. Davoril was entertaining people with a story - Valon was almost certain he heard a reference to a two headed goat but perhaps he was wrong, he thought as he drifted off to sleep.

Valon was woken by Lexana's voice.

Too Long To Die

'I do believe he is coming back to us,' she exclaimed and Endorina turned to see Lonell looking up at them through exhausted eyes.

'How do you feel?' she asked.

Lonell cleared his throat.

'I hurt ... everywhere,' he rasped. 'Did I fight a bear?'

Lonell tried to smile but all he could manage was little better than a grimace. Valon felt his eyes prickle.

'Don't worry,' Lexana reassured him. 'You'll feel well very soon. The worst is over. You've been lucky, although you may not think so at the moment!'

After examining Lonell's wound once more, she turned to Endorina.

'I must go now. I'll return tomorrow. I will try to talk to Saretta about your healing - it was Narthan who wanted to be the only healer and he's no longer here. I don't know if it will make any difference - Saretta is angry with me for ... spending so much time here.'

She stopped and looked down at Lonell, frowning.

'Look after him, Endorina,' she said, quietly. 'And tell Kadell to watch out for him when he's better.'

Endorina heard the unspoken warning but her opportunity to ask questions was interrupted by Valon, his tiredness forgotten at the sound of his friend's voice.

'Is he better?' he asked, worriedly.

'He will recover,' she assured him.

'Shall I sit with him for a while?'

'I'm going now and I am certain Endorina would be glad of a break. If he feels like eating, you could get him some meat juices. I shall tell Kadella,' replied the tall, pale lady, smiling as she gently touched his shoulder.

Valon sat down beside his friend.

'We were worried about you,' he said seriously.

He organised Lonell's bed skins so he could sit up against the cave wall to eat some broth. Despite his complaint that it tasted strange, Valon insisted, saying it would be good for him.

'You've been sick for three nights. There was Death Juice on the arrow. You were lucky that it didn't hit you near the centre.'

He signalled the middle of his chest.

Lonell looked at him in surprise and Valon knew that his friend had no idea of the time since his return to the cave. It was only when Lonell asked, 'Did you carry me?' that Valon realised his friend had little recollection of the last part of their journey back to the cave, so he explained what had happened. Valon noticed Lonell's embarrassment at the thought of being carried and was not surprised when he changed the subject.

'Have you found out who followed us?' Lonell asked him.

'No, but people think there's someone in the cave who's telling Saretta what we're doing. That's how she seems to know everything. But there are some others who just think it's part of her power as High Priestess.'

Valon did not admit that he had also believed it until they were followed on their hunting expedition. Now he realised humans were responsible for what was happening, not some higher power.

'I'm sorry, I keep falling asleep but then I wake up suddenly. I know there's something I need to do but I can't remember ...,' said Lonell, eyes closing as he spoke.

'Don't worry. I'll stay here beside you. You rest,' replied Valon, refraining from uttering the 'We need you well quickly' which was foremost in his mind.

He sat back against the wall and looked out at the cave. He could see why Lonell liked this position: you could see everyone from here and know exactly what was going on.

His thoughts were interrupted by a weak voice.

Too Long To Die

'There is something I want to ask you. Did I see Kara back in the cave?'

'That's what I was going to tell you before you became sick; I'd forgotten. On that morning I found you on the sands, Tordano came over to tell us all to stay in the cave and he brought Kara back with him. We were all shocked because she hadn't completed her three moon cycles. She was crying, afraid she'd failed her Journey to Womanhood, but Tordano told her that she did so well that she didn't need to stay for the full time. Doesn't that sound strange to you?' he asked.

'Mm, it does,' said Lonell. 'I'll have to talk to her when I feel a stronger but now I need to do something else. I've just remembered - there's something I must try. Could you see if there are any old embers in one of the hearths and bring some back here?'

Valon shook his head and gave a quizzical glance but went off to look as asked. No doubt he would soon find out what he was up to; even in sickness Lonell was constantly working out problems. In the middle hearth he found a large piece of charcoal that had fallen off the fire the night before and it was cold. Lonell had pulled himself into a sitting position when Valon returned with the black lump.

'Good,' he said, seeing what Valon had in his hand. The blond man watched curiously as Lonell covered the palms of both hands and the undersides of the fingers and thumb with the charcoal, until they were completely black. He then rolled over and, spreading his hands open, pressed them against the stone wall. He repeated the action three times with the thumbs in slightly different positions and then slumped back onto the bed skins.

'It might be, but it is not very clear,' he mumbled to himself. 'Is Ancient Pel working now?' he asked Valon. 'If he is, ask him for some coloured liquid.'

Valon looked at him, wanting to know why.

'I promise I'll tell you what I am doing, if it works,' breathed Lonell.'

Valon went to find Ancient Pel, also known as the Dyer. He developed vivid colours from local natural resources and, when anyone wanted a special item of clothing decorated, they went to him. The patterns he created and his use of varied colours in one garment were exquisite and, although he was often challenged for his Title, he had retained it for longer than most could remember. His dark, ugly face could frighten the children with a glance but, contrary to his appearance, he was a kind, gentle person who would help anybody in need. He had his own area at one side of the entrance, so that the repellent odours of some of his concoctions drifted out of the cave.

'Dyer,' Valon greeted him. 'Are you preparing any colours today?'

Ancient Pel looked up and broke out into an enormous grin, transforming the ugly face.

'Well, I am glad to have a visitor. I regret that I've been mixing a particularly unpleasant dye today so everyone is busy avoiding this part of the cave!' he chuckled. 'It won't be so bad by tomorrow and, when you see what I am planning to do with it, I'm sure you will agree it was worth the stench, but for now ...'

He waved his hand in front of his face and wrinkled up his nose, eyes sparkling with happiness. Then he turned serious.

'How is Lonell? Is there anything I can do for him?'

'Actually, it is for Lonell. He has one of his ideas – I don't know what it is – but he wanted me to ask if you had any dye he could use?'

'Which colour do you need?' asked Ancient Pel, and when the other man shook his head, he peered into his wooden boxes, each waterproofed with a bison's stomach lining.

'Look, I have a little red ochre left over. I have nothing to use it on at the moment and it's just taking up one of my containers which I could use for something else. So, please do take it. In fact, I think I'll come and see what he's doing. It will get me away from here for a bit.'

The grin returned to the weather beaten face.

They carried the box to the back of the cave. Lonell was still sitting but his skin was clammy and Valon could see the pain in his eyes. Verina had helped him clean the black off his hands. The bowl full of murky water sat on the floor beside him.

'I hope red is suitable,' said Ancient Pel.

'I'm grateful,' replied Lonell. 'It's good to see you.'

'You shouldn't be doing this,' Valon said sternly. 'You should be resting. Let me do it. Tell me what you want me to do.'

Lonell smiled his gratitude and nodded weakly. Following his friend's instructions, Valon moved the container closer and put the palms of his hands into the dye. On the cave wall he made the same marks as Lonell had done with the charcoal. Then he stood back, looking at the result. The red stood out, leaving a clearly defined hand print.

'Spread your fingers apart a bit more and pull your thumbs downwards. Press hard with the thumbs,' Lonell told him and, on seeing the result, the sick man muttered, 'Much better, that's right.' He slumped down into his bed skins.

Valon cleaned off the dye as well as he could, although they remained a dark reddish colour and would do so for a few days. He looked up and saw Lonell give Ancient Pel a murmured 'Thank you', before drifting off to sleep.

The old man did not hear him. He was looking at the hand markings with delight.

'I like this. It's so simple, but exciting. We could decorate the cave in this way and everyone will be able to do it. Your friend is so clever.'

He turned to Valon and laughed at his exasperated face.

'He'll tell you what he's thinking when he wakes up but for now I consider him an artist.'

Too Long To Die

Ancient Pel put his hand in the dye and placed it on the wall, laughing with joy as he saw the result. The children came over to try out the new game and soon most of the tribe was there watching, with some joining in. Valon even held one child up so he could put a mark on the roof.

'I have an idea,' said Ancient Pel suddenly. 'Valon, put one hand on the wall; no, don't put any dye on it. Keep it there.' He picked up some of the red liquid in his cupped hands and flicked it over Valon's hand. He took some more and did it again.

'Now take your hand away carefully,' he ordered.

A murmur of delight followed as Valon revealed the handprint in relief, perfectly formed with red all around the outside. Kadell stepped forward. As cave Leader he was sure that his hand print should be there with the others and he chose to have his in relief, too. The remains of the dye were used up on his print and people began to drift away, but their faces kept turning back to look at the new paintings on the walls. Ancient Pel stood looking at the prints in awe.

Suddenly the old man picked up the container.

'I must go. I have work to do,' he called to Valon, who watched as the Dyer rushed back to his place at the front of the cave.

Valon sat down to clean his hands again in the now filthy water; he shook them off and looked towards where Lonell was lying. He was surprised to see his friend looking at him through exhausted eyes, and he moved over to sit beside him.

'How are you feeling? You've done too much. You're weak.'

'You did most of it. But I have found out something. You know that Narthan was killed by someone who hit his head with a stone?'

Valon nodded and waited for Lonell to continue.

'Well, he was also killed by someone who squeezed the breath out of him.'

Too Long To Die

Chapter Seven

'What, on the Sacred Stones, are you saying? He was killed by two people in different ways?' asked Valon.

Even through his exhaustion Lonell could see his friend was wondering if his illness might be affecting his thoughts.

'Shh, keep your voice quiet.' he urged. 'I don't want others to know we're talking about this. I believe that Narthan was killed in three different ways and by more than one person.'

Valon stared hard into the dark eyes that were watching him intently.

'I'm lost - I can't understand this. You'll have to explain it to me: you think there were three people who all tried to kill him?' Valon asked quietly, becoming more confused by the moment.

'No.' Lonell sighed and started to explain patiently, his voice still weak. 'We all know that he was hit on the head with a stone. Did I tell you I found it?' he asked.

Valon shook his head.

'I've hidden it,' went on Lonell, 'it may become important. But, when I looked at the body when we first found him, I saw other signs. There were bruises round his neck which are similar to the marks you made on the wall, so someone's hands were spread out and put round his neck, which shows that the breath was squeezed out of him as well.'

'So that's what I was doing with the dye on my hands. Everyone in the cave thinks we are artists now! They had no idea you were thinking about Narthan's death.' Valon stopped and thought. 'But you said he was killed three times. You have only talked about two.'

'When I bent over the body I could smell something,' said Lonell, thinking back to the short time he was alone with the corpse. 'There was a bad smell coming from the mouth and the lips and skin around seemed ... bigger than they should have been - swollen. It was unusual but I think he may have been given Death Juice as well.'

'Even if this is right, it could all have been done by one person. Why do you think there was more than one killer?' asked Valon, still trying to grasp the facts.

'Why would one person kill him three times? That wouldn't make sense. But if one person had tried to kill him with ...' he hesitated for a moment, trying to get his thoughts clear in his own head, '... Death Juice, but he didn't die or was making a noise, or it was taking too long, then maybe his neck was squeezed to make him quiet. It is possible that he was hit over the head at the same time but I don't think so.'

Lonell began to lapse into deep thought but he was dragged back by Valon who was totally confused, although he had no intention of telling his friend. He had no idea that Lonell could read it on his face as clearly as if he had shouted it.

'Why don't you think so? And you still haven't said why you think it was more than one person.'

'Don't you remember? You saw the tracks and you said that more than one person had passed that way. It would have taken at least two people to carry the body.'

'Wait,' interrupted Valon, 'Are you saying that he was killed somewhere else and then taken to Mountain Water?'

'Yes. I know there's something else that I have not understood.' Lonell hit his fist against his head, frustrated that his brain would not work it out quicker. 'But something is telling me that he did not die there.'

'But why?' Valon tried valiantly to control his frustration.

'I don't know yet, my friend,' he replied tiredly. 'Could you get me some food? I need to rest now.'

Valon could smell food cooking at the High Hearth but it was only then that he realised his stomach felt empty and it was growling with hunger. He collected two bone plates and wooden spoons and went over to where a huge cooking bag was suspended over the fire. The bag was made of thick aurochs skin and lined with the stomach from the same animal. As it hung over the fire, the bottom of the bag was kept wet which allowed it to be heated, without burning, for long periods of time. Around the hearth milled a group of women who looked up as he approached and it was the tall, dark beauty, Mila, who came over and dished out two large platefuls of stew.

'How is he?' she asked, looking towards the back of the cave, with concerned eyes.

'He would feel better if you went to see him,' replied Valon. 'He's worried that you think he returned Narthan to the earth.'

'What? No, of course I don't. I would never think anything like that about Lonell. I ... I ... like him,' she admitted, the blush on her cheeks making her even more attractive. 'Can I take him his food?'

Valon smiled and handed her Lonell's plate. He headed off to eat his meal by himself so he could think about everything that Lonell had told him. He nodded contentedly as he looked back to see Mila and Lonell together; she was feeding the sick man and he was gazing up at her with that expression he reserved only for Mila. Valon was sure that his friend was quite capable of feeding himself but he would not turn down the opportunity of being looked after by his favourite bed mate.

He watched as Davoril sat at the High Hearth telling his stories, his deep hearty laugh contagious to those around him. Even in the darkest of times, his presence lightened the mood, everyone wanting to be close to him for his humour made them forget. He brought warmth and joy in moments of fear and concern. Valon saw the women bringing him his food and drink; Delina, Kara, even Kadella, fussed after him and he honoured them with a loving smile and a thankful look from his deep blue eyes.

As he observed the interaction between the men and women in the cave, it occured to Valon that he had never before given any deep thought to personal relationships within the tribe. He just accepted them as they were but, as he thought of the deep feelings that Mila and Lonell clearly had for one another, he wondered if they would like to spend more time together, just the two of them. He thought it was probably better that this could never happen - the Pescovari tribe had no concept of a permanent agreement between two people or the fact that they could stay together for life. Love was given freely wherever and whenever they wanted, which suited Valon perfectly; the only rule being that both of the parties must be willing participants. Sometimes two people had feelings for each other that caused them to move their bed skins together for a time, but relationships were usually short-lived and the instant that two people started arguing, they separated, quickly and before any bad feelings became serious. In this way, men and women could remain friends and, perhaps, at a later date, come together again if they both wanted it. Even when two people were 'together', the individuals were free to couple with anyone else; no relationships were exclusive. Some pairs moved together and then moved apart constantly, but in this way there was no matrimonial strife to bring discord to the daily activities of the cave. There were moments of anger but they were short lived and, only rarely did the Leader have to become involved to sort out arguments.

Too Long To Die

Thinking about it carefully, Valon was sure that neither Lonell nor Mila would want to be tied down despite their feelings and, as Valon looked around him at the caring faces, the deep friendships that existed between all the tribal members, he knew he would never want to change it.

He heard laughter and saw children running through the cave chased by another who, Valon could tell, was pretending to be the wolf that lived with the Enlightened Ones. Even the children were happy here, with a feeling of security, of belonging to the tribe. While the mother cared for their child and had the bond with them throughout life, all men had a responsibility to look after and help every child and mother in any way they could. Valon looked at one of the girls whose features strongly resembled the Leader, with the red hair and light skin and he knew that Kadell liked being with the child but there would be no claim on her. The whole tribe was responsible for a child's well-being - they were part of the communal property.

Valon realised he had never before thought in depth about how the tribe lived. All he cared about was that their ways mostly brought happiness and he hated anything that disturbed their harmony. It was for this reason that he felt such anger towards Saretta and the Enlightened Ones for he hated the misery that they were bringing to these people that he loved.

Valon was jolted out of his thoughts suddenly by a small hand shaking his shoulder. He looked up and saw the four children standing at his side. One of them was the child Jadana, with all the pale features of a young Enlightened One, who would soon be taken off to the White Cave as she had already lived four winters; the next one would be her fifth.

He grinned at them but could see from the concentration on the small face that she was thinking hard and suddenly she made up her mind.

'Valon, will you tell us where Cannot came from?' she asked. 'Everyone has heard a different story but mother told me you found him, so you must know what happened.'

Valon smiled as he heard the silly name the children had given to the wolf. Some time before, one of the older boys was heard to say to his mother:

'I think we should call it 'Cannot' because it only comes out with the High Priestess when we are being told 'You cannot leave the cave,' 'You cannot go somewhere,' 'You cannot eat from this tree,' 'You cannot do ... anything!'

This caused great amusement and it was repeated over and over again. Inevitably it caught on and now everyone called the beast by that name, except in front of the Enlightened Ones.

'Come and sit down and I'll tell you,' he said and, using his story-telling voice, he began the tale.

'Two summers past, a trader from another tribe called in here with a fine collection of Sun Stones. You know what Sun Stones are?' he asked them seriously.

They nodded so he continued.

'Well, the trader was invited to stay the night and he told us many exciting stories from his travels. When our High Priestess had completed the exchanges, he told her of a small white animal that he had seen in the foothills of the Great Mountains. He wasn't sure what kind of animal it was but he'd realised from seeing our Enlightened Ones that anything white would be regarded as very special. You do know that's true?' he asked, looking at the children.

They all nodded enthusiastically, especially Jadana.

'Well,' he went on, 'a group of us were sent out to find and bring back this white animal. I went to help, although I was not the Tracker then. The trader had told us where he had seen it so we walked for three days and eventually found the place, by the tall trees in the green

Too Long To Die

valley at the bottom slopes of the mountains. We looked for it for more days than I can count.'

He held up one hand and touched each finger, then another, and then the first one again and then he shrugged and pulled a face. The children all laughed except Jadana who was listening intently and seriously.

'We set out traps with food to attract it and nets to catch it in – we didn't want to hurt it - but we seemed to attract every other animal except the one we were looking for. Eventually we decided to give up although we knew that the High Priestess would not be pleased.'

He snarled as he said this, pretending to be Saretta and then looked scared. They laughed again, more nervously this time.

'We had just packed everything up; our back packs were full of meat and we had rolls of skins to carry and then, suddenly, a small bundle of white fluff ran in amongst us. Poor little thing - it was so frightened that it made it easy to net and we brought it back. I can tell you, it might have been small but it had the sharpest teeth I have ever come across. We all ended up with nip marks.'

Valon bared his teeth and moved towards the smallest child, as if to bite her. She squealed in delighted terror and they all laughed.

'So is Cannot dangerous now?' asked Jadana, a thoughtful look on her face.

'I really don't know,' he replied. 'It's a wild animal but it has lived with men and women for nearly all its life. But one thing I can tell you,' he looked seriously at all the children, hoping that they would believe him, 'I shall not be going up to it to find out and I don't think you should either or you might end up with part of your body missing!'

Tucking one arm behind his back, he pretended it had been bitten off, making three of the children jump to their feet and run away shrieking and giggling at the same time. Jadana was still sitting seriously, a worried expression on her face, and he realised that she was thinking about soon having to share a cave with a vicious animal. He put his arm around her small shoulders.

'I'm sure it's very friendly now,' he said gently. 'Look at how Lexana stands with her hand on it – I think it's more frightened of us than we are of it. You'll probably be able to make friends with it. Would that be fun, do you think?'

The child nodded doubtfully and smiled her thanks but Valon noticed her eyes search out her mother. He saw the tears in her eyes as she walked away and he clenched his fists in rage and grief.

Valon still had his plate in front of him and was on the point of taking it to the cleaning area when, from across the cave, he saw a young woman staring at him. He smiled back and she instantly lowered her head, blushing, as if embarrassed to have been caught out. His heart started beating faster, attracted by this well understood flirting signal.

'Zana,' he thought, 'I will have you tonight. If only you would accept my offer to move your bed skins next to mine.' He sighed, knowing she never would.

Her small, plump figure was topped with a mass of blond hair and she looked at a man as if he were the only man she could ever be with, her beautiful eyes shining with love. They were all taken in the first time but soon came to realise, as she jumped out of one man's bed skins into another's, that she was a free spirit who would not be tied down even for the shortest time. Nevertheless, she was a very popular young woman with all the men and Valon knew he would be lucky to get her for even one night. He beckoned her over and she ran excitedly towards him.

'Oh, Valon. It's been so long since we have been together. I was beginning to think that you didn't want me,' she said breathlessly.

Valon melted into the depth of her green eyes.

'I've been waiting for you ever since we were together the last time.'

Suddenly the spell was broken.

'You promised to come to me soon and did not. You have been a busy girl!' he smiled, slapping her playfully on the bottom.

She grinned cheekily back.

'Well, it's a hard task to keep all the men happy, but it's you I really want to be with.' She tried her charm again.

Their flirtations were interrupted by a call.

'We need more water,' came from beside the High Hearth.

Valon groaned. 'I suppose we'd better help.'

Zana pulled his head down to her level.

'Why don't we go and get some water with the others,' she whispered in his ear, 'and stay there for a while before we come back?' She winked. 'I know a very comfortable place!'

Not waiting for a second invitation and with a wide grin on his face, he grabbed two water bags and they followed the other volunteers up the path to the High Pasture. They lagged behind, holding hands and laughing at each other's words. Zana suddenly stooped down to pick a handful of the small mauve flowers which grew all over the grassland.

'We can have a swim too and get clean, but I think that had better be afterwards. I don't want the coldness of the water to have a bad effect on you,' she grinned as her eyes slid down to the lower part of his body.

'How dare you!' Valon replied, feigning horror. 'Are you questioning my manhood? I'll show you!'

He grabbed at her but she dodged him and ran on ahead, laughing. Within a few strides he had caught up with her and he pulled her round and towards him. She held her face up to him, her mouth parted slightly, waiting for him. His mouth closed over hers and the kiss was so intense that Valon was oblivious to everything including the other water collectors who passed by on their way back with full bags.

She pushed herself away from him.

'Come on. I can't wait any longer,' she breathed.

They ran to the path and almost slid down it in their eagerness. As they reached the level ground of the meadowland, Zana led him away from the usual path towards the lake and he found himself in a small mossy area, enclosed by the rock formations. She took the water bags from his hand and lowered herself elegantly to the ground, pulling him with her.

Valon and Zana returned to the cave just before the Enlightened Ones set out for their Sun Sleep ceremony; they had no intention of passing them on the path.

'Will you share my bed skins tonight?' Valon asked.

He saw her stare into his eyes searchingly, as though looking for the answer to some unspoken question. Then she smiled, nodded and turned away. Realising that he had been holding his breath, Valon let out the air as quietly as he could; he did not want her or anyone else to know how desperately he desired her. He watched her walk gracefully across the cave before he headed towards Lonell's sleeping area, but he only got half way when he was intercepted by Endorina, the Healer, who stopped him. She was smiling.

'I went to give Lonell his potion and I found him with Mila so I left them alone. She can give him better treatment than I,' she winked. 'I don't think you should disturb them either,' she advised him.

He grinned back at her in agreement, wondering what to do with the time before food was ready. He needed a new blade for his knife; he had noticed it was becoming increasingly blunt, but that meant going out to the flint knapping cave and working by himself, and it would be cold. No, he decided, that was not what he wanted to do.

He meandered over to the High Hearth where Vellisco, one of Endorina's sons was showing some of the women how he liked to prepare a roast of deer meat with some unusual flavourings. Valon knew that Endorina had spent years teaching Vellisco all about the herbs and plants that grew in the vicinity, and some that came from much further away, with the dream that he would become the next Healer, but he had taken her knowledge and turned it towards cooking, much to everyone's astonishment and her disappointment. Valon could not understand the attraction for, although like all men, he could cook and prepare food when it was necessary, it was largely considered a female occupation, which caused many people to wonder if perhaps he was one of those who preferred the company of other males. Yet he had surprised everyone: he passed his Rite of Shadows and developed a true dedication for, not only his cooking, but also his recreational time with one woman after another.

Valon was suddenly noticed by Kadella as he stood there.

'Food will not be ready for a while yet,' she said, 'but if you want, there's some cold meat left over from lunch and some vegetables. Help yourself.'

'No, I'm not hungry. I was wondering if I could do something to help. I have nothing to do,' explained Valon.

'Oh yes, you have something to do,' replied Kadella, with a smile.

She went out of the cave and shortly afterwards returned with a large bundle of fur.

'Here are the two goat skins you brought in when Lonell was ... injured. They need to be treated. If you don't do it soon, they'll be useless.'

Thanking her, Valon took the skins to an area at the side of the cave where frameworks were set up. He fetched a scraping tool and started to prepare the skins. One of them was his but he decided that, after being so sick, Lonell could use two new bed skins and these would be perfect. He had no need at the moment for a new skin himself. After scraping them down carefully and removing all the membranes from one side, leaving the fur on the other, he attached the skins to the frames, stretching them as firmly as he could. Then he rubbed in the rendered animal fat to keep them pliant and re-stretched them. It was hard work preparing the skins and, by the time he had finished, the sweat was dripping down his face. He could smoke them at another time which would complete the process. He felt better after the work: it had taken his mind off the problems that faced him and his friend.

Flamina had already provided food for her daughter Marita, when Valon noticed her eyes upon him. He had finished his work and he watched as she brought over a wooden bowl, filled to the brim with the deer meat stew that he had seen Vellisco creating earlier. The different vegetables and herbs that he had put in resulted in an unusual flavour, which surprised Valon but he tucked in with great relish, nodding his thanks to Flamina. She walked away, returning almost immediately with a wooden cup of water and sat down beside him. He could see Marita, as usual, sitting against the wall but she was staring out at the group around the High Hearth, showing an interest in the people in front of her.

'I think that Marita is getting better since Narthan returned to the earth,' Flamina said quietly to Valon. 'She's beginning to show an interest in what is going on around her. She began talking again last night and told me about ... how he treated her. If he were not dead already, I can tell you, I would kill him now.'

Flamina looked down at the ground, ashamed of the strength of her feelings.

Too Long To Die

He put a hand on her shoulder.

'I'm so sorry. I can't understand how we have all let this happen. We are all to blame. It's good she's getting better. I'm very pleased.'

'No, you're wrong. There was only one person to blame ... or rather two. Saretta will come to regret what she allowed to happen.'

Valon was shocked at the venom he heard in her voice. Flamina had always seemed so quiet and inoffensive but this was a woman whose child had been harmed; he saw her for the first time as a she-wolf protecting her cub. He said nothing but let the angry woman take a while to calm herself.

'I wanted to talk to you about making the marks on the wall,' she said, moments later. 'Could Marita try it? She might enjoy it and it could help her if she did it with other people. Could you ask Lonell?'

'It's not his decision,' replied Valon, 'but I'll organise it with pleasure. I'll get some dye from Ancient Pel and Marita will do her painting. It will be good to see her enjoying herself.'

'Thank you,' said Flamina, with tears in her eyes, 'You are a good man.' She rose elegantly to her feet and went back to her daughter.

As he watched her walk away, he thought what a good looking woman she still was, despite all her cares. He jumped to his feet, remembering Zana's promise, took some sand and cleaned out his bowl, swilling it out afterwards with a small amount of water. He looked towards his bed skins; she was not there. In fact, she was nowhere to be seen in the cave. For a moment he felt the deep ache of jealousy but instantly dismissed it, knowing it to be unacceptable. He had no right to expect her to come to him twice in one day, and she had not really promised.

Heading out into the body of the cave, he noticed that more people were sitting around the middle hearth. It would soon be time to move the High Hearth back because the nights were becoming colder, but nobody liked it when that happened because it signified the approach of a long winter. Pallo was there, telling stories about his latest expedition to find new flint and other stones for working. He was the expert flint knapper of the cave, showing a skill that amazed even those used to seeing his work, and he often went away to find new material and came back with amusing tales. There was a certain amount of doubt, however, over the number of adventures he had, and some even wondered if he just went to see a woman in another tribe because sometimes he returned empty-handed. Nevertheless, like Davoril, he could tell a good story, particularly after taking a few drinks, and people crowded round to hear his stories. Even sitting, he looked down on everyone else; it was not just his long, thin legs that gave him his height, his body was longer than anyone else's. Valon always thought it amusing that someone who spent most of his time bent over the tools of his trade, was so tall - he had to almost fold himself up to get into his working position!

Valon joined them by the fire and enjoyed a few cups of the mildly intoxicating drink that was being shared out. Tendo and Davoril showed them a new game, flicking small pebbles at those of the other players. The cave soon rang with laughter, most of the tribe taking part, their worries temporarily put aside, if not forgotten. He stayed until people started drifting away to their bed skins and, reluctantly admitting to himself that Zana would not be joining him, he retired as well. The drink prevented him from staying awake too long, thinking about what he was missing, and he soon slipped into deep sleep.

To Valon it seemed only seconds later when he woke with someone's hand over his mouth and their other arm holding him down. As his eyes came into focus, he saw above him, lit by the flickering flames from the hearth, the dark, sunken eyes of Lonell, who whispered:

'Come on. Quietly! We're going to tame a wolf!'

Too Long To Die

Chapter Eight

For a moment Valon lay absolutely still, eyes opened wide in shock and disbelief. Lonell removed his hand, put a finger to his lips and beckoned him to come. Silently, Valon extracted himself from his bed skins and pulled on his foot coverings. The only light came from embers in the hearths, which cast eerie shadows on the cave walls, and he could see two figures moving around, but the only noises came from the sleeping bodies all around the cave. They crept to the entrance and he followed, passing on one side Kadell and, on the other, the tumultuous snores of Ancient Pel which masked any sounds from his steps. Climbing up the path together, they hugged the rock face, staying on the grassy edges which, although slippery, created less noise underfoot, and they remained silent until they were a good distance away from the caves on the even plateau of the High Pasture.

The paltry light of an overcast moon allowed glimpses of the three shadowy figures and their surroundings. Valon was still mulling over the identity of the third person when Lonell stopped and looked around. He made a sign and they squatted down to talk in hushed tones. Taking the short spear that Lonell was holding out to him, Valon made out Mila's excited face for the first time and he felt deep concern.

'It was Mila's idea,' whispered Lonell. 'I'm losing hope that we'll find out the truth before they sacrifice Sim, so we must get him out of there. Mila thought we could tame the wolf.'

'Tame the wolf? How?' Valon's disbelief was obvious in his voice.

'We'll feed it until it trusts us. Then we can get past it and let Sim out.'

'Will it work?'

Valon was not convinced that giving the huge animal any amount of meat would make it any more friendly. His natural instincts told him that he should avoid wild animals, not walk towards them.

'I don't know, Valon,' replied Lonell, 'but we must try something and this could be the way to do it.'

There was a silence for a moment before Valon asked Lonell, 'But why has she come too?'

'I'm sorry, Mila,' he said, turning to the woman, 'but it's too dangerous. If we get caught we could all be killed. You ought to go back and let us do it.'

'We talked about that - I didn't want her to come either - but the wolf seems more at ease with Lexana than anyone, so we thought a woman might have more chance to get close to it,' said Lonell.

'Look, I've never done anything exciting in my life,' insisted Mila, 'and I can help you with this. I won't go back.'

Even through the darkness, without looking at her, both Lonell and Valon knew that any attempt to talk her out of her plan would be pointless.

Valon sighed and shook his head.

'So what are we doing?' he asked.

'We have some meat which we'll drop bit by bit in front of the wolf as we get closer until it starts to growl,' Lonell explained. 'Then we come away. We'll have to do this every night till it gets used to us, or at least to one of us.' He glanced at Mila. 'Then we can lead it away, let Sim out and afterwards put it back again.'

Silent doubt filled the air around the three figures.

'Lexana managed to tame it somehow so we know it can be done,' Lonell whispered, the determination clear in his voice.

Valon looked up at the stars glinting above and hoped that Lonell's 'helper' was watching down on them.

'We must follow a different path every night,' he said, 'so we don't make obvious tracks. We must be back in the cave early so the night dampness will have time to cover our footprints before the Enlightened Ones come out for Sun Wake.'

'And we can't leave the cave until we're sure everyone is asleep,' added Mila.

'I know,' agreed Lonell, 'the timing is going to be difficult but I can't think of any other way to get Sim out of there, can you?'

He was not able to see their faces clearly but, when there were no answers, he stood up.

'Good. We must go now. Go carefully because there's little light tonight – the Moon is growing smaller. Follow me.'

They took a roundabout path to the top of the slope leading down to the Pit, where they dropped to the ground and looked over the edge. Valon peered upwards again and watched the stars glistening in the clear patches of sky above them. Through the limited light of the waning moon they could just make out the shape of the wolf lying on the ledge. From the cave they sometimes heard him howling in the night and most of the tribe were frightened by it. The sound reminded them that a vicious, wild animal lived close by. Lonell, though, told Valon that all he could hear in that eerie, chilling sound was the deep loneliness of an animal, isolated from its pack. He thought Lonell might be right but hoped it would not decide to howl whilst they were there.

Mila took out the meat from her pack.

'There are no bones in there, are there? The wolf will leave them if there are and they'll know someone's feeding it,' whispered Valon.

'Of course there are no bones,' retorted Mila, angrily. 'I'm not stupid.'

She threw down the first lump of meat which landed a pace in front of the wolf. They waited. Nothing happened immediately but, as she was about to throw the next piece, they heard a snuffling sound and the animal rose to its feet and followed the scent, swallowing the food without even chewing it. They inched down the path, throwing meat with each step, and Mila started talking, her quiet voice quavering.

'Hello, Cannot. I hope you like this food. We're going to bring you some every night and we'd like to make friends with you.'

At first, the wolf's ears twitched and it looked up, straight at them, but they were still far enough away that they posed no threat so it continued eating. Step by step, they climbed down with Mila talking all the time, until suddenly the animal's yellow eyes glared at them and they heard a growl beginning to form in its throat. They backed away quickly but quietly and gave it no more food.

'Sim, can you hear me?' Lonell whispered as loudly as he dared.

'Who's that?' came the weak reply.

Valon and Mila climbed back to the top, leaving Lonell below by the Pit, to explain their plan to the prisoner so he would be ready when they finally managed to bring about his escape.

'You must also talk to the wolf,' Mila said to Valon, 'and Lonell, too. It must get used to all our voices.'

Valon could see her point but he did not know if he could talk to an animal. It was something he had never considered before but if it had to be done, then however stupid he felt, he would do it as well as he could.

'Hello wolfie, what is your name?' he said quietly in a silly voice. His reward was a punch on the arm and a quiet snigger for his efforts.

Lonell suddenly appeared beside them and they could sense his displeasure as he put his fingers to his lips once more and then walked ahead of them. They followed, Valon feeling like a naughty child whose mother had caught him misbehaving. He could hear Mila trying to stifle her giggles for most of the walk back and knew she felt the same.

The following morning, Lonell was feeling the effects of his exertion the previous night. Valon could see him moving as though his entire body ached and he was trembling with fatigue.

'I can't understand what's happened to you,' said a worried Endorina. 'I thought you were better but now ... I don't know. I must get Lexana...'

He put a weak hand on her arm.

'There is no need,' he said. 'I couldn't sleep last night and I'm very tired. That's all.'

Doubt shadowed her face but she changed the dressing on his arm and, when she could see no damage done to the wound, she grunted and gave him a drink to help him sleep. When she finally headed off to look at one of the children suffering from a sore throat, she kept looking back at Lonell, confusion and worry in equal measures.

Valon breathed a sigh of relief when she left and waited until Lonell beckoned him over.

'I don't think I'll be able to come out tonight. The Healer's suspicious and I know she'll be keeping a close watch on what I do,' Lonell said in a low voice. 'I'm sorry but you and Mila will have to go without me.'

'There is an easier way, you know,' said Valon.

Lonell's eyebrow arched. 'Well?'

'We kill the beast. It's simple.'

Lonell looked at his friend.

'Can you be absolutely sure the wolf won't make any noise? If it does, we'll be caught.'

Valon thought for a moment, then shrugged.

'No, you're right. It wouldn't work. Don't worry about tonight. We'll be fine.'

'Do you think you can both remember to be quiet?' asked Lonell, shaking his head in mock exasperation.

Valon grinned.

'Don't worry. Mila and I will have the best time without you!'

He winked and jumped out of the way as Lonell's tired hand tried to swipe at him playfully.

'You rest,' added Valon, more seriously. 'We will be fine. You have to get better; when you're well again you can come with us.'

Having brought breakfast back for his friend, he sat beside him and they ate together in easy silence, until Lonell fell asleep, his plate still half full.

For the next three nights, Mila and Valon crept out of the cave and, taking a different, circuitous route each time, arrived at the Pit. Every night they managed to get a little closer to the animal before it started to growl and, the moment it did, they stopped feeding it. Valon tried to talk to it, but the beast reacted better to Mila as they had originally thought. There were even signs the wolf was beginning to look forward to their visits; the moment they were heard, Cannot stirred its great white body and looked upwards eagerly, waiting for the food. Valon managed to talk to Sim whose voice sounded much stronger than on the first night. He told Valon that he was doing everything he could to get some strength back; although the limited space in the Pit made exercising difficult, he was doing all he could.

Early the next morning, when Valon went to report to Lonell, he was glad to see his friend now completely recovered and waiting for him, restlessly. He was telling him all about their excursion and the progress that had been made when Lonell suddenly interrupted.

'We have a problem,' he said. 'Sim's mother is telling everyone that he's in much better spirits now – that he's eating well and is much more cheerful. We must warn him that he must act as he did before although we'll take him extra food, to make him stronger. It will be difficult for him to hide the truth from Verina, but he must or someone will begin to ask questions.'

'Don't worry. We'll tell him tonight ...' started Valon.

'And I'll be going with you,' interrupted Lonell, with a grin. 'I can't allow you any more time alone with Mila. She might start to favour you more than me!'

'I wish it would be so!' Valon sighed, feigning despair. 'Unfortunately, the best I could hope for would be an occasional night at a festival, but she will always come back to you. It is a hopeless case!'

Lonell looked around the cave and felt the walls closing in on him. He needed to get out but Valon was nowhere to be seen and he did not want to venture out by himself. He saw Tendo sitting at the High Hearth and thought about the small, dark man who was so often to be seen joking around with Davoril. However, Lonell realised, there were two distinctly different sides to the man: the joker that kept everyone laughing with his exaggerated tales, and the person he was looking at now, deep in thought, with a sharp intelligence. This was a man who would be able to hide things, thought Lonell, and he wondered if Tendo might know something about what had happened to Narthan.

Lonell made up his mind to talk to him and wandered over casually to the High Hearth where he sat down beside Tendo, who looked up at him, his face instantly wreathed in smiles, the large nose creased over the bridge.

'Lonell,' he said, 'I am pleased to see you are well again. You have had a difficult time.'

'I'm glad to be through it,' replied Lonell, returning the wide smile. 'I hope I haven't disturbed you. You seemed deep in thought.'

'There's much to think about at the moment,' nodded Tendo. 'I wish they were better thoughts. I was thinking about Narthan ...' his voice trailed off.

'It's hard to discover what happened. So many people had reasons to hate him.'

'That's what I was thinking,' agreed Tendo.

'What did you think of him?' asked Lonell, trying to keep his voice casual.

Tendo's head swivelled round sharply, his eyes staring deep into Lonell's. Then he laughed.

'It is good. You're right to ask. I hope you will ask everyone.'

Lonell nodded.

'I shall. Although some I don't need to ask. Some we already know why they hated him.'

His eyes moved towards Flamina who was busy tidying the plates and cooking utensils. He waited for Tendo to answer his question.

'I hated him because he was cruel to those who could not defend themselves against him. He never hit me or anything like that but his comments about my looks, my nose ... he didn't stop. All the time he called me names and laughed at me. It hurt when I was young.'

He glanced at Lonell, a twinkle of amusement in his eye.

'But that was a long time past. I am now quite happy living with my large friend,' he stroked his nose with affection, 'and it was never enough to make me want to send him back to the earth.'

He hesitated.

'Well, maybe sometimes when I was young but not now!'

Tendo laughed and clapped Lonell on the shoulder. For a while they sat in silence, becoming serious once more.

'Find out, Lonell. For the sake of our tribe, please find out the truth.'

'I'll try, Tendo. You know I'll do all I can.'

He looked around the cave. The children who never seemed to stop were running around wildly, an endless chase of shouting and giggling. Lonell pulled himself to his feet, putting a reassuring hand on Tendo's shoulder and was on the point of leaving him when one of the children crashed into the wall and fell to the ground, one knee catching the sharp edge of rock. The wail which filled the cave alerted everyone, but Lonell, already on his feet, close by, was the first to get there. The knee had a deep laceration from one side to the other and deep red blood was gushing out of it, dripping on the floor. Lonell held the howling child until Endorina covered the cut with her hand to stop the flow and Tendo picked him up and carried him to the back of the cave. Lonell stood staring at the small puddle of blood that had formed. He knew there was something important about it, but its meaning evaded him.

Looking round in frustration, he saw that Valon had reappeared, carrying a pair of large, dark brown birds that he handed over to Kadella. Lonell came up at his side and touched Valon's arm to get his attention.

'Come on!' he said. 'I have to get out of this cave. I want a swim in the Salt Water. I need to get clean. We might do a bit of fishing while we're there.'

At the various caves along the ledge, they gathered up the gear that they would need. Valon picked out a fishing net and baskets while Lonell decided he would take some food and collected dried meat from the store. He smiled at Valon's surprise at the quantity he was taking but made no comment. Then they went into the weapons store. Lonell took the net from Valon and carefully wrapped Sim's spear and a hunting knife in it. He saw the realisation on Valon's face as he finally understood the plan and nodded silently.

Too Long To Die

They made their way slowly to the beach for Lonell's legs were weaker than he would have liked to admit and the wind was blowing hard against them. There was rain in the air but to Lonell it felt like freedom and he breathed deeply, delighted to still be alive. Although he had felt protected by his 'helper' throughout the ordeal, it was still a relief to have emerged on the other side of disaster.

They walked up the beach in the direction of the small cave and, when they were not far from it, Lonell went to the water's edge, removed his clothes and started wading out.

The coastline closest to where they lived consisted of a rocky beach covering a great distance and then extended shallows before it suddenly dropped away into an underwater ravine where the huge Monsters of the Salt Water lived. However, close to Lonell's secret cave, the water came right in leaving only a narrow stretch of sand, littered with rocks and stones. Lonell, in fact, had little intention of doing any fishing that day. When the water reached his waist, he dived under and revelled in the cold, stinging saltiness. Even the pain when the salt washed over his wound did not ruin his enjoyment and he picked up some sand off the bottom and rubbed himself down, including in his hair, cleaning away the sweat and dirt of the past few days. Small silver fish swam up and he felt them nibbling at his legs, tickling, but he brushed them away.

Lonell peered up at the cliffs that overlooked the beach. He could not shake off the feeling that he was being observed but there was no one to be seen and he told himself it was his imagination due to recent events. He washed off all the sand and, as he left the water, dried himself off with his hands, the wind assisting his efforts. He dressed hurriedly, shivering, but feeling refreshed and invigorated.

Valon, meanwhile, waited patiently and, walking up and down the beach, he found some crabs trapped in a rock pool when the tide went out. He pointed them out to Lonell.

'We can take these back to the cave afterwards so they'll think we have been doing some fishing.'

'Good. Let's go to the cave now. We have to get it ready.'

Leaving the net and baskets hidden in a crevice outside, they pushed past the giant boulder and went into the dark recess behind. Lonell produced a bag that Valon had not noticed before and from it pulled some dry kindling. He lit a fire and Valon was able to look around properly for the first time. Lonell had it well organised. There were not just the skins he had seen before – there was a pile of them. A number of tools for making blades and clothing, and cords for bindings were at the rear of the cave, and baskets containing dried food were stashed in the natural nooks and crannies, high in the cave walls, safe from any wandering animals that might try to get at them. There was also a full water bag. Wood was stacked up at one side which, although damp, with the correct kindling, could be used.

Lonell took out Sim's weapons and placed them neatly beside the tools.

'I think we have just about everything he'll need to survive a few days before he can go on,' he said, thinking aloud. 'The food may not be very tasty but he will survive. We should put another water bag in and get some more kindling, although there is quite a lot in this bag. He'll only be able to light fires at night when everyone is back in the caves or the smoke might lead them to him.'

He nodded to himself and looked at Valon, suddenly remembering that he was there. Valon was staring at him. The first time they had visited the cave Valon had not been able to see the contents and Lonell could see his friend's amazement at the number of objects stored there.

'You've been organising this for a long time,' he declared.

Lonell shrugged his shoulders.

'I told you. I knew I had to. Now, we must get those crabs. We can say I didn't feel well enough to fish properly with the net but, at least, we won't return empty-handed.'

He stamped out the small fire and, once more, they squeezed past the boulder and came face to face with Kadell and Kadella. They had the net and baskets at their feet and they were staring at them accusingly.

'I think you had better explain what you are up to, or would you like me to tell Saretta?' threatened the Leader.

Too Long To Die

Chapter Nine

Both men looked at each other with apologetic eyes, each taking the blame on their shoulders. Lonell had sensed they were being followed and had not taken any action, and he knew Valon would be blaming himself for not hiding the net adequately.

'Well,' repeated Kadell, his face red with anger under the ginger hair. 'Are you going to tell us?'

Lonell shrugged, knowing that there was now no alternative but to tell the Leader and his sister the truth. He beckoned them to follow him back into the cave. Valon picked up the net and baskets and, this time, took them with him. Lonell relit the fire and the Leader and his sister looked around them in astonishment at the cave that they had not known was there.

'You had better sit down. We have a lot to tell you,' said Lonell, praying that, once they had heard all he had to tell them, they would support him. If there were anyone in the tribe that Lonell knew he could trust, it was the Leader.

'How much do you already know?' he asked them.

'I heard two people leaving the cave late last night and coming back much later. Of course, I also know that you were shot by an arrow covered in Death Juice, but I don't know why,' admitted Kadell.

'And I know that food has been going missing; also baskets, a water bag and a spare Sun Stone,' added Kadella.

'All right,' said Lonell, 'It's time for me to tell you everything.'

As he talked the Leader and his sister listened carefully, occasionally commenting or asking a question, but mostly in silence.

Lonell told them what he had discovered about Narthan's death, starting with his checking the body when it was first discovered and to the realisation that three methods had been used to kill him. He also explained the hand marks on the wall, which made them laugh despite the serious circumstances. He then went on to the need to break Sim out of the Pit and what they were doing at night, including Mila's help with the training of the wolf. Kadell was amazed to hear that it had been going on for four nights without him realising. This led onto the cave where they were sitting and Lonell explained when he had found it.

'When Sim has escaped he will need somewhere to hide,' he added.

'But it is too close to our cave, isn't it?' asked Kadella.

'No. It's the closeness of the cave that is its strength. When he has gone, Saretta will obviously send us all out to hunt for him, no doubt accompanied by the Guardians. They will never expect him to stay close by; they'll think that he has run as far away as possible, I hope. So he can stay here for a few days until they give up looking for him and then go and search for another tribe to take him in.'

'Poor Sim,' muttered Kadella, 'but I suppose it's preferable to death.'

They all talked again about why the Enlightened Ones wanted Lonell to die but still came up with no better solution than their fear that he would find out the truth. Almost as an afterthought, Lonell added that Tordano had tried to help him by warning him not to try to solve the killing and telling him that Sarril and Valt were out hunting with bows on the day he was shot.

When Lonell finished his explanation, they all sat in silence, thinking, trying to make sense of everything that had happened.

Suddenly, Kadell looked up.

'Why didn't you tell us this before?' he asked.

'Because we didn't want to involve more people than necessary. If we are caught, we'll be sacrificed too, so it was safer for you if you didn't know,' insisted Lonell.

'Are you sure it wasn't that you thought we might tell Saretta what's going on in the cave, that you didn't trust us?'

'No,' answered Lonell and Valon, in unison.

'No, I can truly say that we never thought that, although we know that someone in the cave is giving information to Saretta,' continued Lonell.

Kadell and his sister nodded, and Lonell could see that they were pleased with the reaction to the question and his explanation. As if reading each other's minds, the brother and sister stood up.

'We must get back to the cave now. I have food to cook. At least it will be easier for you now. You won't have to take things without asking anymore!' smiled Kadella.

'I will give you any help I can and tonight I'm coming with you to see the wolf,' said Kadell. This was not a request. As the Leader, Kadell was used to being obeyed and Lonell knew there was no point in arguing.

Valon slid out of the cave to check the beach was empty.

'We'll bring back some nice big crabs so make sure that the boiling pot is ready,' said Lonell, as they left.

The two men watched the Leader and his sister walk along the beach and disappear from view. Both breathed a sigh of relief.

'It's good to know that they are with us,' said Valon.

'I agree, but we must make sure that no one else finds out; the more people that know about it, the more likely our plan will leak out and Saretta will hear about it. We must be even more careful from now on,' responded Lonell.

'Now, where were those crabs?'

Despite the grey skies and high winds which gusted from time to time, threatening to blow them over, the men played like children as they gathered up the large grey crabs which tried to protect themselves with their long, dangerous pincers. These creatures had been known to attack men if they were in a big enough group and one of the most common injuries sustained whilst fishing were 'bites' from the crabs. Luckily the baskets that Valon had brought had lids which tied on with cord, so the crabs were pushed in and tied down. Valon received a nasty nip as he was waving one in Lonell's face and not paying proper attention, which made Lonell laugh so much that he slipped and fell into the rock pool, drenching his clothes and putting himself in danger of being attacked by the other crabs.

Suddenly, a shaft of sunlight broke through the clouds and shone down over the Salt Water. They stopped and touched their brows superstitiously as they watched the golden rays hitting the grey water and reflecting off the white tops of the waves. It lasted brief moments and they did not look at it with the usual sense of dread that men experienced when seeing unexpected natural phenomena; this brought a sensation of wonderment. It was a beam of light in an otherwise grey scenario and Lonell could not help but ask himself if he had just been sent a message. If so, he was sure that it was a good one.

As the clouds covered the light once more, the two men looked at each other, knowing they had shared a special experience. At that moment, it dawned on Lonell; the thing that had been evading him since Narthan's death - it was the blood. It was all wrong. He knew he would have to return to Mountain Water, and soon.

They picked up the baskets and net and walked up the beach together, not speaking, watching the waves increase in size and speed, buffeted by the high wind which had suddenly picked up. Lonell was deep in thought. The two men were almost blown across the High Pasture and down the path and were pleased to reach the protection of the ledge for the sky had turned a deeper leaden grey and sharp needles of rain fell, stinging their skin.

The contentment they felt was instantly crushed as they walked into the cave, almost colliding with Sarril as he stormed out. The furious expressions on the faces of the people looking at the departing back of the Guardian informed them immediately that something was wrong.

'What has happened?' Valon asked Kadell, who was standing beside Delina.

She had tears running down her face but she stood tall and defiant, glaring out at the White Cave. Valon went over and put his arm around her; she relaxed against him, leaning her blond head on his shoulder. He looked at Kadell, waiting for the answer.

'Delina is carrying a child,' he announced, 'but the pale skins will not allow her to celebrate it.'

The tribe gasped, firstly at the thought that the usual festivities, which were celebrated without fail when a carrying was announced, would not take place and, secondly, because Kadell had used the words 'the pale skins' instead of the Enlightened Ones. Only a complete breakdown of respect would cause the Leader to do such a thing.

'I'm sorry,' he continued, 'but recently they banned her from using the bow and she is our Bow Maker. Now they refuse us our right to celebrate a carrying. They don't deserve our respect. This cannot go on much longer.'

The final words were muttered to himself as he turned away in his anger.

The tribe was aghast. Delina had not told anyone of the ban. Valon hugged the young woman.

'I'm so sorry,' he said. 'I didn't know. When did they tell you?'

'After the last wolf hunt,' she replied, sniffing into his shoulder.

'But you brought down a wolf by yourself with the bow. How

could they do that after you showed them how good you were with it?'

Valon was not expecting an answer to his question and he turned quickly when he heard a quiet voice beside him.

'That is precisely why she has been banned. She's too good.'

Lonell put an encouraging hand on Delina's shoulder.

'I'm glad Narthan has returned to the earth,' the young woman said bitterly. 'He was the one that came to see me. He took my bow away – it's in the White Cave now – and he told me that I will never be able to use it again. It's not fair,' she ended, sounding like a petulant child.

'There's one thing that no one can take away from you,' smiled Valon and he put his hand on her stomach.

She looked at him with grateful eyes and Lonell watched Valon's reaction. He hoped Delina would realise Valon was eager to comfort her and he smiled as he turned away, knowing where his friend's bed skins would be later, if she allowed him.

Slowly the cave resumed its normal activity, but there was an atmosphere in the air. Lonell could feel something was different but, at first, even he struggled to pinpoint its exact nature. Up until now, defiance had not been part of an adult's character – it was drummed out of them in childhood - but within each breast it was now beginning to grow. It was some time later, as he watched his fellow tribesmen and women, that Lonell realised the importance of what had happened, that a slight shift in thinking was altering the character of his tribe. Although none of the others recognised it for what it was, only Lonell understood, with a beating heart, that this could be the start of a movement that would eventually bring about change.

Valon suddenly remembered the crabs.

'Delina,' he said, 'would you help me with these? I have some very angry crabs in these baskets that will not have liked being shut in all that time!'

Delina smiled up at him, pleased to have something to do, and she picked up a basket and headed towards the cooking area. Valon took the other one and followed her. They watched the crabs turn from their dull grey to red in the boiling water and Valon left her with Kadella and Vellisco, talking about cooking.

Valon joined Lonell, now sitting alone at the rear hearth. He sat down beside him.

'You do realise,' remarked Lonell, 'that the last wolf hunt was four days before Narthan was killed? Perhaps she wanted to show that she could kill with any weapon, not just the bow. That might explain why he was killed with Death Juice, hands and stone - three different weapons.'

'No. I know she's angry and relieved that he's no longer with us, but I just can't imagine that she would kill someone. Even if you are right, someone must have helped her to carry the body, and she had told no one about her ban...'

'As far as we know,' interrupted Lonell. 'She could have told someone who's not saying anything. Anyway, I was thinking, we ought to keep a watch on her and, since Kadell's coming out with us tonight, why don't you stay here and see what you can find out?'

Lonell's voice sounded deadly serious but when Valon looked at him, he could see his friend's laughing eyes watching him.

Valon played along, with a smile.

'I think that's a very good idea. You never know what information I might uncover overnight.'

'Just remember, she can't stay awake all night. You must let her get to sleep quite early so we can get out of the cave,' Lonell advised his friend, for which he received a punch on the arm and a guffaw of laughter loud enough to make everyone look round at them.

The sound of a small horn brought the cave to a standstill. Kadell put the goat's horn down and beckoned everyone to gather around the High Hearth. Lonell had realised that somehow the Leader would need to attempt to take the individuals' minds away from the strife that was developing between the two caves. Kadell had decided the tribe needed to start thinking about more routine matters.

'We have enjoyed a glorious summer, but the time has now arrived to begin the hard preparation for the bad weather that will arrive soon enough,' declared the Leader.

As if to emphasise his words, the cave was suddenly illuminated by a flash of lightening, followed immediately by a deafening crash of thunder. Two children screamed and their mothers ran to comfort them. Even the men glanced nervously at the cave entrance and touched their brows.

Kadell raised his voice over the sound of the storm and rain which was beating down on the ledge outside.

'We must make our plans for the collection of food and wood. Dinal and Tobin have already left to gather in the seeds from the Sun Flowers and should return tomorrow. They will also be bringing back some plants which Vellisco is going to try to grow on the High Pasture. If he is successful, no one will have to make the journey to collect the seeds in future.'

A murmur of appreciation went around the group and someone slapped Vellisco on the shoulder.

'It was Lonell's idea, not mine,' he admitted, grinning at the other man. 'We'll put the plants in the ground and also some seeds and hope that something grows here. If this works, there may be other plants we can bring here instead of travelling for days to find them. It's an exciting idea.'

Kadell was smiling. His plan had worked. People were no longer thinking about the problems the tribe were facing; they were planning for the future.

'One of the stands of pine nuts is ready to harvest and we need to check on the others,' he continued.. 'Those berries and other nuts, that aren't ready now, will soon be ripening. We've had good hunting all summer but we still need to bring in more supplies. We need to organise a bison hunt on the plains towards Sun Sleep. With one good hunt we'll be ready for the winter. If we can bring in some fish as well, we will be well provided for.'

'And I need to get my healing plants,' Endorina raised her voice. 'I don't care what I've been told; we can't survive a winter without my stores.'

Kadell nodded.

'We'll all help you to get what you need. Maybe we could also move some of your plants that are further away. We'll make plans for that. We need more wood and kindling. I know we have brought a lot in over the last few weeks but we still need more.'

'Don't forget the Cord Plant. We need to harvest that; this is the right time. And we must check the nets. Some are not ...' Lonell was interrupted by another clap of thunder which seemed to shake the cave.

'Let's stop for food now. We can't do anything outside with this weather so we'll spend the time organising our work. I see the women have prepared us some crabs and also ... I believe, Vellisco has some delicious ducks cooking over there which the last traders from over the mountains brought us. I'm hungry!'

He clapped his hands over his stomach, a huge grin on his face, as he strode over to take a plate.

Lonell watched Kadell and realised why this man was a successful Leader. The men and women of the tribe were now all talking about what each of them was going to do to help get the work done and, due to Kadell's good humour, everyone was laughing as they collected their food. This day could have become a disaster but he had turned it around, made it productive and good-natured.

Lonell, on the other hand, was annoyed. He needed to get down to Mountain Water. Now he had made the connection, he had to confirm it, but even if he could leave the cave without attracting attention, he could not perform the test that he needed to make in this weather and get a sure result. So he fretted the late afternoon and evening away at the back of the cave and everyone kept away from him. No one would approach him when he had that expression on his face.

Later that night, when the only sounds within the cave came from sleeping bodies, Kadell joined Lonell and Mila on their nightly trip to the wolf. Despite their intense fear of such a storm, none would admit to it and they made their way to the cave entrance. For a moment they stood on the threshold, breathing nervously, and it was Kadell who took the first step out into the lashing rain, swiftly followed by the others.

Every now and then, the creeping figures were exposed by lightning strikes that illuminated the landscape and streaked down through the sky, stabbing at the earth below. There was no need to keep silent; the sound of the rain and the reverberating crashes of thunder, which seemed to shake the ground they stood on, hid any noise they might make.

When they reached the slope which led down to the Pit, Lonell decided to go down alone. Mila tried to take on the task but Lonell removed the bag of meat from her and refused to be swayed by her signalled arguments. It was a treacherous night to be doing this for if, despite the weather, one of the Guardians were sent to check on Sim and, if the Gods sent the lightning at that moment, he would be clearly visible against the rock face. He would not put Mila in that sort of danger.

Lonell was astonished that, even with the noise, the wolf knew he was coming. The bedraggled, terrified animal squirmed in what the man now recognised as pleasure and he threw the meat down piece by piece, getting nearer with every chunk. As though the wolf thought of Lonell as a lesser threat than the storm, it allowed him to get closer than on any of the previous nights and, as Lonell was beginning to worry that it would let him touch it, the beast became agitated and the man retreated, gratefully. He was pleased and relieved to rejoin the others at the top. He felt a moment of regret that he could not talk to Sim for he knew how miserable the young man must be feeling but he knew it was impossible under the circumstances.

Lonell could not see the faces of the others as they travelled back to the cave. As they removed their soaking clothes and hung them over the hide stretching frames, Kadell signalled that they would talk the following day. Lonell nodded and when he reached his bed skins, he noticed that Mila had taken hers just a short way from his, leaving a gap between them. It was her very definite way of telling him that she was angry with him for not allowing her to show the Leader what she could do. Lonell understood her feelings and would make sure that he told Kadell it was usually her who fed the wolf, but he could not regret his natural instinct to protect her. He sighed and fell asleep wondering what he would have to do to make it up to her the following day.

Chapter Ten

It was morning and the storm had dissipated, allowing sunlight to glint off the rain drops hanging from the cave entrance. The scent of wet grasses filled the air and Valon and Delina decided to escape the confines of the cave; they spent long enough cooped up during the winter that, in the other months, they all tried to spend as much time as possible in the fresh air. They took their knives and short nets; these were much smaller than the net Lonell had used for hunting the goats, but constructed in a similar fashion, albeit with a finer mesh for hunting birds and smaller animals.

The bright sunshine shone in their eyes as they came up the slope to the High Pasture, amplified by the reflection of the light on the wet vegetation. They shielded their eyes with their hands and stared around. Wandering over the flat grassland where the abundant flowers were stretching their soaked petals towards the drying warmth of the sun, they searched for anything that the storm might have flushed out. Tiny animals were ignored – they only took what they could eat – but ground nesting birds tended to leave their sodden nests after a storm and partridge made a tasty meal. As they caught the birds, they wrung their necks and tied them together, slinging them over their shoulders, each determined to catch more than the other.

Delina narrowly missed a bird, her net clipping its wing and she chased it as it fluttered lopsidedly towards the cliff top. She suddenly dug her heels into the ground and came to an instant standstill, her prey escaping whilst her eyes fixed on the beach down below. For a

Too Long To Die

moment she did not move and then she turned, eyes wide, face flushed with excitement.

'Valon,' she yelled, 'Come on! We have to get back to the cave!'

She ran towards him and grabbed him by the arm, dragging him over the High Pasture towards the cave.

'What? Why are we running?' he gasped, as he was pulled along.

'Come on! Quicker!' was the only reply.

'Tell me!' he shouted as, in their speed, they slid down the path to the ledge.

Ignoring him, Delina ran into the cave.

'A Monster! There's a Monster on the beach!' she screamed.

The tribe came to a standstill. Then, as one, they rushed for the entrance, each wanting to be the first to arrive at the beach to see the great Salt Water Monster. The noise brought Sarril out of the White Cave to discover the cause of the commotion and he shouted the news back through the covered opening. Each person knew what to take with them; they had trained often for the moment as everyone understood the importance of this event to the whole tribe.

When they reached the point where Delina had first spotted the Monster, they stopped and stared in astonishment.

'Sacred Stones,' uttered Kadell. 'It's the largest I've ever seen. We won't be able to harvest that by ourselves. Davoril!' he called. 'Take the message to the Fillari, we will need their help.'

He pointed westwards, towards the home of their nearest neighbours, and Davoril did not wait for more instructions; he slid down the rocky path and ran down the beach as fast as he could, soon disappearing out of view.

Kadell led the way across the expansive sands to the shallows of the Salt Water, to where the enormous whale had been flung by the immense power of the storm. Lonell and Valon were among the first to arrive beside the Leader. They stared in wonder at the sight which seemed so much larger as they stood beside the blue-black body, dwarfed by its tremendous height. They craned their necks to look up at the top, wondering how they were going to manage to climb up there. Lonell moved his hand along the side, feeling the rubbery skin, his fingers sinking into one of the deep grooves that ran the length of the creature and he walked towards the head, stopping when he reached the point where the tiny eye, totally out of proportion with the massive body, stared dolefully at him, blank and lifeless. Lonell was surprised at the sudden wave of sadness that invaded him and he swiftly moved on, his hand following the shape of the half-open, giant mouth which, just for a moment, seemed to be smiling at him. He shook his head and gave his own silent thanks to the great beast which would provide him and his people with food and health throughout the coming cold period. Continuing his walk around, he noticed the damage that had been inflicted on the other side and it was evident that, despite its huge size, the Monster had been thrown about in the water, smashing against rocks, which Lonell assumed had ultimately caused its death.

Staring out thoughtfully over the Salt Water, he realised that the beast must have been thrown up from the darkness that lay beyond the clear, shining water in which the tribe now stood. He was unaware of the true depth of the underwater ravine that edged the shallows but he knew, as they all did, that, if you strayed into those darker waters, the temperature plummeted and the sea bed disappeared from underfoot. He wondered if these gigantic creatures often swam close, but unseen, to them as they fished along the beach. When a particularly vicious storm hit, sometimes a creature would be washed up and left lying in the shallows, but to the tribe it was a gift from the Gods: a sign that they would survive the challenges ahead.

Kadell had just finished pacing its length and Lonell saw, from the frustrated shake of his head, that the Leader had lost count of the number of strides taken, when they were joined by the Enlightened Ones. Lonell splashed through the knee-deep water towards the huge tail which lay like a pair of vast unmoving wings, half buried in the sand, as Saretta led the white figures to the head of the beast from where she addressed the Monster.

'We thank you, great Monster of the Salt Water, for surrendering your life so that we may thrive through the coming winter. We honour your life and we honour your death and we give thanks to the Gods for providing us with this great gift.'

Her white face was filled with greed as she repeated the well-known words, her voice totally void of compassion, a perfunctory gesture of gratitude. When finished, she turned to the tribe, her eyes like slits.

'Now, you have work to do. Get started! There will be no stopping until it is finished!'

Every member of the tribe removed their outer garments, leaving men and women dressed in little more than loin cloths, although some of the women had their breasts strapped down for comfort. Some men clambered onto others' shoulders, scrambling to reach the summit of the beast and using their knives to give them purchase by which they could pull themselves up.

As knives began to hack through the blubber, Kadell approached Saretta, his hand pulling nervously on his ginger beard.

'I have sent a runner to the Fillari. They will be here soon to help us.'

'Why?' screamed the High Priestess, her snarling face pushed close to his. 'This is ours! If they come they will want their share. You had no right to call them; we will kill them first! You do not make decisions like that!'

She glared at Kadell, her crazed eyes tearing right through him.

Lonell watched the confrontation from his elevated position and saw Lexana hurrying over to Saretta's side. She held out a wooden cup to the High Priestess.

'Here, Saretta, drink some of this,' he heard her say. 'You must be thirsty.'

The High Priestess took the cup without thinking and drained the liquid contents in one swallow, throwing the vessel to the ground. Her eyes which had swivelled to stare madly down the beach, searching for the arrival of the Fillari, slowly began to lose their sharpness. Lexana looked knowingly at Kadell and nodded in the direction of the Monster. He did not wait for a second signal; he rushed back to the tribe and soon found himself, like the others, up to the armpits in thick yellow blubber. It was cut away in blocks and thrown down into the surrounding water. The older and weaker members of the tribe, including the children, picked up the pieces and stacked them further up the beach, out of the water. The best cuts came from the belly and the tail so most of the tribe concentrated on cutting away the blubber in those areas first in order to access the delicious meat that lay below, while those on top cut down to expose the colossal skeleton. Blood stained the usually clear water a deep red and the stench from the beast attracted hordes of birds, screaming in the skies overhead.

The sun had moved to take its position high above them when Lonell heard a hail and looked up to see Davoril running towards them followed by a group of Fillari men. People briefly stopped work to greet their neighbours. The Fillari saluted Lonell's tribe by tracing two wavy lines through the air with the left hand, which reflected the scars that the Pescovari men wore over their eyebrow and they, in turn, made a diagonal cross with both arms, copying the symbol of crossed spears that the Fillari bore. It was an acknowledgement of something deeper than mutual acquaintance; a demonstration that they were close enough to recognise in friendship the others' tribal markings.

Lonell enjoyed the company of the Fillari; he found it interesting to see how others behaved and to study the differences between the two groups of people, their ideas and manners. The tribes did not come together often but there was an unspoken arrangement that the Pescovari could hunt aurochs and bison on the plains near the Fillari caves and they, in exchange, could come up to these beaches which produced the best fishing in the area. Occasionally in the past, when big herds appeared on the plains, the two tribes had joined up for the hunt and friendships had been formed but, since Saretta became High Priestess, the partnership had become strained and the trust had slowly dissipated. Kadell had risked bringing her anger on himself by the invitation to the other tribe but half the creature would have gone to waste without their help and, when any beast benefited the tribe by giving its life, they felt a responsibility to make that sacrifice worthwhile by using every part available.

From his vantage point on top of the Monster, Lonell watched the members of his tribe, his mind still lingering on thoughts of Narthan's death while he worked. As hard as he tried, he could not imagine any of them taking the life of the Enlightened One. It was not the fact that the man had returned to the earth, it was the manner in which he had been sent. If there had been one strike, then anyone could perhaps have struck out in anger, but three attempts? That was planned and Lonell asked himself who would or could have done that? He watched the blood running into the water and his thoughts returned to the test he wanted to run and he wondered when he would get the chance.

The men and women worked until late in the day, cutting and chopping the meat, tongue, blubber, and intestines, racing against hunger and exhaustion. The bones and the hard, but flexible, material found in the mouth of the Monster, known to the Pescovari as soft bones, would be harvested after scavengers had cleaned the remains over the following few days. With so many hands the task progressed much faster than would have been possible by the Pescovari alone but, even so, they did not manage to remove all they would have liked and flesh was left on parts of the massive skeleton, leaving a feast for the birds.

Communication was easy between the two tribes as most of the Fillari words were the same or similar. In fact, many wondered if they had once been the same tribe and had split for some reason; they were so alike in many ways. The meat was divided equally between the two tribes, with the exception of the brains. Kadell had reached an agreement that the Pescovari would keep this part of the beast and, when they next hunted on the plains, they would leave the brains of those animals for the Fillari. The brains of prey was used to dress hides in order to produce soft, waterproof skins and the Pescovari were certain that the best dressing came from the Salt Water Monsters, so it was of the utmost importance to them to keep all they could from this harvest.

As evening fell, some of the Fillari packed their bounty into nets, loaded as much as they could onto their backs and, bidding farewell with promises to return the next day, set off in the direction of their caves. Those that remained behind moved their shares close to the cliffs and covered them with rocks to keep them safe overnight until they could carry it all back to their home. The Pescovari, meanwhile, trailed back and forth with loads as large as they could carry until only the huge skeleton, large pieces of tattered flesh hanging from the bones, gave evidence of the Monster that had given its life earlier that day.

Their burdens were safely stashed away in the storage caves with gates tied in place for protection against any animals. The smoking would begin in earnest the following day, along with the rendering down of half of the blubber for oil which had a plethora of uses around the cave but the bones, both hard and soft, would be left only to be used when the need arose.

Kadell invited the remaining Fillari to stay with them that night and celebrate the good luck that had befallen both tribes. Like Lonell, Valon was delighted to see the Fillari but for different reasons. His interests lay in learning their hunting and tracking skills and hearing the stories which their traders brought back from other tribes. His only regret was that he had just dressed his two goat skins with rendered-down fat – the result would have been so much better if he had waited until now, when they had the brains of the Monster. He determined that after the next hunt he would claim a skin to make some new and comfortable clothes for the forthcoming cold period.

The sound of two stones cracking together brought silence. Kadell stood at the High Hearth.

'We have been favoured by the Gods,' he said. 'You all know that this gift will bring both our tribes luck through the cold weather.'

'Why is it lucky?' A child's voice piped up, cutting through the hum of appreciation that followed the Leader's words. Kadell looked down at the grubby face of the small boy and smiled.

'Well, Korin, whenever the Gods send us a great Sea Monster and we honour them by eating its flesh, there is always less sickness. So we know we'll live well during the coming cold weather.'

He looked around and saw that the meat had started to cook together with lumps of blubber, providing the much needed fat content, and mixed with vegetables and roots to create a mouth-watering stew.

'I see Vellisco is working his magic with the food. I suggest that we all go and bathe now - we need it!'

Too Long To Die

Everyone laughed and headed off to Mountain Water, torches in hand, picking the Cleansing Flowers on their way which would remove the smell and grease of the whale. With so many people in the water at once, the inevitable childish games began; splashing and dunking was accompanied by screaming and laughter and the tension and fears within the tribe were all but forgotten for a while. It flashed through Valon's mind that Sim would be sitting in the lonely, cramped Pit listening to the distant sounds of happy voices but, since there was nothing that he could do about it, he tried to put it out of his mind and resolved to enjoy himself until he was able to help the young man. For a moment he wondered where Lonell was - he had not seen him for a while - but he then heard his name called and rejoined the game.

Lonell was at that moment watching his friend from a distance, unnoticed by the crowd, only the small flickering light of his torch giving away his position. He had managed to get to Mountain Water before anyone else and was already bathed and dressed. In front of him was a bag which, every now and then, moved violently. Beside it lay two stones. He put his hand into the bag and pulled out a large rabbit which kicked and tried to escape but he grasped it firmly. Holding it on the ground, Lonell spoke:

'I give thanks to you for your sacrifice, that I may discover the truth of the stone. I honour your life and I honour your death.'

With that, he brought one stone sharply down on the side of the animal's head. He heard bone crunch and saw the blood as it spurted out. Lonell picked up the other stone and, holding them side by side, he compared them. Finally, he nodded. He now knew. He still did not know why but he knew what had happened and he felt it was a large step forward.

He waited a while longer until everyone had left the lake, stuffed the rabbit into the bag and carried the two stones back to where the body had been found. Wrapping them both in the large leaves, he buried them in the original hiding place and covered up any signs that the ground had been disturbed. Then he hurried after the others, slipped into the cave behind them and handed over the rabbit to Vellisco who looked at him with a raised eyebrow but made no comment on the strange timing of the contribution.

Everyone was refreshed and feeling ready to eat by the time they had settled down in the cave. A young woman moved from person to person, offering a drink which took the breath away with the first taste but was soon in high demand.

'Bascana!' cried Valon, as she was about to move past him without offering him a second cupful. 'Are you going to ignore this guest?' he asked jokingly, as he clapped the Fillari man beside him on the shoulder, but pushed his cup out first. The girl smiled shyly, keeping her head down and to one side so that one cheek was hidden in the shadow.

She poured them both some more drink.

'I think I ought to warn you that if you drink much more of this, you will not be able to stand up later!' she said and wiggled her little finger in the air before letting it droop again.

'Bascana, I'm surprised at you!' laughed Valon. 'I shall have you know, I can stand up whenever I want to!' he said, thrusting his hips towards her.

She giggled and ran away and Valon saw his Fillari friend watching her admiringly. He felt a deep sympathy.

'When she was a small child, Bascana slipped and fell into the High Hearth and, although she was rescued very quickly, her face remains scarred. Most men here would ignore it for she's a delightful young woman but the High Priestess would not allow her to undertake the

Journey to Womanhood and so she cannot lie with a man,' explained Valon. 'She lives a sad life although we try to make it as good as it can be.'

'I do not like your High Priestess,' murmured the Fillari, 'I think she is...' he searched for the word, '... cruel.' He looked down at his cup and sipped at the contents, slowly.

A sudden revelation hit Valon and he tugged at the other man's arm.

'Come. There's someone I want you to meet.'

He looked around and spotted Lonell sitting apart, eating his food and watching the gathering.

'Lonell, this is Suro. I thought you two should meet.'

The three men talked for a while and Valon explained that he had told the Fillari about Bascana. The expression on Suro's face explained why Valon had introduced him and Lonell listened as Valon told him the events that led up to the imprisonment of Sim. As Valon finished, he watched the two men and waited for a reaction. He saw Lonell suddenly stare hard at Suro.

'I agree. Sometimes it does seem that they should be called the Unenlightened Ones,' said Lonell.

It amused Valon to see Suro's amazement, knowing that the Fillari man must be wondering if Lonell could read what was inside his head. He knew it would unnerve him but impress at the same time; after all, how many times had Lonell done it to him. Valon hoped that a friendship would form and the two men talked long into the night, long after he had drifted away to find Delina.

The sky was already starting to lose the deep blackness of night when the last person went to their bed skins. He was fast asleep when Mila, although exhausted, looked at Lonell inquiringly.

'Not tonight; it's too late,' he whispered to her and they fell asleep, listening to all the familiar noises of the cave and a long, mournful howl of a lonely wolf.

Kadell, once again, accompanied Lonell and Mila to the Pit the following night and Lonell was pleased to see his astonishment at how close Mila managed to get to the animal before it started to become agitated, even closer than he had done in the storm. The great wolf was obviously excited to see them, leaping to its feet the moment they appeared, with its tail waving from side to side - they had noticed that this seemed to be a sign of contentment. The food was quickly thrown down to stop the whimpering noises it started to make. Mila moved her bed skins back to beside Lonell's when she discovered that he had arranged it.

Three nights later Mila finally managed to hold a piece of meat out which Cannot took from her hand. Although still as nervous as she, the wolf edged forward to snatch it from her and then came back for more, becoming more trusting each time. When the meat was finished, the animal sniffed her hand and licked it, causing Mila to jump back but she put her hand out again and received the same treatment. Gingerly she put her hand on its head and stroked the wolf – a bond was forming.

The next night Lonell was also able to touch the beautiful creature which thrilled him more than he would have liked to admit. He was surprised to feel a closeness with the animal, almost as though the physical contact had created a link between them. In the past he had heard tales of men who had lived with beasts and he had always doubted their veracity, but now he could believe and understand the possibility of such a friendship.

Over the next few days the bond with Cannot was strengthened and, whenever possible and taking exaggerated precautions, someone would carry extra rations and wood to the cave on the beach until they were sure that Sim would have everything he needed. Finally,

Lonell was convinced that the time was right; time was running out, the moon was growing fast and everything was in place. During the pine nut harvest, Lonell manage to get Kadell, Valon and Mila together with him as they gathered the precious fruits.

Without breaking off from their work, Lonell spoke to them.

'I think we should let him out tonight, everything is ready and the moon will be covered by the grey, I hope.'

They all nodded their agreement.

'Kadell, you must stay in the cave,' Lonell insisted. 'They must not suspect you. But if you could somehow make sure everyone sleeps early tonight that will really help. Valon, I want you to make a false trail towards the Fillari so they'll think he has gone there. You'll have to get back without leaving tracks that can be followed. Don't come by way of the Sands.'

He put his hand on his friend's shoulder.

'I think you have the hardest job,' he said, smiling sympathetically.

'Mila and I will get Sim out,' Lonell went on, 'and lead him to his cave where we'll explain the plan to him. Unfortunately we must not let his mother know the truth; she will have to think he has gone and mourn his loss or Saretta will think she's part of it.'

'Are you just talking or are you going to help the others get this harvest in?' came a high-pitched shout from Valt who was overseeing the work party.

'That is going too far,' growled Kadell, quietly.

He stood up and glared at Valt.

'And who do you think you are to talk to the Leader in that way, Valt? You are nothing more than Saretta's servant and the sooner you remember that, the better. You have no right to behave as you do – this must stop!' he declared loudly and was surprised to see Valt's face flushing red, not in anger but in shame. There was no apology but, as Valt turned and walked away from the group, Lonell could see his head was lowered and he wondered if, despite appearances, there might still be some good in the Guardian.

The tribe saw the confrontation as a victory for their cave and they worked in high spirits. It was a good crop that would see them over the winter even if the other stands did not ripen in time to gather the nuts. However, to the four involved in the night's activity, the day seemed endless. Eventually they packed up and carried the fruits of their labour back to the cave in large woven baskets, carried between two people. After the evening meal Kadell announced that the following day would be the first day for collecting wood. A groan went up; although everyone knew this was essential, it was the hardest of all the tasks. Chopping the wood with the primitive flint axes they possessed was hard work in itself but carrying it back from the forests was a strain on even the strongest person. Therefore when Kadell, with his newly charged respect from having stood up to a Guardian, suggested that an early night would be in order because they would be starting out at Sun Wake, no one disagreed and, well before their usual sleep times, everyone was in their bed skins, soon to be asleep in preparation for a long, arduous day ahead.

Valon was the first to leave the cave in the darkness. He made his way carefully to the Pit, threw Cannot some meat and had a quick word with Sim. From there he left a trail, making it look as if the person had been trying to cover his tracks but, in fact, making them quite obvious to anyone with skill. Lonell had been correct about the scant light and Valon was thankful that he knew the area so well. He crossed the High Pasture and dropped down into the little valley behind it, then turning westward and heading in a roundabout fashion towards the Fillari lands. He had done the easy part. Now he had to make sure that the trail disappeared so no one could follow his tracks back to their cave.

Too Long To Die

He wandered around until he spotted a large stream. Removing his leggings, he waded through the cold water, following its course. Slipping on the smooth stones of the stream bed and nearly losing his balance, Valon cursed to himself but kept on going. Initially it led him in the wrong direction and, with all his concentration fixed on staying upright, he missed the early warning sounds. Suddenly he realised that he was surrounded by animals, large animals, and he froze. His relief, when he realised that they were wild horses around him which would not try to eat him, was tempered by the danger he would be in if the creatures became frightened and started to run in his direction. He had no way of knowing the size of the herd. The noise built up rapidly; hooves beating on the river stones, distressed neighing as his scent carried on the air. Valon stayed motionless and suddenly the great beasts thundered away into the night, leaving only the sound of the man's terrified breaths.

When Valon recovered he paid more attention to the noises around him as he followed the stream which finally wound back towards the east. Eventually, he calculated that he had covered his tracks for long enough and started, thankfully, to head back. He knew that everyone would be leaving the cave early so he was not concerned about his tracks near the cave as these would be obliterated in the morning.

When he crept back into his bed skins he could see that Mila and Lonell were not yet back and he hoped fervently that everything was going according to plan. In fact, nothing could have been further from the truth.

Too Long To Die

Chapter Eleven

Lonell and Mila arrived at the top of the slope that led down to the Pit. They crawled towards the edge and looked over slowly, a precaution they took every time. Cannot, who had sensed their presence, began to whimper for his food and the company which he was now used to having every night. They were on the point of getting to their feet for the descent when a gruff voice below called out:

'Quiet, you stupid animal! What is the matter with you?'

In the darkness Lonell could just make out a tall, white figure, staring towards their position. The figure stood motionless.

'Is anyone there?' he asked aggressively.

Lonell put his hand on Mila's back to keep her down and he pushed his face close to hers, the fingers of his other hand to his lips. The minutes passed slowly as they waited, hardly daring to breathe, as the tall figure of Tordano scanned the surrounding area with his pale eyes. Lonell felt sweat trickle down his brow and he wiped it away in annoyance - now was not the time to lose his nerve. After what seemed an eternity the Enlightened One turned and they saw him move away, back towards the White Cave. The faint sound of the covering being drawn back told them that he had disappeared inside.

Although thankful it was Tordano keeping guard rather than Valt or Sarril, Lonell had no intention of putting his goodwill to the test and they waited to be certain that he would not reappear the moment they stood up. Eventually they made their move. They crept down the slope as quietly as they could but every sound seemed to bounce off the walls of the crevice, louder than ever before. He took out some of the meat he was carrying and passed it to Mila who fed the excited animal, calming it as best she could, stroking its head and whispering quietly in its ear. Lonell watched her as she untied it from the Pit gate and was surprised to see her wipe her eyes and nose. He knew from their talks that she would miss the contact she had enjoyed every night with this wild but friendly beast but he had not expected such strength of emotion. Then he remembered his sadness at the death of the Monster on the beach and wondered why people felt an attachment to such creatures whose natural instinct would be to eat them.

Lonell turned back to his task and cut the ties on the gate with a flint stone which had been sharpened by chipping off flakes until a cutting edge appeared. It was deliberately primitive and he left it inside the small space to be found after the escape. Sim was waiting and Lonell helped him up the slope to the High Pasture, while Mila reattached Cannot to the gate. As she left the wolf behind her she looked back and said a silent goodbye; it was the end of her nightly visits to the beautiful animal.

Initially they followed the same track that Valon had taken some time before but then changed direction and headed towards the beach. Their pace was slower than expected because, although Sim had tried to exercise within the tiny confines of the Pit, his legs were much weaker than they had anticipated. Lonell and Mila had to support him over the more difficult parts of their journey.

'I'm sorry,' whispered Sim, as his knees buckled once more under his weight.

Mila smiled reassuringly, her hand on his arm, but put her fingers to her lips.

Half-carrying the young man, Lonell suddenly dropped down to his knees, pulling the others with him, and he motioned them to stay still. He could hear movement in the undergrowth behind them. Surely Tordano had not followed all this way instead of stopping them before but perhaps he wanted to see where they were headed. Almost instantly, Lonell discarded that idea. They were not the sounds of a man; an animal was stalking them, perhaps ready to attack at any moment. Lonell was highly aware of Sim who had not bathed for almost a Moon - there would be no hiding from a creature intent on feeding. How could they escape? There was no shelter except for the long grasses in which they were now squatting and there were other considerations: he did not want to kill anything as that would leave their trail visible to anyone looking for Sim. Only if they had no choice. Both Mila and Lonell had their knives in their hands and Lonell also held a short spear ready to throw.

Mila pulled Lonell's arm and made signs of running towards the beach but Lonell knew that Sim did not have the strength to make it. Closer was a craggy rock formation they could climb onto but so, he thought, could the creature - the lower boulders offered little protection and they were still too far away but the group could not stay where it was. With signs, Lonell explained his plan to the others. Mila shook her head vehemently but Lonell held her, nodding his insistence, until she gave in to him. He could see her worried face in the scant light of the shaded moon and he kissed her briefly.

He began to run, spear and knife at the ready, making sure to attract the attention of the creature. He wished he had a net with him, even a small one but he would have to make do with what he had. The animal was following and Lonell knew his plan had worked. He hoped that Mila was already helping Sim down to the beach. Running as fast as he could, the sounds were right behind him, snuffling as the beast followed his scent and the thudding of hard pads on the ground and the scraping of claws on stones. When he reached the rocks, he tucked the knife into his belt so as to have a free hand and jumped, scrambling to pull himself up onto the first boulder and from there to the next higher up. A paw crashed down on the rocks beside him, the fearsome claws just missing his leg and, as he sprung for the next level, he heard the ripping sound of material. He looked around - he could go no higher. He was trapped. Lonell waited, terrified, aware that death was imminent, wondering why this cave hyena was acting so aggressively; their normal fare was the putrefying flesh of already dead animals - they did not usually attack living creatures, although it was not unknown.

Time passed and Lonell listened as the great creature scratched at the ground below him, panting and sniffing. He almost laughed when he thought about his wish for a net. These creatures were vast - a net would only serve as an annoyance. Even a thrust from his spear would, unless extremely lucky, only make the hyena more vicious.

Soon it became obvious that the creature was not going to climb up to him and Lonell sat, wondering why it had not followed. Hyenas were good climbers and, although the rocks were steep, it could easily have pulled its great body up, in which case Lonell would not have stood a chance. Unable to find the tear in his leggings which he was certain the hyena's claws had caught, Lonell was confused. He put his weapons on the rock beside him and loosened the bag at his waist; the bag which, Lonell suddenly realised, held, not only extra dried meat to leave with Sim, but also some chunks of meat for the wolf. One side of the bag was shredded. That was what the hyena was after, the delicious meat which smelt so strongly, and that was why it had not come after him - some of the meat must have fallen out as he climbed. As he looked, the creature cackled its frustration - the meat that had fallen to the ground had been devoured and it wanted more.

Scrabbling to his feet, Lonell held the strap of the meat laden bag. Using all his skills for throwing nets, he hurled the bag away from the direction of the beach. It landed, breaking open and the hyena chased towards it. As fast as he could move, Lonell leapt off the rocks and ran, not looking back, heart pounding, his chest feeling as though it would break open, over the open pasture and he skidded down the rocky slope to the beach, careless to the danger of injury. Suddenly, he was almost knocked off his feet and for an instant thought the hyena had caught him until he realised that Mila was sobbing on his chest.

When they arrived at the tiny opening behind the boulder on the beach, Lonell led the way in and, feeling around, he pulled closed the skin he had fixed over the opening. The darkness was complete but he knew exactly where the hearth was and soon sparks from the Sun Stone lit the kindling which rapidly became an adequate fire. Sim had collapsed onto a natural shelf that protruded from the wall of the cave and was looking around in amazement.

'You will have to pull the skin closed over the entrance when you have a fire. I know it will be smoky in here but it won't be for long,' advised Lonell. 'In fact, the less you can use the fire the safer you'll be.'

He showed Sim where all the stores were kept and then explained the plan that he had come up with.

'You must stay here alone for five days – we will not be able to come anywhere near you. Here, I have made five marks on this,' he said showing Sim a piece of bone with lines carved into it. 'Each day cross one off and then you will know when you can leave – it would be easy to lose track of the days. If it's not safe at that time we will somehow warn you.'

'Where will I go?' asked Sim, forlornly. 'I don't know what to do.'

'Don't worry, it's all arranged. Listen to me. Valon has made a false trail in the direction of the Fillari and we will all be sent out to look for you. Saretta will insist on talking to the Fillari and they'll be able to tell her quite truthfully that you are not there. We're hoping the search will stop soon after they fail to find you there because they'll think you've gone further away. They will never imagine that you've stayed close. Then you can go to the Fillari who are waiting for you – they know what happened and are willing to take you in. They don't have good feelings for Saretta. You must travel by night and follow the edge of the Salt Water as far as you can - the water will hide your tracks. In here you have everything you need, including your weapons and more; take what you need with you, it's all yours.'

When he finished there was a silence and Lonell looked at Sim curiously, expecting some comment. It was only then that he noticed Sim's eyes were full of tears; the young man was trying to control his emotions. Lonell looked away and waited.

'I don't know how to thank you all,' said Sim, his voice shaking. 'The risks you have taken for me – everything you have given me.' He waved his arm, indicating the contents of the cave. 'One day I will repay you. Will you tell the Leader that I didn't do it? I don't want him to think badly of me.'

'He knows,' replied Mila. 'Both he and Kadella know about all this. Two of the nights Kadell even came to feed the wolf.'

There was a short silence again.

'And my mother, will you tell her I'm all right?' the young man pleaded.

Lonell and Mila exchanged a quick look, and told the lie they had known would be inevitable.

'Of course. Don't worry, we'll tell her what has happened and we'll look after her.'

The last part was correct; the whole tribe would help to look after her but, if Sim were to make his escape, it was essential that she thought he had just run off alone. If they told her the truth, the

Enlightened Ones would soon realise she was not grieving like a mother who had lost her son for good.

'We must return to the cave now,' decided Lonell, and Mila nodded in agreement. 'But before I go, I have to ask you, do you know anything about the death of Narthan?'

Sim stared at Lonell, his face horrified.

'I'm sorry, but I'm asking everyone. If I don't ask you, then I will not have all the facts.'

Sim thought for a moment, nodded and answered, 'I know nothing of his death but I am glad. He was ... a bad man. He treated me with cruelty during my Right of Shadows. I cannot feel sad that he has returned to the earth.'

Lonell was watching him carefully as he spoke and when Sim finished he nodded.

'Thank you,' he said simply.

'Is that all?' asked Sim, surprised. 'But I might not have told the truth.'

'But you have,' said Lonell, smiling. 'I can tell from the way you spoke. Good luck, my friend. We shall meet again soon.'

He held out his arm but Sim threw both arms around the older man and clung to him for a moment, speechless, before turning to Mila and repeating the action. They smiled encouragingly at the young man and quietly left him, a mixture of emotions crowding their spirits.

When they finally crept back into their cave and dropped down onto their bed skins, Lonell was unaware that Valon breathed a sigh of relief. He thought that his friend must have been asleep long before, not realising the torturous vigil he had held.

It seemed he had only just fallen asleep when they were being awakened to go on the wood collecting expedition. Every part of his body ached but, despite the exhaustion, Lonell knew it was essential to appear normal. Hopefully they would all be far away from the cave by the time the escape was discovered, which would certainly happen when Verina went to take Sim his food, accompanied as always by a Guardian.

The new day was glorious, a deep blue sky forming the backdrop to the majestic mountains which lined the inland horizon as far as they could see. Despite the cold chill in the air, which told them the cold weather was fast approaching, the strength of the sun was hot on their backs. They were well into their work, the men stripped down to their loin cloths, sweating, as they chopped at the trunks of trees with their flint axes. The women were ranging through the forest to locate any fallen trees and smaller pieces of wood, all of which were piled up, ready to be carried back over the next few days. Their water bags were already being drained when a solitary figure in white appeared amongst them, shouting as he tried to catch his breath.

'Return! You must return to the cave now! The High Priestess has ordered it!'

Kadell straightened up from the logs he had been cutting as if he had just noticed Valt's presence, although Lonell knew the Leader had been observing in detail the approach of the Guardian.

He nodded once and turned to the tribe.

'We are not going to waste a journey back,' he said. 'Each of you, load up with as much wood as you can carry.'

'There is no time for that. Saretta said...' Valt's shout was silenced by the Leader's look and the memory of what had happened only the day before. 'All right, just make it quick,' he finished lamely, clearly hating himself as he saw ill-hidden smirks on the faces of the men and women around him.

Masking his deliberate time wasting, Kadell managed to delay their return by carefully loading up everyone and stopping each time something was dropped. On the ledge they carefully unloaded and stacked the wood in the storage area before returning to their cave.

Saretta was waiting for them beside the High Hearth, fury etched into every line of her face. Even Lonell was horrified and he could see the tribe's anger towards her deepening; she had entered their domain without the Leader's invitation. Although they were used to the ignorance of the Guardians who sometimes wandered in uninvited when they were all there, even they would not have entered had the Leader not been present. What Saretta had done broke an unspoken but vital rule that allowed the two caves to live in relative harmony and, by the discomfort on their faces, it was clear that the Attendants and Guardians were well aware that a line had been crossed. Even the wolf was in the cave, uneasy due to all the strange smells and the angry atmosphere. Lexana held it firmly but looked as if she wished she were anywhere but there.

'I see you have all made yourselves at home in our cave,' accused Kadell, his face scarlet with anger. His eyes fell on Verina who was sitting shaking quietly in a corner, her hands over her face.

'Silence!' shouted Saretta and the noise echoed round the walls of the cave. 'Sim has run away. He was too cowardly to give his life to protect his tribe. He must now be hunted down like the animal he is but I want him alive. We need him for sacrifice or the Gods will punish us. Do you understand?' she screamed. 'He is no longer a man – he is not one of you and you will all suffer if we do not get him back.'

'How did he get out?' asked Kadell, wanting to find out what they knew and whether they blamed Verina.

It was Tordano who answered, and Lonell noticed a bruise forming on the Guardian's left cheek.

'He cut through the gate bindings and somehow got past the wolf. But he has left a trail which I am sure Valon will be able to track. We will get him back.'

He finished, glancing nervously at Saretta and cringed as she stared back with hooded eyes, ready to strike out.

Lonell felt sympathy towards Tordano but better that than they discover the truth. Kadell took command of the situation.

'Valon, you will lead us. Tordano, show Valon where the tracks start and we will all go after him.'

'Should we not split up?' Sarril voiced the question they had not wanted to hear.

'If there are tracks as Tordano has said, there's no point in looking anywhere else, is there? If there's any doubt where he's gone further up the track, then we can split up.'

Kadell looked at Saretta and she nodded.

'Collect your weapons as you go,' she added unnecessarily.

Valon and Tordano led the way, with Saretta and the Guardians next, followed by the Attendants and most of the tribe; Verina stayed behind to look after the children. They filed slowly past Lexana who held Cannot tightly on its leash, the wolf growled quietly until Mila and Lonell passed in front of the animal. Then it started whimpering and its long tail moved from side to side, knocking against Lexana. They both went cold with fear and Mila looked away, but Lonell looked straight at the Attendant and saw her studying them, one eyebrow slightly raised. A hint of a smile flickered over her face and her knowing eyes shone as she patted the head of the wolf and leant down to control it. Hardly able to hide their relief, the two conspirators pushed forward and it was only when they were outside that they dared look at each other.

Valon made a great pretence of searching for the correct tracks and then led them all along the false trail he had laid the previous night. There was one awkward moment when the wolf tried to veer off in the direction of the beach but Lonell dropped back to just in front of Lexana and the animal followed his scent back onto the path they wanted him to take. Neither tribesman nor Attendant acknowledged the other but each was highly aware of the role that the other was playing.

A deep air of melancholy hung over the group of people tracking its missing member, for only five knew where Sim really was. Lexana had also realised that they would not find him by walking in this direction. The rest fretted at the thought of having to hunt him down, the desire to rebel so strong but there was little they could do. They were fast approaching the lands of their neighbours and Lonell could not help but worry that they might have changed their minds about offering help.

Suddenly, as if from nowhere, the Fillari leader and a group of warriors appeared in front of them, dressed in formal leather tunics and leggings, adorned with feathers and sea shells which glinted in the sun light. Despite the decoration and fineness of their attire, the spears they carried clearly demonstrated a readiness for any eventuality, for defence or attack if necessary.

'They're putting on a good show,' thought Lonell, smiling to himself.

There was a tense moment as the two groups faced each other, both heavily armed, but Lonell picked out Suro amongst the Fillari and saw him incline his head slightly in an acknowledgement that all was well. As he watched Saretta approach the Fillari leader, he realised he was sweating, which had nothing to do with exertion. He quickly wiped the dampness off his brow.

'Welcome, High Priestess of the Pescovari,' the Fillari greeted her, his hand drawing the two wavy lines at chest height, but his face not showing the friendship that would normally be expected to accompany the sign.

'What brings you and your warriors to our lands?'

He made no reference to the fact that the Pescovari were there uninvited although it could be read on all the faces. Common courtesy dictated the need to send a runner ahead to ask permission before encroaching on others' hunting grounds and, even though the two tribes maintained friendly agreements, still they were both expected to follow the rules of propriety, which Saretta had ignored entirely.

'We search for an escaped captive,' she announced, with no prior greeting for the Fillari leader. 'We have tracked him down to this place and I want to know if he has been taken in by your tribe. He is dangerous and due to be sacrificed to the Gods.'

Saretta appeared unaware of the intake of breath from both tribes, her lack of courtesy astonishing and unforgivable. The Fillari leader continued smiling although his narrowing eyes betrayed his true feelings.

'If he is such a dangerous man,' he replied, 'perhaps the Gods did not want him as a sacrifice. However, I can assure you that he is not here although ... I believe he was. One of my warriors saw a stranger in the distance. He went to challenge the man but a pack of wolves attacked before he could reach him. I do not know if death had taken him when they dragged him away but he will certainly be with the Gods now.'

Seeing the fury on Saretta's face and concerned at the insults her next words would bring, Kadell quickly stepped forward.

'Great leader of our friends, the Fillari, I greet you in the name of the Pescovari.'

He crossed his arms high in front of his face as if to emphasise his awareness of his spiritual leader's impropriety and he saw the other man smile.

'I regret to ask this favour, but may we see the place where our brother was attacked so the Enlightened Ones might find a Sacred

Stone for his mother? Her grief will be great when she hears and we all feel the pain.'

'You are welcome, great leader of the Pescovari,' was the reply, 'but may I make a request in return? I would prefer the wolf to remain here. If it comes with us it might attract the pack and we will all be in danger.'

At that moment, as if on cue, the wolf threw its head back and howled into the sky. The sound pierced the air and the reply came back almost immediately from the distance. To a man, Pescovari and Fillari touched their brows to protect themselves and they stepped away from the animal. Even those that knew its gentleness were unnerved at the timing.

No one appeared to want to stay behind but Mila and Valon volunteered for Lexana could not be left unprotected by herself. It was agreed that they would return to their cave as the Pescovari could find their way back without them. Had Saretta been able to see them a short while later, she would have been frantic with anger. The three figures walked companionably beside the wolf and demonstrated a levity which had no place following the announcement of the death of a tribal member, although Lexana's heart was heavy with the news she had to impart to Sim's mother.

Meanwhile the rest of the tribe had reached the place where Sim had 'met his end'. Lonell was impressed to see a stain of blood on the ground and a trail where the bloody body had been dragged away. This had not been part of his plan but it was most effective and surely, even Saretta could not argue with the evidence. The tribe was deeply upset at the death of a fine young man with the exception of Saretta who was furious at the loss of her sacrifice but she had to perform her role as High Priestess. Both women and men wept as the Enlightened Ones howled their grief, even though there was no body to mourn over and the wolf pack joined in once more but the irony was missed by most of the observers. The Attendants searched the ground for a Sacred Stone and Talia found a jet black crystal that would later be consecrated back at the cave.

Kadell thanked the Fillari as Saretta swept past them in a rush to return to her cave. Lonell nodded a silent thanks to Suro and, making sure that no one else was looking at him, he held four fingers down the side of his leg, signifying that it would be four more days before Sim arrived with them. On the walk back Lonell thought to himself that Sim would be the only person alive who had a Sacred Stone in his family's collection and it might well destroy his poor mother, which had not been part of the plan.

When a person returned to the earth, a stone was collected usually from the burial place, which was then consecrated and given to the family. If the deceased happened to be a mother of two children, two stones would be found, one for each child, and the mother's collection would be divided between the two. When a man died his stones would be passed on to a sibling if he had one but, if not, they would be buried with him, to continue their protection in death as in life. The Sacred Stones were kept in a small cave on the ledge and each person decorated a box or bag to keep them in. Since the tribe was not able to converse with or pray to their Gods, they talked to their ancestors through the stones, if they felt in need of spiritual help. However, the words 'Sacred Stones' had also jokingly become a curse, referring to a man's most precious physical attributes!

The atmosphere in the cave was crushing. Lonell felt it as an almost physical weight that bore down on him. Verina had been told of her son's fate and there was nothing that could be done to lessen her pain. Overwhelmed by guilt, he stayed by himself at the back of the cave, not wanting to communicate with anyone. The others who knew the truth also felt the burden of responsibility. Kadell asked

Endorina if she had anything that would help and she prepared a mixture of juices which calmed the elderly woman, sending her to sleep.

Those who did not want to sit by themselves gathered around the High Hearth. No one was talking very much; even Tendo and Davoril sat quietly, speaking in muted voices, and so everyone heard when Kara turned to Endorina.

'May I talk to you? I think I may be carrying,' she said.

'Oh, how wonderful! A new life – that's just what the cave needs to hear to bring some happiness,' enthused Endorina, attracting everyone's attention.

Suddenly everyone surrounded Kara, hugging and congratulating her. One person who did not join in was Valon who sat looking at her pityingly.

'Why so miserable?' asked Tendo jokingly, slapping him on the shoulder.

'I'm just hoping it won't be another Enlightened One – we have enough of those already. But she's just come back from the White Cave and that is Saretta's plan. That's why they all have to go through the Journey to Womanhood. She wants more pale skins born to the tribe!'

Chapter Twelve

The silence that followed the outburst was broken by a loud sob. Jadana ran to Jadilla and threw her thin pale arms around her mother's neck, the white head crying on her mother's breast. Jadilla held her daughter, comforting her and glaring at Valon with the intense fury of an angered mother, when suddenly everyone started talking at once. Knowing he had to act immediately to prevent complete uproar in the cave, Kadell stood up and held his hands in the air.

'Quiet!' he shouted and the tribe fell silent. 'Let's all sit and talk about this calmly. Explain yourself, Valon. What are you talking about?'

Valon looked around awkwardly, embarrassed by his comment. He noticed that, at some time, Lonell had moved silently to his side and was now sitting beside him.

'I'm really sorry, Jadana. It's nothing against you, I promise. You are a wonderful person and I don't see why you should have to leave us and move away. I don't want you to go just because your skin is lighter than ours. Jadilla,' he addressed her mother, whose anger had dissipated slightly with his words, 'when you started carrying Jadana, how long had you been back from your Journey to Womanhood?'

'Not long,' she replied. 'Saretta told me I was truly blessed, that the women who started carrying so soon would always be looked after by the Gods. And when Jadana was born they were all so kind to me but I don't know what I shall do when she moves to the White Cave.' Jadilla looked down at the small child still clinging to her and hugged her close, tears falling down her cheeks.

'Minaya's mother had also returned recently from her Journey,' Ancient Pel's voice came from the far side of the circle and, as Lonell turned to look at him, he noticed a distant expression on the wrinkled, ugly face.

'I think Valon is right,' said Lonell. Valon felt his friend's hand on his shoulder, supporting, encouraging.

'There does seem to be a link between the carrying and the Journey. We've always believed that everyone can choose who they want to spend their time with but Saretta is forcing our young women to lie with men they have not chosen.'

Lonell looked around at the bewildered faces in front of him.

'Has no one else noticed this?' he asked in frustration. 'This is not the way we live our lives and yet we're allowing it to happen.'

'But not all the girls who return start carrying straight away – I didn't,' said Kadella, whose face had flushed slightly, embarrassed at her own words.

Endorina, the Healer, stood up from the stone seat she had been sitting on and everyone looked at her. Her face was masked with discomfort.

'No one knows for sure,' she said, 'why some women start carrying after lying with a man and others do not. Perhaps the Gods choose the correct partner at that particular time for each woman. We only know that a woman who does not share herself will never carry a child, but we don't know why. This is a mystery we will never understand, nor should we try to. It belongs to the Gods.'

She stopped for a moment before continuing, anger welling up in her voice.

'The only part of this that a woman has control over is her choice of the man she lies with. That freedom should never be abused. If a man here were to take a woman against her will, he would be exiled from the cave and yet, Lonell and Valon are right, we put up with the Enlightened Ones taking our girls, just as they turn into young women, and forcing them to lie with a Guardian chosen by Saretta.'

She sat down, shaking, relieved to have finished. Although happy to take charge when a person needed her knowledge of healing, she was not used to talking to the whole tribe and being the centre of attention.

Kadell stood up slowly and moved towards her, putting his hand on her shoulder comfortingly. Then he returned to his place in the circle and turned to face the assembly.

'I am ashamed,' he declared. 'I have let the tribe down, particularly the women. I have allowed you to be treated badly and I should not be your Leader. You must choose another.'

He sat down heavily, face in his hands, not wanting to see the accusing looks.

Valon, who had been closely observing all the faces, suddenly realised to his surprise that everyone was looking at Lonell in expectation. He could see that his friend's first instinct was to retreat into his corner. He knew that Lonell would not want to get involved in this but the dark man looked around him and saw there was no way out. He got to his feet, carefully studying the people watching him.

'There is no one better to lead our cave than Kadell,' he said. 'Yes, there are things that have gone wrong but he has only been trying to protect us by not standing up to Saretta. And we cannot throw the blame onto one person – we have all let this happen and none of us has talked about it until now. Maybe we will have to do something now but Kadell must lead us. Nothing has changed the fact that he is the best person to do it.'

'What about you, Lonell?' asked Davoril. 'You always seem to know what is happening and what to do.'

Lonell turned to look at him in astonishment. 'My rank in the cave is very low as you are all aware. I could never lead. Anyway, I wouldn't want to.'

Kadell lifted his head and looked at the other man.

'And what dictates your rank, my friend?' he asked, but although Lonell smiled knowingly, he refrained from answering.

There was a long silence, broken finally by Endorina.

'His skin is dark. It is the natural colour of other tribes in the region. Each of you knows your given rank. I think we should stand up in order, starting with the Leader until we reach the lowest ranked person.'

She looked at Kadell who nodded and stood up. He was followed by Kadella and each member of the tribe stood up in turn. When the final person had sat down again, no one failed to recognise that their rank, given by Saretta, was directly linked to the colour of their skin.

Valon, who had often wondered why his rank was so much higher than his friend's, stood up again to speak.

'Surely rank should go with the value that someone brings to the cave, through their work, not through the colour of their skin? And even that is difficult; who is to say what is more valuable – a hunter or a healer, a knapper or a cook? There should be no rank except for the Leader. We don't need rank.'

He sat down, red-faced, and stared angrily around him.

A rumble of noise broke out and, when no one else took control, Kadell pushed himself slowly to his feet.

'Who will put themselves forward as Leader?' he inquired.

Silence fell over the group and no one stood up.

'Is everyone content that I continue as Leader?'

He looked at each person in turn and received nods from all of them.

'Then I make a promise to you all that these problems will be sorted. We will no longer use rank. From now on, if I need assistance,

I'll ask the people most suited for that particular task. No one is better than the next.'

He stopped for a moment and, taking a deep breath, he lowered his voice.

'The problem of the Journey to Womanhood is more complicated because that involves the White Cave. To stop that we must all stand together and refuse to send our girls to them. It will be dangerous but, if we are serious about making changes, then we'll have to take risks. I will think about the action we must take – are you all in agreement?'

Everyone nodded their assent, as a burning log crashed off the fire and rolled towards Lonell. Kadell pushed it back with the horn implements, used to tend the hearths, but Valon noticed that Lonell frowned and shivered.

'Was this a bad omen?' wondered the blond man as he stared at his friend thoughtfully; certainly there would be trying times ahead, change would not come easily. He felt a sudden twinge of fear but the others started talking and laughing as though a weight had been lifted off them. Kadell put up his hands and silence fell once more.

'Since we are all gathered, there is something else I want to talk about. It has been obvious for a while that someone is informing the White Cave about things that are happening here. I want to know who it is and why they are doing it.'

For a moment no one moved. Some of the faces were shocked, some knew it had been happening but they all looked around at their neighbours and wondered.

'I've been telling them some things.' Ancient Pel's trembling voice broke the silence.

Of all the people in the tribe, Ancient Pel would have been the last guess of most and every member turned and stared at him, shocked.

'Why?' demanded Kadell, as bewildered as the rest. 'We need an explanation.'

'At the back of the White Cave there are caverns that gleam and have shapes of rock and crystals such as I have never seen. Saretta has allowed me to decorate some of the caves but in return she asked me for information about what was happening here. You would understand if you saw them ...'

His voice drifted away as he searched the faces around him. Then he looked directly at Kadell.

'I swear I never told them anything important, only things they could easily have found out by watching from over there or listening. I reckoned that if they thought I was telling them everything, then they wouldn't watch us so closely. Sometimes I had to make things up because I didn't want to tell them what was really going on; for example, they know nothing of any nightly wander...'

Kadell put up his hand quickly to stop the old man. Most people looked confused for a moment but assumed that he must be talking about some romantic activity so they smirked and looked at the Leader to see his reaction to the confession. He thought for a while and looked around the expectant faces.

'Very well. I think we can accept that, as long as you're careful about what you tell them. In fact, it could be useful if we want to feed them information that may or may not be correct.' He grinned. 'We could have some fun with this.'

Ancient Pel was still sitting, shaking, but now he achingly raised himself to his feet and addressed the tribe.

'I have always taken care with what I told them but I ask for you to forgive me. I should have asked permission from the Leader and from all of you. I was only thinking of myself and my art. I hope I can make up for it by passing on what you want them to know in the future. With luck, it may help any plans.'

He sat down again heavily and his neighbour put a hand on his arm in reassurance. No damage had been done.

Kadell took to his feet again and spoke, the authority of the Leader once again returned to his voice.

'This meeting is now over. We have a lot to think about and plans to be made. We will not rush into anything – everything must be carefully worked out before any action is taken.'

People drifted away, some to other hearths, others to their bed skins. Lonell watched Valon approach Jadana and put his arms around her, holding her tight. Jadilla offered him a cup of her berry juice drink that she made and friendship was mended and perhaps even strengthened. There was an expression of hope and determination on her face which had not been seen for many moons.

Lonell had returned to the back of the cave and was sitting with his back against the wall, staring out, when he was joined by Kadell.

'May I talk with you?' asked the Leader.

'Of course. Here sit down on this,' Lonell pushed one of his skins over.

'We must speak quietly,' Kadell said, when he had settled. 'No one else must hear our words.'

Lonell nodded.

'Are you any closer to finding out who killed Narthan?' Kadell asked. 'I think it could be really important. At the moment, we don't understand why Saretta behaved the way she did and, if we can find out what's happening, it may change the way we act. So I can't decide what to do until I know more.'

'I agree. It's vital we find out but, although there are so many people who hated him, either they couldn't have done it or I can't imagine them killing anyone.'

'So let's go over what you do know.'

'All right. As you know, Narthan was given Death Juice, his neck was squeezed *and* he was hit on the head with a stone. I don't know why or whether it was the same person who did all three, but I do know that he wasn't killed where Sim found him. I found the stone and there would have been more blood on the floor if he'd died there, so he must have been moved. Narthan was a big man so either someone very strong or more than one person must be involved, because he wasn't dragged. Anyway, Valon found two sets of tracks so he must have been carried.'

He looked intently at Kadell to check he had followed his reasoning.

'I haven't found anywhere that shows evidence of being the kill site.' he added.

Lonell used a hunting term for want of a better way to describe where the death had actually taken place. He did not mention the results of his stone test because, without an understanding of why, it added no more information.

'So, who do you think hated Narthan enough to kill him?' asked Kadell, frowning in concentration.

Lonell laughed bitterly.

'Almost everyone. At one stage, I did because of the way he treated me. Any young man who had Narthan on his Rite of Shadows and any girl who was 'trained' by him on her Journey, or their mothers; Delina who can't use her bow; Endorina who was not allowed to heal people; Bascana - it was Narthan who stopped her from going on her Journey; Jadilla, whose daughter has to move to the White Cave; the list is huge.'

'Vellisco - Narthan was always saying that he was a woman because he liked cooking.'

Lonell and Kadell looked up, startled, to see Valon standing over them, and the Leader beckoned him to sit beside them.

'Tendo,' continued Valon, pointing to his own nose, unobtrusively.

'The man was cruel to him when he was young.'

'And Dinal,' added Kadell.

Seeing their blank faces, he explained, 'Dinal went out hunting just after he passed his Rites and Narthan forced him to enter a cave by himself even though it was clear that something was using it as a den. The lad was lucky to escape with his life.'

'I'd forgotten that,' said Valon. 'It was a cave bear, wasn't it?'

Kadell nodded.

'An extremely angry but, luckily, very tired cave bear who had been woken from its long sleep. Dinal will carry the reminder with him until he returns to the earth - his arm was clawed badly and he is lucky to have the use of it.'

Lonell nodded in agreement, both remembering the cave's tense vigil as the young man fought for his life.

'I don't know whether this is likely but could it be possible that Alurasta and Finar have returned?' asked Valon, after a moment's hesitation.

The other two men stared at him through the thickening darkness. It was something that neither had considered.

'Is it likely?' The Leader appeared to be talking to himself rather than addressing the others.

Alurasta and Finar had broken the rules of the tribe: they had fallen in love and wanted to become a couple in a monogamous relationship. It might actually have been allowed if Alurasta had not been so jealous, accusing all the other women of trying to steal her man. After weeks of discord, the cave had asked Saretta to make a ruling and she had heard the case, for this was in her earlier years when she tolerated a certain amount of input from others.

While Ancient Brano had made a passionate plea for the couple, who had given their word that no further disharmony would come to the cave by their joining, it was Narthan who convinced Saretta that the changes should not be tolerated. Following his advice, Saretta had exiled the couple from the tribe and they left bitterly, facing a dangerous and uncertain future. If they had been unable to find another tribe to take them in before winter, the chance of their survival was minimal.

It was Lonell who finally broke the silence of their thoughts.

'No, I don't think that is likely - many cold seasons have passed since they left. Either they did not live through the winter or they found a tribe to take them in. But we should keep it in mind.'

He stared at the Leader.

'And what about you? Tell me why you wanted to kill Narthan?'

'What? I certainly did not ....,' blustered Kadell, his face turning red under the ginger hair. He jumped to his feet and glared down at the two men, at which point he noticed the grins on their upturned faces.

'Argh, why do I ever pay any attention to you?' he growled, trying not to laugh as he sat down again.

'However, I suppose I should confess that I loathed the man. It's hard enough to be Leader with the Enlightened Ones looking over everything we do but he always questioned me and showed great disrespect. So yes, you can add me to your list, Lonell, although I did not kill him, but I can't say I'm sorry he's gone! It's your turn now, Valon, tell us why you hated him.'

'Well, this is rather embarrassing,' replied Valon, 'but I hardly had anything to do with the man. I was lucky that he was never in a position to harm me. So, I'm probably one of the few who only hated him for what he did to other people. I'll never forgive him for what he did to Marita.'

'And that's our greatest problem,' said Lonell, staring down at the floor. 'Even if someone did not have a reason to hate him for what he did to them, they loathed him on behalf of someone else. It could be anyone ...'

The three men sat in silence for a while, each trying to come up with an idea of how to solve the puzzle set by the Guardian's death and each knowing the situation in the cave could not improve until this matter was over. They were incapable of ignoring an unsolved death and moving on. Crimes like this happened so rarely that no one alive had ever known the like but they were certain that the Gods would never look kindly on a people who condoned such violence to one of their own, regardless of how the individuals felt about him.

Through the flickering light of the hearth fires, Lonell was staring hard at Kadell and the Leader looked back at him inquisitively.

'What? You have thought of something.'

'No, not really. Do you trust me ... do you really believe that I did not take Narthan's life?' asked Lonell, his eyes penetratingly fixed on the Leader.

'I know you didn't do it, because you would never have let Sim be punished for it if you had,' asserted Kadell. 'Why do you ask?'

'Because I need to leave the cave for a while. I can't tell you where I'm going or why and I'm sure that everyone will think that I have gone because I killed the Guardian.'

Lonell could see Kadell considering him carefully, a frown etching his forehead as he thought, and he could feel himself holding his breath as he waited for the answer.

'Right, we need a reason for you to go.'

Kadell's trust in the unusual man who sat in front of him was absolute. Once he had thought of a valid plan, he did not hesitate.

'We still have some salt that can be traded. We'll say that you have gone to trade with the Burgoni for reindeer meat - that is one thing we don't have in the stores to help us through the cold. Will that give you enough time for what you need to do?'

'I think it will take longer than that, but we can find a reason for me coming back later than expected. I'll do what I need to do and then make the trade.'

He hesitated and was about to speak when Kadell interrupted.

'You will need help to carry the meat back with you. I suggest you take someone with you.'

The Leader grinned at Valon, as the man's face broke into a wide smile and he turned his head back to Lonell.

'Will this help you find out? Will you know the answer when you come back?'

'To be truthful, I don't know, but I'm certain this is something I must do. Saretta will blame you when she finds out that I've gone - you must be careful. She will be angry. I only hope it will be worth it. I'll return as soon as possible.'

'When will you leave?' asked Kadell.

'Tomorrow we'll organise the salt and prepare for the journey. Then I think it would be best if we left while the Enlightened Ones are at the Sun Sleep ceremony. Hopefully they will fail to find out we've gone until after Sun Wake the next day. We'll be far enough away by then that they won't be able to drag us back here, because they will think we are running away.'

'But wait till they see us when we come back laden down with reindeer meat.' Valon laughed quietly, like a young boy with a secret.

Lonell and Kadell looked at him silently, wishing they could be as hopeful and excited but the truth was that both of them felt a coldness in their stomachs and a deep-seated fear of what the future might bring.

Too Long To Die

Chapter Thirteen

The day broke fine but windy and gusts surged through the crevice between the two caves as tasks were allocated by the Leader. Some returned to continue the wood collection which had been so suddenly, but expectedly, interrupted, while others began to gather in Cord Plant and the rest were put to packing the salt harvest.

Lonell rested for a moment. He could feel the heat rasping the back of his throat and he took a long drink from the water skin. Despite the discomfort, he was thankful the tribe lived at the end of land for it was the great expanse of water nearby that provided their most valuable trading commodity - salt. Inland inhabitants had no access to the granular powder which added so much flavour to their meals, other than by obtaining it from traders who came in from the coastal regions so it was very valuable to the Pescovari. Other tribes kept their best goods in readiness for the arrival of the coastal traders for it was a poor tribe that could not flavour their food with salt and word soon spread if travellers had been shown hospitality and offered unsalted food.

Salt had been a priority for as long as Lonell could remember and the tribe had developed an extensive system for its collection which, had the weather been more constant, could have taken place in the open air but, due to the frequent storms, a more protected space was essential. The cliffs that bordered the Sands were riddled with caves and, within many of these, the tribe had dug out, sometimes with great difficulty, shallow basins. In some of the caves part of the stone floors had natural bowl shaped areas which were adopted for use but, in others, the stone had to be chipped away which, given the primitive tools they wielded, was back-breaking, tedious work over long periods of time. These basins were filled with the water which was carried back over the damp, stony ground from the Salt Water. It was time consuming work for the beach extended far from the habitable land and each person could only reasonably be expected to make six trips there and back in a day, bowed down on their return by the weight of water-filled stomach linings, harvested from the larger animals they hunted. It was one of Lonell's least favourite tasks but, like everyone else, he knew it had to be done.

Over time, the water evaporated in the caves until it was possible to scrape the damp sludge together and move it to the drying cave where once again it was spread out. Fires were lit throughout the cave, keeping it dry, while the smoke escaped through fissures in the rock that led to the surface. In this environment the salt dried out and was cut into blocks which were wrapped in finely woven mats made of grasses, keeping the salt dry for storage or transportation.

It was in the stifling heat of the drying cave that Lonell and Valon worked throughout the morning, the sweat dripping off them as they cut and packed the valuable goods, and later they helped carry the packages up to the storage cave on the ledge. Hot and exhausted, when the last package had been stacked away, the whole team headed down to Mountain Water to bathe and soak away the salt which seemed to permeate every inch of their skin. The muted atmosphere which had enveloped the group all day was still in evidence even as they tried to relax in the water. In each person the air of tension was almost palpable, with a sense of communal holding in of breath, waiting for something or someone to break.

Lonell and Valon cleaned themselves off quickly and sat beside the lake to dry off in the warm wind. Lonell was aware that his friend was waiting for some information about their trip. He was surprised that the blond man had managed to last the entire day without saying anything but he had felt Valon's questioning but silent gaze on him many times.

'I'll tell you who ... what we're going to see when we're away from here,' said Lonell quietly. 'I think it's safer ...'

'Lonell, Valon!'

They heard the cry from behind them and turned to see Davoril, his long, thin legs moving as fast as they could, bringing him over the meadow towards them.

'Kadell sent me,' the words tumbled out as he reached them. 'He thought you ought to know straight away. I saw Sarril leaving.'

'Leaving?' asked Valon instantly.

Davoril nodded. 'He was dressed for travelling and carried a large bag with a spear *and* a bow. I think it was the one they took off Delina.'

'Why?' muttered Lonell, almost to himself. 'What is she doing?'

'Who? Delina?' asked Valon.

'No.' Lonell shook his head, impatiently. 'Saretta. Come on! We must get back to the cave.'

He was aware that Valon and Davoril looked at each other and saw Valon shrug his shoulders but he had no intention of sharing his thoughts. He put on his clothes, trying to calm the anger that he could feel building up in his chest. As a man who could normally work out problems, he was not used to finding himself in this position, unable to understand events. He was beginning to doubt that he would ever uncover the truth, either about Narthan's death or what Saretta had planned for the tribe. Of one thing he was certain - it would not be pleasant.

Back at the cave, they discovered that Kadell and his sister had already prepared the travelling backpacks, filling them with salt packages, a selection of shells which were highly valued and quantities of dried food: nuts, berries, acorn cakes, dried fish and meat, all of which would keep them going when they could not catch fresh meat and were light to carry.

Kadell took Lonell on one side.

'I don't know why Sarril has left but you must be careful not to run into him. He headed towards the Great Mountains.'

Lonell frowned at his Leader.

'I was concerned about leaving before but now, I am seriously worried. We have no idea what Saretta is doing. Perhaps I should not go ...'

'You must,' interrupted Kadell. 'It may be our only chance of making sense of what's happening to the tribe but return as fast as you can.'

For the first time, Lonell thought that Kadell was beginning to look older, that fear for his tribe had aged the Leader rapidly. Lonell nodded and turned away to complete the preparations for departure.

By the time the two men had added their warm clothes and tied on their bed skins and shelter, the backpacks were heavy as they tried them on to check their balance. Reindeer skin was used for its strength and durability and the skin had been worked many times to give it the waterproofing that was necessary and yet a softness for comfort - tribesmen and women walked many miles carrying inconceivable weights in order to trade for items that were necessary or desirable for their survival. In addition, they would also have to take enough water to last them until they reached new sources, which were abundant until they reached the mountains when they would have to search for places to refill the bladder-lined skins high up amongst the craggy rocks. They would also be carrying the weapons they needed for hunting and their safety.

Most of the tribe had returned to the cave by the time the sun started to dip down behind the first peaks to the west.

Too Long To Die

'They have left for the Sun Sleep ceremony,' Tendo's voice called softly across the cave.

Until then, very few members of the tribe knew anything about the 'trading journey' that Lonell and Valon were about to undertake. Kadell had planned it so, in an effort to maintain the secrecy of the mission from the Enlightened Ones. Only the Leader knew that there was, in fact, another motive for their departure, although even he was unaware of its true nature. If anyone was surprised at the timing of their trip, no one mentioned it; to most of them, it seemed in keeping with the strange atmosphere that hung over them. Not long before, they may not have been happy with many aspects of their lives but they had known the order of things; now, nothing seemed to be in its proper place and unexpected events were ceasing to take anyone by surprise.

Farewells were said and the two friends departed, laden down with their burdens. Each man carried a long spear, a knife tucked into his belt and, packed in with the salt, was a hunting net. They took a circuitous route, constantly watching out for the white figure of Sarril and maintaining a good distance from the Mountain Water meadowland where the Enlightened Ones were completing their ceremony. By the time they had returned to the White Cave, completely unaware that two tribesmen had hurried inland towards the Great Mountains, Lonell and Valon had already arrived at the tree line and disappeared amongst the tall, elegant pines and willows and the short, stubby oaks. However, with no way of knowing whether their departure had gone undiscovered, they continued at their fast pace, aiming to put as much distance as possible between themselves and their home, but constantly alert to the danger of sighting Sarril.

Just before complete darkness fell, the friends stopped and put down their bed skins. There was a warm humidity under the trees and the wind had blown itself out during the day so they had no need for a cover. Deciding not to light a fire for fear of it being seen by those they thought might be searching for them, they settled down to eat some of the travelling food that Kadella had given them.

'Will you tell me now where we're going?' Valon asked his friend through the darkness, impatience overcoming him.

The silence flowing from Lonell was broken only by the sound of small, scuffling animals moving through the fallen leaves of the forest. Valon was starting to wonder if the other man had heard him when he coughed gently and began to speak.

'I told you before that I first began to realise I was different when I had passed four winters. This is true but it wasn't until after the seventh winter that I understood more about what was happening to me.'

Lonell halted for a moment and laughed dryly.

'Perhaps 'understood' is the wrong word because even now I lack understanding. But it was something that happened just after my seventh winter that developed my senses. I have never spoken of this so it will be difficult to explain, but I'll try.' He took a deep breath. 'The tribe decided to make a hunting expedition into the mountains to get the white pelts from the animals that live in the snow. Do you remember?'

'Yes, I do remember you all leaving. I was unhappy at being left behind,' Valon confirmed.

'I was taken along for I was just large enough to help with the skinning and carrying of the skins on our return home. You were too young and stayed behind with those that could not travel.'

Valon remembered his fury when everyone, except the smallest children and the old and sick, left the cave to go on an adventure and he felt deserted. Even his hero Lonell had been allowed to go and he had felt jealousy for the first time.

'I thought it was unfair I had to stay and I was so bored while you were away. They gave me little tasks to keep me occupied but I wanted to be out with you, and there was no one to play with!'

'There were times I wished I had stayed with you,' admitted Lonell. 'It was a hard journey for someone so small. The climb into the mountains seemed endless and it was the first time that I'd ever felt the biting cold of the snow and the wind when you're so high. Although the new experiences were exciting at the start, I soon tired of ice forming around my mouth as I breathed and constantly having to melt ice for water. And I'd never shaken with cold before, when it was difficult to control your body and impossible to use your hands properly.'

Valon was starting to realise that this was to be their destination and he was almost wishing that he had been left behind this time too when Lonell added, 'We're going into the Great Mountains with the sun higher in the sky this time so I don't expect it to be as uncomfortable. It will be cold but, I hope, not freezing.'

Another silence followed and Valon realised Lonell had lapsed into his own thoughts once more.

'So, what happened in the Great Mountains all those years ago and what are we going to do there this time?' he asked, to bring his friend back to reality.

When it resumed, Lonell's voice seemed to come from far away.

'The older ones went to hunt the goats with the long, white fur and the mountain foxes whose pelts are so beautiful. I was told to wait at the camp but I grew cold and bored so I went exploring. That was when I found it.'

Lonell stopped.

'What? What did you find?' Valon almost shouted, exasperated at yet another pause.

'A cave. It was hidden from sight like the cave on the beach. I only found it because I was dragging one hand along the rocks and suddenly there was a gap. I squeezed in through the opening and found myself in a large space with light shining down from a hole above. There were many different markings on the stones.' Lonell leaned forward, intently. 'They weren't pictures like Ancient Pel paints - they were lines and shapes that I'd never seen before, and I haven't seen anything like them since. I have no idea what they were showing me but somehow I knew they were ... special.'

Valon felt the other man grab his arm and he jumped.

'Valon, there was a feeling, an atmosphere, in that cave. It was so beautiful, lit up by the sun, and yet it felt stifling. I didn't know whether I wanted to run away or stay there forever - I've never experienced anything like it since and yet I feel it in my dreams.'

'So we're going to look for this cave again, are we?'

'Wait, I haven't finished. I was walking around peering at the markings, trying to make sense of them when I heard the voice. You know, the silent voice I told you about?' questioned Lonell.

'Yes, I remember,' answered Valon. He shivered involuntarily and felt bumps creeping along his arms and down his neck.

'It called me! It used my name and it called me! It seemed to come from the side of the cave so I went to look. I could hear the sound of my feet moving over the rocks and a thumping in my centre,' - he put his hand on his chest - 'but when I was there I could see nothing. The voice spoke to me again - it said, *'Look harder.'* I stared at the wall, searching, and suddenly in front of me there was a ... shadow. I know that this is going to sound ridiculous but it looked like a skull, and it just appeared ... from nowhere.'

'Sacred Stones! What animal was it from, this skull?' asked the younger man.

'I don't know. I'm not even sure what I saw. I thought it might be a skull but it wasn't an animal I'd seen. It might even have been a man but it didn't look like bone. It was a shadow and yet somehow I had the impression it was solid and clear, like frozen water but perfectly clear. I thought it might be ice and put out my hand but it was warm to the touch. I pulled off my hand coverings to be sure and touched it again. Soon my hands were hot and I felt a shock go through my whole body, through the head, down to my feet and the warmth spread through me. Then I ran. I couldn't stay any longer. I was frightened. How could a shadow be solid and look like ice but be warm? Nothing made sense.'

Valon realised he had been holding his breath as Lonell talked and suddenly gasped for air, as his friend continued.

'I left the cave and ran back to the camp where the hunters had returned and had just started to look for me. Kadell was still a young man and not yet Leader but he was formidable, even at that age. He shouted at me for leaving the camp and, when he discovered that I'd lost my hand coverings, I was punished by being given a double watch at the coldest time of night.'

'That must have been dreadful,' sympathised Valon, imagining the misery.

'No. You don't understand. My body stayed warm during the entire night and throughout the rest of the time until we came down from the mountains but I wasn't stupid enough to tell anyone! They all thought I'd taken my punishment very well without complaining about the freezing temperature but, in fact, I hadn't suffered at all! I would love to be able to tell Kadell one day but I know that day will never come. This isn't something you can share with other people.'

He stopped for a moment and Valon felt his friend's hand on his arm.

'I am aware that by telling you and showing you what we're going to see, I'm taking you into a life of secrecy. If you tell people they will think you're head-sick and yet it will always be there, like a wall between you and them. What we are about to do will change you.'

Valon was silent when his friend finished, wondering whether he was ready to hear Lonell's secret, whether he would be able to live with the burden of this truth, but suddenly he knew the answer.

'It's strange.' Valon spoke quietly and yet he heard it loud in his head. 'If you had told me this story before, even when you first told me about the voice you hear, I don't think I'd have believed it. I would have thought you were head-sick. I don't know why but now it just seems to explain everything about you. I should doubt what you've told me but I don't. I can't understand why I think this way - perhaps because everything has changed. Nothing is as it was before Narthan's death. It's as though our whole world is changing and maybe I'm already changing with it. I think we're going to find the 'skull' again - is that the reason we're heading into the Great Mountains?'

He heard Lonell breathe a sigh of relief and Valon realised, with a jolt, that Lonell must have been nervous about telling him. His friend had finally confided in someone, explained something of what made him the man he was and he, Valon, had accepted the truth and the consequences to himself that the knowledge brought with it.

Valon suddenly saw how difficult Lonell's life must have been, living with this secret, unable to share it with anyone. He hoped that, by his reaction, he had made his friend's life easier and it was confirmed when he heard Lonell laugh, a light, gentle sound that, given the circumstances, seemed an odd reaction, but he understood it. Lonell was happy.

'Yes, that's my plan,' he answered Valon, his voice now more animated. 'It is a long walk but I feel that I must now face the shadow, the skull, whatever it is ... again and try to find some answers. I think it's calling me and I wonder if it's calling you too. You say you've changed - maybe that's the reason. We have much to find out, my friend.'

He patted Valon on the shoulder.

'It's time to sleep now,' he said. 'We have many long days ahead of us - we need our rest.'

Valon, although he knew the wisdom of these words, thought he would struggle to sleep. 'I have so many questions. You have so much to explain to me. I'm certain I'll be unable to sleep tonight.'

'I think you will surprise yourself. Lie down and relax, now.'

Valon could hear the smile on his friend's lips as he reassured him. He pushed his bed skins into a comfortable position and looked up at the stars, glowing gently in the sky above, obscured from view every now and then by the swaying trees that surrounded them.

'I shall never be able to get to sleep,' were his last thoughts, as he was enveloped by the comforting folds of oblivion.

Too Long To Die

Chapter Fourteen

After two days of trekking eastward under the trees, the two men were certain that no one was following them and they began to experience a feeling of liberation which increased with each step that separated them from the spiritual leaders of the Pescovari. However, they did not forget that Sarril was also out there somewhere, and although they saw no trace of him, their spears were readied, not just for the animals that inhabited the forests.

Beyond the trees lay a swathe of green, lush grassland, protected from the vicious winds which blew in from the Salt Water by the trees on one side and the tall mountains that disappeared into the mists on the other. The contrast was extreme between the vivid colours of the valley which spread up the lower foothills and the craggy mountains, whose rocks had been bleached white by high winds and sun; jagged rocks, jutting skyward as far as the eye could see. It was these mountains that divided the inland regions of the peninsula from the coastal lands and Lonell began to wish that he could just carry on walking, leaving behind the worries that were preying on his mind.

As they walked, they caught rabbits and other small animals or birds that they flushed out of the undergrowth. They wasted no time trying to bring down larger prey as they had no desire to carry the excess meat - it was easier to catch only what they could eat at one meal. Their food was supplemented by the fruits, pine nuts and berries that hung off trees and shrubs, along with edible fungi that grew plentifully at the base of the trees, all of which they ate on the move.

They stopped as little as possible for they had to cover far greater distances than expected by their tribe so they kept up a fast pace. Each night, once darkness fell, they lit a fire and cooked the fresh meat they had found during the day. Only on one night did they have to put up their shelters for the skies had been overcast all day with a heavy greyness which held the promise of a downpour. They were prepared and their belongings under cover by the time the rain started to fall; great thick droplets which bounced off the ground and instantly soaked everything within reach.

The two men had always been drawn together in friendship despite Lonell's reserved and private nature, now explained to Valon. Neither had a sibling but the bond between them came close to that experienced by two people born of the same mother. Now, with the revelation of the true nature of their journey, they felt their connection strengthened; they were two men charged with the burden of a secret that must never be divulged and yet, perhaps, it was the answer to the dangers and unrest being suffered by their tribe.

Their journey was taking them eastwards and each day they climbed higher into the mountains. On their fourth day they began to notice signs that humans had been in the area: the remains of extinguished fires, branches taken from trees and the odd remnant of a meal.

'This could the tribe we want to trade with. These signs aren't old - they have been here recently,' observed Lonell.

It was then that Valon's skills as Tracker came to the fore and the following day he led them into the territory of a people that neither had met before but they had heard of them from traders who had passed through on their own missions. As unannounced visitors it was customary to make their presence known before arriving so both the men picked up stones and cracked them together, calling out 'Hallo!' as they approached the cave, and then they waited, desperately

Too Long To Die

hoping that Sarril would not appear.

It was not long before a figure emerged. At first glance the man seemed to be of average size but as they approached, Lonell and Valon could see that he was tiny, just over half their size, but his headdress almost doubled his stature. Made of a long piece of hide which had been wound into a tall funnel, it was painted with red and black zigzag patterns and decorated with small bones, tied down the sides of the headdress; the result was a rattling sound as the small man moved his head from side to side. He was the most extraordinary sight and it took Lonell and Valon a few seconds before they averted their staring eyes and remembered their manners. Still at a short distance, they placed their weapons on the ground and held their hands out to the front in the familiar gesture of greeting, followed by the signal of the two wavy lines which signified their tribe. Then they turned slowly around so their host could see that they bore no hidden weapons and had come in the spirit of friendship. As they completed their turn, the diminutive leader was walking towards them, a huge welcoming smile on his face and the headdress rattling above him. He came to stand before them and stretched up to put his hands first on Lonell's shoulders, then Valon's. He said something that neither could understand and beckoned them to follow him back to the cave while he trotted in front. The two friends exchanged amused looks but their faces betrayed relief that they had been greeted with such warmth.

Others came out to see the visitors and guide them into the cave. The two Pescovari men were surprised at the size of the cave which was illuminated by many small stone bowls filled with animal fat, burning in shallow crevices around the outside of the living area. It gave off a distinctive but not unpleasant odour, very different from the grease they obtained from the creatures of the Salt Water, which the Pescovari usually burnt at home. The numbers of inhabitants were similar to their own tribe and they were instantly made to feel at ease as they were welcomed in. As they unburdened themselves of their backpacks, plates made from the shoulder blades of large animals, piled high with reindeer meat and vegetables, were pushed into their hands. Smiling faces looked down at them as they nodded gratefully and dug into the food with fervour. After their days of living off hastily cooked small game, the meal was delicious but they were happy to notice that something was missing - and that was the flavour of salt.

They could understand little of what was being said around them but a few words seemed familiar. They looked up as they heard shouts and into the cave, accompanying the leader, who had disappeared as soon as the two travellers had sat down with their food, came an older man with greying hair but a strength and presence about him that made him stand out from others. The tiny leader stood beside the new arrival but, even with his head gear, he did not reach his height. Lonell and Valon pushed themselves to their feet and were delighted to hear the stranger greet them in their own language.

'Welcome to the home of the Burgoni. It is good to see strangers passing through our lands.'

The man's voice was deep and he spoke with a distinctive, guttural but clearly understandable accent.

'What brings you to these lands? Where are you headed?'

Lonell and Valon had already discussed how to reply to this question that they knew would be asked.

'Thank you for your welcome,' replied Lonell. 'I am named Lonell and my friend is Valon. We are people of the Pescovari and are making a short journey to trade before the cold weather comes in and also to investigate what lies in this direction. Some winters have passed since anyone from our tribe has travelled this way.'

'I am glad to see you and to renew our friendship,' said the Burgoni man, 'for I have met with your traders before - I am Marcot, the trader for the Burgoni - although I have never journeyed all the way to your caves.'

'You speak our language well,' said Valon, his face showing his admiration of the man's ability to learn another's tongue.

'I was fortunate to join up with your Trader, Rafin, on a number of journeys. I understand he has now returned to the earth.'

He passed his right hand in front of his eyes, a gesture to the Gods, when he spoke the words.

'He was a good man and we spent much time together. He stayed with us here once when the bad weather caught us unexpectedly early. We taught each other our tongues although he always had difficulty with some of the sounds in our language!'

The man smiled, and Lonell could see that he was thinking back to those enjoyable passed times with fond memories.

'He has been missed greatly by all of us. He had much experience and he returned to the earth unexpectedly. He had not yet completed the training of a replacement so our trading has been less successful. We found ourselves with no reindeer meat which our tribe likes to eat through the cold times and we volunteered to travel as Lonell had been this way before, although only as a child,' said Valon.

'So, you want to take away some of our highly valued meat,' said Marcot, and both men knew that trading had begun. Valon had often watched Rafin trade when visitors came to their caves and always felt the excitement when there was a successful exchange of goods. He had studied the manner of conducting the negotiations, although he had never had the chance to take part and so, it was he who took over when trading began. He knew that Lonell was quite content to sit back and observe for he had admitted to Valon that he felt uneasy through the bargaining.

The tall Burgoni translated for his Leader who looked excitedly from one man to the other. He had obviously never mastered the expressionless face that was habitually worn for trading; no one wanted to appear too eager for that weakened their position. The Leader led them to what was clearly his area of the cave. Lush skins covered the floor and seats cut from tree trunks were draped with thick furs. The four men sat down and Lonell watched as they began to talk. The rest of the tribe realised what was happening and watched the proceedings from a close distance. When Valon bought out the packs of salt there was a gasp and some clapped their hands together in excitement, only to be glared at by Marcot; they had ruined his chance of driving a hard bargain and the trading was completed in half the time that it would normally take. The usual gambits of 'Well, we do not really have any need for what you are offering' or 'We never use that - we do not have a liking for it' could hardly be used after the tribe's reaction.

The result was that Valon had traded a little over half their salt and a small amount of decorative shells for as much meat as the two of them would be able to carry back, using a large skin tarpaulin, provided by their hosts which they would bear between them, in addition to what they could carry in their, by then, empty backpacks.

'I would ask you a favour,' requested Valon, looking at the Leader while Marcot translated.

'May we leave the meat with you while we continue to explore the lands further on and then collect it upon our return?'

This was soon agreed and it was clear that the Leader was delighted with the transaction. Although Marcot was not quite so happy, even he was unable to be unaffected by the contagious excitement of the little man who rushed around talking to everyone, laughing and slapping people on the arm as the bones on his extraordinary headwear jingled and rattled. The affection for the Leader was tangible; everyone wanted to be near him, to talk to him, to draw his attention, and the energy he exuded appeared to invigorate and enliven each person he talked to.

Despite the large meal that Lonell and Valon had eaten when they arrived, it was clear that a celebration was being planned and delicious aromas were emanating from the bulging skins that were hanging over the large cooking hearths. Marcot showed them the area around the cave, pointing out various places and Lonell was interested to see a mountain goat tethered to a post nearby. Wondering why it was being kept in such a way, he questioned Marcot.

'The Leader likes to drink the beast's liquid,' he answered, a smile on his face.

Both Lonell and Valon expressed horror at the thought and Marcot gave a great shout of laughter, realising he had given the wrong impression.

'Wait here,' he said, and disappeared inside the cave where they could hear him talking. Waves of laughter followed his words and the tribe spilt out of the entrance to watch Marcot, now striding back towards them, cup in hand, a wide grin on his face. The two men watched with a certain amount of trepidation as he squatted down beside the goat and started to pull on the drooping sack that hung down underneath the animal. As the thin, white liquid spurted out, Lonell looked at Valon in amazement but when Marcot offered him the cup to drink from, he took a step back, waving his hands in front of him. Valon was braver and took a sip. He wrinkled his nose in disgust and everyone cheered and pointed at him. Clearly, the only person who liked the drink was the tiny Leader who pushed forward, grabbed the cup and drained it, rubbing his stomach in appreciation.

'What is it?' Lonell asked Marcot. 'Why is this liquid in the animal?'

Marcot looked around and his eyes settled on a young woman, holding a baby. Smiling, he beckoned her to come forward. She walked shyly towards them and Marcot showed the baby and pointed at her breast. She blushed scarlet as Lonell exclaimed, 'Oh, I see,' and

Valon nodded his head, grinning at the group of watching people. Lonell knew he would enjoy telling the story when they got back home.

Back inside the cave, Marcot introduced them to everyone and translated as they answered a multitude of questions, asked by the smiling faces that surrounded them.

The two friends were exhausted by the time they unfolded their bed skins, having eaten far more than they needed or even, in truth, wanted. They had also drunk rather more than was sensible of the fruity, alcoholic beverage and it was remarkable how they were able to communicate without the help of Marcot once they had taken a few drinks of the potent mixture. Despite his spinning head, Valon had not had any problem encouraging a pretty young girl to accompany him to his sleeping area and when Lonell was about to roll over and go to sleep, he felt someone crawl in beside him. He was amazed to see the most attractive young lady lying beside him, dark hair shining in the fire light and large hazel eyes looked at him shyly from underneath long eyelashes. When he awoke in the morning, looked at the gorgeous face beside him and remembered the tender, sensuous love-making, he thought that, despite the ache that was now thumping in his head, he had just experienced one of the best nights of his life.

The Pescovari men were not the only ones suffering the after effects of the party. The Leader had not put his headwear back on and his face bore a greyish tinge but he was still smiling, albeit somewhat lopsidedly. Food was put out by ladies who moved very slowly and purposefully, and everyone tried to eat a little, without much success. The only man who did not seem to be suffering was Marcot. Lonell remembered that he had not seen the trader after the meal and wondered where he had gone but, when the older man appeared and began to talk about their continuing journey, he forgot and asked his host about the terrain to the east. He did not mention climbing high into the mountains but he found out useful information about the area.

'Lonell,' said the tall Burgoni man, 'I must warn you. There are groups of dangerous men who have sometimes been seen in the mountains. We don't know where they come from but we know of one man who was beaten hard by them and they took everything he had with him. They are bad men. Be careful. If you see them, go in the opposite direction.'

Before long they were joined by an exhausted Valon, who groaned as he hoisted on the backpack but, despite their distinctly delicate state of health, the whole tribe turned out to wish them well on their journey and a speedy return. Lonell could not help but think of the difference between their departure from their own tribe and the Burgoni. It made him even more determined to rectify the problems that assailed his home, as he turned his face into the wind and started the trek towards his ultimate target.

Throughout the next three days Lonell and Valon headed eastward and each step took them higher into the Great Mountains. On the second day, the cold began to penetrate their furs and they found snow under their feet and at this point the effort to keep going became ever more intense. Every now and then, Valon glanced at his friend, hoping for a hint about their final destination but Lonell kept his head down, pressing onwards, keeping up a fast pace and saying little. Their only break from routine came when they were on the point of leaving behind the tree line. Following Lonell's instructions, Valon searched for two sturdy branches about the length and width of a man's arm. The other man, meanwhile, was looking for the thick pine resin that leaked from the trees and could be broken off in chunks. One particular species produced huge amounts of the sticky sap that hardened on contact with the air and it was for this that Lonell searched because it was the perfect fuel for torches. They both also picked up sticks and twigs for the fires they would need over the next few days and Lonell gathered any loose animal fur and grasses until he had a good few handfuls of the mixture.

They continued their journey, leaving behind the protection of the last few trees and, as the sun sank behind the mountains at the end of the third day since leaving the Burgoni, Valon was starting to despair. The cold was really affecting him; he was beginning to lose the feeling in his hands and feet and he thought it possible that he would not be able to accompany Lonell much further. Valon remembered Lonell telling him that this would not be as cold as his first visit to the area and he wondered how anyone had survived that trip. As they set their fire in a sheltered area, protected by an outcrop of the mountainside, the older man suddenly looked up at Valon.

'You can stop worrying,' he said. 'Tomorrow we will be at the cave. We are very close now but I will need light to find the entrance with help from my hangbone.'

'Hangbone?' exclaimed Valon. 'Do you really think that children's game will help you?'

'Tomorrow you will see. It will lead us to the place.'

Valon tried to remain positive and, if asked, he might have admitted that he hoped Lonell was not putting too much faith in the delicate object. It had been a long time since his friend had first found the place that was so essential to them now.

It was important to keep themselves busy until they tried to snatch a few hours of freezing sleep. They built up the fire, higher and hotter than on previous nights and Lonell found a large stone, naturally hollowed out into the shape of a shallow bowl. He took out the large lumps of tree resin and placed them in the bowl which was heated until the contents were malleable and then he added the grass and fur.

Too Long To Die

After a while the mixture could be stirred together, the liquid resin covering the other contents. He picked up the two branches and covered one end of each with the glue like substance. As it cooled, he moulded the resin with his hand until content that the torches would burn well enough to provide them with sufficient light once they were in the cave.

Neither man could sleep for any more than a few uneasy minutes at a time and to both it seemed the longest night of their lives. After a hasty breakfast of dried food, they packed their kit, put the loads on their backs and Lonell took out his hangbone. Valon watched as his friend concentrated on the small piece of bone that spun one way and then the other; then it settled. As Lonell moved to his left, the bone started spinning to the right.

'Come on, Valon. This is the way,' he said over his shoulder.

Whenever the bone stopped or started moving in another direction they knew they had veered off course. They were led to the face of a cliff, almost at the top of the mountain, where the bone stopped swinging as suddenly as if someone had reached out his hand and held it. Lonell looked around him and nodded.

'This is it, my friend. We've found it. Let's light the torches.'

'Where? I can't see a cave.' Valon searched with his eyes but, hard as he tried, he could not see an opening.

'Trust me,' said his friend. 'You're about to see something that you will never forget.'

Each holding their branch, resin flaming, Valon followed Lonell around an edge of rock that had been invisible to him before and they plunged into the darkness. The flickering torches threw strange shapes over the walls of the narrow tunnel and, as it opened onto the huge cavern that lay beyond, Valon gasped.

Chapter Fifteen

The two men held their torches high to obtain the maximum effect and were rewarded with a sight that took their breath away. Even though Lonell had seen it before, he stood and stared in amazement, sensing that any movement would break the moment of magic. The walls of the cavern were smooth and shiny, unlike any stone surface they had seen before and the rocks which were strewn around the interior appeared to have been carved into shapes unseen in nature and, thus, unrecognisable to the men. Bright sunshine shone down from above, illuminating the centre of the chamber but the air seemed thick and heavy. Throughout the cave, strata of red and black veins cut through the almost white background which glistened as the light of the torches fell upon each area. Evenly spaced around the cavern were groups of strange markings, row upon row of black lines and curls that meant nothing to the two men who stood spellbound. There was an open area in the centre with a completely flat, even floor and Lonell suddenly had a picture in his mind of a group of beings standing there, looking out at the walls and somehow he knew this was a place where they had met to share knowledge and make decisions; and yet, the people did not look like any humans he had seen in his lifetime.

Lonell shrugged off his backpack and let it slide to the floor, with a thump.

'Come,' he said, as he turned to look at Valon and felt the urge to laugh. Valon's mouth had dropped slightly open and his eyes stared around him in astonishment. As he put his hand to his forehead to ward off evil, his hand shook and his face had turned pale and clammy.

Relieving the other man of his pack, Lonell pulled at his arm and led the way round the edge of the pale, glittering walls. As they went, he noticed that there were candles evenly spaced around the walls and he lit them from his torch as he passed by, which filled the air with the scent of lavender, a scent known well to the men but they could not have given it a name. Valon followed as though in a trance, unable to take in fully what he was seeing. Lonell suddenly saw Valon begin to pull at his clothes, loosening the belt. Then he realised that he was no longer cold, that a deep warmth was permeating his clothing and his skin was tingling to its gentle touch. It was evident that Valon was feeling the same.

'It's hot in here,' Valon whispered to his friend.

'Why are you whispering?' laughed Lonell, his voice filling the chamber.

It was his turn to be surprised when his voice echoed back from all directions, startling them both.

'Halloooo!' he shouted out and the noise vibrated back to them, the sound clear and pure. Valon joined in and the two men filled the huge cavern with sound. They had both heard echoes before in the mountains but neither had experienced the build up of volume that this cave allowed. As suddenly as they started, they stopped. Neither knew why but the solemnity of the location abruptly brought it to an end, as though the cavern were a living, breathing entity that directed the activity within. The silence that fell was as overwhelming as the noise had been and the two men stood motionless, hardly daring to breathe. How long they stood there neither man knew but it was Lonell who finally broke the spell. He beckoned to Valon who looked back at his friend and, appearing to take a few seconds to come back to reality, suddenly shivered and then grinned sheepishly, as though embarrassed by his lapse.

They silently continued their way around the edge, Valon sliding his hand over the even surface of the walls. Lonell was almost as fascinated watching his friend as seeing the inside of the cavern again. He knew it would not occur to Valon that perhaps the cavern had not been created by natural events, he would assumed that it was one more marvel that he had never seen before but Lonell's questions probed deeper. Neither of these men had travelled any further than this point and their knowledge of what lay beyond their usual horizons was limited to the stories narrated by travellers and traders who passed through their tribal lands. They had heard of great wonders; water falling from great heights, earth moving and red hot liquid thrown into the sky from the top of a mountain, among others. Many stories were enjoyed but not truly believed; everyone knew that storytellers always wanted to have the most exciting and extraordinary descriptions to share with their audiences and exaggeration tended to play a part. Only other travellers knew the truth and, then, only if they had followed the same routes, so those on their first journeys were uncertain of what to expect. Lonell suspected that had Valon heard of this cave in a story, he would not have believed what he was being told, but now that he was seeing it with his own eyes and knowing it to be true, Lonell could see that his friend was marvelling at the power of nature, as he had as a young boy.

However, Lonell had other thoughts niggling in his head, thoughts that told him that this could not be natural. Although it was well beyond him to explain what might have created the work of art in which he now stood, he knew that natural stone was never this smooth and yet, he also knew that man did not possess the tools to create such perfection. Somehow, though, this did not matter to him; he accepted it in the same way that he acknowledged the existence of the voice and its influence over him.

Lonell came to the place where he thought he had seen the shadow-skull on his last visit and he halted.

'Wait. We must wait here,' he was now whispering.

They stood for a while and nothing happened. Lonell could feel a knot of worry growing in the centre of his body. What if he'd dragged them all the way here for nothing? What if he didn't discover anything from this visit? He had relied on obtaining some new insight into the death of Narthan. He wondered how he would break the news to Kadell that he had failed. His breathing was becoming faster, panic was overtaking him; he was unable to control it. He was being crushed by the stifling atmosphere that he remembered from his first visit, thicker now with the aroma of lavender. There was a weight on his shoulder and he looked down and saw Valon's hand, reassuring and comforting, and he felt the calmness return, seeping through his body. Lonell turned and smiled at his friend; words were unnecessary. He marvelled that he had such a friend; they always managed to comfort and give strength to each other when necessary.

So they waited. Time passed, how long neither knew. Suddenly Lonell turned to Valon.

'You must go into the centre of the cave and wait there. I must stay here alone.'

He patted the younger man on the arm and nervously watched his back as he walked away. He could see that Valon had lost his fear, that he was now quite content to explore the strange stone shapes he had noticed before and he wandered around, trying to make out what they were and touching the beautifully tactile objects that littered the inside of the chamber. There was nothing he was able to recognise but Lonell watched as he explored the objects, enthralled by their beauty. Valon had clearly recovered from his shock on their entrance to the cave and now looked completely at ease in this strange environment. After a while, seeing a large stone that appeared to have been cut into the form of a seat, Valon sat down to wait for his friend. He seemed entirely relaxed as he sank back into the luxurious comfort of the stone seat.

Although Lonell was feeling less nervous now, he glanced over at the blond man from time to time, wishing he were still standing beside him, and noticed that he had fallen fast asleep. His torch was lying beside him on the floor. Lonell's had also extinguished but that did not matter - the beam from the unseen source in the ceiling and the candles shed ample light on the cavern and its contents. He turned back to look at the wall and there in front of him was the shadow. How had it appeared from nowhere when there was nothing solid to cast a shadow? Lonell was certain that he had been looking at that exact spot before and there had been nothing to be seen, but now the shadow was there and slowly it formed itself into the shape of a crystal head, its outline undulating in the candle light.

'I remember you, Lonell.'

The voice echoed loud in the man's head but, had Valon been awake, he would have heard nothing.

'You have returned here because you seek help. Tell me what is troubling you.'

'I need to know,' Lonell could feel his heart thumping in his chest, 'Who ...what are you? Why ... are you here? Where are you from? Why do you know who I am?'

He had so many questions, he was not sure where to start.

'Where I come from and what I am is irrelevant,' communicated the shadowy form. *'But I shall tell you this: I came here many, many moons ago - more than you can possibly imagine - and I am not alone - there are others like me in distant lands.'*

'But why are you here?'

'To look after this world. Man is a powerful creature and will become more so as he develops but he must take care of the land that he lives on. There is a danger that he will forget this. There is good and evil within everyone and I am

here to ensure that good prevails. Man must remain close to the earth that nurtures him or he could lose his connection with all that is pure and natural; he will lose connection with himself. Already he has forgotten so much.'

Lonell was not at all certain he had understood anything that had been communicated but the overall impression that something or someone was there to look after the people filled him with joy and relief. He wanted to ask what had been forgotten but his priority was to discover facts about the voice he often heard and why he had been picked out. He was uncertain of how to word his question but he need not have worried.

'I did not choose you, remember,' the shadow said, as though it had read Lonell's thoughts. *'You found me when you wandered into my cave as a child. You already had the gift - that was why you came to me.'*

'What gift?' asked Lonell, trying to think of something that he had been given.

'Do you not realise that you are different? Do you not think more deeply than the rest of the people you know?'

'But that started after I saw you the first time.'

'No.' The shadow fluctuated and the skull-shape disappeared for a moment before flickering back. *'You were aware of your individuality from a very young age. You were already marked. Your mother knew it, as did others of your tribe. You also know that I speak the truth, do you not?'*

Lonell had to admit it - he had even confided as much to Valon. He had become aware that he thought differently to others when he had passed only four winters but in his mind he tried to blame his uniqueness on the voice which he wanted to believe had originated from his visit to the cave.

'So, why am I different? If this is a gift, there must be a reason that I have received it. What is expected of me?'

'The truth, Lonell. You are the searcher for truth. That is your destiny and it is your fate to be needed by many. You will travel far in your quest for the truth.'

Lonell was shaken by this revelation. He had always imagined that he would grow old within his own tribe, perhaps see children who looked like him when he was old enough, and spend more time with Mila. And Valon; would he have to do this alone or would his friend go with him? He hated the thought of leaving behind the man that he thought of as a brother.

'The man who sleeps nearby is a faithful friend. He will not let you journey alone,' the voice in Lonell's head reassured him.

'How will I know where to go?' he asked.

'Events will unfold to reveal your path but that is in the future. Now you must think about the present. Your gift is needed at this moment. If true evil is allowed to go unpunished, it spreads. You must prevent that.'

Lonell hesitated for a short time, trying to formulate the correct questions, knowing that the answers that followed would show him how to proceed with his investigation into Narthan's death.

'Will you tell me who killed the Enlightened One, Narthan, in our tribe?' he asked.

'No.'

The simple response caught Lonell off-guard. It was not the reply he had expected or wanted and he quailed at the thought of returning to Kadell with no answers.

'Can you tell me how he was killed?'

'You already know that.'

Lonell pushed his hands through his long hair, exasperated. 'Why was he killed?'

'Many wanted to harm him but only one was evil enough to do so, but they were not alone. An occurrence took place of which you are unaware. Find this out and you will discover the truth.'

'Will you not tell me what happened?' the man asked in desperation. 'How am I expected to solve the problem without your help?'

Too Long To Die

'You will always have my help but I shall not resolve your problems. That will be up to you. You have the ability to work them out yourself and, with each solution that you find, greater knowledge will come.'

'Can you tell me nothing more?' begged Lonell, 'You must help me. My people are waiting for an answer and they expect me to give it to them. Please help me,' he cried out but the intense silence gave him his answer.

He waited until he was sure there would be no reply.

'I am frightened,' he whispered.

Had Valon been nearby he would not have considered admitting to his fear but with this entity that he was facing, it was different. He felt he could bare his very soul to the shadow-skull and not be judged.

'That is to be expected but it will not prevent you from doing what you must.'

The tone of the voice in his head had changed. It was like velvet, soothing his dismay, and he felt himself buoyed up with a courage that came from the very centre of his being.

'Go, sit with your friend and consider what you have been told,' the entity ordered gently.

'Will I see you again?'

'There will be no need. I shall always be in you but you know where to find me. Tell no one, for if others come here they will find nothing. Now go.'

Lonell knew that this signified the end of his audience. He turned towards the centre of the cavern and started to move, glancing over his shoulder to the place where he had just stood. He was unsurprised to see the shadow was no longer there but, as he had been told, he still felt its presence within him. Seeing a stone like the one that Valon was sleeping upon, he sat and closed his eyes.

'Just for a moment', he told himself, 'I'm exhausted and I need to think. Then I'll look around the cavern at all the wonderful shapes to see if I can understand any of them.' As he fell asleep, the last thing he heard was the voice in his head.

Too Long To Die

'You are searching in the wrong place,' it said.

Valon stretched and opened his eyes. He had just enjoyed the most refreshing sleep he had ever experienced. He felt animated and eager to continue their journey and then he remembered that this was their destination. He wondered where Lonell was and, looking around him, saw his friend slumped on a rock, fast asleep. It was then that he noticed the change. Gone were the glistening walls and the smooth, tactile shapes that had so fascinated him; gone were the strange markings and the bright light shining from above. Now, the only light came from the two torches they had made which were abandoned on the floor but still burning. Valon was certain that he had seen his go out not long after they entered the cave, but then again, the cave they had entered had not looked remotely like this. He contemplated waking his friend but then decided to let him sleep. It was warm in the cave and he himself had felt the benefit of his rest so he decided to leave Lonell alone. He would only wake him when the torches began to extinguish and, at the very moment these thoughts came to him, the light started to flicker and dim.

Valon tried to wake the sleeping man.

'Come on, Lonell. We have to get out of here.'

He shook him but there was no reaction. Quickly Valon made a decision: he picked up his friend and carried him out of the cave and into the fresh air, where he gently lowered him down against the side of the mountain. He returned just in time to retrieve their backpacks for, as he left, the last torch sputtered and extinguished itself.

Valon took out the bed skins, wrapped the still sleeping Lonell in his and then he made a shelter from the extra skins they carried for that purpose. He thought about making a fire although they had used up most of their wood but, strangely, he still felt the warmth of the cave and decided to leave it until it was really necessary.

Too Long To Die

Valon wondered what to do. He felt so refreshed from his sleep that he had no need of more but, he thought, for now he would sit and watch over Lonell. Then he realised, he knew suddenly, with no doubt, that this was to be his role from this point onwards. He never asked himself why he had come to this realisation - all he knew was that he was responsible for looking after his friend, the Dreamer, to keep him safe and he felt honoured to have been handed this burden. Had he any idea of what this responsibility would entail, he might well have questioned his own ability and steel but, as it was, he settled down to safeguard his friend.

Too Long To Die

Chapter Sixteen

As Lonell lay in a deep, dreamless sleep, Valon decided to investigate his surroundings and pass the time searching for something to eat. He had been sitting beside his friend for what seemed like an age and he noticed that the sun was beginning to sit lower in the sky. He realised they would be staying in the lee of the mountainside for the night and hunger began to gnaw at his stomach. He took his spear and a small hunting net from his pack and, wondering if he would find anything edible this high up, set off in search of the local wildlife. Small animals scurried under the light covering of snow, pushing the icy granules in front of them as they headed for their burrows. Valon was surprised to see that even at this altitude, scrubby little bushes grew out of the stony ground and cracks in the rock walls. He picked some and piled them ready to collect on his way back; they would be needed to replenish the firewood that they had expended.

Most of the larger wildlife lived further down the mountain, closer to the trees and vegetation. However, Valon was certain that some of the caves he could see would probably contain bears. Although these huge beasts were vegetarian, they towered over even the tallest of men and their very size was fearsome. They would also not hesitate to attack if they thought that another creature was taking food they considered theirs, and Valon knew only too well that man rarely prevailed in a confrontation with a cave bear. He thought it too early for them to have retreated to their dens to sleep through the cold season and he kept a wary eye out for the tell-tale signs of their presence.

Too Long To Die

It was not only Valon that was hungry in the harsh environment. Small stoat-like creatures dived in and out of the bushes, searching for smaller prey, their fur beginning to turn from the summer brown to a shining white. Birds of prey also hovered overhead, watching for the slightest movement that would give away the presence of their next meal while Valon stood quietly observing their actions. He chose a spot and quietly crept towards it; then he squatted down and waited for his moment. It was a long wait; his movement had disrupted the hunting methods from above and the smaller animals had gone to ground on hearing his almost silent footsteps. It took a while for them to forget his presence but, suddenly, a hare broke cover and, at the same moment a large hawk fell out of the sky, talons ready to retrieve its catch. Instantaneously, the net flew. Valon had hoped to trap the bird but, by luck, the net came down over both animals. The man ran towards the fluttering, screaming chaos, his spear at the ready. A thrust and the hawk lay still but the hare still squealed until his life was terminated by a slash from the flint knife.

Valon picked his catch up in the net and covered the blood-stained ground with fresh snow, giving thanks to the earth for the sustenance provided. He headed back to where Lonell was still sleeping soundly and settled down to prepare the food. The dexterity he showed when skinning the hare was matched only by the speed with which he plucked and gutted the hawk. He decided to keep the talons and some of the feathers - the beautiful markings of the larger feathers would make them valuable for trade - and the soft pelt of the hare would weigh nothing and might come in useful some time. So he packed his prizes in the skin and put them in his backpack. Unable to dig a hole in the hard, rocky ground, he found a fissure in the mountain wall and placed the animal detritus inside. Picking up the scrub wood that he had stashed nearby, he built a fire and staked the meat over it to cook. As he waited, he started to collect fresh snow, forcing it through the neck of the water container, which he placed beside the fire to melt.

He was soon appeasing his growling stomach with a mouth-watering mixture of hare and hawk meat and, as he lay back sated, he decided to let Lonell sleep until he woke naturally with no encouragement. Darkness was falling as he wrapped the remaining cooked meat in snow and patted it down into hard ice blocks, hoping that this would protect it until morning and with that done, he settled down to rest, surprised at how tired he felt again.

Lonell was the first to wake in the morning and he jumped up from his bed skins, stretching and taking deep breaths of the clear, chill air. A light sprinkling of snow was covering them and yet he showed no sign of feeling the cold. A deep rumbling that betrayed his hunger sounded loud in the quiet landscape and he laughed aloud. He shook his friend awake.

'I'm starving. I'll go and catch something to eat.'

'Not necessary,' replied Valon, groggily opening his eyes. 'Light the fire. There's wood under the skin over there.'

He pointed to a snow covered pile against the mountain wall. He pulled himself out of his bed skins and uncovered the frozen packages of meat. He cracked them open and was astonished to find that the food had also become hard. Placing the food on the rocks around the fire to defrost, he rubbed some snow onto his face to shock himself fully awake, hoping the meat would become soft again in the warmth of the fire.

As they enjoyed their breakfast, Valon waited for Lonell to speak but his friend sat, deep in thought, silently. Overnight, the memories of the cave had blurred in Valon's mind and he was now confused. It had seemed so clear before but, try as he might, he could no longer recall exactly what had happened or if, in fact, it *had* really happened.

'Was it a dream?' he blurted out. 'Were we really in an extraordinary cave with objects and markings that I've never seen before, that shone like the sun? Or was it just a dream, Lonell?'

His friend's words snatched him out of his thoughts and he stared at Valon for a moment as though he did not know him. Then a gentle smile crossed his face.

'I don't know,' he replied. 'We were there together - we both went into the cave. We saw the same things, so it must have been real, mustn't it?'

'But the cave disappeared!' cried Valon. 'When I woke up we were just in a normal cave ... I think. I carried you out.'

He tried to put the pieces of his memories together.

'I don't even understand why I brought you out here into the snow. We could have stayed in the warmth of the cave but I knew I had to get you out. I can't explain it.'

'I'm not sure it matters that we remember all the details. The important thing is to take the messages that we were given and use them.'

'I wasn't even given any messages ... nothing ... so why was I there?'

'Are you sure?' asked Lonell. 'Has nothing come into your mind since we were in there?'

'No,' insisted Valon, stubbornly, but through his brain passed the realisation that he was fated to care for the man in front of him; he had received a message but he did not intend to divulge it. What he did not realise was that there was no need - Lonell had noticed a difference in the younger man already. He did not know what had happened to his friend in the cave but he knew that something had, deny it as the other man may.

'What happened to you?' Valon asked, hoping to divert the attention from himself. 'I think I fell asleep so I didn't see what happened? Did you see the ... er, skull?'

'Yes.'

Valon waited for more and when nothing further was offered, he threw his hands in the air and rose to his feet, exasperation written over every inch of the man.

'Well? Tell me! Did you get the answer? Do you know who killed Narthan and why?'

He paced up and down waiting for the answer.

'No.'

'Sacred Stones! You are the most infuriating person I know!' shouted Valon.

Lonell looked at him surprised, grinned and stood up to join the angry man.

'I'm sorry,' he said, intending to appease his friend. 'As you are finding, it's difficult to remember and to make sense of what happened to us. I was told I was looking in the wrong place, and that something happened that we don't know about. I have to find out what this ... thing ... was and that will lead us to the killer. Only one person actually killed him but others helped.'

'You said you thought that more than one person was involved - you're right. But wouldn't he give you more information?'

It was strange, thought Valon, that they both thought of the shadow-skull as a 'he'; there was no proof as to its gender, or even what it really was. He had not heard the voice in the cave nor, obviously, could he tell what Lonell listened to in his head and he had not been told it was masculine. Perhaps it was the natural air of authority that surrounded the entity but it was ridiculous that they even considered it to have human-like properties.

Lonell shook his head and answered his friend.

'Not about this killing; he only said I had the ability to discover the truth myself. But he did say that in the future I would travel far to look for the truth.' He hesitated. 'I didn't understand his words fully but he also told me that you would not let me go alone.'

Valon's face had changed from a frown at the thought of losing his friend to a wide grin when he knew he would not be left behind. He had known that he was to look after this strange, dark-haired man and now he was sure that they would journey together.

'We shall clearly have many adventures and stories to tell,' he laughed.

'But for now, I still have to solve the problem in our cave,' said Lonell. 'What did it mean - I am looking in the wrong place? I must think while we walk. It's time to go back.'

Lonell began to gather their belongings. The fire had already dwindled but he moved the stones away so soon there would be no sign of anyone camping there; they did not want to attract any attention to this place. Lonell had told Valon that it was vital the skull not be discovered by others; not now, maybe in the future, but for the present they had to keep it secret, safe from the world.

Packs secured on their shoulders, the two men looked back at the sight and knew that any evidence of their presence there would soon be obliterated by the weather and the movement of animals. Valon's eyes searched the cliff face for a sign of the opening to the cave but in vain; there was nothing to hint at a break in the rock formation.

They took a different route down the mountain, not wanting to double back on their footsteps for fear of making a trail from the cave. Lonell estimated that Kadell would soon begin to look out for them but that they had a few days before he began to worry - they could always say that the Burgoni had insisted they stay for longer than expected.

They spent two more nights on the exposed mountainside but neither felt the effect of the deep biting wind or the sleet that threatened. It was harder here to find a protected area in which to light a fire and, had it only been for the need for warmth, they would not have bothered to expend the time and effort. However the need for protection from wild creatures that roamed nearby made it an essential activity; they had no desire to be confronted by a hungry animal and it was only flames that kept them at a distance.

Their fears were confirmed on the final night. Neither man woke as the fire burnt down. Lonell thought he was dreaming. Someone was pulling at his arm, they were telling him he had to go with them but he did not want to move. Feebly he tried to push them away and then he felt the pain as sharp teeth sank into his arm. With a cry he leapt to his feet. Valon already had his spear in his hand and he thrust at the wild pig which squealed in anger and terror, as the spear blade slashed its side.

'No!' cried Lonell, his large hunting knife in his hand. 'Don't kill it!'

He stamped his feet and shouted, trying to chase the beast away. The confused pig stared wildly around it and made a bolt for freedom away from the weapon wielding men.

'Why? It could have killed you and it would have been good to eat.'

Valon stared at Lonell in desperation.

'I don't understand you.'

'It had no tusks,' Lonell said in explanation.

'And so .... ?'

'It was a female. They only attack when they have young to feed. They must be hungry. I won't take a mother from its young unless I must.'

He turned away and pulled up the sleeve of his tunic have to look at the teeth marks. They were not deep. He thanked his Sacred Stones that he had woken in time but he needed to clean them. Valon was already at his side, a handful of pristine snow ready to place onto the wound.

'This should wash it out,' he said quietly and Lonell knew his friend had understood him. While Valon bathed his arm and bound it with a rabbit skin he had prepared a few days before, Lonell pictured his mother, the woman who had been taken from him in a hunting accident when he had only passed five winters, the woman who had protected him from the others and loved him, even though she did not understand him. When she died, no one else had really wanted to care for him - he was just too ... different. The tribe members had been kind to him, had not let him want for anything, but there was no closeness, no bond, and his life of solitude and separation had begun.

The late afternoon of the following day they reached the tree line for, in these lands, the tall pines grew higher up the mountains. They were further east than where they had started their climb and Lonell was uncertain of the best route to take, so they settled down early to spend the night under the trees. They caught two giant squirrels and slowly cooked them, together with freshly picked roots and mushrooms, in a hole in ground until the meat fell off the bones. It was a luxury to have the time to enjoy well prepared food and the two men were savouring every mouthful when Lonell heard a rustling in the undergrowth behind him. He was holding his hand out towards Valon to alert him when figures stepped out and showed themselves. Lonell and Valon leapt to their feet and faced the warriors who had approached so silently. There were eight men, dressed only in loin cloths, tied on with soft skin belts, their bodies streaked with mud. Some had leaves embedded in their hair and all bore short spears in their hands with knives tucked into their belts.

There was no time for the Pescovari men to grab their spears which were propped up against a tree and, although nothing showed on their faces or in their bearing, they were afraid that they had been caught by the roaming group of thieves the Burgoni had told them about.

'Lonell, it is Lonell, isn't it? And Valon? I can't believe it!'

Too Long To Die

A man stepped forward and gave the Pescovari greeting of two wavy lines. They stared at him without recognition, until Valon suddenly realised who the man was.

'Finar, is it you? It is impossible to recognise you under all the mud!'

They greeted him in relief.

'I didn't think we would ever see you again,' said Valon. 'I'm so pleased but I see you have joined a warrior tribe.'

Finar grinned and translated Valon's words to the others. They all roared with laughter and, one by one, came forward and put one hand on their shoulders, while Finar explained.

'We go into the woods to exercise. Someone is the prey, the others the hunters. We spend days out here and when one is found, another becomes the prey. There are two winners at the end: the man who evades capture for the longest and the man who discovers the most prey. It's a game but it also sharpens our hunting skills, so we have fun, get fit and learn at the same time. We have four of these exercises through the warm period - this is the last one until next summer.'

'So, who are they? Have you been with them ever since you left the Pescovari? And Alurasta, how is she?'

The final question brought a sour look to Finar's face but he grinned.

'There's so much to talk about and you must tell me everything that's happening with the Pescovari. I miss everyone so much ... well, not quite everyone!'

Then he turned and talked rapidly to another of the scarcely clad men who stepped forward and slowly addressed them in their own language.

'I am Corazin, son of leader of our tribe, the Estrondi. I greet you.'

He made the formal gesture and Lonell and Valon signed their reply.

'I am ...' Corazin hesitated over the word and then remembered, 'pleased to invite you to spend time at our home. We go home now.'

Lonell thanked him and accepted.

'You speak our language well. Did Finar teach you?'

'Yes,' replied the young man proudly. 'He try very hard, work with me long time, but he learn Estrondi better. Most of tribe now speak some Pescovari, not good but some.'

'Most speak better than Corazin,' someone said with a laugh. 'He is so slow at learning. It is good he is best hunter!'

There was still some food left which Valon offered to the hunters. Although between the eight of them each only had a little, the Estrondi were grateful after their activities and asked to be shown how it was cooked so they would not go so hungry on their exercises in future.

'Estrondi men do not cook,' explained Finar. 'So we usually get very hungry when we are exercising. We live off only what we can pick.'

The Pescovari men had not yet unpacked their belongings for the night so it took no time to ready themselves to follow the Estrondi. Corazin started out at a good pace and after a while, the leader's son let out a whoop. A man appeared out of the ground, startling both Lonell and Valon and they saw the grin of appreciation on the face of Finar. The ground ahead of them appeared to be a low mossy bank, covered in the woodland vegetation and, from a distance, no entrance could be seen. Suddenly the ground beneath their feet started to slope downwards steeply and within a few paces they found themselves at a long opening in the hillside.

Lonell had expected the leader to be a woman since Corazin had referred to himself as their son. However, the strongly-built man who came to the entrance and gave Corazin a bear-hug, was clearly in charge. A deep, booming voice welcomed everyone back and, after Corazin had spoken quickly to him, he turned to the visitors, welcomed them in their own language and invited them in. The floor continued to slope downwards until they were in a large, spacious cavern with many small hearths spread throughout. It was clear that spaces were allocated to each person, for the bed skins were left out, together with personal belongings. To Lonell and Valon who were used to a person having only essential belongings and sleeping wherever he wanted which meant that bed skins tended to be rolled up during the day and cleared away, the scene was one of total, disorganised chaos. It was only once people settled down in their family groups that it was obvious how it all worked together. Very little natural light entered the cave and torches were stuck into the ground at regular intervals, throwing flickering light over the untidiness around.

'Come, you must share my hearth with me,' said Finar, coming up beside them, 'and then we are going to wash ourselves off. Would you like to bathe too?'

'That would be wonderful,' Lonell said with a heartfelt sigh.

He had been wanting to bathe ever since they went up into the Great Mountains but there had been no falling water to be found. He was certain that he must smell terrible.

Dropping off their packs, they followed the men back out of the cave. Daylight had disappeared but each man took a torch which was already prepared and they filed down a path until they arrived at a large pond. Tall trees provided a canopy, sheltering the area below from wind. The air did not move and the smell of rotting vegetation assaulted the senses. The water seemed so black under the trees, despite the torches, that the two strangers were uneasy about going in.

'Don't worry about the darkness, shouted Finar.. 'It is clear fresh water, as good as Mountain Water. You will enjoy it.'

Not wanting to be seen to be hesitant, they swiftly removed their clothes and jumped in. Someone handed each of them some flowers and they crushed them to make a soapy mixture. Lonell was sure that he could feel days' worth of dirt falling off his body and hair and he lay back in the water and felt himself relax. Valon was playing some sort of game with the others, throwing a round object made from the rushes, from one to the other. Lonell made no attempt to join in.

'There is so much to find out,' he said to himself. 'Finar must have many things to tell us.'

Suddenly he remembered the words that had so confused him.

'Finar,' he shouted and, when his host had extracted himself from the game, Lonell asked the question that had been playing on his mind since their arrival.

'You must explain something. Corazin said he was the son of the leader. How can that be if the leader is a man? A man can only be the son of a woman.'

Too Long To Die

Chapter Seventeen

Finar and Lonell stood in the black water, savouring the refreshing touch of cold liquid against their tired bodies. Lonell smiled at the man he had known in what seemed like another life and an age ago. Finar had known Valon better - Lonell suspected that he had always seemed rather remote and perhaps a little frightening to the man beside him, but he was used to that reaction. However, from the smile on his face, Lonell knew it must be good for him to see anyone from those days - nostalgia would bring back his happy memories - and he would surely be delighted to receive news of other friends he had left behind.

'I know what you're thinking. When I first came here I found it difficult to understand that a man could accept a child as his son or daughter, but it's part of the linked life of this tribe.'

Lonell shook his head, frowning.

'Sorry, I don't know that word - linked,' he told Finar.

'I'll try to explain,' he said. 'You know that Alurasta and I had to leave the Pescovari because we wanted to stay together, not sharing ourselves with others, but Saretta wouldn't allow it.'

Lonell nodded.

'It was a difficult time,' continued Finar. 'After we left we were alone a long time, wandering in search of a people who would take us in. Sometimes we thought we would never find a new home, that we would return to the earth on the mountains. We were almost despairing when we came across the Estrondi who were out hunting and they took us back to their cave. We soon found out that their custom is to live as a man and woman together. You know that was what we had wanted to be,' he searched Lonell's face, making sure that the other man was following his words.

'I still don't understand why Corazin said he was the son of a man,' insisted Lonell.

'Well, it's not like the Pescovari. Here each man and woman has their own hearth and any child born to the woman also belongs to the man. As he takes on responsibility for the woman, he also does so for her offspring and they are considered his children. That's what they call a link.'

'How long do the man and woman stay together?' asked Lonell, fascinated by this alternative way of living but, equally, disturbed by the thought of it.

'All their lives - it's called the life-link,' replied Finar. 'Or, until they make a formal request to Stovat to be link-broken.'

'Stovat?' inquired Lonell.

'That's the name of the leader.'

'Surely, he must get many requests. I couldn't stay with one woman all my life!' exclaimed Lonell, the very idea repelling him.

'Some do break the link but it's frowned upon and considered unlucky to the tribe. It destroys the peace of the cave but, then, so too does quarrelling between man and woman, so a link-break is usually allowed if the relationship is considered to have totally broken down.'

'I'm sorry. I just can't imagine tying myself down like that,' admitted Lonell. 'Are they allowed to share themselves with others?'

'No, definitely not,' said Finar forcefully.

Lonell shook his head. He had never understood Finar and Alurasta's desire to keep to themselves. Although he loved being with Mila, he always felt he was free to spend time with others and so was she.

'But most men do. Unlinked young women are very attractive!' Finar interrupted his thoughts, smiling through the darkness. 'It is actually harder on the woman; she is expected to obey her man at all times. Somehow it is not considered serious if a man shows interest in another woman, but everyone is horrified if a linked woman strays from her hearth. That's the only time a man may beat his woman in public.'

'A man can beat a woman?'

Finar did not appear to notice the disgust in Lonell's voice.

'Yes,' he said, 'and he may request a link-break. If it's granted under those circumstances, he can keep the children or send them away with her if he wishes; it's his choice. As in most things here, the woman has little say in what happens. It is a good life for the men here!'

Lonell felt himself grow cold and he knew it was nothing to do with the temperature of the water. The thought of the women of the Pescovari having to obey anything that a man might say, or to receive a beating, public or not, was hard to grasp; in his mind no one had the right to treat others so badly - as if they were worth less. That was the reason for the anger against the Enlightened Ones - they were imposing their wishes upon the people, whether they agreed or not. It would not be tolerated for long.

'So you are life-linked to Alurasta now?' he asked, struggling to keep his voice neutral.

'No, thank the Great Bear.'

The Estrondi phrase leaked into the Pescovari language, Lonell noticed.

'I said that our time before we reached the Estrondi was hard. Well, she did not stop moaning and crying the whole time. Then she started blaming me, although it had all been her idea.'

Finar laughed loudly and threw his arms in the air.

'By the time we arrived here we were hardly talking and certainly did not wish to spend any more time together. So, when the son of the leader asked to life-link with her she accepted immediately and shortly afterwards found she was carrying a child.'

'I am pleased. Corazin seems like a good man. Is she happy?' asked Lonell.

'No,' replied Finar. 'She made herself very unpopular, thinking she was so much better than all the other women, telling them how good it was to be linked to such an important man and how that put her on a higher level than everyone else. And it wasn't Corazin, it was his brother. Unfortunately for her (and everyone else, for he was a good man), he was killed in a hunting accident just after the birth of her daughter.'

'That is sad,' commiserated Lonell. 'Who looks after her now?'

'She had to move to the hearth of his mother and father, which is the custom. She is terrified of both of them and her husband's mother spends her time looking after the child while telling Alurasta that she is useless and scolding her. She has to do all the work - she's like a slave to the older woman. I think I'm the only person in the cave who feels remotely sorry for her, even though she brought it on herself.'

'Poor Alurasta,' Lonell pitied the girl but remembered the disharmony she had caused back at home and he could understand the bad feeling that she had obviously generated in her new cave.

'I must get out of this water - I am freezing!' he said, hoping to change the subject and, as he climbed out, others took it as a sign that the time had come to return to the cave. Lonell and Valon started reluctantly to put their old, filthy clothes back on when the men all started talking. Finar stopped them.

'Unless you are really attached to those clothes,' he said, 'you can leave them here and we will provide you with clean trousers and tunics, if you wish.'

Lonell had rarely been more grateful and, as the ten naked men trooped back towards the cave, he tried to reconcile these generous, warm people with men who would beat their women and eject children from their hearths.

Once back inside and dressed in clothes, similar to their own style but with a slightly longer tunic, Lonell, Valon and Finar were invited to eat at the hearth of Stovat, the leader. This was somewhat uncomfortable for the two Pescovari for it was Alurasta who was serving them and, after they had greeted her warmly, she was shooed away to get back to work by the leader's woman. Lonell had to admit that had he met her without knowing the history, he would not have recognised her. The gaunt, sad expression on her face and her now bony frame tore at the hearts of both men although neither had really liked her before she left. Valon tried to smile encouragement to her but her face remained blank and lifeless. Finar just ignored her and talked to the leader and one of the other young men they had met before, who turned out to be another of Stovat's sons.

A stew made of a meat that they had never tasted was served and, after the first couple of nibbles to test it, the two men wolfed it down as though they had never eaten before. They even managed to extract some smiles from the leader's woman by showing great interest in the meal and, when told that they had just dined off the meat of a cave bear, they were suitably impressed and asked about the trapping and preparation of the beast. By the time they had taken a few drinks of a mellow grape juice and finished a delicious plateful of sweet berries after the stew, it was a relaxed and cheerful group that sat around the leader's hearth. It was Valon who first noticed that here too, there was an absence of the flavour of salt in the food and they asked Finar to translate, for there could be no misunderstanding in trading procedures if they wanted to remain friends afterwards.

Valon went to find their backpacks, put all the goods into one and brought it back, while Lonell spoke to the leader.

'We have brought with us valuable items for exchange and trade. It comes from the Big Water, far towards Sun Sleep and takes many months to harvest and prepare.'

He could see Stovat's eyes open with interest briefly and then rapidly half close to slits of cunning. This was the true trader's expression and Lonell welcomed it. Although Valon was a much better trader and he sometimes felt uncomfortable, he could not deny the excitement that accompanied the banter which flashed backwards and forwards between the two sides until a bargain was struck that neither side appeared to be happy with, but usually both were quite content. He would leave Valon to do that part of it.

'Do you have anything to trade,' he inquired, 'that might be worthy of exchange for our fine goods?'

The leader leant over and spoke quietly to his son who, grinning, left the circle and disappeared into the back of the cave.

Valon still had the backpack in front of him but he kept the goods out of sight until the young man returned with a bag of his own. Lonell stood up and moved away from his friend to show that Valon would be the man undertaking the negotiations for their side and at that point the bag was put down in front of the leader. The two men faced each other, expressions untrusting and aggressive, but everyone knew this was part of the game.

Valon removed one of the packs and unwrapped it. There was the struggle to keep the eyes unmoving; it was exactly what the leader had hoped it would be but he must not show that on his face. His woman put her hands together and was instantly glared at by her man and her sons. She looked away, embarrassed.

Stovat smiled cunningly, as though he knew he had the upper hand in this trade. He slowly opened up his bag and produced a lump of grey material about the size of a large, elongated apple. He put it down in front of himself triumphantly and looked up. He was shocked at the genius of the Pescovari traders. He looked from Valon to Lonell, amazed that neither of them betrayed any emotion; in fact they managed to seem most unimpressed.

It was Finar who realised what was actually happening.

'Do you know what this is?' he asked.

When Valon shook his head, he then looked at Lonell who shrugged his shoulders.

Someone giggled and the tension of the moment, the intensity of serious trade was broken.

'Could someone,' asked Valon, 'please tell us what we are supposed to be so impressed about?'

All those who understood laughed and explained to the others and even Stovat had difficulty in maintaining his stoic expression.

The leader said something rapidly and four men moved in the direction of the back of the cave. Immediately they reappeared bearing a variety of weapons; knives, arrows and short spears were all brought into the hearth. Both Pescovari stared at the weapons carried by the men. It was now their turn to attempt to keep their faces blank. The blades and arrow tips were all made of a shiny, black substance that they had not seen before. Lonell squatted down and leant his hand forward to touch the arrow head. The stone, although he instinctively knew that it was not the same substance as any form of stone he had come across before, was black and shiny and glinted like the eyes of a wolverine. Lonell shuddered; he sensed death and despair within it. Valon touched the finely honed sides of the blades and felt the sharpness. He stroked the glossy material and realised that, although brittle, the fineness and the cutting power of these blades would be invaluable.

Valon could hear his heart beating with excitement as he started the bargaining.

'I see that this looks pretty but its sharpness would be lost as soon as it was used. It would break straightaway. I do not think we could use this.'

Stovat countered with his own.

'You tasted our food. There was none of this seasoning in it and it was delicious. We would not waste our valuable goods by exchanging them for salt.'

'We already have extremely sharp weapons and they do not break easily. When your life depends on a good weapon, I would far prefer to have a strong stone blade on it that I could rely on, rather than a pretty one.'

'There will be other traders that come through our lands bringing salt. We are in no hurry and I can see we could strike a better deal with them.'

The cross-exchange continued, strike and strike again, until both men sat back content that they had reduced the value of the other man's offering as much as they possibly could. They then took out all their items and Valon managed to swap all the packs of salt for eight lumps of obsidian to take home. In addition, the beautiful decorative sea shells bought them a smaller lump and the promise that the next day, their best blade maker would show them how to work with the material.

Both sides being inwardly content with their own bargaining powers and delighted with their purchases, everyone settled down and Lonell took the opportunity to ask Finar about the 'stone' they had just acquired.

'I don't really know about it,' said the other man, 'but come, I'll introduce you to someone who does.'

Lonell and Pulanor, the Estrondi trader talked for a long time. They soon discovered that they did not need the help of Finar as

Too Long To Die

Pulanor spoke the Pescovari language very well. Pulanor told Lonell of his meeting with traders who had come from a place far to the east of them and they had told him tales of many magical things including a large mountain, near a never ending sea, which threw flames and yellow, burning liquid from its belly. The new, black material had come from this region and the traders had called it the Death Stone, so they had kept the name in their own language.

'It doesn't feel like stone but I have never seen any material like it. It is more like the resin that comes from trees when it's really hard.'

'I agree, but we don't know what else to call it. It is interesting; I was watching you when you first touched it and I noticed that you shivered,' observed Pulanor.

'It is strange that it's called the Death Stone because that's what I felt.'

'That is why it has that name. Many men have the same reaction to it. I do too; it made me feel quite sick when I first touched it, but it makes unbelievable cutting edges. You'll be amazed when you discover how useful it is. You traded some large shells along with the smaller ones, didn't you? Well, I was told that the people who live by the water make tools from the Death Stone to open the shells and, because it is possible to give it such a sharp edge, it is perfect for wedging the two sides apart. For anything that needs a really sharp point or edge, this is the perfect material. Its only fault is that it breaks quite easily.'

'I thought it would, but I still think it will be useful. It's not like any stone I've seen before.'

'No. I agree it's different but, on an arrow it's a fearsome blade and so light that it does not affect the flight,' continued Pulanor. 'Did you know that it was Finar who brought us the idea of bows with arrows. Of course it was just the basic idea but we have worked to develop it.'

'Yes, he left our tribe just as one of our women had invented the weapon but it was still at its earliest stage and not ready to use.'

'He got the idea from a woman?' exclaimed Pulanor. 'He didn't tell us that! He let us think he had made the weapon.'

Lonell laughed and told the story of the bow's creation. Then he explained that women in the Pescovari tribe were equal to the men, a concept the other man found difficult to accept but Lonell tried to describe how their system worked and that it was very successful. He did not mention the Enlightened Ones or the problems that now faced his own tribe.

They talked well into the night and Pulanor told him about the many trading journeys he had taken and some of the tribes he had met. He also mentioned some roaming groups of, usually, just young men who were looking for some excitement in their lives. He told Lonell that most of these were quite harmless but warned him that others were not friendly and it was best to avoid them.

Lonell had suddenly developed an interest in discovering what he could expect when he travelled, following the information the skull had provided. He also realised that he should begin to learn other languages if the opportunity presented itself and so he asked the Estrondi man to teach him some of his words. To start with, it was difficult to make some of the sounds of the new language but soon he was making progress and Pulanor was delighted with the speed that his pupil learnt.

Many people had already retired when Lonell realised how tired he was and, bidding his new friend 'Good night' in the other man's language, he made his way over to his backpack. He found Valon and Finar fast asleep so he unrolled his bed skins and settled down. Despite his tiredness, his brain was spinning. He had heard so much, there was a great deal to think about and he lay on his back staring at the roof of the cave, his mind turning over the new found information until he drifted into a restless sleep.

Too Long To Die

Chapter Eighteen

Despite his tiredness, Lonell was keen to be started the next morning. As soon as he heard movement around him, he crawled out of his bed skins and rolled them up, ready to be tied onto his backpack when they left later that day. It was still early so he decided to return to the pond to wake himself up fully in its cold embrace. The water was black, even in daylight, despite the sun's rays filtering down through the trees but he plunged in without a second thought. As he surfaced, he heard a stifled scream from the water's edge and looked round to see a group of young women holding their clothes in front of them to cover their naked bodies. Within seconds Alurasta appeared beside him in the water.

'You must get out now,' she said urgently. 'This is the time for the women to bathe and men are not allowed to come near. You must leave. Don't look back as you go. And cover your body quickly when you get out so the women can't be accused of looking at another man. You're putting us all in danger,' she added, fear making her voice shake.

Lonell did has he was told without a second thought or a glance behind him. He ran into the bushes covering his body with his tunic and, when he was out of view, he put his clothes back on. Realising that he dare not be seen arriving back at the cave with wet hair and clothes, he took a circuitous route back, taking in the surroundings while he dried off.

The cave was just on the edge of the forests and the lower slopes of the mountains were covered in lush meadow grasses at this time of year. He noticed plants that he had never seen before: great purple and red flowers on long stalks which bent over under the weight, orange spiky plants that were sharp to the touch, and delicate blue and white flowers that grew close to the ground. He wished Endorina were there to tell him what they were. The trees seemed larger and more densely packed than where he lived and he could hear bird calls that he did not recognise. Over the meadow fluttered thousands of small yellow butterflies like a cloud and for a while he sat and marvelled at the extraordinary beauty of the place, enjoying the deep relaxation. Eventually, when he felt dry, he stirred and decided to return to the cave, assuming it would now be safe.

However, as he walked towards the entrance he could see a gathering of people. A large man, still strong although his hair had turned white, held a terrified woman by the arm, his long fingers digging into her flesh. She was shaking her head and weeping. At his side stood Stovat, the leader, a stern expression on his face, waiting for the Pescovari man.

It was the other man who spoke, his voice rough with emotion and anger:

'You bathed in pond with my woman. Is this true?' he accused.

Lonell recognised the girl as one of those who had been on the water's edge and her imploring eyes bore into him.

'No, I did not bathe with her or with anyone's woman,' he replied, feigning horror at the very thought. 'I went to the pond because I did not realise that it was reserved for the women in the morning, for which I apologise.'

He looked steadily at the leader.

'When I heard women's voices, I left quickly, and took a walk around the meadows, watching the butterflies. Your land is very beautiful.'

To this point, he had spoken the truth but the next question was not as simple to answer truthfully.

'So you did not see women without their clothes?'

He had seen them but they had their clothes held in front of them and he had only seen Alurasta's head above the water.

'No, I have seen no women here without their clothes,' he answered, hoping they would accept this and ask no further questions.

For a moment the tension hung in the air and Lonell held his breath. The white haired man looked at Stovat who nodded and Lonell was astonished to see the man let go of his woman and come towards him with a smile on his face. Lonell had not realised how tall this man was. He towered over the Pescovari and put his hand round the visitor's shoulders.

'Come, my woman make breakfast for you.'

'Thank you,' mumbled Lonell, as he was guided into the cave and towards his host's hearth. He passed Finar on the way in, who looked at him from under a slightly raised eyebrow, and Valon, his face showing huge relief.

At the hearth, the woman gave him a hurried, grateful glance and, nursing a badly bruised arm, provided him with a meal of small loaves made from a coarse grain that was new to him, and honey. Lonell wanted to apologise to her for his mistake but knew that any attempt would only cause more grief, so he nodded his thanks, trying to convey his deeper feelings in the gesture.

After he had thanked the huge man for his generosity, wondering how he had not seen him the night before as he overshadowed everyone around him with his height, he left to find Finar and Valon. He had not noticed anyone come up behind him so he was startled when he heard a voice behind him.

'If you are going to travel, the first thing you must learn is that you never go off by yourself until you are sure you know all the customs of your hosts. This is even more important than the language.' Lonell turned to see Pulanor, the trader, beside him, a conspiratorial grin on his face.

'How many times have you got yourself into trouble?' Lonell asked, quietly.

'Only once, like you, and I also managed to talk my way out of it. I know that you will have the sense to heed this lesson for it will stand you in good stead in the future. Now, let me take you to the stone cutter. I am also interested to see him work the Death Stone.'

Gathering up Valon on their way, they left the cave and were led towards an area where leather hides had been pulled between the trees to act as walls. Rolled up and tied to the trunks were other skins which could be dragged over the top as a roof. Underneath was a large space where work could continue even in the worst conditions. This was one of the tasks that could not be carried out inside a cave due to the sharp pieces of stone that flew off and were a danger to others. A large tree trunk served as a work surface and other smaller trunks were the seats.

The stone cutter, Serin, sat on one of these. His round, friendly face was weather-beaten from hours spent working in the open air. He grinned at them broadly, showing gaps where teeth were missing, clearly delighted to show his skills to strangers who had not seen him at work. First he demonstrated his dexterity with other forms of stone, asking them about their knowledge of stone knapping. When they explained that they were not stone workers but would take what he could teach them back to their knapper and try to pass on a little of his expertise, Serin seemed sad that they would not appreciate the full intricacies of his creations. Lonell could see that he obviously thought of himself as an artist, and appreciated it when Serin settled down to show the laymen as much as he could, so the obsidian they had bought would not go to waste.

'Now I am going to work with the Death Stone. One thing you

must remember is that the chippings are sharper than other stone and they can fly off in any direction if you are not careful. It is important to protect your eyes and to do this I have made these.'

He held up two smooth sea shells, each of which had a hole pierced through its centre. He held them up to his eyes to show the observers and then passed them around. As each man put them up to his own eyes there was an exclamation of amazement. Not only would these prevent any chips coming through but it appeared that, by looking through the hole, the eye was more focused, the item was clearer. Immediately Lonell thought about how this could help people doing any detailed, intricate work, particularly as they grew older and they had more difficulty in seeing.

'I regret that I only have this one pair,' said Serin, as he stuck them around his eyes sockets with a smooth yellow glue. 'You will have no problem in finding shells where you come from. But for now, you must be careful to make slits of your eyes while you watch me, but even so, do not get too close.'

He held the dark grey nodule in his hand reverently and his eyes searched its surface.

'I am looking for a natural flaw in the stone, a line that might eventually develop into a fissure.'

He showed them what he had found and picked up a flint chisel and a large smooth stone which he held in the palm of his hand. He tapped the nodule smartly and it fell into two parts. The black, shiny glass-like material was exposed and Serin then showed them how to use the hand stone and the tip of an antler to take flakes off. The smaller the flakes, the sharper they were but he also showed them how to put a sharp edge on a larger blade. Tiny flakes were chipped off all around the edge until the whole large blade had the sharpness of a small flake but the greater strength of a large piece.

They were truly impressed by his skill and his ability to make it seem easy, for when they tried themselves they were unable to get anything that resembled a fine blade. Whenever Lonell tapped it, the flake broke off in unusable pieces or just shattered into small crystals. However, Valon created, by chance, a flat piece of the glassy material.

'Look. I can see my eye in this,' he exclaimed, as he stared at it.

They each held the piece in turn and, laughing, tried to look at the reflection of different things in the stone.

'Can you imagine, if you could get a really large piece of this? Women would use it to look at themselves, to make sure they looked good!' said Lonell.

'Yes. It might be better if we did not tell them about it or they will expect us to search for huge rocks and drag them back to the cave, just so they can look at themselves. And it might stop them from working and looking after the men!' added Finar.

His words proved that Finar was now far more Estrondi than Pescovari and they brought Lonell and Valon back to reality. They broke up the gathering, saying that they must get on their way if they were to get back home within the expected time. The stone cutter wrapped the usable flakes and remains of the nodule in a piece of hide and added one of his antler tools for, he assured them, they would not be able to obtain the fineness by using a flint tool. They gave Serin heart-felt thanks and promised that the next time someone came this way, they would send more of the correctly shaped and sized shells for eye protection.

Their backpacks were heavier with the grey nodules than they had been with the salt, but the two men knew they had discovered something new and immensely valuable for their cave. Alurasta had put in a pack of dried meat and some of the delicious bread that Lonell had eaten for breakfast - Lonell hoped she would not be caused any more distress for her generosity. As he said good bye to her, he saw tears in her eyes. He wanted to put his arms around her and tell her to come with them but he knew she would never leave her child behind and he grieved that there was nothing he could do for her.

While they prepared to depart, one by one the men came to take their leave and wish them well. It was clear that Valon had made many good companions amongst the younger men while Lonell had been conducting a more serious conversation with Pulanor who he now counted amongst his friends, a label bestowed on few people. Lonell happily bid farewell to these people in their own language which surprised many of them, including Finar. The leader, Stovat, gave them an invitation to visit whenever they wished and Lonell returned the gesture on behalf of the Pescovari, although he secretly hoped none would take up his offer in the foreseeable future. Despite Lonell having almost caused a serious incident, they departed on the friendliest of terms and were quite sad to leave behind some of their new acquaintances. For the first time, Lonell began to appreciate the lure of travel. He had always wondered how traders were able to endure what he had seen as the loneliness of their long journeys - he had never taken into account the friendships forged in distant territories.

In his mind, Lonell could not reconcile the two faces of the Estrondi; he struggled to balance their generosity and warmth on one side, and the cruel treatment towards their women on the other. They were an enigma and Lonell somehow knew that their paths would cross again which pleased him. He looked forward to being able to attempt to unravel the character of his latest acquaintances.

'You have to feel sorry for Alurasta. She's ruined her life,' commented Valon, as they walked along.

'I agree. I'm trying to understand why they treat their women like that. They are such kind people in every other way,' replied Lonell.

'They're very jealous of their women. The men are judged by the behaviour of their link-mate. If they don't behave properly, the men lose the respect of the tribe. So each man competes in showing his complete control over his woman.'

'Yet they are unhappy and the men don't seem to care about it.'

'No. The women like to be kept in control that way so their man is well thought of. They share his status so they know the need for him to punish her when she misbehaves.'

'Do you really believe that? Didn't you see the fear on their faces and the bruises on their bodies?'

Lonell felt his anger rising at the very thought of the injustice and also at the idea that Valon, his friend, could begin to think like the Estrondi men.

'Well, that's what I was told and I would think that men of their own tribe understand the situation better than we do', insisted Valon stubbornly, but Lonell could see that his friend's face was showing some doubt about the men's interpretation of the women's feelings.

'I think we can agree that they're a most welcoming and generous people and I look forward to meeting them again in the future.'

Valon grunted, acknowledging the comment, but his unhappy expression revealed an unwillingness to confront a feature of the Estrondi he had tried to ignore, even though, deep down, it had disturbed him.

They made good time for they walked mainly on the flat, through meadows or on the edge of the forests where the trees and undergrowth offered little resistance to their passage. The trees thinned out as they walked towards Sun Sleep and it was only two days later that they began to notice familiar sites that told them they were fast approaching the land of the Burgoni. When Lonell saw a clear stream running beside them, he suggested they stop to eat. They chewed on the dried meat and drank thirstily from the brook.

'You know that we mustn't mention to the Burgoni anything about our time in the mountains. I think it may also be wise to say nothing about the Estrondi,' said Lonell.

'Why do you say that? I don't see any reason not to tell them about their neighbours?' questioned Valon.

'I'm not sure but I remember Rafin, who traded for the Pescovari for many, many moons, do you remember him?'

Valon shrugged.

'Only vaguely,' he said.

'He told me that he'd once made the mistake of saying to one tribe how friendly and generous their neighbours were. It turned out that the two tribes hated each other and he was banned from their land. I remember he was so angry with himself because it had been a valuable trading route and after that, he had to walk far greater distances to get to the tribes beyond.'

'Now I see your point,' agreed the younger man. 'We don't want to upset the Burgoni - they may be useful in the future. I'm beginning to see that trading is quite an art. You have to be so careful not to upset anyone ... especially by going swimming at the wrong time!'

Lonell laughed and threw a clump of grass which stuck in the other man's blond hair. Valon retaliated and the assault developed into a wrestling match. Accompanied by shouts and laughter, the two men expended their natural excess energy by trying to get the other into a position from which he was unable to extricate himself. This time it was Valon who was the victor and it was only as they rolled onto their backs, puffing with exertion that they saw Marcot, the Burgoni trader, leaning on a sturdy oak staff and watching them, that they realised they were not alone.

They jumped to their feet, hastily making their tribal sign of greeting and looking rather sheepish. Marcot returned the greeting in his own manner.

'I remember the days when I could wrestle like that,' he said, 'but I think my bones would snap in half if I tried it now! Welcome, I hope you have enjoyed your journey.'

'Indeed we have,' claimed Valon. 'We have seen many things that are new to us: animals and birds - some of an enormous size - and plants. We wished our Healer were with us. She could have told us what some of them were - she seems to know the names of everything that grows!'

'And butterflies. I have never seen so many, like yellow clouds that would suddenly rise up and then settle all at once. It was a marvel,' added Lonell, hoping that Marcot would not want any more details, but it appeared to have satisfied the Burgoni.

'We were rather worried when you left. We forgot to warn you about a tribe that lives along the route you took. They are an extremely cruel and jealous people. They treat their women harshly and, also, anyone who looks at the women in what they see as an inappropriate way. I am exceedingly glad that you did not come across them. To your people, like mine, freedom of choice is essential and it is difficult to accept the way some tribes live.'

'No,' lied Lonell, painfully aware of Valon's gaze. 'We didn't meet up with anyone although we did see signs that man had passed that way recently. We were worried that we might come across a group of those men you told us about, so we took different paths.'

He felt that this made it seem a little more likely since Marcot knew that they had followed the route that would have passed through the Estrondi territory.

'I am glad,' replied Marcot. 'Come, we must return to the cave. Everyone will be delighted to see you again.'

The Pescovari men walked beside their host, a deep unease within them. Even though it was not meant in any harmful way, the lie weighed heavily on Lonell's spirits. Although he would happily avoid a subject or fail to give all the details about something, thereby hiding the complete truth, he found it hard to actually tell a lie, particularly to a person he respected.

However, if Marcot noticed their reticence, he said nothing and soon the two men were embraced, once more, by the warmth and hospitality of the Burgoni.

Too Long To Die

Chapter Nineteen

Another morning and another aching head; Valon felt rather glad that he did not live with the Burgoni. He was not sure his body would survive long but, despite that, he had made it his business to find out how the potent drink was made. Lonell had spent the evening learning as many Burgoni words as he could but Valon was not certain that he would remember much, for he had never seen him drink as much before. It was therefore a great surprise to him when his friend approached him with no sign of tiredness or headache.

'The meat is all packed and I'm ready to depart,' said Lonell. 'The Burgoni have been extremely generous - we shall not have to hunt before we reach our cave. Have you eaten yet?'

Valon grimaced at the question and held his stomach.

'I don't need anything. Perhaps some fresh air will do me good.'

They left the Burgoni, once more, knowing they had made good friends and there were many that they were sad to bid farewell to, not least the girls who had once again shared their bed skins. With promises to return when the cold period was over, they made their way in the direction of their home. Their backpacks, already heavy with the stones, were filled to the brim with reindeer meat and, between them, they carried a large bundle of meat packed in hides. It made movement quite difficult, particularly over rough, stony ground but they knew it would be worth it in the end.

Valon kept looking at Lonell out of the corner of his eye. The man was striding out, no appearance of tiredness or suffering. After a while he could take it no longer.

'Lonell, how do you do it? I have never seen you drink so much and yet you don't seem to be feeling any after effects. But I feel as though I'm about to empty my stomach with every step I take.'

'I did drink rather a lot last night,' replied his friend. He stopped and looked at the grey face of his companion and Valon waited for an explanation but there was only silence.

'Oh, come on, Lonell!' said Valon, completely exasperated. 'Tell me how you do it.'

Lonell looked at him, his mouth twitching with amusement.

'Yes, I enjoyed the drink.' He paused dramatically. 'It's remarkable how refreshing water is on a warm night.'

He laughed out loud at the other man's expression and dodged the pathetic attempt at a punch.

For three days they walked, through the lush greenery of the valley but Lonell did not see the beauty that surrounded him. The weight that he felt bearing down on him became heavier and heavier with each step and his mind dwelt only on the problems he faced. On the third day they knew they were once again in Pescovari territory and Lonell was ashamed at the lack of enthusiasm he felt. There were many people he would be glad to see again but he had a task to complete and he was not sure how he was going to do it. When he set out he had been so certain that he would be returning with the answers but he had failed: he had no more knowledge about Narthan's death than when he had started out. He did not even know where to begin and his frustration weighed him down.

They reached the place where they had all gone to cut down the trees for wood and they could see that the tribe had worked hard to gather in more. They stopped for one final meal before reaching home and were on the point of packing up when they sensed rather than heard Tendo approaching. They were about to hail him when

Too Long To Die

Tendo put his fingers to his lips to warn them into silence. He gave them no greeting but indicated a spot which was hidden from the open path. The distress on his face pulled at Lonell's insides.

'I wish I could greet you with better news,' whispered Tendo. 'Terrible things have happened since you left.'

'What? Tell us!' Valon somehow managed to keep his voice low.

'The day after you left, Saretta was furious that permission for your departure had not been requested. She came into the cave and shouted at Kadell - can you imagine? She shrieked and screamed and knocked over all the dried foods. Then ...,' Tendo swallowed hard and Lonell was sure he had seen a tear in the man's eye, 'then she ordered Valt and Tordano to take Verina to the Pit. Think how she must have felt going to where her son had been kept all those days? And she still thought he was dead.'

'Is she still there?'

Tendo shook his head.

'All the time we could hear her howling and moaning and the White Ones kept guard over us in the cave.'

'White Ones, not Enlightened,' thought Lonell, his eyes opening wide with shock, but he said nothing.

'Even when a person needed to leave the cave for hygiene reasons,' continued Tendo, 'they were accompanied. One moment, it seemed she thought that you had escaped and were never coming back, and that we would all try to leave too; the next, she was sure that you would return with warriors from another tribe.'

'Didn't Kadell tell her that we had gone to trade for reindeer meat?'

'Yes, but she didn't believe him. There's no way to reason with her. Even Lexana can't make her listen now. Even so, we couldn't believe what she had done.'

'What?' asked Lonell, his stomach churning with fear.

'Sarril - you remember that he'd left?' Lonell and Valon nodded their reply.

'He returned, but not alone. He brought men. I don't know where they come from - they are Outlanders, cruel, wicked men. Saretta says they are there for our protection but she lets them do what they want. We have all been shouted at, knocked down, some beaten by them, and the women, they take them when they want.'

Tendo was trying to hold back his emotions but a tear escaped down one cheek and he wiped it away, angrily.

'What happened to Verina?' Lonell hardly dared to ask.

'At the time of the Sun Sleep ceremony, we were all taken, even the children, to the High Pasture, to the place that looks down over Mountain Water. They dragged Verina down with them and, while two of the Outlanders held her arms, Saretta pulled back her head and ... slit her throat.'

By this stage, there was no disguising Tendo's tears. Lonell gasped and felt his own eyes prickle, a deep guilt filling his chest. He put his arm around the shoulders of the dark, stocky man and felt him shaking. Valon sat with his head in his hands, his body rocking to and fro in his grief.

'Why?' asked Valon, his voice cracking, fury and grief competing within him.

'She said it was to appease the Gods for the death of Narthan and, since Sim had been too cowardly, they would take his mother instead. But that's not all. Kadell is no longer Leader; Saretta is our only Leader. She's taken all our weapons. And Kara started to bleed - she lost the baby she was carrying.' The words poured out of Tendo's mouth, stopped finally by a choking sob.

There were no words, nothing that could be said that could have calmed Lonell's grief and guilt. Certain his actions had brought about this horror, his mind recalled the moment the log had come crashing off the fire as they decided to stand up to Saretta. He had known it was an omen; he should have spoken up. He should never have left on his ridiculous quest to find the skull. It was all his fault - he had known his departure would bring down Saretta's wrath on the tribe. And, to make matters worse, he had returned with no new information.

He wiped the spilling tears with the back of a rough hand.

'Lonell, no one blames you,' said Tendo, as though he had read his mind. 'None of this is your fault. But it's not safe for you to return. If you've found somewhere to live, go back there. There's no saying what Saretta will do if she sees you. You must go too, Valon.'

Both men uttered the word 'No!' at the same time and they exchanged looks.

'We will *not* run out on our tribe. Whatever happens to the tribe, happens to us,' asserted Lonell, and Valon nodded in agreement.

'Kadell told us that's what you'd say when we found you but he doesn't know how to keep you safe.'

He saw confused looks on the faces of the travellers.

'There's someone on every possible approach route, working but really waiting for you. Saretta believes we can do no harm if we're alone and this has worked in our favour. I'm cutting more wood and the others are picking and gathering whatever's in their position. It was vital that you knew what had happened before you arrived back at the cave.'

'How many Outlanders are there?' asked Lonell.

'We don't know. They've set up camp on the hill above Mountain Water,' Tendo pointed, 'and there always seem to be new ones.'

'I only hope we can do something to help but now we must plan. As you see, we've brought back much meat but we also have something else that will be valuable to us and I don't want Saretta to know about it. It makes fine weapons.'

From the bottom of the two backpacks the men brought out the grey stones. The wrapping hides had prevented the meat juices from seeping out over them and their dull grey cases hid the black magic within.

Tendo looked at the stones and a glimmer of humour returned.

'Don't worry,' he said. 'I shall never tell anyone!'

He rubbed a hand over his large nose and a shadow of a smile crossed his face.

'You'll be amazed, Tendo, when you see it worked. But for now it must be hidden,' said Lonell seriously. 'Can you carry it back with the wood and hide it in the storage cave? You must take great care with it. We'll arrive back at the cave with the meat which should be distraction enough for you to smuggle it in afterwards.'

'Do you have a spare piece of hide?' asked Tendo.

The intensity of Lonell's expression was enough for him. He wrapped the stones in the hide making a long tube and then surrounded this with sticks and branches and tied it all together. He casually put this over his shoulder and picked up his other large bag which was filled with smaller pieces of wood.

'I don't think they'll give me a second glance, do you?' he asked.

'No, it should be safe, but don't follow us immediately. Wait till you think we've reached the start of High Pasture before you follow.'

The two men replaced their backpacks and picked up the heavy load of meat.

'Our thanks, Tendo,' said Lonell. 'We'll see you at the cave. May good fortune go with us all.'

Tendo nodded. 'We'll need it.'

Their presence went unnoticed until half way across High Pasture. A shout went up and a horn blown, signalling their arrival. The two men could see the tribe being herded onto the flat land by the

Outlanders, using spears. Lonell watched the strangers as they approached. They were tall and wore their hair loose, the long unwashed tresses blowing in the wind. Their bare chests were covered in tattoos, crudely drawn, and the leggings below were torn and dirty.

Saretta rushed to the front and halted, a mountain cat waiting for its prey.

'Act as though we know nothing.' Lonell spoke quietly to Valon, hardly moving his lips.

He fixed a smile on his face and put his hand in the air.

'Hallo,' he shouted. 'See what we have brought.'

As they got nearer they were shocked at the appearance of the tribe. The adults seemed to have aged during the short time they had been gone, none of the women had attended to their hair and the men stood hunched over, looking at the ground, while the children cried, a cloud of terror hanging over them all.

The travellers came to a sudden standstill a few paces from them and dropped their burden, as though they had just noticed that something was amiss.

'What's happened since we've been away? It's clear there's been a tragedy. And we have guests?'

He knew his words sounded unnatural. He hoped she would not notice. Leaving the last question hanging, he looked directly at Saretta. The flesh on her face had shrunk, pulling the skin taught over the cheek bones, emphasising the wild, glazed eyes. She stood chewing viciously at her lip, drops of blood running scarlet down the white chin. Her appearance made Lonell's skin crawl, although he tried his utmost to hide it.

She glided crookedly towards them until she stood a few paces in front. For a moment she said nothing and then she shrieked into their faces,

'So you've decided to come back, have you? And alone. Couldn't you find any warriors to bring with you?'

Blood-tinged spittle flew through the air and hit Lonell on the cheek. He took a step backwards and wiped his face with the back of shaking hand.

'I don't know what you're talking about,' he replied, nerves straining his voice. 'We've brought back reindeer meat from our friends, the Burgoni. We have enough here,' he pointed at the large package at his feet, 'to last through the cold period. We don't know anything about warriors.'

'Liar!' she shouted, her face aggressively thrust forward towards his. 'Valt, Tordano, check the meat and search their backpacks. We will see what you have really brought back with you. If there is anything I don't like, we shall have more sacrifices for the Sun Sleep ceremony.'

Two Guardians came forward. Lonell could feel Valon begin to shake beside him and he was surprised that it was Valt who looked at them with an apologetic stare; Tordano kept his expression completely neutral. In fact, Lonell could see in his body language an anger about Tordano, not towards Saretta, but aimed at them.

Despite the fear, his mind was questioning. 'Why is Tordano angry that we've returned? Have I been wrong about him? I always thought of him as an ally. Was I mistaken? Perhaps he's just worried that our arrival will put the tribe in more danger.'

He was surreptitiously studying the tall, pale figure when he heard a whisper.

'Go and join the others quietly. Don't do anything that will make her pick you out from the rest. She may forget...' Valt peered at Lonell, trying to convey the urgency.

The two men did not wait to be told twice. They moved slowly towards the tribe, not making any sudden movement, until they found themselves in amongst their friends. Saretta stood by herself, her face pointed to the sky, arms outstretched as she swirled around, oblivious to all around her. Her body began to twitch and she fell to the ground, jerking, the spasm growing in strength. Her arms and legs thrashed and a deep groaning sound came from her mouth as Tordano ran towards her to hold her down.

'Help!' he shouted to the other white figures. 'Help me hold her down or she will damage herself!'

Lonell noticed the reluctance as they moved towards the thrashing body on the ground. He could see the Outlanders standing, uncertain, but when Lexana, who had been standing with the Enlightened Ones, made a movement with her hand and Kadell gently started to move the people towards the path down to the cave, they suddenly started pushing everyone towards the path that led down to the cave as though it had been their idea. Lonell saw an Outlander strike out at someone and he heard Mila cry out, nursing her arm. He started towards the attacker, his entire body quaking with anger, but found himself held back. He turned sharply to find Kadell holding his tunic. The ginger head shook.

'Do nothing. You will only make things worse.'

Lonell stared at Kadell, unable to believe that the tribe had reached a point where they could not even defend themselves. Lonell's eyes followed Kadell's as he looked at the figures filing past them and he noticed, for the first time, that almost everyone showed bruises or other signs of ill-treatment. He turned his attention back to the Outlander. He saw the lack of facial tattoos, showing that he belonged to no tribe, but down one cheek ran a long, jagged scar. The nose was pushed over to one side, the result of a fight in the past, and one front, yellowed tooth was broken half way down. Lonell was not, by nature, a violent man but the strength of his reaction surprised him as he swore to himself that one day he would get his revenge.

Valt moved quickly towards Lonell and touched his shoulder.

'Take the meat and store it.' He hesitated. 'I can inspect it later.'

He did not look at the other man as he spoke. Then he turned and almost ran back to the gathering around the High Priestess. Lonell grabbed Valon's arm and together they quietly collected the large hide package and carried it down to the cave.

Once inside, Kadell rushed over to them and held each one by the shoulders for a moment.

'I'm so sorry that none of our people met you,' he said in a low voice. 'I had men out to warn you, to stop you from returning.'

'We met Tendo,' smiled Lonell. 'Do you really think we would run away when the tribe's in serious danger? He told us everything that has happened. I hope you can forgive me.'

Kadell blinked and looked at the ground. The man who had been so imposing when they left now seemed a shadow of the Leader Lonell knew so well, but he gathered himself.

'None of this was your fault. It had been building up and I was too blind to see it. It would have happened whether you had gone or not. Your leaving was only the excuse - she would have found one somewhere. But we don't have much time to speak. There is now always at least one of the Guardians in the cave with us and an Outlander standing at the top of the path. We can't get out without being seen and we have little privacy. It's only because of Saretta's sickness that no one's here. They don't know what to do if they aren't told - they're animals.' He spat out the last words. 'So we must make the most of this time. What did you learn on your travels?'

Kadell looked eagerly into the face of the strange man that he had put so much faith in and Lonell felt his guilt and despair overwhelm him. He knew that Kadell could see his failure too.

'I am sorry, Kadell. I was so sure I knew where to find the answers but I return with nothing. Forgive me, Leader.'

'I am no longer Leader, nor do I deserve it. A good leader would never have allowed his tribe to be brought to this.'

He nodded in the direction of the people and the two men looked around the cave. Everywhere men and women were sitting watching them, hope hardly daring to glimmer in their eyes, an air of defeat hanging over each of them.

Lonell took a deep breath.

'It seems we are both to blame, Kadell. But you *are* our Leader - without you we only have Saretta - and that ... well, I can't even think of that. I would rather die than live like this. I can see that you have all lost the will to fight. We must relight the fire in our bellies and get our decent life back.'

'Since Verina's ... death, we have not had the heart to do anything.'

'And yet you sent out people to warn us and they were willing to do it although it put their lives in danger.'

Kadell looked up at Lonell who, to his amazement, could see a glimmer of change. It was as though his words had caused a surge of hope, a spark, rising, within the breast of the Leader. He felt the strength returning to Kadell, who looked around the cave, cautiously hopeful for the first time in days, that he could still help these people he loved.

'We may not have much time to talk and there is much you must know,' said Kadell, a fresh urgency to his voice.

'What I need to know is first, who are the Outlanders?' Lonell responded, anger still coursing through his body.

'We don't know. They treat us like animals. I have never come across men like them before. They won't talk to us. Even when they take the women they don't say anything they can recognise - it's possible they don't speak our language.'

'I think they must be the people that the Burgoni warned us about. They attack people and take everything they have. They don't seem to live anywhere settled,' said Lonell.

'And Saretta knew about them and sent Sarril to get them. She must be giving them something for being here,' added Valon.

'How many of the White Ones are now on Saretta's side. I've noticed a difference in Valt - he seems more friendly - but Tordano appears to be less so. And what about the women?'

Lonell hoped that Kadell would say they were all sympathetic to the tribe.

'That's the problem. We don't know who Saretta fully controls and who just stays with her out of fear. It's impossible to find out without asking them.'

'Don't you think we can trust Lexana? She didn't give us away when she knew that we'd made friends with the wolf and helped Sim.'

'Perhaps. Yes, I think you're right. We must start with her,' Kadell began to plan.

'And those who don't take our part, who side with Saretta, we must take action and rid ourselves of them or we'll never live in peace. There are far more of us and we only need to exile them from our lands - we don't need to kill them.'

'There's something more,' groaned Kadell. 'She's taken all the weapons. Whenever we leave here, to hunt or to go harvesting, we have to ask at the White Cave for our spears and knives - that's where she has them kept now. Even cooking knives - she controls them and they have to be counted and handed back. It's hopeless, but without weapons, we don't stand a chance, and she knows it,' he shrugged, apathy beginning to take control once more.

At that moment Tendo walked into the cave. He looked around to check who was there and then nodded at Lonell, his face grim. Lonell beckoned him over, put his arm around Kadell's shoulder and with a look at Valon, headed towards the back of the cave.

'Sit. We must talk. There is something we've brought back - Tendo helped us. We'll have to be very careful but it could give us a chance.'

Too Long To Die

Chapter Twenty

Kadell and Tendo sat, their anxious eyes fixed on Lonell.

'Wait,' said Valon. 'Shouldn't we invite Pallo to this meeting? We'll need him.'

'Is he to be trusted?' Lonell looked inquiringly at Kadell, who nodded without hesitation.

While Valon scurried off to find the flint knapper to bring him back to the dark corner where they sat, Kadell searched the front of the cave with his eyes. Once reassured that at least two people were keeping watch for any approaching Guardians or Outlanders, he stood up, pacing, waiting impatiently for the knapper.

Lonell remembered that Kadell and Pallo had been Nothings together; that is, they had suffered through their Rite of Shadows together which always created a bond between men. Lonell thought back to his Rite when he, like all boys, was tested to his very core and broken down in order to be rebuilt as a man. He had lived with the dread that he would fail to complete his Rite of Shadows for the humiliation that went with such failure was unimaginable. At least he had no mother who would have had to live with the shame.

He had hated wearing the shaved head which showed the tribe that he was Nothing (neither child nor man) but he had looked forward with eager anticipation, formed of fear and curiosity, to the series of ordeals, developed over the generations to discover whether a youth was ready to take his place among the men. From the moment his hair was removed, a moon before the physical trials began, no one was allowed to speak to or help him in any way   he had to be totally self-sufficient, easier perhaps for Lonell than for most.

Only those who were lucky enough to have a companion taking the trials at the same time had anyone with whom to share their misery and pain and Lonell was sure that Kadell had been thankful for Pallo's company. Their closeness was obvious to all.

Lonell had had no such companion and every trial was etched forever on his mind. The practical elements had started with exercises to show his ability with weapons, both against man and in the hunting field, followed by trials of strength that became ever more difficult and dangerous. Rocks which had to be dragged great distances became large cliffs to be scaled using only the strength of his arms. He had been taken into the mountains and forced to enter caves, unarmed, without knowing whether animals, vicious or otherwise, were living in them. He now knew that the men running the Rite had checked these out before but the Nothings were always told that no one had entered them in many years. As much a trial of the mind as of the body, it lasted for a whole moon, and ended with the Rite of Shadows, the most feared test of all. Taken to a huge cave which, he had been told, was the earthly home of the Gods, he was left alone and told to sit motionless in its centre. He sat by a large fire, with extra wood beside. The only movement he could make was when he built up the fire for if it extinguished, the result was failure.

The cave was situated in such a position that the wind blew right in through the entrance and skins, unseen to the participants, were attached high up in the roof. The Nothings were always told that this was the final judgement and if the Gods did not consider them worthy, They would come down into the cave, move around them and, in the worst cases, take the failures away with them; stories were told of many young men who were never seen again after they had entered the Cave of the Gods. Whenever the wind blew, the skins moved, casting shadows from the light of the fire, over the walls of the cave and creating terror in the hearts of the Nothings. The entire night Lonell, like all those who had suffered through the Rite, sat and watched the shadows, waiting to be grabbed by a vengeful God but in the morning he was dragged out, exhausted and shaking, declared to be a man, given the mark of the Pescovari and sworn to secrecy, never to reveal the details of the Rite of Shadows. It was a period that no man would ever forget and Lonell knew that Kadell's had been made easier by having Pallo at his side.

When they were all there, Lonell produced, from inside his tunic, a fragment of the Death Stone. He held it hidden in his hand.

'Tendo, will you tell them what we brought back with us?' he said.

The long nose twitched as he looked first at Lonell and then at Valon who was sitting smiling at him.

'They brought back with them some lumps of stone, just plain grey stone. It's now hidden in the wood store. And an antler,' he added, shrugging his shoulders, not knowing what else to say.

It was then that Lonell produced, as if by magic, the large, black flake which glinted in the fire light. The men sat forward, fascinated by the item in Lonell's hand. Pallo stretched out to touch it and gasped as he felt the smoothness. Lonell handed it over and the knapper stroked the glassy substance reverently. Kadell held out his hand and took it, feeling the edge which, although it had not been worked, was still sharp. He looked up in wonder and his eyes rested on Tendo, who was now feeling a little foolish. Pallo was also watching the expression on the young man's face.

'Don't worry, Tendo. I wouldn't have recognised the worth of this if it were wrapped up in a plain grey stone covering. It is a lesson that all knappers are taught but we tend to forget: never judge a stone by the part you can see - anything can be hidden in the middle, both good and bad.'

He turned his head to peer at Lonell.

'But what is it? I've never seen a stone like this.'

'They call it the Death Stone and it comes from a land far towards Sun Wake, much further than we went. We obtained it from a people who had traded for it themselves - they really wanted our salt! No one knows exactly what it is, but when it is worked, the edges are sharper than anything we have seen before.'

Valon could not keep quiet any longer.

'They had knives, spears and arrow heads made of it and, although it breaks easier than flint, the sharpness cuts through anything.'

'Yes, it is extraordinary.' Lonell was trying to remain calmer than Valon but even he could not keep the excitement out of his voice as he talked about the Death Stone. 'They showed us how to work it, although we could not do it properly. I'm sure you will be able to, Pallo. They also gave us an antler tool to use.'

'You have to use an antler to flake off the very fine slithers,' Lonell explained, seeing the confusion on Pallo's face. 'It will break if you use stone. Valon and I will show you what we know. We brought enough to make many weapons and there's wood in the store for shafts and handles.'

'I wish we had bows like the White Ones',' said Tendo, a frown lining his forehead.

'We do have one,' said Valon, looking at Lonell.

'So we do,' replied his friend, recalling the cave on the beach.

'If we can get to it ...' Kadell thought out loud, aware that Lonell had hidden one down there before Sim's escape.

'But how will I get to work on the Death Stone. There's always someone watching us. We've been lucky to have this time.'

'Does someone stay in the cave overnight?' asked Lonell.

'No, but they are usually here until the darkness is complete,' answered Kadell. 'And then they look in on us every now and then, watching to see if we are doing anything.'

Lonell thought deeply for a moment, his eyes drawn to the entrance of the White Cave across the crevice. Then he looked around and noticed one of the small, natural inlets into the side of the cave.

'Look over there,' he nodded in its direction. 'If we covered that with skins at night, Pallo could sit and work in there with some candles. We'll have to find a way to hold the skins in place.'

'Yes, but what about the noise.'

Valon thought for a while.

'I think Lonell and I will have to develop terrible coughs that we've brought back with us. We could cover the sound if we cough all night.'

'Yes, and if Saretta thinks you are both ill, she may not observe you so closely. In fact, the White Ones may want to stay away if they think they might start coughing too,' contributed Tendo.

'Go! Quickly!' Kadell said suddenly to Tendo and Pallo.

Mila had signalled that there was movement outside the cave. They hurried away and Kadell scrambled to his feet but, leaning over the two returned travellers, he ordered them to cough as Tordano walked through the entrance.

The show put on by the two conspirators was impressive. If other members of the tribe wondered why the engrossing meeting had broken up so suddenly and two of them had suddenly begun to be racked by painful coughing, nothing was said. However, Lonell worried that Tordano could not fail to notice the shift in the energy of the cave; the atmosphere had altered. It was subtle but there was no doubting that something was changing. He saw the Guardian peer around him suspiciously but all that he could see of any difference was Kadell leaning over the two men who had just returned and they appeared to be ill, from the noise coming from them. Hopefully, Lonell thought, he would think that what he had noticed was the tribe's fear that the two men had brought back a terrible sickness.

'What is wrong, Kadell? Are they ill?' Tordano called out, loathe to go any nearer.

'I think so,' he replied. 'Could Lexana come and see them, please?' he asked politely.

Lonell could see that Tordano was thinking desperately. It was clear that he was trying to work out a way in which none of the White Cave would have to come into contact with the unknown illness. Everyone was aware that sickness had been known to wipe out entire tribes and since Lonell and Valon had returned from a place that was unknown to him, Tordano was desperate to keep himself safe. In order to do that, he would have to make sure that no one from his cave came into contact with the sick men. His eyes came to rest on Endorina.

'She can treat them. If she needs any healing potions or plants, she can shout over to Lexana. Someone will leave them on the ledge for her to collect.'

'But Saretta has forbidden Endorina to practise her healing,' said Kadell, his face betraying no emotion.

'I am sure she will agree to it under these circumstances.' Tordano glared at Kadell, hating the insolence of the man who was no longer the Leader. 'I shall now go and report this ... to the High Priestess.'

He tried to retain his composure as he turned his back on them and stalked off around the ledge until disappearing behind the heavy drapes of the White Cave.

Endorina hobbled over to where the two men lay prostrate on the floor, pain and worry etched into her skin. She bent over Valon who opened his eyes, stopped coughing and winked at her. Not knowing whether to laugh or hit him, she looked over at Lonell who was propped up on one arm, grinning at her. Instead, it was Kadell who received the full force of her anger, although conducted in a whisper.

'That was a dreadful thing to do, Kadell. I was desperately worried. Why are you doing this?'

'It will be extremely helpful if they' - he nodded his head in the direction of the other cave - 'keep away from us for a while. Actually, we were only thinking about covering up some noise but if they are too worried to come in here, that's better for everyone. Maybe they'll leave us alone for a while. You must help us,' he begged.

'No doubt you'll tell me what it is all about one day.'

She gave Kadell a sour look but sat down beside the men and pretended to be looking at them carefully.

'It's amazing,' thought Lonell, as he watched her. 'Like Kadell she's feeling better, stronger because there is a plan, even though she doesn't know anything about it.'

He had seen a flicker of excitement on her face although she had the sense to mask it quickly. He followed her eyes as she looked around the cave and could see that even those who were unaware of what was taking place appeared more animated. She pushed herself to her feet, no pain now in her movement, only hope. She made her way to the entrance, aware that all eyes were on her, and followed the ledge round to the White Cave where she slapped her hand against the skin curtain. Almost immediately, Tordano emerged.

'Go back', he said, his hands shooing her away. 'I told you to call over, not to come close.'

'But it's really serious,' sobbed Endorina, enjoying her pretence. 'If Lexana doesn't give me the healing plants, it could spread throughout the cave. I have heard of a sickness like this. I was told it was the end of a people.'

She fell on her knees and made a grab at Tordano's hand.

'Go back to the cave!' he shrieked in terror, pushing her away. 'Do not come here again! What you need will be put outside for you.'

Endorina picked herself up and, head bowed, followed the path around to her own cave, where she struggled to hold back the laughter. A murmur erupted around the cave, silenced immediately by Kadell who waved his hands in the air to quieten everyone. No words needed to be spoken. It was now obvious to all that there was a plan, that they must play along with this pretence that had been thrust upon them almost by chance. It was a surprisingly long time before Tordano reluctantly left the safety of the White Cave and left a small package half way along the ledge. Tendo went to collect it, his face and manner suitably disturbed.

The Healer looked inside. She took the package over to where Lonell and Valon were lying. Lonell thought she looked pleased, and a little guilty.

'Lexana has given us the best treatments,' she said.

She unwrapped a small pouch of the sweet smelling plant that bore the small white flowers in the warm season which was one of the best relaxants that could be found, and another bigger bag filled with large dried leaves. She held it out to Lonell, trying to remember for she had seen it before. She racked her brain and suddenly recalled the tall, deep red flowers that were so hard to find.

'Blood-spike, yes, that was the name,' she said out loud.

It was the lowest, longer leaves that were picked, that grew out from the woody root and it was a marvel for relieving coughs. The next package she did not even have to unwrap fully as the smell of wild garlic filled the air when she took the first layer of leaves away.

'These are quite fresh,' she said. 'They will make wonderful poultices,' and put her hand on her chest as though imagining the soothing effect it would have.

The last item was a small skin bag which held a clam shell, tied together with the narrow tendrils of the Cord Plant. Endorina removed the ties and opened it to reveal a piece of honey comb, its thick, yellow sweetness oozing out. Lonell was touched; like

Endorina, he realised that this had no doubt come from Lexana's own ration but she had kept it for healing, knowing that someone would have a greater need for it than she.

Lonell was surprised that the lady had not come out herself but then, he realised, she had probably not been allowed to. He felt sorry for Lexana - she was a decent person who had done her best for those she thought were suffering. If she had become High Priestess, the tribe would still be a happy place to live. He watched as Endorina went over to the hearth to put the water on to heat, pretending to prepare the soothing tea, for she did not know if they were being watched. Then she went back to where the two men were still lying, calmly resting and coughing every now and then for effect. She moved Pallo out of the way for he had returned and was talking quietly to Lonell. Calmly, she took a stone and laid the garlic on top. It was Lonell who realised what was about to happen.

'If you think you are going to put any of that evil-smelling plant on me, you can forget it,' he hissed and Valon, beside him, agreed whole-heartedly.

'Now, what would happen if one of them came into the cave and did not smell garlic?' she asked, smiling happily at him. 'I regret that I must put some on each of you.'

'You aren't sorry. Of that I'm certain. In fact you're enjoying this,' he growled. 'Wait! You can put some on a bit of hide - you do not have to put it on us!'

The Healer pretended to be very reluctant to do this but eventually gave in to the two complaining men.

'I suppose I have now taken my revenge for the shock you gave me earlier,' she said, as she walked away, a bounce in her step.

Lonell sat up, his back against the wall and stared out at his people. His eyes kept being drawn to the white skin curtain that covered the opposite cave. He tried to think about the individuals of the tribe, mulling their characteristics over in his head, trying to work out who could have killed the Guardian. It was not enough to wonder who wanted to see him returned to the earth - almost everyone was guilty of that and most with good reason. However, he was unable to concentrate. Every few moments, his eyes returned to the White Cave. He shook his head with annoyance and frustration until he heard a voice.

'Why do you ignore what you know? You are searching in the wrong place.'

Lonell swivelled round to see who had spoken the words in his ear but knew he would see no one.

They were the same words, *'You are searching in the wrong place,'* that he had heard inside his head ever since they left the cave in the mountains but he had not understood them until this moment. Suddenly he knew the meaning. He wanted to jump up and shout with relief but he had to stay calm and quiet. He grabbed Valon's arm.

'The answer is in the White Cave,' he said, excitement mounting in his voice, but his friend looked back at him, blankly.

'That's what the skull told me. It said I was looking in the wrong place. And where have I been looking for the answer to Narthan's death?'

Valon squinted at his friend.

'You've been wondering about everyone in the cave, asking who had a reason to kill him?' he answered, his voice full of doubt.

'Yes, that's exactly what I've been doing and I've been thinking all wrong.'

'Well, where else should you be looking?' asked Valon.

'There!' said Lonell. 'Over there!' His eyes were glued to the gleaming hide that hid the White Cave from view. 'That's where the answer lies, not here!'

Too Long To Die

Chapter Twenty One

Lonell rolled onto his back, his mind racing.

'Are you saying they know who killed the Guardian?' asked Valon. 'If they do, that means they've known from the beginning and ...' his voice trailed off.

He looked at Lonell, his face flushed with anger.

'Yes, I believe they've known all the time and Saretta was willing to sacrifice Sim, despite that. She was fully aware that she would be putting to death a man who had done nothing wrong. But, remember, she always wanted it to be me.'

Valon's hand moved upwards and Lonell saw him put his two fingers to his brow in an attempt to protect himself from the evil that controlled his tribe.

'But why? None of this makes any sense. Do you think she killed him? I always thought Narthan was her favourite.'

'I'm not saying she killed him, although ... '

A cough rang out from Davoril who had been given the task to watch for movement from the other cave. Lonell and Valon began to display their 'symptoms' once more and a reluctant Tordano edged round the side of the entrance. In his right hand he held two spears and in his left, two knives. He placed them carefully on the ground.

'I bring an order from our High Priestess,' he cleared his throat nervously.

'Oh, Tordano,' Endorina's voice rang out, full of false sympathy. 'Is that a cough? Let me look at you.'

It gave her great pleasure to see his discomfort, although she knew

Too Long To Die

it was wrong.

'No, stay away. Do not come any closer. I have no cough,' he tried to convince himself, taking a step backwards. 'Listen, Lonell and Valon must leave the cave, now, and they must stay away until the sickness has left them.'

'Where can they go?' asked Kadell.

'That is not our concern but they must leave our lands and any other person who is taken with the sickness must also depart.'

'So you would just leave them to return to the earth alone, with no help?'

Tordano shuffled his feet uncomfortably and looked round at the entrance to the White Cave. There was no one there to help him deal with this situation.

'They can take what provisions they need but they must go now, before they pass it on to others.'

There was a moment's silence broken by a sudden cough. However, it did not come from where Lonell and Valon were lying. They looked over and saw Pallo doubled over, clutching his throat. Endorina took the hint and rushed over to him.

'Oh, Pallo, no. You have the cough too. You will need some healing.' Her words sounded strained even to her but Tordano, in his fear, did not notice.

'He must go with the other two. You have enough healing plants to treat them all before they leave.' Tordano's eyes scanned the people in the cave. 'Surely you can now see it is necessary or more of you will be taken by the sickness. There is no more to be said! I shall return soon to check that they have departed,' and with this, he scuttled back along the ledge and in through the white curtain.

The cave burst into hushed action. Kadell congratulated Pallo on his quick thinking. Tendo left the cave and came back shortly with the package that he had made up earlier in the day.

Too Long To Die

'This should give you enough firewood to last for tonight,' he said in a clear voice. 'You will have to gather your own from there on. Where will you go?'

'We shall return to the forest which will provide us with food and shelter,' Lonell said weakly, and then mouthed 'Sands' at Kadell who dipped his head slightly to acknowledge the message.

Ample food and water was loaded for them and Lonell and Valon found themselves, once again, with a heavy pack on their back. Each of them held a spear and a knife and Pallo bore the large bundle of 'firewood' in front of him. They made a show of bidding everyone farewell from a distance, coughing from time to time, and left the cave with promises to return when they were better.

The Outlander guarding the path tried to stop them, but when the three men began to cough and hold their chests, the startled man stood back and put his hands in front of his face, as though to protect himself. They crossed the High Pasture, making noise and coughing, aware that the Outlanders would be listening and watching so as to know which route they had taken and therefore avoid it for the foreseeable future. Lonell was sure that Tordano would tell the other White Ones that they were most unlikely to ever be seen again.

When far enough away, they circled back quietly, not knowing where the Outlanders might be but hoping they would have retreated to their camp. They took the circuitous route that Lonell had followed when he guided Sim to the cave on the beach. It was hard to believe that Sim's escape had taken place so recently - so much had happened since then and, most of it, bad. Pallo did not know where they were going so they reassured him that they had a place to stay. He expected to have a long walk ahead of him and was astonished when they dropped down to the beach and, shortly afterwards, were safely concealed in a comfortable, if rather damp, cave.

No one had been inside since Sim's departure and he had left it immaculately tidy so all they had to do was sweep out some sand that had blown in, although there was very little due to the shape of the entrance and the skin that was draped over it. They quickly built a fire and, since they knew that no one would come near to the beach this late in the day, they could leave the drape pulled back to let the smoke out. They lit some candles, put down their bed skins and opened up the packs of food to see what had been provided for them. They were surprised to find not only the usual dried food but acorn patties, fruits and, best of all, a bag of goat stew, ready to be strung up over the hearth to heat.

They talked long into the night. Pallo had known nothing of this cave so they explained how it had been prepared and used for Sim's escape. Lonell also showed him the bow which he kept there, together with some arrows and the knapper decided that the first things he would make from the Death Stone would be arrow heads for use with this bow.

'I have to admit, I didn't expect to be sleeping here tonight,' said Lonell, feeling more cheerful than he would have expected.

'It's strange how events have led us to be isolated here when we needed to be alone to make the weapons. It was clever of you to pretend to be sick too, Pallo, so that you would be sent away with us,' Valon smiled at the other man.

Pallo laughed.

'There was nothing clever about it on my part. Lonell had the idea and we discussed it before Tordano returned. We hoped they would exile us from the cave. Now we can work on those rocks you brought back with no worry!'

He rubbed his hands together in glee.

'Except for the Outlanders. They could come round here at any time. We'll have to be careful,' warned Lonell.

'No, we're lucky. We couldn't be hiding in a better place. One thing we've learnt about them is their fear of the water,' said Pallo. 'They never even wash,' he wrinkled up his nose in disgust, 'and they won't go anywhere near the Salt Water.'

'So, unless they see us from the cliff tops, we're safe,' said Lonell, thoughfully.

'Well, your plan is not perfect, Lonell,' said Valon. 'We should have got some of the girls to cough as well. It will be a bit lonely down here on the Sands, just the three of us!'

'Trust you to find something to complain about! You'll just have to make up for the time you've wasted when we 'recover'!'

'May I see the stone?' Pallo interrupted the friends' banter, trying to keep the impatience out of his voice.

'Wouldn't it be better to leave it until we have the light in the morning?' Valon said, but Lonell had seen Pallo's face and realised that the knapper was desperate to touch the stone again. There was almost a physical connection, Lonell thought, between Pallo and stone. His need to examine and find out about a new material was the same as Lonell's need to be able to think and work things out. To say to Pallo that he could not see the stone until Sun Wake would be the same as telling Lonell not to think during that time.

He wondered briefly why each man was drawn to a different path; was he born that way or did the people around him influence him, and did he have any choice? He would have to give that some consideration but, in the meantime, he jumped up and fetched the bundle of wood. He put an old skin on the ground and laid the wood down. As he cut the cord that held the bundle together, the pieces fell apart and the package within them was revealed. Pallo opened it carefully, his long, slim body bent over the pieces. Lonell noticed the reverence the knapper paid to the large, grey nodules as he lifted them out and studied them one carefully, one by one.

'It is remarkable,' said Pallo, holding one piece in his left hand and running his right hand over it, 'how even a rock tries to protect itself.'

'Protect itself?' asked Valon, a bemused frown lining his forehead. 'What do you mean, Pallo?'

The older man looked at him.

'Birds and animals take on the colouring of their surrounding so that their enemies won't be able to see them. Some, like the fox, even change colour when it snows.'

The other two nodded their agreement, still unsure where he was taking them with his thoughts.

'Now, look at this. Who would be bothered to pick up a boring lump of stone like this? It's impossible to tell that this holds a treasure possibly as exciting as the discovery of Sun Stone, and yet most men would walk by it without a second glance. Nature has given it a way to protect itself!'

While Pallo had been talking, Lonell had picked up a nodule himself and was feeling it. The strong sense of death and despair that he had experienced when he first touched the stone had diminished. The stones that were still completely covered with their grey layer had no effect on him and where the black obsidian was exposed, all that remained was a slight dizziness and sickness deep in his stomach. He wondered if Pallo would have a reaction, given his strong bond with the material.

'I don't imagine that it'll be as important as Sun Stone but I'm sure that we - or, rather, you - will be able to create weapons with the finest of blades. I also think that it could have a use in more delicate situations, like sewing.'

'And skinning and preparing hides. Can you imagine how much faster that could be done with a really sharp knife?' added Valon, beginning to realise the practical advantages that this could bring to other areas, not just weaponry. 'Pallo is right; this could be really exciting.'

'But, for now, we must concentrate on making weapons,' Lonell said, in an attempt to prevent them all from getting carried away on a tide of creativity. 'I think we should put them away now and get some sleep. Tomorrow, the first thing we must do is find shells for eye coverings.'

'Eye coverings?' questioned Pallo.

'We'll show you tomorrow. And I have thought of a method of holding them in place that is far better than the glue that Serin used.'

'Who's Serin?' asked Pallo, trying to make sense of what he was being told.

'He was the stone worker who showed us how to knap the Death Stone - he was brilliant,' replied Valon, already wrapped in his bed skins.

Lonell lay awake long after the other two were snoring gently, his mind going over what Pallo had said about nature disguising what was inside. Until that moment he had assumed that the person responsible for Narthan's death would be someone he could imagine as a killer. Perhaps he was wrong; maybe 'looking in the wrong place' meant he was looking at the wrong people.

He tried to make a mental list of those that he thought would never harm anyone: both the healers, Lexana and Endorina - they spent their lives caring for people - surely they would not take a life, but Narthan had banned Endorina from healing and perhaps he had done the same to Lexana in the White Cave. Would that be enough to kill for? Or if he had threatened someone they loved? Then, yes, they could. Lonell was surprised that he was so certain.

Talia and Minaya. He really didn't know anything about Talia. She seemed harmless but who knew what was going on in that silent head. But who would have helped her? She was always alone. Then Minaya. So sweet and so sad, but inoffensive. Was there someone left that she loved enough to protect by killing Narthan? Lonell didn't know, but maybe. What was she hiding on the inside?

Kadella, Ancient Pel, Tordano. Kadella looked after people and was kind and sweet. But he had seen her anger and if someone had threatened Kadell - possibly. Ancient Pel - he was surely too old now and usually by himself, but maybe he felt a hidden bond with someone he would kill to protect. Tordano - until recently, Lonell would have said, no. But now, he had shown more anger but perhaps it was fear. Lonell had always thought well of him before and he could see no reason why he would kill Narthan.

The list went on and, as he finally drifted into sleep, Lonell realised two things. Firstly, how little he really knew about the other members of his tribe and, secondly, he was certain that any one of them could have returned Narthan to the earth to protect a person they loved.

The weather was perfect when they awoke. Not the beautiful azure sky that Lonell loved so much, but a grey miserable day with the rain beating down on the surface of the crashing Salt Water and gusts of wind blowing intermittently along the sands. Unlike the coastline that lay closer to the home of the Pescovari where the beach stretched out for miles before sinking under the water, the land in front of the small cave where they were staying almost disappeared when the tide came in. For that reason it was not often visited by the tribe, even at the best of times, and the weather ensured that none of the White Ones would venture down there today. In fact, Lonell was almost certain that they would remain inside their cave all day, using the wind and rain as an excuse but, truthfully, so they could avoid the tribe, any of whom might have been affected by the feared sickness. Lonell doubted that the Outlanders would go anywhere near the cliffs with the wind blowing in so hard but, even so, he knew they must keep a watch out for them.

Valon and Lonell left Pallo to prepare for work. The knapper removed the skin that covered the entrance, put down the old hide on the floor in the natural light and took out all his implements. Pallo never let his precious tools out of his sight and kept them in the cave which had made it very easy to roll them in his bed skins when they left the cave. The two other men swam briefly in the salty water, buffeted by high waves, and then they searched the beach. The rough sea, which had battered the shore during the night, had deposited all manner of debris on the land including a plethora of shells of every shape and size. The men sorted through them and were soon rewarded with a selection of suitable eye protectors which they took inside to prepare.

'Each of these,' Lonell pointed to the six best shells, 'needs a round hole in the centre about the size of ....' he looked around him and saw a tiny pebble on the floor: 'this.' He held the small white stone up so that Pallo could see it clearly.

At that point Valon added, 'They need holes on either side as well.' He showed them where.

'We can then tie them - one short cord between the two shells to go over the top of the nose and then a cord on each side which we can knot behind our heads to secure them in place.'

'Good idea, Valon,' exclaimed Lonell, bringing out a tangle of cord that was stored at the rear of the cave.

'You don't have to seem so surprised,' retorted his friend, vainly attempting to feign indignation. 'I do have some good ideas; not many, I admit, but some!'

The sound of their laughter was drowned out by a thunderous crash. All three men ran outside to see an entire tree which had been deposited onto the beach close to their cave.

'Sacred Stones!' cursed Lonell. 'That's not good. As soon as the weather is better, everyone will come down here to have a look at that. They're bound to discover us.'

'Can we get it back into the water?' asked Pallo.

'If we remove this,' said Valon, pointing to the one branch that stuck out from the trunk, 'then we should be able to roll it. Luckily, all the other pieces have already been broken off. It'll be heavy but between the three of us, I think we could manage it. But first we have to cut this branch off.'

Lonell had disappeared back into the cave and came out brandishing three knives of various sizes.

'How many weapons do you keep in there?' asked Pallo, astonished. 'Were you planning to go to war?'

The uncertainty in his voice showed that the question was not entirely frivolous.

'I used to come down here when I wanted to be alone and I'd spend my time working on tools as I sat and thought and enjoyed the peace. I regret that they're not as good as you would make, but it's lucky that I didn't just sit and gaze at the water!' replied Lonell, handing them out.

Pallo spent the morning hacking at the wood and grumbling, clearly upset that he had to waste precious time on this when he could have been learning how to work the Death Stone. The sweat dripped down the three men and they were beginning to feel the hunger of the midday when they finally removed the offending tree limb and carried it to the water to be pulled away as the tide went out. Next they had to roll the enormous trunk in the same direction.

When the tree had come crashing down it had embedded itself in the sand and pebbles so the most difficult part of moving the gigantic log was to free it from where it was buried. After that it was a case of getting the initial momentum and then keeping it rolling until it splashed into the water. It took all their strength but eventually the tree was released and it rolled over to show a split that stretched up its centre. The giant fir tree had been dying from the inside out for many years and the trunk was quite hollow.

'I remember this tree,' exclaimed Valon. 'It grew way up the coast. It used to hang over the cliff and we hid things inside it when we were children.'

'Yes, you're right,' said Lonell. 'I remember once, when I was very young, I wanted to hide and I tried to get inside this tree. But the gap was too small and I got my tunic caught and tore a great hole in it. My mother was furious - she wouldn't let me out for days.'

He turned back to the tree.

'But I'm sorry to see the storm has finally taken you, old friend.', he said, patting the trunk. 'What are you doing, Valon?'

The blond man was peering into the gaping hole and inserted his arm to feel around.

'I wondered if someone had hidden something in there recently and I thought I saw something ... Arrh, there is something. I can touch it but I can't hold on to it.'

'Let me,' offered Pallo, making no effort to hide the fact that he was desperate to finish this job so he could get back to the stones.

He pushed his arm in, up to the shoulder, and with a satisfied grunt, brought out a leather bag. It had been beautifully prepared; patterns decorated its surface and its softness was still noticeable despite the time it had obviously spent inside the trunk.

'There must be something very important in a bag like this,' said Valon, his excitement reminiscent of when he had played childhood games. 'Let's have a look.'

He shook the bag but could not hear anything, against the wind and rain. Then he released the tie that held it closed and pulled from it a roll of yet more fine leather. He put it on the ground and unrolled it gently, revealing the precious contents: the tiniest mummified body of a human baby lay looking out through its empty eye sockets and Lonell had the strangest feeling that it was staring at him.

Chapter Twenty Two

Valon and Pallo jumped back, frantically touching their brows for protection.

Lonell looked down at the delicate features covered by the thinnest, brown, leathery skin and wondered how they all knew instinctively that this was human for it was far too small. Of course, animal corpses and skeletons were seen all the time: when man killed for food they stripped the meat off carcasses and they frequently came across the bones of creatures that had died natural deaths in the wild or had fallen prey to other animals. What the men and women of the Pescovari saw rarely, and then only briefly, were the bodies and bones of other humans for, when someone died, the Enlightened Ones removed the bodies rapidly and dealt with them. Yet, they all knew that this was, without doubt, the remains of the tiniest baby.

Lonell had never before questioned what happened to the remains of someone who died. They returned to the earth; it was quite simple and it had never really concerned him. He knew that bodies were buried or placed in the Salt Water. Anyone who had seen a dead body knew that the essence of that person was no longer present once they had died. Lonell believed that somehow his body would once more become part of nature when his spirit had moved on. It was this that upset him; not that the child was dead but that, by wrapping it in a skin and hiding it in a tree, the remains had not returned to the earth.

Still squatting, he turned to the others, the lightweight bundle in his hands.

'I think I should return it to the earth,' he said, over the noise of the elements, the statement almost a question, and he waited for their reaction.

When he saw their eagerly nodded agreement and their relief that he would do it, he stood up and carried the leather wrap to the edge of the Salt Water where he knelt, insensible to the wet as it soaked through his leggings, and let the minute body fall into the waves. He watched as the miniature corpse sank to the bottom and was dragged away by the briny, swirling water.

He turned and walked back to the others.

'He has now returned to the earth, as is right.'

There was a moment's silence. Then he retrieved the leather bag, pushed the wrappings inside and took it back to the cave. Lonell saw Pallo watching him, could feel his eyes on his back and he was aware that the knapper wished he had thrown the leather away, but he hoped the items might help him unravel the mystery of the death. Lonell knew without a doubt that something quite extraordinary must have happened for someone to put the baby in a bag and hide it in a tree.

So many questions raced through his mind. Why was the child not dealt with in the customary way? Who was the mother? Why was the corpse so small? His superstitious mind had prevented him from examining the body as carefully as he would have liked but it had had all the appearance of being empty, and why was it not just bones like all the animal remains they frequently saw?

As if there had been a sign, all three men turned back to the tree without a word, determined to rid themselves of it as fast as they could. No one considered keeping some of it as firewood; they never wanted to see it again. They pushed with all their strength, gritting their teeth and grunting with the effort, glad to be doing some physical work to take their minds off what they had just seen. After a while, they succeeded in rolling the trunk and kept going until it was in the water.

'It's not being taken,' said Valon, as the huge log lay unmoving on the rocky bottom. Lonell saw the more slender end sway slightly.

'Since I'm already wet,' he sighed, 'I'll take it further out. I should be able to manage - the wood will float when there's enough depth.'

He removed his tunic and leggings and plunged, naked, into the sea, breaking through the waves, and he took hold of the log.

'Push,' he ordered the others and he pulled with all his might,

It took a few attempts, while the great white birds of the Salt Water seemed to laugh at them as they screeched overhead. Suddenly the trunk surged towards him, pushing him over. He surfaced, spluttering, and guided the now floating tree further out to sea. Finally it was torn out of his hand and taken away on a strong current, down the coastline and away from their lands. Lonell clambered out of the churning water and joined his friends who were making an effort to disguise the signs of the human activity on the sand, although they knew that the weather would take care of most of it. He stood in front of them, dripping onto the beach but, to be fair, he was not a great deal wetter than they were. The constant rain had penetrated every inch of clothing and their long hair was as completely soaked as Lonell's.

'Let's light a fire and try to dry off our clothes while we have something to eat. Then we can finally return to the work we were supposed to be doing this morning,' suggested Lonell, knowing that they needed something else to think about.

With a large fire blazing in the centre of the cave, the men were soon warmed as they huddled around the hide, on which were laid the broken pieces from the nodule that they had practiced on back with the Estrondi. Pallo had set out a variety of his own tools and beside them lay the antler horn which they had been given. Lonell and Valon had told Pallo everything that they had been taught and Valon showed him the technique with the antler that Serin had employed when working the black, shiny material. There was nothing more they could do. It was now down to the knapper to work out his own method and get the best out of the obsidian. Valon sat beside him, watching the expert, fascinated by way he was able to feel the stone, to understand how to get the best out of it, even though he had never worked with it before.

Lonell found it difficult to stay within the airless confines of the cave, with the tap, tapping as Pallo worked and the hot fire suffocating him. He fretted at the enforced inactivity and slid outside, the cold wind and rain once again hitting his body and bringing sharpness back to his mind. He walked back and forth along the beach trying to concentrate. He knew that the discovery of the tiny body had been important, even vital, in his search for the truth but the link with facts he already knew continued to evade his grasp. Time passed as he walked up and down, not feeling the cold, forgetful even of the danger of being seen. His mind far away, he collected fish that had been thrown up out of the threshing water onto the beach, where they had spent their last minutes on earth, struggling to breathe.

His mind turned over everything that had happened recently: how did this baby fit in? Or was it nothing to do with the death of Narthan? It might not even be a child of the Pescovari but, as much as he tried to tell himself that the two events were unconnected, he knew they were.

'An occurrence took place of which you are unaware.'

Those were the rather stilted words he had heard from the skull and Lonell was certain that he had, by pure chance, stumbled across the evidence of that 'occurrence'. Now he had to make it fit in with the other facts he knew and, therein, lay the problem. Why could he not see the connection? He stared up at the flint-grey sky, hoping for inspiration but nothing came. Every time he had the answer to a question, another slid into his mind. Finally, he gave up and returned to the cave, carrying the fish he had collected, which he left just outside the entrance.

As he stepped inside, he cursed. A slither of obsidian sliced through the thick skin of his foot, evidence of its incredible sharpness. This was the reason that knappers were not allowed to work in caves; the shards that chipped off were a danger to everyone. However they did not have the luxury of extra space. Even if the weather had been pleasant, they would not have dared let Pallo work outside for fear of discovery. He sat down, sighing, and picked out the slice of stone. Valon came over to check on his friend.

'Sacred Stones, you're frozen through, Lonell,' he exclaimed.

'I'm fine,' he replied, although he had just started to feel the cold penetrate his bones. 'We must remember to wear foot coverings at all times. That is really sharp.'

He held up the slither and marvelled at its fineness. Black, shiny, blood, death all around. The tapping echoed round the small cave and Lonell shivered. Valon was by his side with a thick skin, wrapping him in it but he felt nothing.

'This will keep you warm while your clothes are drying,' said Valon. 'What have you been doing out there?' he asked and received no answer.

Lonell had slipped into the Dreamer's walking sleep, as Valon had called it. The man's mind was occupied somewhere else and he was unaware of activity around him but his body continued to function. It was never any use discussing things of importance with him in this state; he would answer but later he would have no recollection of anything that had happened. Nevertheless, Valon sat beside him and watched his friend absent-mindedly stroking the hair of the skin draped round him and decided to talk about the day's find in the hope of bringing Lonell out of his 'dream'.

'I have seen babies when they have just been born and I'm surprised at the size of their bones. I know babies are small but they don't look that tiny. I would have expected the body to be bigger.'

There was no answer from his friend but Pallo looked up briefly from his work.

'Some babies are smaller than others,' he said. 'When I was away trading for Sun Stones once, a woman gave birth to two children at the same time.'

'Two at the same time?' asked Valon. 'I've never heard of that.'

'They told me that women have been known to have up to four at once but it is rare for either mother or babies to survive that. Anyway, the babies were much smaller than any I'd seen before - I suppose there was no room inside the mother for them to be the size of single babies.'

Pallo stopped for a moment, recalling the excitement of the tribe he had been staying with.

'But they were still much bigger than the one in the tree,' he added.

He touched his forehead again. It had been an unnerving discovery and he wished he could forget what he had seen. Tap, tap, tap. Concentrate on the stone.

'Perhaps, this was one of four,' offered Valon, hopefully. 'Maybe the others survived and just one returned to the earth.'

'We'll never know so there's no point in worrying about it,' said Pallo, shrugging his shoulders, clearly hoping the others would forget the incident too.

'No!'

Valon and Pallo jumped as Lonell's shout echoed off the cave walls.

'I think I know! I need to ask Endorina …' His voice trailed off again.

'What, Lonell? You can't leave it like that. Tell us what you're thinking,' begged Valon.

Lonell's eyes rested on his friend and came back into focus, as though released from a spell. He shivered, noticing the dampness in the air and he pulled the thick wolf skin closer.

'I may not be right ...,' he started. 'But I was thinking ... we all know women who have started to bleed before a baby is ready to be born. I don't know how a baby grows inside a woman, but maybe there's a time when the baby would be big enough to be properly formed but still too small to live. I need to ask Endorina; I'm sure she would know. If I'm right, then the baby we found may have been born early and not survived.'

'And does this help? Is it anything to do with Narthan's death?'

'I think there's a connection but I can't find it yet,' confessed Lonell.

He was aware that the tapping of stone had paused when Narthan's name was mentioned but it started up again almost immediately.

'Are you making any progress with the stone?' he called to Pallo, to change the subject.

'You should see what he's done, Lonell!' exclaimed Valon. 'This man's a genius! Come and have a look!'

'Let me put on some foot coverings first - I don't want to carve my feet up any more.'

They squatted down beside Pallo's work space and Lonell could see that he had already finished some pieces. To one side Pallo had pushed the broken, misshapen pieces that had obviously been produced when he started to learn how to work the Death Stone. On another side were three beautifully crafted arrow heads. Lonell picked one up and felt the edge to test its sharpness; the red drops that appeared on his thumb bore witness to the true cutting ability of the stone and he gasped in amazement. None of the three had ever seen any edge as keen as these.

'As you can see,' explained Pello, 'I've made each of these arrow heads of a different thickness. The edges are still as fine but we need to try them to see which works better, or which doesn't break as easily. Obviously, the thinner I can make them, the more blades I can get out of one stone. I'm now making a blade for a knife.'

He showed them a larger object, that gleamed black in the fire light, the edges thinned to an almost transparent dark grey.

'I'll make three of these and three spear heads in the same way. Then we must test them so that I know which to make more of. The larger pieces that are not as good can then be cut down for arrow heads so very little material will be wasted.'

'We can make knife handles from the branches that were wrapped around the stones,' suggested Valon.

'And, at the back of the cave are some spears. We can remove the blades attached now and replace them. When someone comes down with the drinking water, I must ask them if they can bring us some glue,' added Lonell.

If Pallo had heard he might have wondered how anyone would know where to bring them the water, but his thoughts were focused only on the stones in his hand.

'Thank you both,' he said to the two friends. 'If you had not found this, I would never have had the opportunity to work with such ... magnificent stone. I can't tell you how exciting this is for me. I'll be able to make the finest weapons and tools with it and, amazingly, it is so easy to work with. You have to be careful not to hit too hard or it will fracture but using the antler horn, it removes the harshness of the strike and just flakes off where you want it to.'

'You're being too modest, Pello,' Lonell put his hand on the knapper's shoulder. 'It isn't so easy. Remember, Valon and I tried and could do nothing with it. It's your skill that makes it easy for you.

Look, you've been working with it since we came in and you don't have a cut on you. I've touched one piece and cut myself and put a piece through my foot! You have a way with stone that is enviable.'

Lonell saw Pallo blush at the compliments. Most people just accepted that he had been working with stone all his life and so they expected him to be skilled. Lonell knew that it would give him great pleasure to have his ability praised and he hoped it would give him encouragement for the work ahead.

He shrugged off the skin he was wrapped in. His clothes were still slightly damp but were drying fast. Bending down to pick up the skin, he suddenly saw it with new eyes. It was Pallo's words about the coverings hiding what was inside that played on his mind. What if it were the other way round - that a wrong covering was put on to disguise the truth? He looked at the dark skin in his hand and remembered the body of Narthan wrapped in one very similar. It was like a flash of lightening hitting him: the skin wrap and the stone. 'Clever,' he thought. 'Clever, but rather insulting.'

He opened his mouth to speak but Valon touched him on the arm and held his hands to his mouth. In the silence, he could also hear the sound of someone stumbling down the beach, their feet crushing shells as they walked. Lonell quickly pulled up the skin that was still attached to the wall and he held it over the entrance. He winced as he thought of the fish that he had left piled up outside the cave and hoped that the rocks that jutted out, masking the entrance, would prevent them from being found.

Pallo very quietly pulled another small skin over his work place and they all sat hardly breathing, willing the person outside to keep walking past but their wishes went unheeded. The footsteps stopped and a weight fell against the hide covering.

'Come on, Lonell! Let us in. Do you know how bad the weather is out here?'

Too Long To Die

The voice was desperate and when Lonell pulled back the skin, Kadell and Tendo fell in through the gap. They headed straight to the fire and squatted down to warm themselves, dropping two full bladders of water and a bag by the wall. Tendo, who hadn't seen the cave before, quickly took in his surroundings.

'As far as I was concerned,' said Kadell, 'you could have gone without fresh water in this weather but my sister insisted we come! There's also some more food for you in the bag, although seeing the huge pile of fish at the door, I think you're managing quite well by yourselves.'

He grinned at the three men he had come to see.

'Why don't you take some back with you? There's plenty out there. It was all washed up by the storm. You can say you got it further up the coast. It's good to see you.'

'I can take some back in the bag,' said Tendo, 'because I'll be making my return by way of the High Pasture. If I am seen, they'll think I've been working down on that part of the beach or in the Salt Caves.'

Lonell looked first at Tendo and then at Kadell, his question written over his face.

'We come and go alone, in case we're being watched,' explained the Leader. 'I'll go back the longer way on this day and approach the cave from inland. They don't seem to stop people when they're alone, only when they are with others.'

Kadell added that no one had seen or heard from a White One since they had left the cave the day before and even the Outlanders had disappeared, presumably trying to keep dry. However, they were going to maintain their precautions on their trips to the beach cave. It was quite possible that they were being watched even though they could not see the Outlanders.

Kadell had news of the tribe; spirits were so much better now that there was a sense of hope again. In fact, he said, they would have to be careful; when the White Ones did finally realise that they would not all return to the earth due to the coughing sickness, Saretta might start to notice a change, so they would all have to be warned to act as though they still felt defeated.

Lonell told them about their day but he did not mention the tree or the grim discovery that they had made, aware that Valon and Pallo would be wondering why he was keeping it to himself. All the while Lonell could see Kadell peering around.

'Well, have you done any work on the stone?' the Leader demanded when he could bear the waiting no longer.

Pallo removed the top cover to reveal his handiwork. The two visitors stared in silence for a moment and both stretched out their hands at the same time.

'Be very careful,' said Lonell. 'It's very easy to cut yourself.'

He held up his thumb dramatically, and grinned. As if the tension had suddenly broken, they were all laughing and talking, marvelling over the pieces that Pallo had created. They discussed the testing of the blades and the making of weapons. Lonell asked Kadell to bring or send them down some glue. They made the adhesive from goats' hooves so, after a hunt, one of the jobs was to boil these down until a gelatinous lump was left. Lonell was aware that he could have made some from the brown algae that was so abundant in the area but he knew that once it had been boiled down it had to be kept for a time to build up the strength. Since he knew there was already an ample quantity of the glue up at their home cave and he wanted the best, he decided it would be better to wait until it could be delivered to them, even though it meant a delay in the production of working models. Tomorrow he would start collecting wood that had been thrown up onto the beach - there was bound to be some that would make good staves or could be cut down for arrow shafts, although the latter was tedious work. However, with only one bow available, they only had to make a few arrows.

The already limited daylight was failing when Kadell and Tendo departed, with a reminder to keep watching out for the Outlanders. Just before they left, Lonell had taken Kadell on one side and requested that he ask Endorina a question, which he promised to do, although he did not understand why the man should need such information.

They took out three beautifully cooked venison steaks and a plentiful supply of acorn cakes from the bag and filled it with fish, before the two men left the comfort of the warm cave to face the continuing deluge outside. They promised to return the next day with more supplies, glue and answers.

Too Long To Die

Chapter Twenty Three

The trio worked solidly for five days with rain and high winds battering the beach and cliffs almost continuously. The sound of crashing waves and debris carried on powerful gusts kept the men inside the cave for most of the time, the confinement eating away at Lonell's patience in his need to discover information. When he had nothing to do he paced up and down, six paces one way and six paces back, until the others could bear it no longer and made sure he was kept busy.

The tests conducted during a brief lull in the weather on the second day showed them the optimum thickness for each weapon. Once this was known, Pallo continued to fashion the obsidian blades as fast as he could. Valon and Lonell spent their time making the shafts of various sizes. They cut branches down to size, checking the weight and balance of the spears and maximising the handle comfort of the knives by using sand to smooth off the wood. Only short shafts were made for the spears which, although not ideal, would be far less likely to be discovered by the White Ones; hiding a full length spear would be near to impossible.

Lonell and Valon cut deep slots into the end of spear shafts and covered the blunt ends of glinting blades with the thick, mucous glue which was warming by the hearth. Protecting their fingers with pieces of hide, they pushed the blades into the slots and bound them round with cord. The difficulty was the fragility of the sharp blades but they soon discovered that when the blades did become chipped, the new edges created were still able to cut through even the toughest of material. It soon became a competition between the two friends, the desire to make the best, the most perfect, but Pallo refused to judge the results of their work.

They made covers to protect the spear blades when they were bundled together for transportation and, with a sense of regret, Lonell allowed his soft goat's fur to be cut up to make tiny caps to cover the each of the arrow heads. It was simple to make these coverings: the skin was cut in a tall triangular shape and then glued down one side. Valon came up with the idea of making a sheath out of stiff hide to cover the blades of the knives and they cut two slots into each sheath so that a person's belt could be threaded through it, thereby holding the weapon securely in place and with the blade protected.

Each of the three men now bore a lethal weapon on his belt but one night, after they had finished the hard work of the day, they removed their clothes and placed the knives on the ledge in the cave. Having braved the lashing rain to take a swim in the pounding waves of the Salt Water, they returned, refreshed, to the cave and realised that none of them knew which knife was theirs.

It was Pallo who came up with the novel idea of decorating the sheaths so they would always be able to recognise their own. Lonell, after much thought, drew an eye on his, which the others agreed was suitable because the Dreamer saw things differently to others. Valon chose a mountain goat and Pallo drew an antler, showing how attached he had become to the new tool. They cut fine lines into the hide with one of the sharp obsidian blades and then charcoal from the fire was rubbed into the cut which made the drawing stand out vividly. Finally some meat fat which had cooled hard was rubbed over the sheath which had the dual advantage of protecting the art work and making the whole item more waterproof.

As each new knife was created, a sheath was also made and, by the fifth day, they had a knife ready for every adult in the tribe. According to Kadell and Tendo, the Outlanders had not been seen since the three men had left the tribal cave, but whether it was due to the rain or the fear of sickness, no one knew. Regardless of the reason, it gave the two visitors the opportunity to smuggle back the arrows, bow and short shafted spears wrapped up in bundles of wood each day, with little danger of being caught. They had to remove the cord from the bow so that it became straight, in case they were spotted carrying the 'wood' but it was replaced once back at the cave. All that remained was to move the knives back, and Lonell kept a pair of spears and some knives in the beach cave, just in case they were needed.

The three men sat, listening out for the arrival of Kadell and Tendo on their final day in the beach cave. They had finished the work and the tension in the cave was growing, the waiting weighing down on them.

'Where are they?' fretted Lonell, beginning to pace. The visitors had appeared at more or less the same time on each of the previous days and they were late.

'They'll be here soon.' Valon tried to reassure his friend but he could not hide the concern in his voice.

Time passed agonisingly, their ears straining for some sound of human activity outside and Valon was on the point of leaving to look down the beach once more, when Kadell pushed his way past the hide that covered the doorway.

'Something's happening,' he said, not bothering to greet them. 'We heard loud voices this morning - an argument between Sarril and the Outlanders. We don't know what was being said because it was in their language but now the Outlanders are out in the rain and stopping everyone, taking their anger out on all of us.'

He moved his head and the light revealed a vivid, darkening bruise forming on his temple.

'So Sarril speaks their language,' mused Lonell. 'Perhaps they are his people. He's not Pescovari but I've never known where he came from.'

'Nor I,' agreed Kadell. 'But Tendo may not get here. He was carrying the food.'

The silence that filled the cave was heavy with dreadful imaginings of what they would do to Tendo if they found the contents of his bag. Suddenly the hide was pushed back once again and a breathless Tendo fell in through the entrance. He grinned at them as he regained his composure.

'That was close. I almost walked into one of them but luckily he was relieving himself so he couldn't run after me until he'd finished! I ran and hid until I was sure he'd gone but then I took the longer path to be certain he wasn't following me.'

He looked round at them all.

'Is everything ready?' he asked.

Lonell moved towards the recent arrival and put both hands on his shoulders, the relief clearly visible on his face. Then, as though embarrassed by this unexpected show of emotion, he cleared his throat and turned, pointing at Pallo who held their new knives in his slightly shaking hands. The atmosphere lightened instantly with the exclamations of pleasure from Kadell and Tendo. They were delighted with the ingenuity of the sheath and were invited to put their own mark on the hide. Kadell drew the two wavy lines of the Pescovari, together with a spear, and Tendo, after much thought, suddenly snorted loudly, picked up his knife and carefully cut the shape of his nose into the hide.

'I think you've started something here!' exclaimed Kadell, when the laughter subsided. 'Each person can have a sign which belongs only to them and they can put that on their knife.'

'It could be very useful,' Valon said, thinking like the tracker he was. 'If someone wants to show others the trail he has taken, he could leave his mark at intervals.'

'And in a hunt, a person can put their own mark on a kill they have made. It could stop all the arguing over who killed what animal,' added Tendo.

'I imagine we'll find all sorts of uses for these signs!'

Kadell grinned at the others, before his expression became serious once again, the responsibilities of leadership hanging over him.

'Now we have to talk about more urgent matters. You've finished making all the weapons. The time has come for your return to the cave.'

'How are we going to manage it?' asked Pallo, his voice full of the disappointed acceptance that his time working with the miraculous Death Stone had come to an end.

Lonell was eager to get back. Although Kadell had returned with Endorina's answer the day after the discovery of the tiny body, he still had many other questions that he needed to ask. Without those answers he could get no further in solving the puzzle that his mind dwelt on constantly.

'If you come to the High Pasture tomorrow when the sun is high, I shall make sure that Endorina is out there collecting her healing plants, even if it's still raining. She can look at you and agree that you're all fit to return to the cave. I thought that Tendo and I would take all the last weapons when we went back today but, with the Outlanders searching everyone, that's impossible.' As he spoke, Kadell stroked his ginger beard absentmindedly, deep in thought.

'Don't concern yourself with that,' said Lonell. 'We'll get them back to somewhere close to the cave.'

There was a pause.

'Can you bring Endorina earlier, after the morning meal?' he asked. Kadell nodded, like the others wondering what plan he had thought up. Tendo had opened his mouth to ask when Lonell held up his hand to silence him.

'Kadell, will you give me a few days before doing anything?' he asked. 'I'm close to working out the events that led to Narthan's death but I just need a little longer.'

'What does it matter? Once we've rid ourselves of them, it surely won't matter who killed him. He deserved it,' said Pallo, much to Lonell's concern.

He turned to Kadell.

'What are you planning to do?' he asked. 'Do you intend to exile all the Enlightened Ones? Surely, it's only Saretta who deserves to be forced to leave.'

'And what about Valt and Sarril? Even Tordano has become vicious recently,' added Tendo with a shrug of the shoulders.

'This is the problem. At the moment we don't know who's just following Saretta because they're frightened and don't see any other way, and those who actually agree with the way she is behaving and therefore think like she does. It's only the last group who must leave, not all of them, surely,' Lonell looked beseechingly at his Leader.

'What's going to happen if you find out that someone we love killed Narthan?' asked Valon quietly. 'Someone in our cave or Lexana? Or Minaya or Talia? They've done no harm to us. Will we exile them along with Saretta?'

'Lonell is correct,' said Kadell. 'That's why we need to know the truth before we take any action. Only then can we make the right decision.'

The others looked at him, a question on their faces.

'I know I'm the Leader but such a decision that affects the future of the whole tribe can't be taken by just one man. I will take into consideration the feelings of everyone and then I'll give my judgement.'

Too Long To Die

There was a silence as Kadell considered Valon's questions and he looked at Lonell.

'Do you think the killer may come from the White Cave, then? That it's not one of us?' he asked hopefully.

'I'm beginning to think they might,' replied Lonell, 'but I'm not yet certain. I need to talk to Endorina and then, somehow, I must have some time with Lexana. She's the only one there that I trust completely because she didn't betray us before.'

He did not add that he also liked her very much and that he was still finding it difficult to imagine her doing such a thing. He was sure that she was not involved; well, almost entirely sure, and he so wanted to be certain. He looked at the other men and realised they were all thinking the same, all hoping desperately that Lexana was innocent.

The meeting broke up with the agreement to meet early the next day on the High Pasture. Tendo and Kadell were sorry to hand back their knives but they knew they dared not return with them. So, reluctantly, they allowed them to be taken by Pallo and wrapped up with the rest. They bade the others a tense farewell, knowing that the events of the following day would be vital to the success of their plans. If anything were to go wrong - and, with Saretta's irrational behaviour, that was easily possible - disaster could come crashing down on the tribe.

After their departure, Lonell suggested a swim and they all headed out to the beach. The rain had finally stopped and the last diminishing gusts of winds were pushing the dark clouds over the horizon; the sight of the first blue sky for many days filled Lonell with a renewed sense of hope - the weather had looked after them so far.

The tide was out so they picked their way over the rocky terrain down to the sea. Lonell plunged in swiftly, gasping as he resurfaced. There had been a noticeable drop in the temperature over that last few days. Salt Water was never warm but, since the recent bad weather, there was an iciness to it which heralded the approach of the cold period. People would not be swimming here for much longer, he thought to himself, and even Mountain Water would soon become a necessity rather than a pleasure.

Lonell pulled himself out and saw that Valon and Pallo were already resting on a rock by the cliff face to dry in the gentle wind. It seemed warm, sitting in the pale, glimmering sunlight, after the chill of the water. He revelled in the peace and tranquillity of the scene, thinking of the difficulties he had to face before he could once more experience such calm, if he survived. His eye was caught by the glint of silver in the water and he watched a vast shoal of fish pass by. He wondered how many were there but his mind, which struggled with numbers greater than ten, could not begin to calculate the quantity and he soon gave up and, relaxing, just enjoyed the spectacle.

'What a shame we can't take some fish back to the cave,' he thought, but he did not want Saretta to know that they had been living down by the beach. If she found that out, she would no doubt order a search for the cave and he did not want anyone, other than the few who were already aware of his secret place, to find the things he kept in there. His mind started to buzz with details of their return and a feeling of dread overcame him as he thought of the events which would soon be put into action. The peace had vanished and, sighing with regret, he started to walk back to the cave.

They were soon dressed and the fire had been built up to heat water for a warming drink, made with the dried leaves that Endorina had sent down to them. Lonell took a sip and, although he could not recognise most of the flavours, he could pick out the delicious mint taste he always enjoyed. He felt the hot liquid travel down his throat and into his stomach, the warming effect instantaneous.

Lonell explained his plan to the others and, after a few questions and a helpful suggestion from Valon, they agreed that they would depart when the Sun had lowered itself to sleep behind the mountains beyond the lands of the Fillari. None of the three felt any hunger, apprehension showing on all their faces but, as they talked, they forced down the food that Tendo had risked so much to bring them. Then they sorted through all the items in the cave, deciding what to take back with them. In the end, most was left, neatly stacked, ready for whenever the cave was next needed. Lonell watched Pallo as the tall figure stooped over a skin on which were placed the two remaining nodules of Death Stone and the antler tool which he was now so adept at using. He saw the knapper's long fingers hover gently over the items and gently wrap them into a secure bundle which he stored lovingly at the back of the cave and he knew that Pallo would feel bereft until he could return to work on the Death Stones once more.

They sat, waiting, their back packs ready with bed skins attached, and the knives, wrapped in three skins to divide them between the men. Every now and then Valon stood up and peered outside, returning to sit once more to wait. They talked, making certain that they all had the same 'memories' of the last few days. It was vital that they all tell the same story about where they had been and how their sickness had progressed or someone would realise they were covering up the truth. When they had finished talking it through a second time, silence fell and the wait continued. Valon stood up once more and returned with a strained smile on his face.

'It is time,' he said.

As they stepped out of the cave in the darkness, Lonell realised with horror, that the skies, now clear after so many days, would allow the light of the Moon to shine down on them, leaving them visible to any watchful eyes.

'Please, do not fail us now,' he whispered to no one in particular but the wavering vision of a skull, its outline blurred against a shining, white cave wall, swam before his eyes as he spoke.

He signalled to the others, pointing at the white orb which shone above them, and grimaced. They stayed close to the cliff wall as they walked along the beach in single file, placing their feet carefully on rocks whenever they could to disguise their tracks. They felt relatively safe until they arrived at the rocky path the led up from the beach to the High Pasture. At the top of this they had no idea what they were going to find for no one knew where the Outlanders went when darkness fell. They might be keeping watch over the area, particularly after the confrontation with Sarril earlier that day.

They crept up the path, aware of every noise they made, grimacing as pebbles were dislodged, rolling gently down the slope, the sound magnified in their minds to thunderous intensity. At the top Lonell slowly pushed his head up, eyes and ears straining for any movement, hardly daring to breathe and, instantly, the Moon disappeared behind an unseen cloud, dimming its revealing light. Lonell smiled to himself and gave silent thanks. Once convinced there was no one around, they emerged carefully on to the High Pasture and began to make their way towards the path down to Mountain Water, their bodies crouched low to the ground but moving as fast as was possible. Half way over the silent plateau, they heard a cry and dropped like stones to the earth, disappearing among the tall grass. Slowly, fearfully, their heads reappeared searching for the source which was immediately evident. They could pick out far away, under the first canopy of the woodland high above Mountain Water, the glimmering light of a camp fire and they heard cries, tempered by the distance. The three men remained motionless, watching, although it was impossible to see anything other than the tiny glow but the sounds carried through the silent air.

'Do you think they're all there?' Pallo's whisper made Lonell jump and he was about to reply when the sound of remote shouts swelled.

Different voices could be heard roaring and bellowing, which mingled with cheers that grew in volume.

'Now, while they're busy. We go!' ordered Lonell.

The three men ran bent double, not stopping until they reached the path leading down to Mountain Water. They slid down quietly and at the bottom, Valon guided them to the secluded area where Zana had taken him on a much happier occasion. Their first action was to gather as many loose rocks as they could find by the still dim light of the Moon and they built up a pile against the rock face, carefully hiding their precious burdens of knives inside.

They took turns to keep watch that night and thanked their Sacred Stones that the rain had ceased. Their sleep was fitful and disturbed with unwelcome thoughts and they greeted the arrival of the new day with relief. Light began to break through and they heard the Enlightened Ones come down the path, taking their places for the Sun Wake ceremony. Lonell peered carefully round the edge of the outcrop which protected them from view. He saw the three Attendants, with the wolf, standing in a line behind the High Priestess, the Kalia Headdress fixed crookedly on her head, and the Guardians took their positions five paces behind the Attendants, all holding weapons. However, what interested Lonell more were the Outlanders who stood some distance behind, spread out, their spears held ready, protecting the small group before them. Lonell could see their eyes moving over the surroundings and he was amazed that they appeared so alert after the activities of the night before.

The ceremony completed, Mountain Water was deserted once more, except for the unseen presence of three men. Lonell explained what he had seen while they ate some dried food and waited to hear the sounds of people moving about on the plateau above.

It was with a mixture of excitement and trepidation that Lonell led the others out onto the High Pasture. On the other side, towards the cave, he saw people heading towards them, empty water skins in their hands, and he cupped his hands to his mouth.

'Hallo!' he shouted.

Amongst the people, Lonell could pick out Kadell, Endorina, Tendo, Davoril and Bascana. To one side, stood the solitary figure of Tordano and two Outlanders stood apart, watching. Endorina was the first to show any reaction for she had not known that the return was planned. Despite her advancing age she almost ran towards them and then, realising that, had she not known that their illness was pretence, she would have been more wary, she slowed down.

She greeted them.

'Do you still suffer from the sickness?' she asked formally, still at a short distance from them. 'Are you still coughing?'

'No,' Lonell replied for them, aware that Tordano was listening to their every word. 'The cough went on the third day but we stayed away for longer to make sure that we had completely recovered. Did anyone else fall sick?'

'No, we were lucky. The sickness passed us all by.'

With the Guardian and Outlanders behind her, Endorina was safe to show the large grin that covered her face as she reached them. She made a great show of inspecting them before turning to the others.

'They are clear of the sickness. They will not pass it on to others,' she announced, whereupon Tordano approached.

'Welcome back,' he said, his insincerity ringing in Lonell's ears. 'You must wait here until I have spoken with the High Priestess.'

He turned to leave but Endorina would not let him go that easily.

'Why should they wait? I have declared that they bring no risk to anyone. Now they are well they must be allowed to return to the cave.'

Tordano wracked his brain for a valid reason.

'Saretta may want Lexana to examine them. She has knowledge of all sicknesses and cures, so her judgement will count.'

Too Long To Die

'I was a good enough healer when you Enlightened Ones were too afraid to come anywhere near the tribe, when you all remained quivering in your cave. I was allowed to treat people then but now ...'

The tone of her voice as she used their name and the derision for their fear was startling to everyone so Kadell stepped forward and put his hand on her shoulder to stop her from saying any more. His eyes warned that now was not the time.

'We shall all wait here,' he said to Tordano. 'They will be happy to be looked at by Lexana.'

They watched the Guardian walk away and Lonell could tell from his gait that he was uncomfortable, that he was aware of all the eyes watching his retreat.

'I am sorry, Kadell,' apologised Endorina. 'I just cannot talk to any of them now without showing my disgust.'

'That's understandable. However we must wait. All will be resolved soon...'

Lonell was sure he saw Kadell bite back the words 'I hope' but he made no comment.

'In fact, Lonell wants to talk to Lexana so it will be good if she comes out to look at him. You may have to accept that she's in the cave sometimes over the next few days.'

'Oh, I don't mind Lexana. She's a good woman and I know that she would have come out to treat them if they had let her. I would be pleased if she stayed in the cave with us. It's interesting to talk with someone else about healing.'

Suddenly she fixed her gaze on Lonell.

'Was my answer helpful?' she asked him, quietly.

'Yes,' he nodded, 'but I need more information.'

'Come. Help me look for this.'

She held up a small blue flower on a thick stem with leaves that were covered in what Lonell thought looked like animal fur.

'It relaxes the body and calms a painful head,' she replied to his unasked question.

He placed his backpack on the ground and the two moved away from the others, bent over, searching for the plant as they began to talk.

'You asked me how small a baby could be and still survive its birth. Why did you need to know?'

As Lonell told her about the discovery in the tree, her hand flew to her brow and her eyes filled with compassion.

'Your answer to my question was about the size of two blocks of salt, length to length - any smaller than that and an infant would be unlikely to survive. Well, the body we found was perhaps the size of one salt block.'

'Then it is likely that the mother did not carry it for the full time. Perhaps it died inside the mother or, for some reason, she rejected it earlier than expected. It sounds very unlikely that the child would have lived at all.'

Lonell thought hard.

'It appeared perfectly formed to me, just tiny. Can you work out how long in the carrying the woman must have been when the baby died?'

Endorina shook her head.

'There is no way of ever knowing that. You would have to be able to look inside a woman!'

'The skin was like a very thin, dried out hide, but you could almost see through it.'

'It had skin still on it?' asked the Healer. 'I thought you were talking about the bones. Perhaps it was fairly recent - I don't know enough about this. You must ask Lexana. As a member of the Enlightened Ones, she would know more about this.'

The two continued to talk as they searched. When Lonell was sure that Endorina could tell him no more about the infant's death, he turned the subject to plants and began to test her knowledge. Once he had started the Healer off on her favourite subject, she only stopped to draw breath and answer his occasional question.

He had not yet found out all that he wanted when he was aware that the sounds coming from the other group had stopped. He looked up and saw the reason: Saretta and Lexana, surrounded by the three Guardians, were walking towards them, and two more Outlanders accompanied them.

Too Long To Die

Chapter Twenty Four

'How dare you return, bringing the sickness back to us?' spoke Saretta, her voice barely audible over the short distance between the two groups.

Lonell noticed that the question was asked without conviction as though she knew they were well but was searching for an excuse to keep them away. Saretta had changed since they last saw her, only seven days before. The savageness of her actions and stridency of her voice had mellowed and her face bore a blank, vacant expression. Lonell recalled the drink that Lexana had calmed her with at the harvesting of the Salt Water Monster.

However it was her clothes that attracted most attention. This was the woman who would never appear in public without her beautiful robes and regalia, immaculately groomed. Now her tangled hair blew wildly in the wind and the white tunic she wore was covered in dirt and old food. Lonell wondered how he had failed to notice this at the ceremony but realised that he had been distracted by the Kalia Headdress she had been wearing and the presence of the Outlanders.

Endorina stood forward.

'I have examined them and found them to be clear of the sickness,' she told the High Priestess. 'There is no reason why they should not return to the cave with us.'

'However, it might be sensible for Lexana to inspect them to be certain that I have not missed anything,' she added, glancing at Lonell.

Lexana was watching her closely, a frown creasing her brow, and their eyes met for a moment.

'That would be wise,' agreed the Attendant. 'It is evident from observing them here that they are very much improved and, since no one else contracted the sickness, I think it will be safe for them to return to the cave. I shall attend to the High Priestess and then bring my healing plants over if I may, Kadell?'

A flicker of annoyance passed over Saretta's face as though she knew that something was wrong with Lexana's words, but it was Tordano whose expression revealed his fury at the fact that Kadell was once again being treated as the Leader. However, he was in no position to correct an Attendant Priestess and so the Guardian pushed his clenched fists behind his back, bit his lip, and remained silent. A twitch of a smile touched the corner of Lexana's mouth as she turned to Saretta.

'Come, High Priestess. I shall guide you back to the White Cave so you can rest.'

The vapid eyes of the mad woman looked at her gratefully and Lexana held out a hand to her.

'Have we found someone to sacrifice yet?' Saretta asked in a loud, conspiratorial whisper.

Lexana put a guiding arm around her. She looked back over her shoulder sadly, as they walked away.

Back in the cave the three men were welcomed warmly and with an air of withheld excitement. Everyone knew about the weapons that had been smuggled back and they were eagerly awaiting some action in the hope they would soon return to a happier way of life. Kadell had already told everyone to be patient but it was difficult for the undercurrent of bubbling eagerness to be kept under control. Lonell went straight to the back of the cave to wait for Lexana and he took the time to observe the men and women that made up his tribe.

'Am I right?' he asked himself, 'or is there someone in this cave who's involved in the killing of Narthan? If there is, am I in danger, along with Valon and Pallo?'

His eyes scanned the area around the hearths where people were getting ready to eat the food that was the source of the delicious aromas he could smell and then he looked towards the entrance. Ancient Pel was sitting by himself, staring down at the floor in front of him. Due to the odours that some of his dyes emitted it was not unusual to see him alone but he was normally busy, bustling around over his pots, a gentle smile on his ugly face. Now he was the picture of misery, no sign of the simmering emotions that were affecting everyone else.

The call for food went up and people began to pick up a wooden or bone platter from the communal area and head towards the cooking containers. Ancient Pel made no move. Lonell claimed two plates and waited to fill them with the deep red meat that he recognised as bison. This was a treat as the stores of bison meat were kept for special occasions only and the very smell brought back memories of the last time they had hunted with the Fillari. It was a great success - the plains had been filled with more of the enormous animals than anyone could remember in their lifetimes and the humans, puny besides the great beasts, had suffered no losses. The valuable meat had been dragged back over many days and the cave was full of drying meat for so long that everyone declared that they never wanted to see or smell or eat any part of a bison again. Now that was all forgotten; the meat had been rehydrated through soaking and the resulting stew was delicious beyond belief.

Lonell carried his two full plates over to Ancient Pel's area and when the old man did not look up, he sat down beside him without invitation. He pushed a plate into Ancient Pel's hands and told him to eat. Nothing was said but the Dyer began to eat, slowly at first but increasing in speed with every mouthful, shovelling the food into his mouth until there was none left. Then he sat back and let out a huge belch, before subsiding into his morose attitude once more. Lonell wondered how long it had been since Ancient Pel had eaten and he waited, hoping that something would be said but nothing was forthcoming. He gathered up the plates and took them to the cleaning area. Mila had been watching him from a distance and recognised his intense expression. She hurried over and took them from him.

'It's good to see you back,' she smiled up at him. 'Is there anything I can do to help?'

'No. Well ... thank you for doing that.' He nodded at the plates. He put his hand to her cheek and felt his usual physical reaction to her.

'No, now is not the time,' he said to himself. 'Hopefully later.'

He smiled back at her, his eyes full of the passion he was feeling.

'Go back and try to talk with him. He's been like this for many days. That's the first time I have seen him eat in ... I can't think how long. Why don't you take him to your place at the back of the cave? There aren't so many people there - less eyes will be on you both. I'll bring you some fruit and a hot drink.'

Mila felt his need but realised that he was driven to talk with the old man, to sort something out, and she knew that must take priority.

Following her advice, Lonell invited the old man over to his sleeping area where they sat and talked about generalities. Initially, Ancient Pel answered Lonell's questions about his work in monosyllabic answers, picking at the dried fruit and nuts and sipping the soothing infusion that Mila had brought over for them. Suddenly, the old man's eyes filled with tears and he began to talk.

'I loved Minaya's mother. I know that we're not meant to have strong feelings for others but I could not help it with Cali. She was beautiful - every time she looked at me I could feel the beating in my chest and it was hard to breath.'

He inhaled deeply.

Too Long To Die

'I was excited when she went away to her Journey to Womanhood. I was so looking forward to enjoying her as a woman, and she loved me, I know she did. But she was different when she came back ... quieter and ... less happy. Then she found out she was carrying and she became her old self again until Minaya was born. Don't misunderstand me,' he grabbed Lonell's arm, emphasising his words, 'she loved Minaya as only a mother can but when she saw her white colouring, I think something died inside her. I stayed with them as much as custom would allow - in fact, probably more - and I also came to feel deeply for the child. So when she had to go away I mourned for her alongside her mother. Then Cali just drifted away from her life. I tried everything but I couldn't reach her. When she returned to the earth I thought of walking out into Salt Water myself and never coming back but I lacked the courage.'

He stopped, his eyes focused on the past, and Lonell wondered why Ancient Pel was telling him this but he said nothing, waiting for the Dyer to continue. They sat in silence for a while until the old man shuddered and looked at Lonell, desperately.

'One day, Lexana came to me,' he continued. 'I think she'd noticed how sad I was and guessed the reason. She told me about the White Cave and asked if I'd like to see it. So, with nothing better to do, I agreed, not expecting to see anything unusual. But I was wrong. The place is extraordinary and as I wandered through those glistening white caverns I felt the need to paint, to create, and that was when I started going over there regularly. Of course, it also gave me the chance to spend time with Minaya, or at least to see her. Sometimes she would come into the place where I was working and watch me. I loved those times, but mostly she was kept busy and I would just see her every now and then. She was never happy over there ...' his voice trailed off.

Lonell waited for him to continue but the man had retreated once more into his own thoughts.

'Do you still go over there?' he asked gently, in an attempt to extract more of the story from the lost, old man who, Lonell realised, he had misread all these years. He had always thought of him as contented, enjoying the great skill he was born with, a man always ready to joke and have fun. Now, however, he realised that this had all been a pretence; he had covered up his true emotions with joviality but perhaps he had used the odours from his dyes to keep people away deliberately.

Ancient Pel looked up absentmindedly.

'Sorry,' he said. 'I missed your question.'

'Do you still go over there?' Lonell repeated.

The old man's face crumpled.

'No,' he sobbed. 'They won't let me in now.'

'Is that because of the sickness?'

He shook his head.

'They stopped me before that. While you and Valon were away. One day, they just said that I'd decorated the caves enough and I wasn't to go back any more.'

He looked at Lonell with tear filled eyes.

'It's not the painting that upsets me; it's Minaya. I know she only kept her strength up because I went over there. Now, I dread to think what will happen to her.'

Lonell thought about the young Attendant. He had seen little of her since she entered the White Cave but that was not so strange. She was still young and had a lot to learn even though she had been initiated as an Attendant two summers previously. She appeared when all the Enlightened Ones did - at ceremonies and some gatherings. There was no doubt that she was extremely beautiful and she always held herself composedly and with elegance, but her face showed no expression. She never made eye contact with anyone, he recalled, and he could not remember hearing her speak since she had been taken. Suddenly he felt glad that Ancient Pel had been going over there to give her some comfort.

'Why has she been so unhappy? I mean, I know it is difficult to be taken from your mother so young, but surely by now she should be content with her life?'

The old man shook his head.

'She's never been happy, but she bore it, sometimes better than others. There were periods when I would not see her for a long time; once three moons passed without a glimpse of her and I was becoming frantic. Then she reappeared and told me she'd been in seclusion as part of her training. I was so relieved, but she'd changed. It seemed as though something was worrying her all the time but somehow she managed to keep going.'

He looked up at Lonell with terrified eyes.

'That was, until the death of Narthan. Then she became someone I couldn't recognise. She wouldn't come to where I was working or even speak to me when we passed; she wouldn't even look at me.'

'That was when they stopped me from going over there,' he added.

He put his head in his hands. Lonell looked across the cave and managed to make eye contact with Mila. He held up the drinking vessel and pointed at Ancient Pel. She instantly got the message and quickly brought over another drink for both of them. Lonell smiled his thanks.

'Ancient Pel,' he said, putting his hand on the other man's shoulder, 'You know that there will soon be changes within the tribe?'

He saw the old man's head nod in acknowledgement.

'How it will work out, no one knows but things will change for the better, we hope. Now is the time when we need all our strength. That includes you. Minaya, and others will need you to be strong. The tribe as a whole will require your wisdom to help us through this and you must be there for Minaya.'

'But you are determined to discover the truth about Narthan's death,' wailed Ancient Pel. 'Why can't you leave it alone?'

Lonell went cold inside and felt the hairs on his arms bristle.

'Are you saying that Minaya was involved?' he asked, not certain that he wanted to hear the answer.

'No, I'm not saying anything,' the old man shook his head violently, spilling some of his drink and retreating into a deep silence.

Lonell took the vessel from his hand and placed it on the ground.

'Ancient Pel, listen to me.' The old man looked at him, hostility waning. 'If Minaya is in some way involved, I'm sure there is a good reason. She's probably been forced into something she didn't want to do. I can't imagine her doing anything wicked but we must find out the truth. You yourself said that she's changed since it happened. She must be bearing the guilt of something that is, perhaps, not her fault but, until the truth comes out, she will continue to suffer. She can't continue to live a life of such grief - it must be sorted out, for her sake. Don't you agree?' he added gently.

'Yes, you're right,' replied the Dyer, after a moment's silence. 'I'm sure she can't be held responsible for this death. If anything, she has been forced into hiding the truth. Yes, we must find out in order to help her.'

Lonell could hear Ancient Pel convincing himself as he talked and was pleased to see, for the first time, determination in his eyes.

'You must be strong for Minaya,' he repeated.

'I shall. I have been of no help to anyone recently but that must change.' The old man stood up and Lonell copied him.

'My thanks, Lonell. Without you I'm not sure where I would have gone - probably followed Minaya's mother back to the earth. That will happen soon enough but not now. I am needed. I'm grateful - you are a true friend,' he said as he turned and walked back to his area where he began to sort through his equipment.

Lonell hoped that he would feel the same when the truth was revealed.

Everyone in the cave had been carefully getting on with their own tasks. Some had been sent out to gather in more Cord Plant, others to a stand of pine nuts that had just ripened and yet more had gone down to the beach to collect some of the large clams that were such a delicacy. The storms of the last few days would have pushed a variety of creatures out of the depths, to be held in rock pools until liberated by the hungry birds that flocked over the large expanse of rocky beach or by human beings intent on feasting on the easily harvested shellfish. Everyone wanted the tasks that took them down to the beach for the Outlanders would not go there, close to the Salt Water.

Those that remained inside were each busy working on something for the benefit of the cave, whether it were the preparation of food or the creation of utensils, mats or gathering baskets. However, busy as they were, none could resist the odd glance to see what Lonell was doing. Kadell had not left the cave because he wanted to know what was happening and when, shortly after he had returned to his own area, Ancient Pel picked up a basket and left, the Leader was ready to move in. He knew that it would be some time before the old man returned for he had gone to gather shells on the beach which would be used for decoration or to grind down for texture and colour in his mixtures.

'Well?' he asked. 'No one has been able to get a word out of him for days and as soon as you arrive, he starts telling you the story of his life. What is his problem?'

'He's worried that Minaya is very unhappy. He says that she always has been and that's why he liked to go over there. He was able to see her and sometimes talk to her but now he's been banned.'

'Has he?' exclaimed Kadell. 'I wasn't aware of that. I wonder why?'

'Do you think they knew we'd found out he was giving them information and that we were going to feed them with false news about the cave? The 'sickness' was not the cause - it happened before then. But he is certain that something is wrong with Minaya.'

'She probably suffered as badly as her mother when she was taken away but I'm surprised that she is still unhappy. It has been a long time since she moved over there and they don't have a difficult life. She has no responsibilities. She doesn't need to find her own food or water or wood or anything. We provide it all for the White Cave. They only join the hunts if they want to and she never does. I have occasionally seen her picking flowers but that's all. I would say it is a very easy life,' Kadell finished.

Lonell was not entirely certain that the Leader was seeing the whole picture.

'Nor does she have any freedom. We don't know what restrictions she is under over there. Of course, she has to keep herself pure as an Attendant so she cannot choose to spend time with a man if she wants to. She can't talk to a friend or play with others. We never hear laughter from the White Cave. I would imagine it's a rather boring life with no freedom and now, with Saretta as she is, it's probably frightening.'

'Yes, that's true but by now, surely she should be used to it. I can see no reason for Ancient Pel to get so upset about her. However, you seem to have calmed him down. He'll be fine from now on,' declared Kadell.

Lonell wished he could be so sure. Kadell needed to take this more seriously.

'Ancient Pel is worried that Minaya had something to do with Narthan's death,' he informed his Leader.

Too Long To Die

Chapter Twenty Five

The Leader and the Dreamer sat side by side contemplating the idea that Minaya, the beautiful child who they had all loved so much and who had turned into such an elegant young lady, could have killed the Guardian, Narthan.

'Did he give any reasons for thinking she might be involved?' asked Kadell.

Lonell shook his head.

'He only talked about how unhappy she was and how she seemed to have got worse since Narthan returned to the earth. But he was definitely worried that she had some part in it. I told him that perhaps she'd been forced to keep quiet about it and so her guilt was weighing her down and that she would need him to stay strong for her. It seemed to make him feel better.'

'Is it what you think?'

Lonell's silence told him the truth and he sighed.

'You know, there are times when I wish I weren't the Leader,' he said heavily. 'When will you know?'

'I must speak with Lexana. I'm surprised that she hasn't come over sooner,' insisted Lonell, fretting over the missing pieces of the puzzle that he was trying to solve.

'She'll be here when she can,' reassured Kadell. 'She probably had to prepare something for the Sun Sleep ceremony and I would imagine that she has to stay close to Saretta to keep her under control.'

'I think I'll go and find Endorina. There's something else that I forgot to ask her before,' said Lonell, glad that he had something to do that would take him out of the cave.

The sun was just beginning to drop behind the mountains when he found the Healer. She straightened up from picking the varied selection of plants which she would use to make healing drinks, infusions and poultices for the inevitable sicknesses that would strike them down over the cold period. Rubbing her back, she groaned.

'Are you feeling sick?' asked Lonell.

'No,' she replied, her grimace replaced by a gentle smile. She was genuinely moved by the concern in Lonell's voice.

'It's just that I'm getting too old to be bending down over my plants for so long and my back is complaining! I've been thinking that I must start to train someone and they can then pick everything I want.'

'May I ask you something?' Lonell wondered if she felt strong enough to help him.

'Certainly. I've finished for today. I can no longer see too clearly and when the sun goes down, things become a little ...' she searched for the words, 'faded at the edges. It's important that I pick the correct plants or I could end up giving someone Death Juice instead of curing them!'

Lonell remembered how clear his sight had become when he looked through the holes made in the shells and he grinned.

'Remind me later. Valon may have something that will help you to see things more clearly when they're close up. I warn you, you might feel ridiculous wearing them at first but they really do help.'

'What are they?' she asked, her curiosity piqued. 'You have my interest.'

'If I tell you, you'll think I am wrong in the head,' he laughed, 'so you'll have to wait until you see them. But now I want to ask you about a plant.'

He looked around to make sure no one was within hearing distance and saw an Outlander, leaning on his spear, picking at a rotten tooth. He was clearly bored and too far away to know what they were saying even if he did understand their language, which Lonell doubted. On the other side of them, at about the same distance, stood Valt, staring out towards Salt Water, paying no attention to those on the High Pasture.

'If you wanted to give someone Death Juice, which plant would you use?' he asked quietly.

Endorina looked up at him sharply.

'Why do you ask?'

Lonell saw her face and could not stop himself from laughing.

'No, I don't intend to kill anyone. But there is something that I haven't told you.'

He took a deep breath.

'When I found Narthan's body, I noticed that his breathe had a bad smell; it was really bad - bitter!'

He shook his head, his face twisted in disgust at the memory.

'I believe this means that he was given Death Juice, am I right?'

'I heard that you thought he'd had the breath squeezed from him.'

He did not stop to wonder how she had come by that information.

'Yes,' he replied. 'He had bruises around his neck, which I think was the reason he returned to the earth, but he also had that smell and his mouth was swollen. I can't see why someone would need to do both but perhaps you can tell me something that will help.'

'Oh, Lonell,' sighed Endorina. 'There are so many plants that can make Death Juice or can kill by being eaten. Some can be dangerous if they are just touched. You know to be careful when you pick the fungi in the woods because you were taught when you were young which ones you must not eat. Some of those are deadly and they could be served to someone instead of the edible ones. No one would know when they've been prepared.'

'Would they make the mouth swell?' the man asked.

'I'm not sure ... there are so many, it's possible.'

She stopped to think.

'Even some of the plants I use to treat illnesses, if they're prepared incorrectly they can cause great damage. For example, I used the root of a plant with a small pink flower to treat you when you were shot. That can be extremely dangerous if used in the wrong way. And then ...'

She stopped again and Lonell could see in her eyes that she had thought of something.

'Come, we have just enough daylight.'

She grabbed his arm and pulled him across the High Pasture in the direction of the line of trees that led down towards the forest. They heard a shout and Lonell felt the crash of a spear shaft strike his back and fling him to the ground. He rolled over, trying to catch his breath and saw Endorina leap at the Outlander, pounding at his tattooed chest with her fists.

'Leave him alone, you animal!' she screamed.

The tall man looked down at the old lady who was attacking him and laughed, an ugly guttural sound lacking any humour. He drew back his spear to strike her as Valt rushed between them, placing himself in front of Endorina. Equally small, he stared up at the Outlander.

'No! Leave them!' he shouted.

At another time the confrontation between the diminutive, clean, white figure and the lanky, unkempt creature might have been amusing but now it was extremely dangerous. For a moment, Lonell was not sure whether their attacker would strike Valt but slowly, he lowered the spear and, scowling, turned and strode away.

Lonell struggled to his feet and put his arm around Endorina who stood, shaking in fear, her anger having passed.

'Our thanks, Guardian,' he addressed Valt formally, showing a new respect for the small man in front of them. For a moment, Valt stood, unmoving, as though in shock at what he had just done. Then he breathed deeply.

'Where are you going together?' he asked, trying to hide the quake in his voice. 'You are not allowed to go off with others anymore,' he said, and Lonell thought he could hear a note of discontent.

'It's my fault, Guardian,' replied Endorina, before Lonell could speak. 'I'm getting old and my back was paining me, but there are some plants that I promised Lexana I would find. I asked Lonell to help me pick the last ones. They're over there.'

She pointed with a shaking hand to an area towards the rear of the High Pasture where the grassy plateau was bordered by rocky cliffs, the side of the formation from which their Mountain Water flowed.

'You could come with us, it won't take long.' she suggested innocently, and Lonell hoped desperately that he would refuse the offer.

Valt looked round at the other people within sight.

'No,' he replied, making his high-pitched voice as authoritative as possible. 'You can show me the plants when you return. Be quick!'

They walked away from him, hoping the Guardian would not change his mind, both now nursing sore backs. Endorina took Lonell to a place he had never seen before. The natural formation of large stones that jutted out of the earth created a protected enclosure where the marshy ground stank of rotting vegetation. In one corner grew some plants which Lonell did not recognise. Rising as high as his waist, each plant had pointed, oval leaves and a few long, tubular flowers. Lonell thought instantly how ugly they were with their dirty purple colour but on most stems the flower had died and in their place grew a single, shining, black berry.

'I call that the Darkness because it's one of the most evil plants I know and, just looking at it, I feel a coldness inside me, as though any happiness had been taken away. I don't know why; perhaps it's this place but it somehow suits the plant.'

She shivered.

'And it makes Death Juice?'

'Yes,' she nodded seriously. 'The whole plant is the most dangerous of any I know,' she repeated. 'I've only once seen someone who had eaten this. It was a young man who was so hungry on his Rite of Shadows that he decided to eat some of the black berries. It was a terrifying death.'

'Could you describe it to me? It might help.'

She thought back.

'He was really hot but not sweating - his skin was completely dry. He had vomited but some must have stayed in him. He was shouting, babbling, nothing made sense, as though an evil spirit had taken him - I was only young and very frightened. It took him a long time to die.'

Her pained eyes looked up at Lonell and was surprised to see, instead of horror, an expression of triumph.

'This is what you were looking for, isn't it?' she asked.

'I think it is,' he said excitedly. 'The only piece that's missing are the swollen lips.'

He shook his head, annoyed that the he could not find the link.

'Oh no, that's not missing. If this plant touches any part of your skin, it will swell up and erupt. Did you look at his hands?'

'They seemed unhurt except that ... some of his finger tips had what looked like small blisters on them. I didn't think anything about it - they didn't look serious at the time. That would have been the fingers that he picked the berries up with. Endorina, thank you. We must return to the cave now. Let me carry your basket for you.'

'Wait!' She pulled up some other plants. 'I need something to show to Valt.'

'What are these?' asked Lonell. 'How do you use them?'

'I have no idea,' replied Endorina, laughing up at him. 'I don't think they have any use!'

As they walked back, she glanced up at the silent man beside her.

'Is that it?' she asked. 'Do you know who killed him?'

'Almost,' he answered quietly. 'Almost.'

Food was being served up when they arrived back at the cave. Lonell walked in and realised he felt different. Excitement was coursing through his body, an eagerness that gave him a lightness in his step. His eyes roamed over the cave and everything seemed more defined and colourful. He knew that his movements were faster, sharper than before, and he was sure that everyone must be noticing the change in him. He looked around the cave in his new found confidence but no one paid him any attention; most were too busy eating and Kadell was sitting in a corner in deep discussion with Tendo.

Lonell sighed, deflated, and joined the others waiting for a platter full of meat with fresh root vegetables which was being served out by the cook. He wondered how Vellisco was able to put up with the endless cycle of preparing food. It was a never-ending task and food that had taken all day to prepare was wolfed down in no time at all. He, Lonell, would find that unbearable but Vellisco was moving from person to person, asking them how they found the food and describing his methods of cooking to anyone who would listen, a great beaming smile on his face.

'A lucky man,' thought Lonell, 'a man who really loves his path in life.'

Sitting down in his usual position at the rear of the cave, Lonell saw Tendo shaking his head vigorously and wondered what he and the Leader were talking about so intently. He was still watching them when Valon joined him.

'You know something,' asserted the blond man. 'I can tell. Have you worked it all out?'

Lonell rolled his eyes in mock despair but secretly delighted that someone had noticed a change in him.

'I wish everyone would have a bit of patience. I'm not able to do everything at once.'

He grinned at his friend.

'However I have discovered something. I talked to Endorina and asked her ...'

At that moment conversation in the cave ceased as the tribe looked towards the entrance. Lexana was standing there, her bag of healing plants and treatments in one hand and Cannot, the wolf, held firmly by the other. Kadell left his meeting with Tendo and, greeting her cordially, invited her into the cave. He pointed in the direction of Lonell. People backed away, not from the Attendant Priestess but from the wolf, as they passed through the cavern.

Mila took a piece of meat from the hearth and, wanting to renew her friendship with the animal, also headed to the back. More than two moons had passed since he had seen the three people who used to give him food. He was slightly wary for a moment but then, recognising their scent, he happily greeted them with a cold nose pressed into their hands. Everyone was astonished as they saw the wolf take meat gently from Mila's fingers while Valon and Lonell patted the great shaggy beast. In the cave, only Kadell could understand how they were able to do this for he had gone to the Pit with them; everyone else wondered if they had special powers.

He returned to his talk with Tendo - he would find out afterwards if Lexana had been able to provide the information that Lonell needed.

Too Long To Die

It was obvious that Lonell wanted to talk to Lexana alone and Mila and Valon offered to take the wolf away. However, it was decided that it had better stay with the Attendant in case anyone looked out from the White Cave. Lexana was certain that the animal would be killed if Saretta no longer saw it as a useful tool to keep the tribe in order. She had only brought it over with her now in order to protect it; she dared not leave it alone for, although the High Priestess was in a deep sleep now, she had the habit of unexpectedly waking up and demanding something totally unreasonable. Lexana had seen Saretta's eyes lingering on the luxurious coat of the wolf and she had no intention of returning to the White Cave to find that one of the Guardians had killed the magnificent animal for its pelt.

She sat beside Lonell, making the wolf lie down quietly beside them and pretended to be examining the man. Her pale eyes stared into his and for a moment Lonell felt fear. This woman had seen so much, had so much knowledge and had the all-powerful link to the Gods. She was fond of Saretta, that much was obvious and, for an instant, he felt uncertain that she would help but his doubt disappeared when she smiled encouragingly.

'Ask, Lonell,' she said. 'Ask me what you need to know.'

He took a deep breath.

'This is the first time that I've come across human death in its physical form, except for very briefly. Usually you, the Enlightened Ones, remove a body so fast that we hardly see it. Don't misunderstand me, I'm more than content that you do, but it means I have no understanding of what happens to a body ... afterwards.'

'What do you want to know? I am not sure that I can give you all the answers, but I shall try. We remove the body and then prepare it with a spiritual ceremony. After that we place it in the ground or in Salt Water.'

'Do you know what happens to it once it's in the ground?' asked

Lonell, rather uneasy. Superstition told him that this was not a subject to be discussed but he needed the information.

'I know that the flesh breaks down and eventually disappears leaving only the bones. I once saw a burial place that had been dug up by a wolf. What had not been eaten by the animal was full of insects and small creatures. I assume they were devouring the flesh.'

Lonell was beginning to wish that he had not eaten so much; his stomach was churning and his skin started to itch as he imagined his corpse crawling with tiny creatures. He had never thought that one day he would become food for insects. He was struggling to bring his imagination under control when he felt Lexana's cool hand on his.

'I know it is a shock to begin with but, once you start thinking about it, it is right. We know that all life exists by feeding off other forms of life. All animals either eat other animals or grass, leaves or something that is or has been living. And we do the same so why should we be excluded from the process? We finally give back to the earth some of what we have taken from it during our lives.'

When explained like that it made absolute sense to the man, whose natural curiosity was piqued by this morbid, new idea. The practical reasoning of it overcame the superstition and he would have liked to continue talking about it but he remembered the questions that needed to be answered.

'When would a body not break down after death?'

Lexana stared at him, deep in thought. This was something that she had not considered before and there was no reason why she should. Unlike Lonell, she had never seen a mummified corpse, but she was interested enough to attempt an answer.

'I suppose, if it were kept in a place where there are no insects.' She hesitated. 'I do not know but if, say, the body was not buried in the ground; if it was kept dry, maybe in a dry cave.'

'If it was wrapped and then put in a stone cache inside a dry cave, then perhaps. Yes, that must be the answer,' said Lonell, gazing into the distance.

The comments were made for his own benefit but he realised that Lexana was staring at him. He read confusion on her face and it came to him that she had no idea why he was asking. He surprised himself with the strength of his own relief that she was not involved in what had happened to the baby.

Then he took another deep breath, aware that he was about to touch on a subject that the tribe would not be expected to even think about.

'Attendants are expected to remain pure for the Gods, I mean, they must not go with any man, isn't that correct?'

Lexana nodded.

'Are those rules ever broken?' he continued, trying to pick his words carefully.

He saw her eyes widen briefly and knew he had uncovered a truth. He was almost certain she had turned paler than usual, although it was difficult to tell.

'If an Attendant had a child, what would happen to her?' he pushed on, his questions probing deeper.

'She would be sacrificed to the Gods, along with her child. But that would never happen.'

Lonell formed the question with his eyes.

'There are ways; ways to rid oneself of an unwanted baby. Plants that can be taken.'

She saw Lonell's horrified face.

'But life is sacred,' he spluttered.

'When you know that the child will die regardless of your actions and the alternative is the loss of your own life as well, then you see the teachings in a different light. If you could save the child then you might think differently but, as it is, there is no hope.'

'Then why take the risk? Why go with a man when it exposes you to the chance of creating an unwanted child?'

'Could you imagine living your whole life without having the pleasure of someone to give you comfort? That is the life of an Attendant and it is not an easy path. The Guardians have the task of mentoring girls through their Journey to Womanhood although they are expected to remain pure the rest of the time. Perhaps that makes it worse for them because they know what they are missing.'

There was something in the tone of her voice that caught Lonell's attention.

'But they don't stay pure, is that what you're saying?' he challenged her.

'And if the Guardians do not, to whom must they turn in order to take their 'pleasure'?'

'It can only be people from other tribes .... or ... or the Attendants.'

Lonell was feeling uncomfortable - a picture was forming in his brain that he desperately wanted to shake off. His skin began to crawl at the dreadful thoughts.

'And what if they do not want to?' Lexana whispered the question.

'You are not saying the Attendants are forced?'

The horror sank home and surged through Lonell's insides. He looked at the sad lady in front of him.

'Not you?' he asked gently.

'No, thank the Gods. Although sometimes I wonder if They have deserted us.'

The last words were addressed to no one, very quietly, as she stared into the air. There was a moment's silence.

'Are you telling me that you know there was a child?' As Lexana spoke she stared at Lonell but did not wait for his answer. 'I tried to protect her but I could not be there all the time. She was so beautiful ...'

Her ravaged eyes stared at the ground and tears ran down her cheeks. Lonell beckoned to Endorina, who was beside them in an instant.

'Do you have a soothing drink for Lexana? She's had a bit of a shock.'

'It seems to be in constant demand these days,' grimaced the Healer, 'so I have some that will be ready soon.'

She bustled off to check on the preparation and, with a quick glance back at the shaken woman, she added another pinch of her special mixture.

After a while, the Attendant left with somewhat unsteady steps and glazed eyes, the wolf leading her back to her cave. Lonell had managed to remind her to say nothing back at the White Cave for the consequences would be unimaginable. By the time she left she had almost convinced herself that she had checked Lonell and the others and found them fit, and that she had then stayed to talk about her healing plants, while taking a few drinks. However, she had not realised that the seemingly innocuous beverage had been stronger than she thought.

No other White Ones were in the cave because Lexana had been there to watch the tribe so, once she left, Lonell joined Kadell, Tendo and others who were sitting around the hearth. Silence fell instantly and everyone heard his words.

'Tell everyone to prepare for the sleeping hours as normal; we must not raise suspicion. But once we are certain that there is no activity in the White Cave, we must have a tribal meeting.'

'Do you have all your answers?' asked the Leader.

'Yes,' replied Lonell. 'And everyone must attend the meeting. We have to prepare ourselves. Tomorrow will be the day.'

Too Long To Die

Chapter Twenty Six

No one else doubted Lonell's right to give the call to action but he looked at Kadell to check that he had not overstepped his position. Kadell nodded his agreement and leant forward intently.

'Spread the word to everyone,' he said. 'Settle down quickly. Tell the mothers to get the children to sleep. But don't do anything unusual. If we are being watched, they must think we're behaving normally.'

Most of the cooking utensils had already been sorted away but it was some time before the cave had been completely tidied for the night. One by one, people drifted away to their sleeping areas and settled into their bed skins or joined other people for the short time they had to relax. Lonell had just lain down when he felt Mila put her skins down beside him and he welcomed her in.

'We have no idea what will happen when Sun wakes,' she whispered, a nervous tremor revealing her true feelings. 'Make this time special, Lonell.'

All around the cave it was clear from the sounds that people were relieving their tension in the well-established manner but soon silence descended, the cave disturbed only by even breathing and an occasional snore. Lonell lay still, Mila's head cradled in his arm. He stared at the shadows on the roof, thrown by the light from the glowing embers at the three hearths. He tried to prevent himself falling asleep by planning the forthcoming confrontation with the White Ones but he must have succumbed for the next thing he felt was his shoulder being shaken by Kadell. His eyes flew open instantly and he joined Kadell in waking the others; only the children were left to sleep.

Tendo and Davoril were already silently creeping along the outside ledge to bring back the spears and bow with its arrows; the knives would be collected later. This was the first time the tribe had seen the new blades and hushed expressions of wonder were instantly stifled by Kadell's gestures. Lonell took the bow, fixed the cord and took it over to Delina. She looked up at him with thanks, her eyes brimming with excitement but when she saw the arrowheads she had to put her hand over her mouth to prevent herself from letting out an exclamation of delight. Her fingers stroked the silky black Death Stone points until Lonell mouthed the word 'Careful!' to her and showed her the scar that could still be seen on his thumb. Each person was handed one of the short-shafted spears which they hid in their bed skins and then they all crouched down in as small a circle as they could make, towards the rear of the cave.

'Lonell now knows who killed Narthan,' Kadell's whisper seemed loud in the cave and no one else made a sound. 'Therefore when the Sun wakes we shall face the White Ones and the Outlanders to reclaim the life we used to have in this tribe.'

All eyes moved from Kadell to Lonell and back but everyone knew better than to speak.

'They don't think we have weapons,' continued Kadell, 'and if we face them when they are at the Sun Wake ceremony, they won't expect it. Lonell saw them at the ceremony on the day of his return so we know what to expect. I've thought of a course of action which I'll now explain. If anyone has any questions or other ideas, when I have finished, put your hand forward and I'll invite you to speak. That way we won't have everyone trying to talk at once and making noise.'

The Leader talked for what seemed a long time. Every now and then someone would push out their hand, unable to wait until he had finished. He let them speak and eventually the plan was understood by everybody. Each one knew what they had to do, where they had to be. Flamina had been selected to stay behind with Marita and the children and had finally agreed to do so. Naturally, she wanted to see justice done and not miss anything but Kadell worried that her loathing for the High Priestess might cause her to act in haste and ruin the plan which relied on stealth and patience. More than one person asked Lonell to reveal what he knew but he just shook his head. Even Kadell, as Leader, only knew part of it.

'What if I am wrong? Sacred Stones, let me have the right answer,' Lonell prayed silently.

'Remember,' Kadell emphasised, to finish off the meeting, 'we may have weapons but we do not want to use them on the White Ones. Our aim is to bring the guilty ones to justice and to rid ourselves of Saretta and the Outlanders, but no Pescovari need return to the earth. If anyone uses this as an opportunity to take revenge, I will make sure they face their own punishment. Do you all understand?'

He stared hard at each person through the darkness and they nodded in turn.

'Now return to your sleeping areas and ready yourselves for the morning.'

This time every person knew that sleep would be hard to come by and they were resigned to the time passing slowly. Lonell felt the cave walls closing in, crushing the air out of him and he had to get out so he volunteered to climb up to the High Pasture to watch the skies and judge the moment when the tribe should move out. Mila accompanied him and they crept along the ledge and up the path, every sound seemingly magnified, their nerves tingling. At the top, Lonell was pleased to see the fire and hear the loud voices of the Outlanders in the same place he had seen them on his return from the beach cave. He put his hand down and felt the grass. A heavy dew was beginning to form - this was something they had not planned for. If they waited to make their way later, as they had planned, the White Ones would surely see their footprints when they left for the Sun Wake ceremony. Lonell left Mila in the darkness and returned to the cave. A few short words explained the problem and soon everyone was on their feet, prepared for a cold, damp night outside but relieved that the plan was in motion. Leaving their bed skins in place stuffed with other skins, they moved out silently, each knowing exactly where they had to go. Kadell was the last to leave, with a few final whispered instructions to Flamina.

Valon left the cave first and when each person arrived at the bottom of the path down to the meadow by Mountain Water, he handed them their own knife which they strapped to their belt. It took time for the whole tribe to cross the High Pasture. One by one, the crouching figures moved out, a long gap between each, while Lonell fretted. His nervousness spread to Kadell and Tendo as they stood, waiting for a cry of alarm to break the silence. None came and finally the tribesmen and women were all in their positions in the meadow to begin their cold, silent vigil.

The moon had moved across the sky and the light of day had appeared over the horizon when the White Ones filed past the entrance to the cave. As they glanced in they were unsurprised to see everyone still in their bed skins. The only person moving around to rekindle the fires was Flamina and she did not even look at them which alarmed no one; they were well aware of her hatred of them. They filed over the High Pasture, the damp soaking up their white robes which wrapped about their ankles as they walked. The rising sun glowed orange through the early morning mist as the Outlanders joined them. There was no sense of danger - just another day about to start, the routine ceremony to be completed. The white figures climbed down the rocky path onto the open meadow beside the lake.

Saretta appeared quite lucid as she took her place at the front. She had changed her filthy robes for clean and replaced the Kalia Headdress. In her right hand she held the Sun Staff, beautifully crafted with painted suns spiralling down the shaft. The three Attendants stood behind the High Priestess in a line. Lexana held an agitated wolf, that pulled at the cord tied around its neck, whimpering, hackles raised. Saretta turned and fixed her with a withering stare and, although it took all Lexana's strength, she managed to control and calm the animal. The Guardians took up their position five paces behind the Attendants and beyond them the Outlanders.

The White Ones stood waiting, eyes closed, their faces turned skywards and, as they did so, the first man died without a sound. Tendo was the first to strike: he rose silently from the long grasses behind the Outlander, clasped his hand over the mouth, pulling the man's head backwards, and the black, glinting blade cut through the soft flesh of the throat. The small, dark man held his much larger victim in a vice-like grip as he tried to struggle but the life drained from him with the spurting blood and the body was lowered gently to the ground by Tendo's blood-spattered arms.

Three other Outlanders quietly but unwillingly gave their lives to the figures hidden in the long grasses.

As the early morning light hit them, Saretta opened her arms wide but it was Lexana who cried out:

'Great God of the Sun, you have brought us your gift once more and we thank you for it. Look down on us during this period of light and help us to live according to your wishes. Let us keep this, our land as you would want it kept, let us treat nature with respect knowing that its power is far greater than ours and let us also honour the animals that provide us with our food.'

Another Outlander fell, brought down by Kadell and Valon.

Silently and deadly, they held him down and dispatched him quickly, like a wild animal, with a thrust of a spear into the neck. The two tribesmen crouched quietly in the tall grasses, hoping for more time but they heard a call and, peering out, they could see one of the Outlanders looking around him. He was approaching their position so they crawled away in the direction of the White Ones, making as little disturbance as possible.

The ceremony continued, the White Ones unaware of encroaching death. Lexana turned to the others.

'Now each Attendant must offer the Sun their own thanks,' she said. 'I shall begin: I thank you for our lives and those of our brothers and sisters in the tribe and I ask that you care for them as you do for us.'

The remaining Outlanders were now searching for their friends, their movements becoming more urgent as they realised something was wrong. Another one was dragged down, his blood staining the earth below him.

Lexana held out her arm and touched Talia on the shoulder. The tall, thin young woman stared avidly at the sky, unable to utter her wishes aloud, but voicing them internally and hoping that the God of the Sun would hear her. In turn she, touched Minaya who, although she was expecting it, jumped nervously.

'Great God of the Sun,' her quiet voice strained out the words, shaking. 'Protect us all from the evil that is around us and ... and ... let me do no harm this day,' she finished in a rush.

Outlanders were running, searching, calling. They met in the centre to question each other.

The Guardians became aware of noise behind them and looked round, realising something was wrong, but not daring to speak. Entirely engrossed in the ceremony and her own unstable thoughts, Saretta swivelled round to take her place facing the Attendants. She glared at the shaking girl before throwing her head back and crying, her voice harsh and uncaring:

'Look down on my people and protect the strong. Teach the weak their proper place and let this tribe accept that only by shedding those who want in strength shall we become a better and more powerful race. Now,' her voice became louder and more strident with every word, 'now, the time has arrived for your cleansing, great Sun God. The tribe has no weapons with which to defend itself and so we shall rid ourselves this day of those who do not have the strength to fulfil your wishes.'

Lexana let out a gasp and Minaya slumped to the ground sobbing. Talia showed the horror she felt, slapping her hand over her mouth. In their disbelief the three remaining Guardians forgot their position and stared at the High Priestess.

The Outlanders split up and began searching again in a more ordered fashion, each taking an area through which to hunt for their lost members.

'You,' screamed Saretta, pointing at the crumpled Minaya.

'You are not fit to be an Attendant Priestess of the new Pescovari. However, I have decided that you will be spared because of your skin - you will be useful for breeding.'

Her crazed eyes glided over to Talia.

'You too must bear children with our colouring - that will be your duty, and your children will be honoured by all. You are too old to be useful,' she pointed viciously at Lexana.

Talia shook her head wildly and her mouth opened with a silent scream. Minaya's sobbing became a wail and Tordano ran to her side, dropping his spear, as the wolf began to growl, instinctively bearing its teeth at Saretta. Lexana felt the cord cut through her hand as she held the animal back, preventing it from leaping at the demented figure in front of them.

Too Long To Die

A shout went up from one of the Outlanders - he had discovered the body of Tendo's victim and the others ran towards him. It was the moment they had waited for. Out of the waving grasses rose up the tribal hunters. The Outlanders turned but they were on them. Spear clashed against spear, stabbing and pushing. The superior blades of the Pescovari cut deeper when they made contact but the Outlanders were tall and strong, vicious in a fight. One fell with an arrow in his chest, blood oozing from the side of his mouth. Unable to get a clear shot at any of the others for they were surrounded, Delina moved back towards the gathering of the White Ones.

Saretta was still oblivious to the battle going on close by. She waved the staff menacingly.

'Yes, Tordano, yes,' she screeched. 'Make her stop! Silence her! You know how to do that well enough, but that's our secret, isn't it? That's why you must do what I say!'

'I don't care anymore,' the Guardian shouted back at her. 'You will do no more harm to Minaya!'

From underneath his tunic he grabbed a knife and charged at the High Priestess. Mad as she was, she was still fast on her feet and, side-stepping the man, she brought the staff crashing down on his head knocking him to the floor. Valt jumped forward to wrestle the staff from her hands and Tordano pushed himself to his feet, blood running down the side of his face. The knife was in his hand. So focussed on Saretta was the strange group, that only the booming shout of 'No!' from close by made them stop and look around. Only then did they realise they were surrounded by armed men and women who had risen from the long grasses and stepped out from behind bushes and rocks.

Davoril rushed forward and knocked the knife out of the hand of Tordano, momentarily frozen in the confusion. Sarril moved too fast; his spear slid deep into the side of Davoril who sunk to his knees. As he toppled over, gasping in pain, an arrow sliced into Sarril's body and he crashed to the ground. The tribe moved forward, their spears pointing towards the pale figures, black blades glinting in the early morning sunlight. Lonell stepped forward and secured Saretta. Holding her hands, he pushed her to the ground, as she screamed and thrashed against him.

Another Outlander died with Kadell's spear through his eye, dropping instantly and the last two, with blood running from their wounds and thinking only of saving their own lives, fled.

'Let them go,' ordered an exhausted Kadell. 'They will tell the others. They won't return.'

'Tendo!' Lonell's voice shouted from the group of white figures, surrounded by members of the tribe. 'Come, quickly.'

Tendo's view was obscured by the tall grasses so he could not see the man lying on the ground but he crossed the distance as fast as he could. Throwing his spear to one side, he dropped to his knees beside his closest friend.

'Davoril! No! Stay with me, my friend!'

Davoril's limp hand held Tendo's arm and he groaned as Endorina examined his injury. He started to speak but a blood-filled cough wracked his body and his arm dropped down to his side. He cleared his throat weakly and whispered, 'My brother,' as the life drained from him, a smile no longer on the handsome face of the blond man.

The intense silence was broken only by the sobbing of both men and women; even Saretta had temporarily stopped her wailing. Then the whole tribe, White Ones and tribesmen and women alike stood and howled their grief, the sound echoing off the rock faces that surrounded the Mountain Water meadowland.

Mila, tears running down her face, made her way towards Lexana and held out the package that she had been responsible for since leaving the cave so many hours before. The wolf's nose twitched and, teeth bared, it turned towards Mila. She pulled a piece of meat out of the package and held it out, gingerly. The black nose sniffed and Cannot took the offering, and then another. The young woman stretched out her hand and stroked the animal's neck, its hackles dropping, so she unwound the cord from Lexana's bleeding hand and led it away from the circle.

Saretta took the removal of the wolf as the signal for her to resume her tirade, incorrectly assuming that Kadell was there to support her since the tribe had prevented Tordano's attack. She shrugged off Lonell's hands and pulled herself to her feet.

'Dead! You are dead, Tordano!' she shrieked. 'Take him to the Pit. He will be sacrificed tonight!' Her order was directed at Valt but, when no one moved, she looked around, frowning in confusion.

'Nobody is going to be sacrificed today, Saretta,' insisted Kadell, gently but firmly. 'In fact, no one is ever going to be sacrificed again.'

'And what gives you the right to decide that? I am the High Priestess and I say what will happen, not you.'

Her eyes were slits as she watched him.

'No longer, Saretta. Everything is changing from this day.'

For a moment she said nothing, made no move, and then suddenly she lunged at the Leader. One hand made contact with his red beard and the other slashed at his face, his eyes the focus of the attack. A snarling, vicious animal, Lonell and Valt pulled her off and held her arms until she was surrounded by black points of death, digging into her clothing. Her eyes dropped to the spears and when she raised them again they were full of disbelief.

'Weapons,' she said. 'But you have no weapons.'

She tried to push a spear head away and her hand sliced open on the blade. She wailed as she saw the red blood well up and drip down the front of her white ceremonial robe. Lonell looked at Tordano and saw his confusion; he knew the other man was trying to work out where they had come from.

'The blades are ...' Tordano searched for a word, unable to help himself, '... magnificent.'

Pallo smiled at the Guardian in appreciation, before he remembered and replaced the expression with a glare.

'So what are you going to do now?' the sneering voice of Saretta cut into Kadell's indecision.

'Soon we are going to hear the truth. Lonell knows what happened to Narthan and he will tell us who killed him. Then I'll make a judgement over our future. There is no need for anyone else to return to the earth this day, but no longer will this tribe be ruled by injustice and cruelty.'

Kadell looked around at those who had been known as Enlightened Ones. The women were still too shaken to show any reaction; they were huddled together for protection and comfort. The men stared back at him with expressions he could not understand but Lonell recognised Valt's as relief. Tordano was more difficult to read but Lonell could sense the fear that lurked beneath the mask.

'Now we must deal with those who have returned to the earth. Lexana,' Kadell addressed the Attendant as Endorina tied the hide bandage into place around her hand, 'Would you see to the ceremony?'

Tendo stood forward.

'Davoril always said he wanted his body returned to the earth in Salt Water. Could we ...' He turned away, overcome with grief and Kadella put her arm around his shoulders.

Kadell looked at Lexana who nodded, and then he spoke.

'We shall bear Davoril to the Salt Water for his proper rites. The Outlanders and Sarril can stay where they fell. Animals will take care of them. They deserve no better.'

Too Long To Die

The Sun was high in the sky by the time the men and women of the Pescovari, weary in mind and body, crossed the High Pasture towards their home. Tendo clutched at the shell-shaped stone that Lexana had found, and which had been given to him as Davoril had no mother or siblings. Lonell, walking beside him, saw Tendo open the palm of his hand to reveal the shape of the stone dug into his flesh from the tightness of his grip, but there was now a calmness in his face, a steadiness, and Lonell wondered if these stones that held the spirit of those returned to the earth also passed on some of their strength. Whatever the reason, Tendo was now back in control of himself and his expression marked him as a man with a purpose. Lonell wondered what that purpose was.

Everyone had taken the opportunity to wash off the dried blood in the Salt Water so they felt cleaner but, still taut with emotion, the tribe kept their weapons at the ready, in case of trouble. Kadell suddenly held up his arms to stop everyone and turned to address the White Ones.

'At the cave we'll hear the truth of Narthan's return to the earth and the future of the tribe will be decided. Don't try to do anything stupid - you have seen our weapons and there are many here who would like to use them on you. If you make it necessary we will bind your arms but I don't want it to come to that.'

As if on cue, Saretta tried to grab a spear. She had been quietly observing those around her and selected Bascana as the weakest. It took everyone by surprise and only the disfigured girl's deep hatred gave her the strength to knock the woman to the ground and reclaim her spear. She stood over the now cringing creature on the floor, spear poised to strike, but with great force of will she stopped herself. Visible to all, loathing gave way to horror, shaken by the strength of her feelings, at her desire to take the life of the pathetic figure at her feet. Lonell nodded approvingly when she turned away rapidly so as to do her no more harm.

Tendo and Valon pulled the almost unrecognisable Saretta to her feet and took some of the cord offered by Lonell. They tied her hands firmly behind her back while she screached and wriggled trying to escape them, but to no avail.

'Go on ahead and tell Flamina the news and that we are on our way,' Kadell called over to Mila.

Girl and wolf took to their heels and ran across the High Pasture, relieved to escape the tension for a while. The run calmed the wolf, now content to be with Mila who always seemed to have food. When they reached the cave, she gave the fretting Flamina the message but she could see that everything was already prepared.

'Why have you taken so long? ' Flamina asked, dreading the answer. Hearing Mila's reply, she sat down heavily, weeping until the tears dripped off her chin onto the cave floor, the joy of the victory nullified by the loss. There was no one who had not loved Davoril.

While waiting, Flamina had moved all the bed skins to one side of the cave. Dried meats and small acorn loaves were ready on platters with bowls of dried fruit and nuts beside them and the hungry girl took a loaf and pushed it into her mouth.

The children had just been sent to the rear of the cave and told not to move when they heard clattering on the outside ledge. Since Saretta's last escape attempt, the short walk back had taken place without incident and soon every member of the Pescovari was inside the cave. The six remaining White Ones were seated on stones facing the cave entrance, looking up at the four men who stood before them: Valon, Lonell, Kadell and Tendo, still grey with sadness but a look of determination on his face. These men had put aside their spears but the others who stood behind and to the sides of those to be judged still bristled with weapons.

Food had been offered to all. Saretta refused, snarling and spitting at Flamina as she held out the dish. She was offered no more but the others were grateful and began to relax a little. Once again, Lonell recognised the skill of the Leader.

Kadell used the Sun Staff, taken from the High Priestess and knocked the end on the ground three times. The sound echoed through the cave.

'Quiet!' he said, unnecessarily, for a tense silence had fallen over the cave. 'It is time to hear what Lonell has to say. He will now tell us about Narthan's return to the earth.'

Too Long To Die

Chapter Twenty Seven

Lonell was surprised at how nervous he felt. He had never spoken in front of so many people and the future of his tribe could depend on his words. Faces turned to him, some hopeful, some frightened, all expectant. His mouth felt dry as he started to speak.

'It was clear to me from the start that something was wrong about this death, aside from the obvious fact that it was unnatural. Afterwards, when I thought about the search, I realised that it had been planned for me to find Narthan's body.'

His eyes scanned over the men and women seated in front of him.

'It was a huge shock to you when Sim claimed the find and not me. In fact, Valt, you were terrified of what Saretta would do because you had failed to make sure I was held responsible. It was only due to Sim's eagerness that you had no choice but to hold him for sacrifice instead of me. Even for you, Saretta, it would have been too obvious if you'd swapped us over for no reason but, thinking about it now, perhaps you should have done.'

His dark eyes, cold with anger, bore down on High Priestess who was looking at him, a sardonic smile on her face.

'That was your second mistake. Your first was in letting me see the body and giving me time to look at it which showed that this was a very complicated death.'

He looked at the people standing in the cave and scratched his head, wondering how to explain it all simply.

'Many of you know some of the things that happened but I'll try to explain it all. There were three things that I noticed: firstly, there were bruises around his throat which were the same on both sides. To begin with, I didn't recognise what it meant. Secondly, Narthan's lips were swollen and the ends of some of his fingertips had blisters on them and his mouth smelt bitter. And finally, it was obvious that he'd been hit on the head with a stone or something hard. In fact I returned later and found the stone which I've hidden and can produce if necessary but I used it to test out an idea I had.'

He took a deep breath.

'Let me take you through these one at a time,' he continued. 'Ancient Pel, you helped me solve the bruising around the neck with your dye.'

The old man looked confused and Lonell smiled at him.

'Do you all remember the hand marks you made on the walls?' he asked the tribe.

A murmur of agreement and appreciation filled the cave which stopped as soon as Lonell began to speak again.

'I was trying to copy the marks on Narthan's neck and it proved to me that it was caused ...,' he turned to Valon next to him and placed his hands round his neck, 'like this.'

Lonell turned back and faced the tribe.

'He had the breath squeezed out of him.'

Muttered comments filled the air and some turned round to look at the 'art' they had made, perhaps not as pleased with it as before.

Lonell held up his hand and the noise ceased again.

'But there was more to it than that. It was also clear from his lips and the smell that he had been given Death Juice or part of a plant that kills. Endorina showed me a plant which would have caused the signs that I found on the body. This plant is so deadly that even touching part of it can make your body swell and break out in blisters.'

He turned to Kadell.

Too Long To Die

'I think we should show everyone what this evil plant looks like so they won't pick it by mistake and we should destroy any that we find.'

The Leader nodded, glancing at Tendo.

'And, as if this were not enough,' said Lonell, 'the man had been hit on the head with a stone. It was a large stone but any of us could have picked it up so it did not help to tell me who the killer was but what was interesting was that it had only a small amount of blood on it. I killed a rabbit by hitting it with a similar stone and there was much more blood. Endorina helped me with this too - she agreed with what I had thought from the beginning: if Narthan had been alive when he was hit, there would have been more blood so, for some reason, the killer hit the head of someone who had already returned to the earth, which made no sense to me at the time. It was only much later that I realised that this was connected with the skin.'

'What skin?' asked Kadell, wondering why he had not heard about it before.

'The skin the body was wrapped in.' Lonell looked at Kadell's blank face. 'Don't you remember when we brought the body back it was wrapped in an old, dark wolf skin?'

'I thought you had wrapped him in that,' replied Kadell, a little embarrassed.

'No,' continued Lonell. 'He was in something that we might use,' he pointed at his own clothes. 'He wasn't in a white skin as you might expect, and for a long time I couldn't understand why. I was thinking what the killer wanted me to think.'

He looked round the cave over the heads of the six figures in white.

'Only one of *us* would use a dark skin to cover the body and, if we did kill someone, we'd be likely to do it in the easiest manner, like hitting the person with a stone. The stone even came from this cave, from the storage shelf.'

He glared down at the remaining Enlightened Ones.

'Do you really think we are all so simple?'

All but one of the white figures in front of him cowered slightly at the anger directed at them. A murmur of annoyance bubbled up in the cave until Kadell brought the staff down on the ground, once more.

Lonell pushed a shaking hand through his dark hair.

'It was all done to make us think the killer was one of us, that he or she was one of the tribe. And for a long time, I admit, I believed it. I spent my time wondering who would want Narthan dead. Of course, as we all know, nearly everyone in this cave had a reason to hate the man. He inflicted pain on so many people that it could have been anyone here and I wasted many hours agonising over my thoughts, not wanting any of you to be the killer.'

Lonell turned his head to look at Valon, his eyes communicating a silent warning.

'It was only after Valon and I returned from our trip away, which I went on, not only to do some trading, but also to clear my head, to think more clearly. It's remarkable how you can see things better from a distance and, when we returned, I was able to see the truth. Someone sitting down here in front of me had made every effort to prevent me from looking at the members of the White Cave.'

He pointed at them, moving his hand along the row until it came to rest on Tordano.

'You tried to stop me. You warned me not to look for the truth, that I would be killed if I did, and then you found the opportunity to tell me that Valt and Sarril were out with their bows on the day I was shot.'

'I thought you were helping me, that it was Saretta who did not want the truth to come out because she would look bad if I could prove that it was not Sim who killed Narthan, that she had made a mistake.'

Valt was glaring at Tordano.

'I have not used a bow for many moons,' said Valt, a hesitation in his voice. Even Kadell noticed the difference and took a step forward to stand in front of him.

'Now is the time to be telling the truth if you wish to have any chance of a future with this tribe.'

Valt closed his eyes briefly.

'I admit,' he said, 'I have used my bow but not then, not on that day. I swear to that. I had nothing to do with your injury, Lonell.'

Lonell nodded and Kadell stepped back again.

'I tried to stop you but you wouldn't leave it alone. You had to keep on looking for the answers. Why couldn't you just accept that we were all better off without Narthan? He was no loss to anyone.'

The hatred in the Guardian's voice took nearly everyone by surprise but Lonell was one of the very few who understood it.

'He hurt her, Tordano, didn't he? Every day you had to listen to her pain and could do nothing.'

'He was a beast,' he shouted in reply. 'He didn't deserve to live.'

Great tears began to fall down Minaya's white face.

'We all know what Narthan was capable of,' Lonell said slowly. 'We saw what he did to Marita and ...' - he paused to make the dreadful revelation more dramatic - 'he did the same to Minaya.'

The cave gasped, unable to believe what they were hearing. If anyone was in doubt of the full significance of what he had said, Lonell's next words ensured they understood.

'Marita went there for three moons and we saw the effect he had on her. Minaya went over there,' he pointed behind him at the White Cave, 'to spend the rest of her life.'

'As an Attendant Priestess it was her duty to remain pure to honour the Gods but Narthan respected nothing; no rules, no person.

Too Long To Die

I don't know when he first started using her - I presume it was when she became a woman. He forced her and, I'm guessing that he threatened to tell Saretta ...'

'It was earlier than that. She was still only a child,' interrupted Tordano, his voice close to breaking. 'He was going to tell Saretta that I was the one using her. We would both have been sacrificed. She would have believed him - she thought he could do no wrong.'

Minaya was rocking backwards and forwards on her seat, holding her knees.

'It wasn't my fault. It wasn't my fault,' she repeated, over and over again.

Tordano moved from his place and squatted down beside her, placing his arm around her shoulder. No one stopped him. Lonell looked around the cave. The women were crying and some of the men seemed close to joining them while Lonell could see that others were battling to hold down the thunderous rage that they felt.

'Seven winters came and went and during this time she had to put up with his constant ... attention,' Tordano continued the ghastly tale, as he stroked her white hair to calm her. 'She could do nothing and nor could I. Then she ...'

'No, Tordano, please,' begged the girl.

'It's over now. We have to tell the truth. It's the right time,' he reassured her, his voice gentle and soothing. 'Then Minaya discovered she was carrying. At first she did not realise what was happening - she had no way of knowing what the changes in her body meant. We had to ask Lexana for help and she provided some herbs to dislodge the baby.'

Tordano heard the gasps and groans behind him and he turned to face the tribe.

'We had to do it or Saretta would have sacrificed Minaya and the baby.'

Too Long To Die

He turned back to the four men in front of him.

'It was quite large, bigger than we'd expected - it almost seemed to be alive but it didn't breathe. We went deep into the caves and built a rocky grave where no one would find it.'

'Many moons later, Saretta announced that Ancient Pel was going to use that same cave for his painting so we went to dismantle the grave, expecting to find nothing. We both thought the body would have rotted away but when we took the stones away we found..., we found ...' Tordano put his hands over his face.

'You found the tiny baby intact - dried out but still whole,' Lonell finished for him.

Tordano looked up at him and nodded, tears in his eyes.

'Then you took the body, wrapped it in a piece of very fine skin and put it in a beautiful bag. Does Minaya know where you put the bag, Tordano?'

'Yes, we were together but that was not meant to be its final resting place. We were disturbed. Tendo, you were leading a hunting party and had chased a wild pig right down to the cliff edge. So we hid the bag, meaning to go back, but we never got the chance.'

'The baby has not returned to the earth,' wailed Minaya.

'Yes, it has,' Lonell assured her, gently, and explained that he had put the tiny body into the Salt Water to be taken back to the earth. He briefly told the tribe about the discovery on the beach but he was vague about the exact place for he still wanted his cave to remain a secret.

'One thing I don't understand,' said Lonell. 'After all that time, why did you kill Narthan then and not before?'

There was not a sound in the cave. They all now knew who had killed the Guardian but there were still certain pieces of the puzzle that needed to be explained.

'Minaya bore the abuse to save me but when she lost the baby she ... changed. To begin with he left her alone - I think her carrying may have frightened him - but then he started again with the additional threat that, if we did not do exactly as he said, he would tell Saretta that I had been the cause of her giving birth.'

Tordano looked up at Kadell, tears coursing down his cheeks.

'Minaya could bear it no longer,' he cried. 'She thought there was no other way out. I told her we should leave and find another home. I'm certain we could have found somewhere before the winter. I thought she'd agreed that we would go but, the next day, when I returned from gathering provisions for our journey, I heard sounds coming from Narthan's cave, terrible noises. Minaya was watching him as he thrashed around. He was shouting nonsense and groaning and she just sat beside him, not moving, just looking at him. Her face was blank, no emotion, and then she said...,' he swallowed hard, the words sticking in his throat.

'She said, 'He is taking too long to die.' That's all she said. 'He is taking too long to die.' I knew I had to do something to make him quiet before the others returned so I put my hands around his neck and squeezed until he made no more sound.'

As though all the air had been dragged out of him, Tordano crumpled. His body shook and he cried out his grief for all to hear. Endorina brought a cup and, cradling his head in her arm, she made him drink. Gradually he calmed down and lay motionless but conscious on the floor. She also allowed Minaya a small drink of her infusion but, wanting the girl to remain alert, she kept it to a few sips. Lonell was grateful that Endorina had thought to prepare the draught the night before and, glancing at the man standing next to him, he wondered if she had allowed Tendo a small taste of it before he had to face the tribe.

Lonell realised that he could expect no more from the Guardian so he filled in the details as he knew them for the rest of the tribe.

Too Long To Die

'They hid Narthan's body in the caves and later, Tordano must have taken a skin out of our storage cave. Then, during the night, they took the body down to Mountain Water. Of course, Saretta, you must have known Narthan was missing that night because he failed to attend the Sun Sleep ceremony but you waited to see if something happened that you could use to your advantage. I imagine you discovered the truth, you probably saw them carry the body out, and have used it control them with threats ever since. You didn't care that one of your own had returned to the earth and I'm sure you knew what Narthan was doing before but you saw it as an opportunity to get rid of me and gain greater control over your Guardians, who all hated the way that Narthan behaved. Even if they did not know about Minaya, everyone knew what had happened to Marita.'

'Very clever, but you are too arrogant, Lonell,' the harsh, cackling voice exclaimed. 'Why should I, Saretta, High Priestess, care about you? Why should I need to get rid of you, as you put it? You are nothing to me.'

'You have always been uneasy with me, Saretta,' he replied, staring straight into her mad eyes. 'I am the Dreamer - I think differently to others and that frightens you. You knew you couldn't control me quite as easily as the others and that's why you wanted to sacrifice me. Instead you managed to kill a poor, innocent, old woman who was grieving for the son she'd lost.'

He took one step towards her, his fist clenched in anger.

'You must be very proud of what you've done, you head-sick creature. You will no longer be able to hurt anyone. And I'm pleased to tell you that Sim is alive and living with the Fillari,' he finished with a sneer.

No one had seen Lonell really angry before and, in the stunned silence that followed, he turned his back on Saretta to gaze out of the cave entrance, trying to regain his composure.

Too Long To Die

It happened so fast that no one could prevent it. Saretta rose from her seat shrieking and dived towards Lonell, head down, hands still bound behind her back. Her head hit him in the small of the back and the momentum took them both out through the entrance and over the ledge.

Her screams echoed around the crevice for what seemed like an age until a distant thud brought silence.

Too Long To Die

Chapter Twenty Eight

'Lonell!' screamed Mila.

The whole tribe surged forward towards the ledge. Valon threw himself down, peering desperately over the edge into the abyss below. He urgently tried to push the Cord Plant away that was growing down the rock face and obscuring his view. Nothing moved below: there was no sign of life, no sign of his friend.

'Lonell!' he shouted, desperation filling his voice. 'Lonell, answer me, please!'

Other voices joined in calling his name over and over again. Nothing. Valon felt hands on his shoulders, someone trying to pull him away from the edge.

'It's over, Valon. He's gone,' came Kadell's agonised voice.

'No,' yelled back Valon, shaking him off. 'It's not possible. You don't understand. Lonell and I are going to travel together. He can't ...'

He felt Endorina kneel beside him, a cup in her hand, and he saw a tear drop hit the earth beside him. He could hear the crying and moaning of the tribe and he put his head down on the cold stone ledge and wept.

Suddenly Tendo held up his hands.

'Quiet! Listen!' he shouted.

The silence that descended was instant and absolute. No one moved and from out of the depths of the chasm, they heard a groan and a weak call.

'Help!'

'Lonell! Where are you?' Valon cried out.

'Below you.'

'I can't see you,' Valon shouted back.

'I'm hidden ... by an overhang.' Lonell's voice was filled with agony.

'Can you climb back up?'

'No. Send me down a cord ...You'll have to pull me up ... I can only use one arm.'

Delina was already returning with the longest cord she could find.

'Quickly! I can't hold on much longer.' Pain was audible in every word.

The line snaked down the cliff face below them and they felt it taken up.

'Tell us when you're ready and we'll haul you up.'

They waited, breath held, hoping that the cord would be strong enough. Moments passed and there was no sound.

'What's happening?' shouted Valon, beginning to worry again.

'I can't do it,' came the weak reply. 'My arm .. it's too painful. It's caught in the plant - I can't tie the cord ... I can't pull myself up.'

Valon looked round desperately and saw men and women dragging the hunting nets out of storage. Pulling them to the cave, they spread them out and people swarmed over them, tying them together as fast as they could.

'Hold on, Lonell! It won't be much longer. I'm coming down to get you!'

There was no answer and Valon's insides churned in fear.

He rose to his feet and went to help with the nets. Everyone knew that each moment that passed increased the chance that Lonell would never return to the cave but they tied their knots carefully, ensuring their strength.

Once finished, a row of bodies lay on the ground holding the top of the netting which was thrown down towards the injured man.

Pallo was still holding the rope and he was joined by Mila. Valon began to climb down over the edge, partly using the netting but, to take some weight off it, he also held on to the growing Cord Plant. Slowly he lowered himself and suddenly felt his feet swinging in the air, unable to touch the rock face.

'The overhang', he thought, and peered underneath. He could see Lonell, the Cord Plant looped round one shoulder, pulling it up into an ugly position, while his other hand gripped the cord they had sent down. Valon climbed down further until he was beside his friend. At first he thought he was too late, that Lonell was already gone, but he saw him shift and cry out in pain.

'I'm here, Lonell,' he said and saw the other man turn his head to stare at him, disbelieving.

Valon wasted no more time on words - he could see Lonell would not last for much longer. He held his friend while he moved his hand to the netting and, tying the long cord round the other man's waist, he shouted up to Pallo to be ready to take more weight on it.

'Hold on hard,' he ordered, making sure that Lonell obeyed him. Then he cut through the cord that held the shoulder, bringing a groan of pain from his friend which he did his best to ignore. He placed himself below the injured man until Lonell was sitting on his shoulders.

'Now! Pull!' Valon shouted to the people above.

With Valon pushing upwards from below and Pallo and Mila pulling from above, Lonell steadied himself as best he could with his uninjured arm and, in this way, they crept up the rock face, painfully slowly. Half way up Valon's foot broke through a weak point in the netting, and nearly fell, his hands scrabbling at the cords, ripping the skin from his fingers. At the last moment he caught hold and saw, with relief, that the long cord had held Lonell. He pulled his way back up, suffering as he did so, every time his bleeding hands grabbed out for the next hold. At last they were close enough for Kadell to reach down and grasp the back of Lonell's tunic, hauling him back onto the ledge. Lonell groaned as he rolled over and passed out.

Valon was helped back onto the ledge by Tendo who grinned and slapped him on the back as Endorina and Lexana pushed their way through to the prone man, whose misshapen shoulder jutted forward at an unnatural angle. They looked at each other and grimaced, aware of what they must do.

'It's good that he's sleeping - this will be painful,' said Endorina as she moved his arm at right angles away from his body. Lexana placed her hands behind the shoulder and Endorina guided the arm upwards and back. The pain of the first excruciating attempt woke Lonell with a cry but, at the second try, the shoulder popped back into place and the agony was replaced by instant relief which flooded through Lonell's body. Lexana took some hide and tied the arm, bent at the elbow, across his front.

'You must keep this strapping on,' she said, her voice shaking. 'If you try to use your arm, the shoulder could come out of position again and we shall have to repeat the replacement.'

'Once is enough, thank you,' he said, through gritted teeth.

He lay for a moment, unable to move until Pallo and Kadell carried him carefully into the cave where he sank back onto his bed skins and his eyes closed.

He woke with the two Healers beside him, Endorina holding out a cup of her infusion.

'No,' he said groggily, pushing it away. 'I must keep my head clear. I have to think.'

'Just a little,' she insisted gently, 'to keep the pain down. It will help your body to heal.'

As he reluctantly took a sip, he looked up at them and noticed the tears and grief on Lexana's face.

'You are sad for Saretta,' he stated. 'Lexana, I can't understand how you, of all people, can regret her death. She was evil.'

'No, Lonell, not evil. She was head sick and there was nothing I could do to help her. I failed her. As she became worse, all I could do was try to keep her calm with my healing plants but I could not cure her. It was as if there were two people inside her and, at times, the person I had known as a young girl would appear. Then we could sit and talk about everything but, at other times, most of the time at the end, it was the monster that controlled her body. She could do nothing about it, Lonell. It is the young Saretta that I mourn.'

The whole cave had been listening to her words and the anger that each person felt began to mellow. It was just the start; the healing process would take time, but it had begun.

Everyone was milling around, wondering what was going to happen, when Kadell resumed his place silhouetted against the light shining in through the entrance and the staff rang out again through the cave. They all looked at him, waiting.

'Lonell, do you have anything to add?' asked the Leader.

'I think I have said enough.' Lonell shook his head tiredly.

Kadell cleared his throat.

'I shall have to consider everything that has been said this morning and talk to others before I make any decisions. I am willing to hear from anyone if they have a valid point, from both sides.'

'Now, we should all have something to eat. I, for one, am starving so Vellisco, please prepare some food. We will all feel better with some stew inside us.'

He had taken a step away when he halted.

'And I think the spears can be put away in the storage cave now, as long as I have your word that you will stay here peacefully until I have given my judgement.'

He looked pointedly at the dejected figures in front of him. They all nodded without hesitation. A buzz of activity filled the cave and it was not long before the aroma of meat drifted into the air.

Kadell sat and spoke with Lexana for a while. He brought some food and left her, hunched over a platter of meat which lay untouched in her lap. Then he called Tendo and they headed to the back of the cave where Lonell was sitting, trying to get comfortable. Valon, his hands now bandaged, and Mila were with him and by his side, much to Kadell's astonishment, lay the wolf. Mila held up her hand to stop the Leader and went over to Vellisco. She returned with some pieces of meat which she gave to Kadell and Tendo.

'Give it the meat. It seems to like people who feed it,' she grinned, 'because that seems to be a sign that you are a friend.'

As the Leader, Kadell did not want to show the fear that was curdling his insides and so he stepped forward and held out a chunk of goat's meat. The large beast clambered to its feet, nose twitching and gently took it from the man's hand. It did the same with Tendo's offering but the younger man's nerves betrayed him and he jumped slightly, his hand touching the animal's cheek. The wolf bent its head towards the hand as though to rest it there and, for a moment, the two stared into each other's eyes, transfixed. It was the wolf that broke the contact as it circled lazily and settled down once more and the men had the strangest feeling that they had just been granted permission to join the group.

'Do you feel up to talking, my friend?' Kadell asked Lonell, who nodded his answer. At that moment, Endorina came over to dispense some more healing drink to soothe the injured man's pain. When she gave him the cup Kadell put out his hand.

'I hope that isn't too strong,' he said. 'I still need to hear his opinion. He's no good to me if he's asleep.'

Endorina grinned at them.

'Then you'd be better to only drink a little, as you did before. Keep the rest for later, Lonell.'

Lonell was far more alert this time and, although he drank only a few mouthfuls, he could feel the gently numbing sensation creep over his body. He laughed as the pain disappeared from his shoulder and surrounding muscles. For a moment, all he wanted was to put his head down on his bed skins and go to sleep, but he saw a flicker of annoyance pass over his Leader's face and he forced himself to stay wake.

'I'll be better when I've had something to eat,' he tried to reassure the people around him, unaware that his slurred words sounded as though he had been drinking the strong liquor they made for celebrations.

Mila rushed off and brought back substantial platters of food for all of them, while Tendo collected a water bag and horn vessels. Little was said as they delved into the food, forgetting for an instant the decisions that had to be made.

Replete and with the empty platters removed, Kadell opened the meeting. They talked throughout the afternoon and into the evening. Various people from the tribe asked to talk with the Leader; most gave useful opinions except Flamina who insisted that they all be exiled or worse. Seeing her daughter suffer so dreadfully and also having lost her friend, Verina, she was in no mood to consider anything other than the most extreme vengeance.

Finally, Lexana approached them. Kadell was pleased because there was still something he did not fully understand but he had not wanted to summon her. He was aware of her suffering.

'I know we have already spoken, Kadell,' she said. 'But I have seen you looking at me and know you have more questions.'

'Thank you.' He smiled gently at her as she sat in front of him.

'Can you tell us why Saretta brought in the Outlanders?' he asked and everyone waited with interest for her answer.

'Saretta was sure you would find out the truth,' she replied, nodding at Lonell.

'She even ordered Tordano to return you to the earth. He did try to warn you off first, but, it seemed, nothing would stop you. One night, she became hysterical, screaming and crying, insisting that you were a danger to her, you would defeat her. Sarril said he knew of a group of men from his old tribe who would fight for her, in return for food and as many women as they wanted.'

Lexana swallowed hard and stared at the ground.

'Despite my pleading, she sent him off to find them, and from that moment she would not listen to me anymore. Only my infusions calmed her but sometimes she refused to take them. She was out of my control and I could do nothing. So many dead and I should have been able to stop it.'

She put her head in her hands and wept.

Daylight was failing and the evening meal being prepared when Kadell knew they had considered all the facts and every possible solution. He made his decision. Word went round that he would speak when everyone had finished eating. He passed the time walking on the High Pasture with Tendo and Kadella at his side, glad to escape from the suffocating cave for a short time.

They heard the clattering from below which told them that the meal was being cleared up and then a hush descended. It was time. The Leader turned to the others.

'Are you both certain?' he asked.

They nodded, illuminated by a full moon that shone its gentle light down onto them. Kadell looked up at the silver orb and hoped that it was a good sign, that the Gods were pleased with his choices.

Inside the cave everyone waited silently. The three figures had appeared as if by magic out of the darkness and, as Kadell started speaking, the only sound was that of a child being hushed by its mother.

'You all know that I've given this great consideration and listened to all who wished to speak with me. Saretta has returned to the earth and, although some may mourn for the person she once was, I'm sure that most will agree that her death has relieved us of a terrible burden. I'm only too glad that she failed to take Lonell with her and thank Valon for his courage.'

Sounds of agreement and elated stamping erupted from every part of the cave.

Kadell held up his hand.

'Our problem is what we should do with the others that were formally known as the Enlightened Ones. That is my first decision and I think we can all agree that they do not deserve to bear that title. The men are no longer Guardians and the women are not Attendants or Priestesses; they are just men and women, the same as us.'

Muted sounds betrayed their fear.

'Who will speak to the Gods on our behalf if we have no Priestess?' Ancient Pel asked the question they were all thinking.

'I will come to that later but we shall not be abandoned by the Gods, I promise you that. We have some in front of us here who have done nothing wrong except for supporting a cruel and wicked woman, for fear of their own and other's lives. Some performed their duties with ... relish, enjoying their power and another, Lexana, did it to protect others. She was told that if she did not follow her, Saretta would sacrifice one of us each day until she learnt to obey.'

He paused for the tribe to fully understand what he had just told them.

'And then we have two people who killed to protect themselves. I

Too Long To Die

had to decide whether what they did was justified and whether they would kill again and are therefore a danger to us. Do we exile them which, because of their skins is almost the same as sacrificing them? Their chances of survival if we turned them out would be ... poor.'

Kadell stopped for a moment and looked around the cave.

'I received mixed advice from you but this is my decision: they will all stay with us. They will remain a part of the tribe. In fact, they will now be real members of the tribe for they will live with us in this cave; they will have no rank, they will have to undertake the same basic tasks for which we are all responsible. The killing of Narthan, which cannot be forgiven, for it is the greatest crime that can be committed, was nevertheless, understandable and perhaps inevitable. Tordano added to his guilt by allowing others to suffer for his actions and even trying to take Lonell's life and, for this reason, his punishment is the most severe. Lonell has agreed that you may stay here but, you, Tordano, will never be allowed to bear a weapon of any sort. If at any time you need to use a knife, or any other tool with a blade, it will be under the strictest supervision.'

Due to the period of time the tribe had spent without weapons they realised the full implications of this punishment. Danger surrounded them in the form of many wild animals and, without the protection of a weapon, if Tordano left the cave, he would be in peril. Therefore, whenever he wanted to go outside, even for his most basic needs, he would either have to ask someone to accompany him or run the risk of injury or death. Any pride left completely drained from the pale, young man as he nodded his head in acceptance, but Kadell had not finished with him.

'In addition, if at any time you break our rules or cause any problems whatsoever, within a period of twelve moons, you may be exiled from the tribe and this period may be extended if considered necessary.'

Kadell moved his attention to the girl who sat beside him.

'Minaya.'

She started when she heard her name and looked up at the Leader with fearful eyes, threatening to overflow once more. Kadell's voice became more gentle.

'You have also committed a terrible crime but there are few people here who can bring themselves to blame you. I spoke to Lexana and we all feel that your ... experiences have affected your head, which is understandable. Kadella has agreed that she will look after you until you are able to live a normal life within the tribe and I know Ancient Pel will be at your side whenever you need him. However, it is only fair that you are put on the same twelve moon trial period as Tordano. Do you understand?'

There was no reaction to his question. She continued to look up at him but he was not sure that she had taken in his words.

He leant towards her.

'We are going to look after you,' he said kindly.

Kadella stepped forward and, putting her arms protectively around the young woman's shoulders, helped her to her feet and led her away to the farthest hearth where Ancient Pel joined them moments later.

'Valt and Talia, you will also be given twelve moons to prove yourselves but you will be accepted as part of the tribe. You, Valt, might find that there are certain people to whom you should apologise for past actions and I advise you to do so.'

Kadell looked past them to the people behind.

'His apologies will be accepted, I hope,' he said, a warning in his voice.

'And Lexana, will you come and stand beside me?'

She was startled but pulled herself to her feet and walked over to him. He turned her to face the tribe.

'This woman has done nothing but try to help us and she has

risked her own wellbeing to keep us safe. She should have been our High Priestess when Saretta took over but I hope she will take on the position now.'

Lexana's head snapped round to look at Kadell. Tears coursed down her cheeks and her acceptance was drowned out by cheers and the traditional stamping of appreciation that came from the men and women, relieved that their spiritual lives would finally be looked after by someone they could trust.

Kadell held up his hand for silence.

'It will take some time for the details to be worked out exactly but I intend for us all to live together in this cave. It's quite large enough. We'll decide what to do with the White Cave later but we shall no doubt find a good use for it. In the meantime I want to lay down some basic rules for all of us to live by. From now on there is no rank, with the exception of the Leader and, in spiritual matters, the Priestess. Our skins and hair colouring make no difference whatsoever. Each person will be judged on their merits and what they bring to the tribe. No one is 'better' than another. We'll continue to compete for our skills titles for that keeps us wanting to improve ourselves but we must all learn to live peacefully together.'

The tribe was beginning to get a little restless and Kadell became aware of the growing background noise. He held up his hand once more.

'I have only two more things to say. Firstly, Lonell. That man,' he pointed to the back, 'is responsible for us being here this day. Without him we would still be suffering the injustices of Saretta's rule with no end in sight. He has always been known as the Dreamer but I do not think this is a fair title. He does not just sit and dream; he thinks things through and then takes action.'

'Yes, sometimes he flies off cliffs,' shouted Pallo from the back which raised a barrage of laughter and stamping of feet.

'I think we should rename him the Thinker,' declared Kadell and the stamping became louder and louder until the cave was filled with noise and laughter.

'And finally,' shouted Kadell over the noise, his face becoming serious once more. The cave gradually quietened down. 'Finally, I have decided that this is a good time for the tribe to have a fresh start. I have made errors as Leader, as we all know, but I'm certain that I'm doing the right thing now. I have named Tendo as the new Leader and he will take our tribe into this new life that we have begun here. I offer him my help, if he needs it, but I know he will lead us wisely and bravely. You all know him well and appreciate the fine man that he has become. I ask you to give him your support. Tendo is the Leader of the Pescovari from this day onwards!'

The momentary silence and shock on the faces of the tribesmen and women was rapidly replaced by nods and growing sounds of agreement. The noise built up to a crescendo, billowing out of the cave and down into the abyss where, far below, it washed over the broken body of a mad woman, already forgotten by the people she had terrorised for so long.

THE END

Too Long To Die

Acknowledgements

I really never thought this book would be finished and it certainly would not have been without the help of so many people:

Annette Cattle and Claire Ambler who spent hours trying to find all the mistakes (any left are purely down to me - they did their best with a near impossible task!).
My brother, Johnnie Braithwaite, for making it possible for me to spend time on my writing.
Laurence Kennedy and Sally Seward at Convergences for doing all the technical bits so brilliantly - it's hard to help someone who, in this day and age, has to ask the question: 'What's a blog?' Laurence and Sally somehow managed!
Helen Edwards who read the manuscript with no prior knowledge of content or genre and for giving wonderful feedback.
Thomas Stofer who, so long ago that he probably doesn't even remember, looked at the first draft and offered many suggestions for improvement - which I hope I have taken on board.
My husband and daughter for their patience.
And, of course, Rhonda Fraser Brown, who kept me writing, always demanding the next chapter. Her enjoyment of the story and her faith in me are why this book was finished. And yes, Rhonda, the second book is on its way!
All those other people who have supported and encouraged me.
My everlasting thanks go out to all these people.

Printed in Germany
by Amazon Distribution
GmbH, Leipzig